DEBBIE MACOMBER

is a number one *New York Times* and *USA TODAY* bestselling author. Her books include *1225 Christmas Tree Lane, 1105 Yakima Street, A Turn in the Road, Hannah's List* and *Debbie Macomber's Christmas Cookbook*, as well as *Twenty Wishes, Summer on Blossom Street* and *Call Me Mrs. Miracle*. She has become a leading voice in women's fiction worldwide and her work has appeared on every major bestseller list, including those of the *New York Times, USA TODAY, Publishers Weekly* and *Entertainment Weekly*. She is a multiple award winner, and won the 2005 Quill Award for Best Romance. There are more than 100 million copies of her books in print. Two of her Harlequin MIRA Christmas titles have been made into Hallmark Channel Original Movies, and the Hallmark Channel is launching a series based on her bestselling Cedar Cove series. For more information on Debbie and her books, visit her website: www.DebbieMacomber.com.

LINDA GOODNIGHT

Winner of a RITA® Award for excellence in inspirational fiction, Linda Goodnight has also won a Booksellers' Best Award, an ACFW Book of the Year award and a Reviewers' Choice Award from *RT Book Reviews*. Linda has appeared on the Christian bestseller list and her romance novels have been translated into more than a dozen languages. Active in orphan ministry, this former nurse and teacher enjoys writing fiction that carries a message of hope and light in a sometimes dark world. She and her husband live in Oklahoma. Visit her website at www.lindagoodnight.com. To browse a current listing of Linda Goodnight's titles, please visit www.Harlequin.com.

#1 *New York Times* Bestselling Author

DEBBIE MACOMBER

The Gift of Christmas

Recycling programs for this product may not exist in your area.

ISBN-13: 978-0-373-18071-4

THE GIFT OF CHRISTMAS
Copyright © 2013 by Harlequin Books S.A.

The publisher acknowledges the copyright holders of the individual works as follows:

THE GIFT OF CHRISTMAS
Copyright © 1984 by Debbie Macomber

IN THE SPIRIT OF…CHRISTMAS
Copyright © 2005 by Linda Goodnight

Printed in U.S.A.

CONTENTS

Dear Reader,

It's that time of year again—the holiday season. And if you're anything like me you're wondering where the months went. My advice is to take a deep breath, sit back and relax with a good book. By golly, you've got one in your hands right now!

Everyone loves a little something extra, an expected gift—and this volume has it, in the form of an additional story. *The Gift of Christmas* was one of my early stories, written back in 1984 (never mind the months, where did the *years* go?). I've refreshed the story, and this volume also includes a wonderful novel by Linda Goodnight titled *In the Spirit of…Christmas.*

This was the first Christmas book I ever wrote and as you're probably aware it became a tradition for me to write one nearly every year since then. I've lost count of the number of Christmas-related books I've published, but this is the one that started it all.

I hope you enjoy meeting Ashley and Cooper and Webb. And if you haven't read Linda Goodnight before, then you're in for a treat.

Merry Christmas!

Debbie Macomber

P.S. Hearing from my readers is a joy to me. I read each and every letter and website message and value your feedback. You can reach me at my website at DebbieMacomber.com or on Facebook or at P.O. Box 1458, Port Orchard, WA 98366.

THE GIFT OF CHRISTMAS

#1 *New York Times* Bestselling Author

Debbie Macomber

To Rachel Hauck, Roxanne St. Claire,
Virelle Kidder and Martha Powers, my Florida sisters.

Chapter 1

Ashley Robbins clenched her hands together as she sat in a plush velvet chair ten stories up in a Seattle high-rise. The cashier's check to Cooper Masters was in her purse. Rather than mail him the money, Ashley had impulsively decided to deliver it herself.

People moved about her, in and out of doors, as she thoughtfully watched their actions. Curious glances darted her way. She had never been one to blend into the background. Over the years she'd wondered if it was the striking ash blond hair that attracted attention, or her outrageous choice of clothes. Today, however, since she was meeting Cooper, she'd dressed conservatively. Never shy, she was a hit in the classroom, using techniques that had others shaking their heads in wonder. But no one doubted that she was the most popular teacher at John Knox Christian High School. Cooper had made that possible. No one knew he had loaned her the money to complete her studies. Not even Claudia, her best friend and Cooper's niece.

Ashley and Cooper were the godparents to John, Claudia's older boy. Being linked to Cooper had pleased Ashley more than her friend suspected. She'd been secretly in love with him since she was sixteen. It amazed her that no one had guessed during those ten years, least of all Cooper.

"Mr. Masters will see you now," his receptionist informed her.

Ashley smiled her appreciation and followed the attractive woman through the heavy oak door.

"Ashley." Cooper stood and strode to the front of his desk. "What a pleasant surprise."

"Hello, Cooper." He'd changed over the last six months since she'd seen him. Streaks of silver ran through his hair, and tiny lines fanned out from his eyes. But it would take more than years to disguise his strongly marked features. He wasn't a compellingly handsome man, not in the traditional sense, but seeing him again stirred familiar feelings of admiration and appreciation for all he'd done for her.

"Sit down, please." He indicated a chair not unlike the one she'd recently vacated. "What can I do for you? Any problems?"

She responded with a slight shake of her head. He had always been generous with her. Deep down, she doubted that there was anything she couldn't ask of this man, although she didn't expect any more favors, and he was probably aware of that.

"Everything's fine." She didn't meet his eyes as she opened the clasp of her purse and took out the check. "I wanted to personally give you this." Extending her arm, she handed him the check. "I owe you so much, it seemed almost rude to put it in the mail." The satisfaction of paying off the loan was secondary to the opportunity of seeing Cooper again. If she'd been honest with herself, she would have admitted she was hungry for the sight of him. After all these months she'd been looking for an excuse.

He glanced at the check and seemed to notice the amount. Two dark brows arched with surprise. "This satisfies the loan," he said thoughtfully. Half turning, he placed the check in the center of the large wooden desk. "Your mother tells me you've taken a second job?" The intonation in his voice made the statement a question.

"You see her more often than I do," she said in an attempt to evade the question. Her mother had been the Masters' cook and housekeeper from the time Ashley was a child.

He regarded her steadily, and although she could read no emotion in his eyes, she felt his irritation. "Was it necessary to pay this off as quickly as possible?"

"Fast? I've owed you this money for over four years." She laughed lightly. Someone had once told her that her laugh was one of the most appealing things about her. Sweet, gentle, melodic. She chanced a look at Cooper, whose cool dark eyes revealed nothing.

"I didn't care if you ever paid me back. I certainly didn't expect you'd half kill yourself to return it."

The displeasure in his voice surprised her. Taken aback, she watched as he stalked to the far corner of the office, putting as much distance between them as possible. Was it pride that had driven her to pay him back as quickly as possible? Maybe, but she doubted it. The loan to finish her schooling had been the answer to long, difficult prayers. From the time she'd been accepted into the University of Washington, she had attended on faith. Faith that God would supply the money for books and tuition. Faith that if God wanted her to obtain her teaching degree, then He would meet her needs. And He had. In the beginning things had worked well. She roomed with Claudia and managed two part-time jobs. But when Claudia and Seth got married, she was forced to find other accommodations, which quickly drained her funds. Cooper's offer had been completely unexpected. The loan had come at a time when she'd been hopeless and had been preparing to withdraw from classes. They'd never discussed terms, but surely he'd known she intended to repay him.

A tentative smile brushed her lips. She'd thought he would be pleased. His reaction amazed her. She attempted to keep her voice level as she assured him, "It was the honorable thing to do."

"But it wasn't necessary," he answered, turning back to her.

Again she experienced the familiar twinge of awareness that only Cooper Masters was capable of stirring within her.

"It was for me," she countered quickly.

"It wasn't necessary," he repeated in a flat tone.

Ashley released a slow breath. "We could go on like this all day. I didn't mean to offend you, I only came here today because I wanted to show my appreciation."

He stared back at her, then slowly nodded. "I understand."

Silence stretched between them.

"Have you heard from Claudia and Seth?" he asked after a while.

Ashley smiled. They had so little in common that whenever they were together that the conversation invariably centered around Claudia and their godson. "The last I heard she said something about coming down for Christmas."

"I hope they do." His intercom buzzed, and he leaned over and pressed a button on the phone. "Yes, Gloria?"

"Mr. Benson is here."

"Thank you."

Taking her cue, Ashley stood. "I won't keep you." Her fingers brushed her wool skirt. She'd been hoping he would notice the new outfit and comment. He hadn't. "Thank you again. I guess you know that I wouldn't have been able to finish school without your help."

"I was wondering…" Cooper moved to her side, his

look slightly uneasy, as if he was unsure of himself. "I mean, I can understand if you'd rather not."

"Rather not what?" She couldn't remember him ever acting with anything but supreme confidence. In control of himself and every situation.

"Have dinner with me. A small celebration for paying off the loan."

"I'd like that very much. Anytime." Her heart soared at the suggestion; she wasn't sure how she managed to keep her voice level.

"Tonight at seven?"

"Wonderful. Should I wear something…formal?" It wouldn't hurt to ask, and he hadn't mentioned where he intended they dine.

"Dress comfortably."

"Great."

An hour later Ashley's heart still refused to beat at a normal pace. This was the first time Cooper had asked her out or given any indication he would like to see her socially. The man was difficult to understand, always had been. Even Claudia didn't fully know him; she saw him as dignified, predictable and overly concerned with respectability. In some ways he was, but through the years Ashley had seen past that facade. He might be refined, and sometimes overly proper, but he was a man who'd been forced to take on heavy responsibility at an early age. There had been little time for fun or frivolity in his life. Ashley wanted to be the one to change that. She loved him. Her mother claimed that opposites attract, and after meeting Cooper, Ashley had never doubted the truth of that statement.

Ashley chose to wear her finest designer jeans, knowing she looked good. At five foot nine, she was all legs. Her pink sweatshirt contained a starburst of sequins that extended to the ends of the full length sleeves. Her hair was styled in a casual perm, and soft curls reached her shoulders. Her perfume was a fragrance Cooper had given her the previous Christmas. Although not imaginative, the gift had pleased her immeasurably, even though he hadn't given it to her personally, but to her mother, who'd passed it on. When she'd phoned to thank him, his response had been clipped and vaguely ill-at-ease. Politely, he'd assured her that it was his duty, since they were John's godparents. He'd also told her he'd sent the same fragrance to Claudia. Ashley had hung up the phone feeling deflated. The next time she'd seen him had been in June, when her mother had gone to the hospital for surgery. Cooper had come for a visit at the same time Ashley had arrived. Standing on opposite sides of the bed, her sleeping mother between them, Ashley had hungrily drunk in the sight of him. Their short conversation had been carried on in hushed tones, and after a while they hadn't spoken at all. Afterward he'd had coffee out of a machine, and she'd sipped fruit juice as they sat talking in the waiting area at the end of the corridor. She hadn't seen him again until today.

Over the months she had dated several men, and she'd recently been seeing Dennis Webb, another teacher, on a steady basis. But no one had ever attracted her the way Cooper did. Whenever a pensive mood overtook her, she recognized how pointless that attraction was. Whole universes stretched between them, both social and economic. For Ashley, loving Cooper Masters was as impossible as understanding income tax forms.

The doorbell chimed precisely at seven. Claudia had claimed that she could set her watch by Cooper. If he said seven, he would arrive exactly at seven.

A sense of panic filled Ashley as she glanced at her wristwatch. It couldn't possibly be that time already, could it? With one red cowboy boot on and the other lying on the carpet, she looked around frantically. The laundry still hadn't been put away. Quickly she hobbled across the floor and shoved the basket full of folded clean clothes into the entryway closet, then closed the door with her back as she conducted a sweeping inspection of the apartment. Expelling a calming sigh, she forced herself to smile casually as she opened the door.

He greeted her with a warm look, that gradually faded as he handed her a florist's box.

To Cooper, apparently informal meant a three-piece suit and flowers. Glancing down at her jeans and sweatshirt, one cowboy boot on, the other missing, she smiled weakly and felt wretched. "Thank you." She took the small white box. "Sit down, please." Hurrying ahead of him, she fluffed up the pillows at the end of the sofa, then hugged one to her stomach. "I'm running a little late tonight. If you'll give me a few minutes I'll change clothes."

"You look fine just the way you are," he murmured, glancing at his watch.

What he was really saying, she realized, was that they would be late for their reservation if she took the time to change clothes. After glancing down at the hot pink sweatshirt, she raised her gaze to meet his. "You're sure? It'll only take a minute."

His nod seemed determined. Self-conscious, embarrassed and angry with herself, Ashley sat at the opposite end of the sofa and slipped her foot into the other boot. After tucking in her denim pant leg, she sat up and reached for the florist's box. A lovely white orchid was nestled in a bed of sheer green paper. A gasp of pleasure escaped her.

"Oh, Cooper," she murmured, feeling close to tears. No one had ever given her an orchid. "Thank you."

"Since I didn't know the color of your dress…" He paused to correct himself. "…your outfit…this seemed appropriate." He remained standing, studying her. "It's the type women wear on their wrist."

As Ashley lifted the orchid from the box, its gentle fragrance drifted pleasantly to her. "I'm always having to thank you, Cooper. You've been very good to me."

He dismissed her appreciation with a hard shake of his head. "Nonsense."

She knew that further discussion would only embarrass them both. Standing, she glanced at the closet door, knowing nothing would induce her to open it and expose her folded underwear to Cooper. "I'll get my purse and we can go."

"You might want to wear a coat," he suggested. "I

heard something about the possibility of snow over the radio this afternoon."

"Yes, of course." If he remained standing exactly as he was, she might be able to open the door just enough to slip her hand in and jerk her faux fur jacket off the hanger. Somehow she managed it. Turning, she noted that Cooper was regarding her curiously. Rather than fabricate a wild excuse about why she couldn't open the closet all the way, she decided to say nothing.

He took the coat from her grasp, holding it open for her to slip her arms into the sleeves. It seemed as if his hands lingered longer than necessary on her shoulders, but it could have been her imagination. He had never been one to display affection openly.

"Where are we going?" she asked, and her voice trembled slightly, affected by even the most impersonal touch.

"I chose an Italian restaurant not far from here. I hope that suits you."

"Sounds delicious. I love Italian food." Her tastes in food were wide and varied, but it wouldn't have mattered. If he had suggested hot dogs, she would have been thrilled. The idea of Cooper eating anything with his fingers produced a quivering smile. If he noticed it, he said nothing.

Cooper parked outside the small, family-owned restaurant and came around to her side of the car, opening the door for her. It was apparent when they were seated that he had never been there before. The thought flashed through her mind that he didn't want to be seen with her where he might be recognized.

But she quickly dismissed the idea. If he didn't want to be with her, then he wouldn't have asked her out. Those thoughts were unworthy of Cooper, who had always been good to her.

"Is everything all right?" As he stared across the table at her, a frown drew his brows together.

"Yes, of course." She looked down at her menu, guiltily forcing a smile on her face. "I wonder how long it'll be before we know if Claudia will be coming for Christmas," she said, hoping to resume the even flow of conversation.

"Time's getting close. I imagine we'll know soon."

Thanksgiving was the following weekend, but Christmas displays were already up in stores; some had shown up as early as Halloween. Doubtless Seth and Claudia would let them know by the end of next week. The prospect of sharing the holiday with her friend—and therefore Cooper—produced a glow of happiness inside Ashley.

The waiter took their order, then promptly delivered their fresh green salads.

"It's been exceptionally chilly for this time of the year," Cooper commented, lifting his fork, his gaze centered on his plate.

Ashley thought it was a sad commentary that their only common ground consisted of Claudia and the weather. "Yes, it has." She looked up to note that a veiled look had come over his features. Perhaps he was thinking the same thing.

The conversation during dinner seemed stiff and strained to her. Cooper asked her about school and politely inquired if she liked teaching. In return she asked him about the business supply operation he owned and was surprised to learn how much it had grown over the past few years. The knowledge should have pleased her, but instead it only served to remind her that he was a rich man and she was still struggling financially.

When they stepped out of the restaurant, she was pleased to discover that it was snowing.

"Oh, Cooper, look!" she cried with delight. "I love it when it snows. Let's go for a walk." She couldn't keep the excitement out of her voice. "There's something magical about walking in the falling snow."

"Are you sure that's what you want?" He glanced at the thin layer of white powder that covered the ground, then he looked up, his expression odd as his eyes searched hers.

"I'd forgotten, you'll have to drive back in this stuff. Maybe it wouldn't be such a good idea," she commented, unable to hide her disappointment.

His hand cupped her elbow, bringing her near, and when she slipped on the slick sidewalk he quickly placed his arm around her waist, preventing her from falling. He left his arm there, holding her protectively close to his side. Her spirits soared at being linked this way with Cooper.

"Where would you like to walk?" An indiscernible expression clouded his eyes.

"There's a marina a couple of blocks from here, and I love to watch the snow fall on the water, but if you'd rather not, I understand."

"By all means, let's go to the marina." The smile he gave her was the first genuine one she'd witnessed the entire evening.

"Doesn't this make you want to sing?" she asked, and started to hum "White Christmas" even before he could answer.

"No," he said, and chuckled. "It makes me want to sit in front of a roaring fireplace with a warm drink."

She clucked and pressed her lips together to keep from laughing.

"What was that all about?"

"What?" she asked, feigning ignorance.

"That silly little noise you just made."

"If you must know, I don't think you've done anything impulsive or daring in your entire life, Cooper Masters." She said it all in one giant breath, then watched as a shocked look came over his face.

"Of course I have," he insisted righteously.

"Then I dare you to do something right now."

"What?" He looked unsure.

"Make a snowball and throw it at me," she demanded. Breaking from his hold, she ran a few steps ahead of him. "Bet you can't do it," she taunted, and waved her hands at him.

With marked determination, Cooper stuffed his hands inside his coat pockets. "This is silly."

"It's supposed to be crazy, remember?" she chided him softly.

"But it's not right for a man to throw snowballs at a woman."

"Will this make things easier for you?" she shouted,

bending over to scoop up a handful of snow. With an accuracy that astonished her, she threw a snowball that hit him directly in the middle of his chest. If she was surprised, the horrified look on Cooper's face sent her into peals of laughter. Losing her balance on the ice-slickened sidewalk, she went sprawling to the cement with an undignified plop.

"That's what you get for hurling snow at courteous gentlemen," Cooper called once he was sure she wasn't hurt. As he advanced toward her, he shifted a tightly packed snowball from one hand to the other.

"Cooper, you wouldn't—would you?" She gave him her most defenseless look, batting her eyelashes. "Here, help me up." She extended a hand to him, which he ignored.

A wicked gleam flashed from the dark depths of his eyes. "I thought you said I never did anything crazy or daring?"

"You wouldn't!" Her voice trembled with laughter as she struggled to stand up.

"You're right, I wouldn't," he murmured, dropping the snowball and reaching for her. Surprise rocked her as he pulled her into his arms. He hesitated momentarily, as if expecting her to protest. When she didn't, he gently brushed the hair from her temple and just as softly pressed his mouth over hers. The kiss should have been tender, but the moment their lips met it became hungry and needy. The effect was jarring, as if a bolt of awareness were flashing through them. They broke apart, shocked and breathless. The oxygen was trapped in her lungs, making it impossible to breathe.

"Did I hurt you?" he asked, his voice thick with concern.

A shake of her head was all she could manage. "Cooper?" Her voice was a mere whisper. "Would you mind doing that again?"

"Now?"

She nodded.

"Here?"

Again she nodded.

He pulled her back into his embrace, his eyes drinking deeply from hers. This time the kiss was gentle, as if he, too, needed to test these sensations. Lost in the swirling awareness, Ashley felt as if he had touched the deep inner part of her being. For years she had dreamed of this moment, wondered what effect his touch would have on her. Now she knew. She felt a free-flowing happiness steal over her. He had taken her heart and touched her spirit. When he entwined his fingers in the curling length of her hair, she pressed her head against his shoulder and breathed in deeply. A soft smile lifted her lips at the sound of his furiously pounding heart.

"This is crazy," he murmured hoarsely.

"No," she swiftly countered. "This is wonderful."

Carefully he relaxed his hold, easing her from his embrace. His features were unnaturally pale as he smoothed the hair at the side of his head with an impatient movement. "I'm too old for you." His mouth had thinned, and his look was remote.

Her bubble of happy contentment burst; he regretted kissing her. What had been so wonderful for her was a source of embarrassment for him. "I dared you to do something impulsive, remember?" she said with forced gaiety. "It doesn't mean anything. I've been kissed before. It happens all the time."

"I'm sure it does," he replied stiffly. His gaze moved pointedly to his watch. "I think it would be best if I took you home now. Perhaps we could see the marina another time."

"Sure."

His touch was impersonal as they strolled purposefully back toward the restaurant parking lot. To hide her discomfort, Ashley began to hum Christmas music again.

"Rushing the season a bit, aren't you?"

She concentrated on moving one foot in front of the other. "I suppose. But the snow makes it feel like Christmas. Christ wouldn't mind if we celebrated His birth every day of the year."

"The shopping malls would love it if we did," he remarked cynically.

"You're speaking of the commercial aspect of the holiday, I'm talking about the spiritual one."

Cooper didn't comment. In fact, neither one of them spoke until he pulled up to the curb in front of her apartment building.

"Would you like to come in and warm up? It would only take a minute to heat up some cocoa." Although the offer was sincere, she knew he wouldn't accept.

"Perhaps another time."

There wouldn't be another time. He wouldn't ask her out again; the whole evening had been a fiasco.

Cooper Masters was a powerful, influential man, whereas she was a high school English Lit teacher.

"You'll let me know if you hear anything from Seth and Claudia?"

"Of course."

He came around to her side of the car, opening the door. "You don't need to walk me all the way to my door," she mumbled miserably.

"There's every need." Although his voice was level, she could tell he was determined to live up to what he felt a gentleman should be.

She didn't argue when he took the keys out of her hand and opened the door of her first-floor apartment for her. "Thank you," she murmured. "The evening was..."

"Crazy," he finished for her.

Wonderful, her mind insisted in return. Afraid of what her eyes would reveal, she lowered her head and her blond curls fell forward, wreathing her face. "Crazy," she repeated.

A finger placed under her chin lifted her eyes to his. His were dark and unreadable, hers soft and shining. Slowly his hand moved to caress the soft, smooth skin of her cheek. The gentle caress sent the blood pulsing through her veins, flushing her face with telltale color.

"If ever you're in trouble or need someone, I want you to contact me."

Although he had never verbally said as much, she had always been aware that she could go to him if ever she needed help.

"I will." Her voice sounded irritatingly weak.

"I want you to promise me." He unbuttoned his coat pocket and took out a business card. Using the door as a support, he wrote down a phone number. "You can reach me here any time of the day."

"I'm not going to trouble you with—"

"Promise me, Ashley."

He was so serious, his look demanding. "Okay," she agreed, accepting the card. "But why?"

A long moment passed before he answered her. "I have a vested interest in you," he said, and shrugged, the indifferent gesture contradicting his words. "Besides, I'd hate to have anything happen to Johnny's godmother."

"Nothing's going to happen to me."

"In case it does, I want you to know I'll always be there."

The business card seemed to sear her hand. In his own way, Cooper cared about her. "Thank you." Impulsively, she raised two fingers to her lips, then brushed them across his mouth. His hand stopped hers, gripping her wrist; his look branded her. Slowly he lowered his mouth to hers in a gentle, sweet kiss.

"Good night, Ashley."

"Good night." Standing in the open doorway, she watched until he drove into the dark night. A solitary figure illuminated by the falling snow.

Expelling her breath in a long quivering sigh, she tucked the card in her purse. Why did she have to love Cooper Masters? Why couldn't she feel for Webb what she did for Cooper? Webb was nice and almost as unpredictable as she was. Maybe that was why they got along so well. Yet it was Cooper who occupied her thoughts. Cooper who made her heart sing. Cooper who filled her dreams. The time had come to wake up and face reality. She was at the age when she should start thinking about marriage and a family, because she definitely wanted children. Cooper wasn't going to be interested in someone like her. He might care about her, even feel some affection for her, but she wasn't the type of woman he would ever ask to be his wife.

Troubled and confused, Ashley made herself a cup of cocoa and sat on the sofa, her feet tucked under the cushion next to her. Things had been so easy for her friends, even Claudia. They met someone, fell in love, got married and started a family. Maybe God had decided He didn't want her to marry. The thought seemed intolerable, but she had learned long ago not to second-guess her heavenly Father. She'd given Him her life, her will, even Cooper's safekeeping. Now she had to learn to trust.

She rinsed out the cup, placed it in the kitchen sink and turned out the lights. Her eyes fell on her purse, hanging on the closet doorknob. She wondered if the day might come when she would need to use the card, not that she intended to.

That same thought ran through her mind several days later when the police officer directed her to the phone. She didn't want to contact Cooper, so she'd tried phoning her family first, hoping she would catch her father at home. But there had been no answer.

"Is there anyone else, Miss?" the tall, uniformed man asked.

"Yes," she answered tightly, opening her purse and taking out the card. Her fingers actually trembled as she dialed the number.

"Cooper Masters."

As she suspected, he'd given her his private cell number. "Oh, hi . . . it's Ashley."

"Ashley." His voice carried clearly over the line. "What's wrong?"

"It isn't an emergency or anything," she began, feeling incredibly silly. "I mean, I don't think they'll keep me."

"Ashley," he heaved her name on an angry sigh. "What's going on?"

"It's a long story."

"All right, tell me where you are. I'll come to you, and then we'll straighten everything out."

She hesitated, swallowing past the lump forming in her throat. "I'm in jail."

Chapter 2

"Jail!" Cooper's voice boomed over the line. "I'll be there in ten minutes."

"But, Cooper, Kent's a good thirty minutes from downtown Seattle."

"Kent?" The anger in his voice was barely controlled.

"If you're going to get so mad..." Ashley let the rest of the sentence fade, realizing that the phone line had already been disconnected.

Casting a glance at the police officer beside her, she gave him a wary smile. "A friend's coming."

A smile quivered at one corner of the older man's mouth. "I heard." Looking away, he asked, "Would you like a cup of coffee while you wait?"

"No thanks."

Ashley heard Cooper's voice several minutes before she saw him. By the time he was brought into the area where she was waiting, there wasn't a person in the entire police station who hadn't heard him. She had always known him to be a calm, discreet person. That he would react this way to a minor misunderstanding shocked her. Although…a lot of things about Cooper had surprised her lately. She was standing, her face devoid of color, when he was escorted into the room.

"Can you tell me what's going on here?" he demanded.

His look did little to encourage confidences; she swallowed tightly and waved her hand helplessly. "Well, apparently someone took the license plate off Milligan."

"Who the heck…?" He paused and took a deep, calming breath. "Who's Milligan?"

"Not who," she corrected, "but what. Milligan's my moped. I parked it outside the Mexican restaurant where I work odd hours, and someone apparently took off with my license plate."

"That isn't any reason to arrest you!" he shouted.

"They haven't arrested me!" she yelled in return, and was humiliated when her voice cracked and wavered. "And if you won't quit shouting at me, then you can just leave."

Raking his fingers roughly through his hair, Cooper stalked to the other side of the room. His mouth was tightly pinched, and he said nothing for several long moments. "All right, let's try this again," he replied in a deceivingly soft tone. "Start at the beginning, and tell me everything."

"There's not much to tell. Someone took the license plate, and, since I don't have the registration on me, the police need some evidence that I own the bike. I haven't been arrested or anything. In fact, they've been very nice." In nervous reaction she looped a long strand of curly hair around her ear. "All I need for you to do is go to my apartment and bring back the registration for Milligan. Then I'll be free to leave." She opened her purse and took out her key ring, then extracted the key to the apartment. "Here," she said, handing it to him. "The registration's in the kitchen, in the silverware drawer, stuck under the aluminum foil. I keep all my important papers there."

If he thought her record storage system was a bit unusual, he said nothing.

"There's a lawyer on his way here, I'll leave word at the front desk for him." Without another word, he turned and left the room.

Within twenty minutes she heard him talking to the officer who had offered her the coffee. A few moments later they both entered the waiting area.

"You're free to go," the policeman explained. "Although I'm afraid we can't let you drive the moped until you have a new license plate."

Before she could protest Cooper inserted, "No need to worry. I've already made arrangements for the bike to be picked up." He turned and directed his words to Ashley. "It'll be delivered to your place sometime tomorrow afternoon."

Rather than argue, Ashley mutely agreed.

"If you're ready, I'll take you home," Cooper said.

Shoving her knit cap onto her head, she stood and swung her backpack over her shoulder, then gave the kind officer a polite smile. She wasn't pleased with the way things were working out. If she didn't have Milligan, she would have to take a series of busses to and from work, with a long trek between stops. Surely something could be done to enable her to ride her moped until she could replace the plate. One look from Cooper discouraged her from asking.

His hand cupped her elbow as they walked to the parking lot. Her attention was centered on the scenery outside the car window as they crossed the Green River and connected with the freeway. Wordlessly, he took the first exit and a couple of minutes later pulled into the parking lot to her apartment building.

He turned off the engine, then called his office. "Gloria, cancel the rest of my appointments for today," he said stiffly, his voice clipped and abrupt. Without waiting for a confirmation, he promptly ended the call, and then turned to Ashley. "Invite me in for coffee."

Her heart lodged someplace near her throat. "Yes, of course." She didn't wait for him to come around to her side of the car and let herself out. He gave her a disapproving look as they met in front of the vehicle. He opened the apartment door and returned the key to her. She placed it back on the key ring and took off her jacket, carelessly tossing it across the top of the sofa. He removed his black overcoat and neatly folded it over the back of the chair opposite the sofa.

"I'll put on the coffee." She moved into the kitchen, pouring water into the small, five-cup pot. She could hear Cooper agitatedly pacing the floor behind her.

"Why are you so angry with me?" she asked. She couldn't look at him, not when he was so obviously furious with her. "I couldn't help it if someone stole my license plate. I never should have phoned you, I'm sorry I did."

"I'm not mad at you," he stormed. "I'm angry that you were put through that ordeal, that you were treated like a criminal, that..." He left the rest unsaid.

"It's not the policeman's fault. He was only doing his job," she tried to explain, still not facing him. Her fingers trembled as she added the grounds to the pot, placed the lid on top and set it to brew.

A large masculine hand landed on her shoulder, and she had to fight not to lay her cheek on it. A subtle pressure turned her around. With both hands behind her, she gripped the oven door for support. Slowly she raised her eyes to meet his. She was surprised at the tenderness she saw in the dark depths of his gaze, which seemed to be centered on her mouth. Nervously she moistened her dry lips with the tip of her tongue. She hadn't meant to be provocative, but when Cooper softly groaned she realized what she'd done. When he reached for her, she went willingly into his embrace.

He held her against him, breathing in deeply as he buried his face in the curve of her neck. His hands roamed her back, arching her as close as humanly possible. Ashley molded herself to him, savoring the light scent of musk and man; she longed for him to kiss her. She silently pleaded with him to throw common sense to the wind and crush his mouth over hers. Just being held by him was more happiness than she'd ever hoped to experience. Happiness and torment all rolled into one. An embrace, a light caress, a longing look, could never satisfy her, not when she wanted so much more. Gently he kissed the crown of her head and released her. She wanted to cry with disappointment.

The coffee had begun to perk, and to disguise her emotions, Ashley turned and reached for two cups, waiting for the pot to finish before pouring.

While she dealt with the coffee, Cooper sat in the living room waiting for her. He stood when she entered, taking one cup from her hand.

"I'm sorry, Ashley," he said, his eyes probing hers.

He didn't need to elaborate. He was sorry for his anger, sorry he'd overreacted in the police station, but mostly he regretted throwing aside his self-control and taking her in his arms.

Unable to verbally acknowledge his apology she simply shook her head, letting him know that she understood what he was saying.

"So you work at a Mexican restaurant?" he asked, after taking a sip from the steaming cup.

She wasn't fooled by the veiled interest. He'd commented on the fact she'd taken a second job once before, and he hadn't been pleased then.

"I only work odd hours, less now that I've paid off the loan," she answered, her finger making lazy loops around the rim of her cup.

He pinched his mouth tightly shut, and she recognized that he was biting back words. She wondered how he managed in business confrontations when she found him so easy to read.

Taking another sip of coffee, he stood and moved into the kitchen to put the half-full cup into the sink. "I should go."

She followed his movements. "I haven't thanked you. I...I don't know what I would have done if you hadn't come."

Her appreciation seemed to embarrass him, because his mouth thinned. He lifted his coat off the back of the chair. "I said I wanted you to call me if you needed help. I'm glad you did."

She walked him to the door. "How'd you get to Kent so fast?" Asking him questions helped delay the time when he would leave.

"I was already in the car when you phoned. It was simply a matter of heading in the right direction."

"Oh," she said in a small voice. "I apologize if I inconvenienced you."

"You didn't," he returned gruffly. His eyes met hers then, and again she found herself drowning in those dark depths.

Clenching her hands at her sides, she gave him a falsely cheerful smile. "Thanks again, Cooper. God go with you."

He turned. "And you," he murmured, surprising her.

"Have a nice Thanksgiving."

"I'm sure I will. Are you spending the day with your family?"

"Yes, Mom's making her famous turkey stuffing, and Jeff and his wife, Marsha, are coming." Jeff was her younger brother. John, the youngest Robbins, was working in Spokane and had decided not to make the long drive over the Cascade Mountains in uncertain weather.

Cooper didn't elaborate on his own plans for the holiday, and she didn't ask. "Goodbye, and thanks again."

"Goodbye, Ashley."

As she watched him walk away, she had the strongest desire to blow him a kiss. Immediately she quelled the impulse, but she couldn't help feeling disappointed and frustrated. Closing the front door, she leaned against it and breathed in deeply. She was filling her head with fanciful dreams if she dared to hope Cooper would ever come to love her. Wasting her time and her life. But her heart refused to listen.

As Cooper promised, her moped was delivered safely to her apartment the following afternoon. Webb drove her home from school, and once she dropped off her things, he took her to the Department of Motor Vehicles, where she applied for new license plates. Granted a temporary plate, she was relieved to learn she could now ride Milligan. The moped might not be much, but it got her where she needed to go in the most economical way.

Webb was tall and thin, his facial features almost gaunt, but he was one of the nicest people Ashley had ever known. When he dropped her off at her apartment, she invited him inside. He accepted with a smile.

"Got plans for the weekend?" he asked over a cup of cocoa.

She shrugged. "Not really. I wanted to do some Christmas shopping, but I dread fighting the crowds."

"Want to go skiing Saturday afternoon? I understand the slopes are open."

"I didn't know you skied?" Ashley questioned, her eyes twinkling.

"I don't," Webb confirmed. "I thought you'd teach me."

"Forget that, buddy. You can take lessons like everyone else, then we'll talk about skiing," she said with a laugh. "You could invite me to dinner instead," she suggested hopefully.

"Fine, what are you cooking?"

"Leftovers."

"I'll bring the egg nog," he said with a sly grin.

"Honestly, Webb, how do you do it?" she asked, laughing.

"Do what?"

"Invite me out to dinner, and I end up cooking?"

"It's all in the wrist, all in the wrist," he told her, flexing his hand, looking smug.

Thinking about their conversation later, she couldn't help laughing. Webb was a fun person, but what she felt for Cooper was exciting and intense and couldn't compare with the friendship she shared with her co-worker.

With Cooper she felt vulnerable in a way that

couldn't be explained. But then she was in love with Cooper Masters, and that was simply pointless.

Disturbed by her thoughts, she went to change clothes. As part of her preparation for the coming holidays and the extra calories she would consume, she had started to work out. Following the instructions on the DVD she'd purchased, she practiced a routine that used Christian music for an aerobic dancercise program. Dressed in purple satin shorts, pink leg-warmers and a gray T-shirt, she placed her hands on her hips in the middle of the living room and waited for the warm-up instructions. Just as she completed the first round of exercises, the doorbell rang.

She paused, and with her breath deep and ragged, she turned off the player and checked the peep hole in the door. She wasn't expecting anyone. To her horror, she saw it was Cooper.

The doorbell buzzed again, and for a fleeting second she was tempted to let him think she wasn't home, but overriding her embarrassment at having him see her dressed in shorts and a T-shirt was her desire to know why he'd come.

"Hello," she said as she opened the door.

He walked into the apartment, his brow marred by a puzzled frown as he glanced at her. "Maybe I should come back later."

"Nonsense," she mumbled, dismissing the suggestion. She grabbed a towel to wipe the perspiration from her face. "I was just doing some aerobics. Care to join me?"

"No thanks." The corners of his mouth formed deep

grooves as he suppressed a smile. "But don't let me stop you."

His attempt at humor amazed her. It was the first time she could remember him bantering with her—or anyone. "I think I'll skip the rest of the program," she said and laughed.

"Is that coffee I smell?" he asked as he sat on the edge of the sofa.

"No, cocoa. Want some? If you want coffee, though, it'd only take me a minute to brew a pot."

He shook his head.

Looping the towel around her neck, she sat Indian style opposite him. Her face was glowing and red from the exertion, and she noted the way Cooper couldn't keep his eyes off her. Her heart was pounding fiercely, but she wasn't sure if it was the effects of seeing him again or the aerobics.

For a long moment silence filled the room. "Did you get Madigan back?" he eventually asked.

"Milligan," she corrected.

"How'd you happen to name a moped Milligan?"

"It was the salesman's name. We went out a couple of times afterward, and I couldn't think of the bike without thinking of Milligan, so I started calling it by his name."

Cooper's mouth narrowed slightly. "What do you do when it rains?"

"Wear rain gear," she returned casually. "It's a bit of a hassle, but I don't mind." Why was he so curious about Milligan? Certainly he'd known—or at least known of—someone who rode a moped before now?

"They're not the safest thing around, are they?"

"I suppose not, but I'm careful." This line of questioning was beginning to rankle. "Why all the curiosity?"

Leaning forward, he rested his elbows on his knees, then quickly shifted position, placing his ankle across one knee as if to give a casual impression. "The more I thought about you riding that moped, the more concerned I became. In checking statistics I discovered—"

"Statistics?" she interrupted him. "Honestly, Cooper, I'm perfectly safe."

He closed his eyes for a moment in apparent frustration, then opened them again. "I knew this wasn't going to be easy. You're as stubborn as Claudia," he said, and expelled his breath slowly. "I'm going to worry about you riding around on that silly bit of chrome and rubber."

"I've had Milligan for almost two years," she inserted, feeling the color drain from her face.

"Ashley," he said, his gaze lingering on her. "I want you to accept these and promise me you'll use them." He took a set of keys from his pocket and held them out to her.

"What are they?" her voice trembled slightly.

"The keys to a new car. If you don't like the color we can—"

"The keys to a new car?" she echoed in shocked disbelief. "You don't honestly expect me to accept that, do you?"

"No," he acknowledged with a heavy sigh, "knowing you, I didn't think you would. If you insist on paying me—"

"Paying you!" she cried, leaping to her feet. "I just cleared one loan—I'm not about to take on another." Her arms cradling her waist, she paced the floor directly in front of him. "Don't you realize how many enchiladas I had to serve to pay off the last loan? I can't understand you. I can't understand why you'd do something like this."

He inhaled deeply, his look full of trepidation. "I don't want you riding around on a stupid moped and getting yourself killed."

"You know, Cooper, you're beginning to sound like my father. I don't need another parent. I'm a capable twenty-six-year-old woman, not a half-wit teenager. What I ride to work is my prerogative."

"I'm only trying to…"

"I know what you're trying to do," she stormed. "Run my life! I have to admit, I was fooled." Her hand flew to her face and she wiped a thin layer of moisture from her brow. "You gave me your phone number and told me to call, but you didn't tell me there were strings attached."

"You're overreacting!" Although he appeared outwardly calm, she knew he was as unsettled as she was. Bright red color was creeping up his neck, but she doubted that he would vent his emotions in front of her.

"I'm not overreacting!" she exclaimed at fever pitch. "You think that because I phoned you, it gives you the right to step into my life. Keep the car, because I assure you I don't need it."

"As you wish," he murmured, his voice tight and controlled. Standing, he returned the keys to his pocket, his expression a stoic mask. "If you'll excuse me, I have an appointment."

"I hope the car isn't in the apartment parking lot, because the manager will have it towed away." The minute the words were out, she regretted having said them.

"It's not," he assured her coldly. Brushing past her, he let himself out, leaving her feeling deflated and depressed. The nerve of the man… He seemed to think… Her thoughts faded as she felt a hard knot form in her stomach. Now she'd done it, really done it.

"Happy Thanksgiving, Mom." Ashley laid the freshly baked pie on the kitchen countertop and leaned over to kiss her mother on the cheek.

"Hello, sweetheart." Sarah Robbins placed an arm around Ashley's waist and hugged her close. "I'm glad you're early, dear, would you mind peeling the potatoes?"

"Sure, Mom," she agreed, pulling open the kitchen drawer and taking out the peeler. Ashley had hoped for some time to talk to her mother privately. "How's work?" she asked in what she hoped was a casual tone. "Is Mr. Masters cracking the whip?" Her mother would have thought it disrespectful if she'd called Cooper anything but Mr. Masters, but the formal title nearly stuck in her throat.

"Oh, hardly." Sarah wiped the back of her hand across her apron. "He's always been wonderful to work for. I must say, he certainly loves those nephews of his. There are pictures of John and Scott all over that house, and I swear the only reason he moved out of the condominium was so those boys would have a decent yard to play in when they came to visit. That's all he ever talks about." Opening the oven door, she pulled out the rack to baste the turkey with a giblet broth simmering on the top of the stove. "Have you heard from Claudia and Seth?"

Ashley was chewing on a stalk of celery, and she waited until she'd swallowed before answering. "We chat all the time. I'm hoping she'll be here for Christmas."

"That'll please Mr. Masters. I think he needs a bit of cheering up. He's been in the blackest mood the last couple of days."

"He has?" She hoped to disguise her attentiveness. Her family, especially her mother, wouldn't approve of her interest in Cooper. Her feelings for her mother's employer had never been discussed, but she had sensed her mother's subtle disapproval of even their shared role as godparents more than once. In some ways Sarah Robbins and Cooper Masters were a lot alike. Her mother would view it as inappropriate for Ashley to be interested in an important man like Cooper.

"Did you cook a turkey for him this year?"

"No, he said he'd fix himself something, said he didn't want me fussing, when I had a family to tend to," she said on a soft sigh. "He really is the nicest man."

"I think he's wonderful," Ashley agreed absently, without thinking, and colored slightly when she turned to find her mother staring at her with questioning eyes. She was saved from answering any embarrassing questions by her sister-in-law, Marsha, who breezed through the door full of the joy of the season. She was grateful that she and her mother were never alone after that, and soon the meal was on the table.

Everything was delicious, as all her mother's cooking was. As they sat around the table, Ashley's father asked the blessing, then opened the Bible to Psalms and read several praises aloud. After a moment's silence he asked each family member to verbally state one of the blessings they were most thankful for this year. Tears shimmered in Marsha's eyes as she announced that she and Jeff were going to have a baby. The news brought shouts of delight from Ashley's parents. When it came to her turn she thanked God for the rich Christian heritage she had received from her parents and also that she was going to be an aunt at last.

Later, as she helped with the dishes, Ashley's thoughts again drifted to Cooper. Here she was, with a loving family surrounding her, and he was probably alone in his large house. No, she told herself, most likely he was sharing the day with friends or business associates. But she wasn't convinced.

Hounded by constant self-recrimination since their last meeting, she had berated her quick temper a hundred times. He had only been concerned about her safety, and she'd acted as if he'd accosted her.

"Mom," she said and swallowed tightly. "Would you mind if I took a plate of food over to a friend who has to spend the day alone?"

"Of course not, dear, but why didn't you say something earlier? You could have invited them to dinner."

"I wish I'd thought of it," she said.

When she was all set with a large cooler overflowing with turkey and all the extras, Ashley's father loaned her the family car.

Her heartbeat raced frantically as she pulled into Cooper's driveway in the exclusive Redondo area of south Seattle. She wouldn't blame him if he closed the door on her. He'd purchased the house with the surrounding two acres of prime view property shortly after Claudia had given birth to John. Ashley had never seen the house although her mother had told her about it several times.

Now the large, two-story brick structure loomed before her, elegant and impressive. Adjusting her red beret, she rang the doorbell and waited. Several minutes passed before Cooper answered. He wore a suit, and she couldn't recall ever seeing him look more distinguished.

"Happy Thanksgiving, Cooper," she said with a trembling smile. If he didn't invite her inside, she was afraid she would burst into tears and humiliate them both.

"Ashley." He sounded shocked to see her. "Come

in. For heaven's sake you didn't ride that deathtrap moped over here, did you?"

"No." She smiled and cast a glance over her shoulder to the older model car parked in the driveway. "Dad loaned me his car."

"Come in, it's cold, and it looks like rain," he offered again. He held out his hand, gesturing her inside.

Ashley didn't need a second invitation. "Here." She handed him the cooler. "I didn't know if you…" She hesitated. "Mom sent this along." Might as well jump in with both feet. Being underhanded about anything went against her inherent streak of honesty, but if her mother questioned her later, she would explain then.

Cooper took the cooler into the kitchen. She followed close behind, awestruck by every nook of the impressive home. The kitchen was a study in polished chrome and marble. It looked as clean as a hospital, yet welcoming. That was her mother's gift, she realized.

"Let me fix you something to drink. Coffee okay?" His eyes pinned hers, and she nodded.

After he poured her a mug, she followed him into a room with a fireplace and book-lined walls. His den, she decided. Two dark leather chairs with matching ottomans sat obliquely in front of the fireplace. He took her hat and red wool coat, hung them in a closet and motioned for her to sit in the chair opposite him.

Centering her attention on the steaming coffee, Ashley paused before speaking again. "I came to apologize."

A movement out of the corner of her eye attracted

her gaze, and she watched as Cooper relaxed against the back of the chair.

"Apologize? Whatever for?" he asked.

Her head shot up, and she swallowed the bitter taste in her mouth. He wasn't going to make this easy for her. "I was unforgivably rude the other day, and I have no excuse. You were being thoughtful, and…"

He didn't allow her to finish. Instead he gestured with his hand, dismissing her regret. "Nonsense."

Scooting to the very edge of her cushion, she inhaled a quivering breath. "Will you please stop waving at me as though you find my apology amusing?" she said, fighting to keep a grip on her rising irritation. She bolted to her feet and walked to the far side of the room, pretending to examine his collection of books while struggling to keep her composure. Without turning around she mumbled miserably, "I'm sorry, I didn't mean that."

His soft chuckle sounded remarkably close, and when she turned she discovered that only a few inches separated them.

"Oh, Cooper." Her eyes drank in the heady sight of him. "I've felt wretched all week. Please forgive me for the way I acted the other day."

"Have you decided to accept my offer?" The laughter drained from his eyes.

Sadly she shook her head. "Please understand why I can't."

He raked his hands through his hair, ruining the well-groomed effect.

Ashley's finger itched to smooth down the sides, to follow the proud line of his jaw, to touch him. Of its own volition her hand rose halfway to his face before she realized what she was doing.

Their eyes holding one another, Cooper captured her hand and held her motionless. Even his touch had the power to shoot sparks of awareness up her spine. When he raised her fingers to his mouth, his lips gently caressed her knuckles. Trapped in a whirlpool of sensation, she swayed toward him.

Her movement seemed to snap something within him, and he roughly pulled her into his embrace.

"Cooper." His name was a bittersweet sigh that was muffled as his mouth crushed hers. His hold was so tight that for a moment it was difficult to breathe, not that it mattered when she was in his arms.

Automatically, she raised her hands and linked them behind his neck as their mouths strained against one another. It was as if they couldn't get close enough, couldn't give enough. Ashley's lithe frame was flooded with a warm excitement, a glowing happiness that stole over her. A soft, whispering sigh escaped as he moved his face against her hair, brushing against her like a cat seeking contentment.

"Why is it you bring out the—"

The phone interrupted him, the sharp ringing shattering the tender moment. With a low, protesting groan he kissed the tip of her nose and moved across the room to answer the insistent call.

Ashley watched him, her heart swelling with pride

and love. Their eyes met, and she noticed a warm light she had never seen in him before.

"Yes," he answered abruptly, then stiffened. "Claudia, this is a surprise."

Chapter 3

"Wonderful." Cooper continued speaking into the receiver, his eyes avoiding Ashley's. "Of course you're welcome, you know that. Plan to stay as long as you like."

The conversation lasted several more minutes, but it didn't take Ashley long to realize that Cooper wasn't going to let her friend know she was with him. She couldn't help wondering if she was a source of embarrassment to him. How could he hold her and kiss her one minute, then pretend that she wasn't even there with him the next? The promise of happiness she had savored so briefly in his arms left a bitter aftertaste. He must have sensed her confusion, because he turned away as the conversation with Claudia continued and kept his back to her until it ended a few minutes later.

"That was Claudia and Seth," he told her unnec-essarily. "He's got a conference coming up in Seattle the second week of December. They've decided to fly down for that, then stay for the holidays."

He sounded so genuinely pleased that Ashley quickly quelled the spark of hurt. She didn't know why he'd chosen to ignore her, but she was going to put it out of her mind, and she certainly wouldn't ask.

"That's great."

"It is, isn't it?" He moved back to her side, gently easing her into his arms. "This is going to be a won-derful Christmas," he murmured against the softness of her hair.

His voice was like that of an eager child, and it rang a chord of compassion within her. He had taken over his brother's business when he was barely into his twenties. Over the years he had built up the sup-ply operation that extended into ten western states. Claudia had once told her that his goal was to have the business go nationwide. But at what price? she wondered. His health? His personal life? What drove a man like Cooper Masters? she wondered. Could it be the desire for wealth? He was already richer than anyone she knew. Recognition? Yet he was careful to keep a low profile, and from what her mother and Claudia told her, he seemed to jealously guard his pri-vacy. The man was a mystery she might never under-stand, a puzzle she might never solve.

What did it matter, as long as he held her like this? she asked herself. Her arms around his waist, she laid her head against his solid, muscular chest. The steady beat of his heart sounded in her ear, and she smiled with contentment.

"I feel like doing something crazy," he said, and tipped his head back, laughter dancing in his eyes. "Usually that means taking you in my arms and kissing you like there's no tomorrow."

"I'm game." The urge to wrap her arms around his neck and abandon her pride was almost overwhelming. What pride? her mind echoed. That had been lost long ago where Cooper was concerned.

"Let's go for a walk," he suggested.

Ashley stifled a protest. "It's raining," she warned. A torrential downpour would have been a more accurate description of the turn the weather had taken. She moistened her lips. For once she would have been content to sit in front of the fireplace.

"I'll get us an umbrella," he said, a smile softening the sharp, angular lines of his face.

When he returned, he'd changed clothes and shoes, and was wearing a dark overcoat. A black umbrella dangled from his forearm.

"Ready?" he asked, regarding her expectantly.

He took her red beret and matching wool coat from the closet. He held the coat open for her to slip her arms into the silk-lined sleeves. As he pulled the coat to her shoulders, he paused to gently kiss the slim column of her neck from behind. The tiny kiss shot a tingling awareness over her skin, and she sighed.

"Doesn't this make you want to sing," he teased as they stepped outside. Rain pelted the earth in an angry outburst.

"No." She laughed. "It makes me want to sit in front of a warm fireplace and drink something warm."

Cooper tipped back his head and howled with laughter. She was only echoing his words to her the night it had snowed. It hadn't been that funny. She watched him sheepishly, trying to recall a time she had ever heard him really laugh.

One arm tucked around her waist, he brought her close to his side. "Why is it when I'm with you I want to laugh and sing and behave totally irrationally?"

Wrapping her arm around his waist, she looked up into his sparkling eyes. "I seem to bring out that quality in a lot of people."

He chuckled and opened the umbrella, which protected them from the worst of the downpour. He led her along a cement walkway that meandered around the property, finally ending at a chain link fence that was built at the top of a bluff that fell sharply into Puget Sound. The night view was spectacular. Ashley could only imagine how much more beautiful it would be during the day. An array of distant lights illuminated the sky and cast their reflective glow into the dark waters of the Sound.

"That must be Vashon Island," she said without realizing she had spoken out loud.

"Yes, and over there's Commencement Bay in Tacoma." He pointed to another section of lights. But his gaze wasn't on the city. Instead she felt it lingering, gently caressing her. When she turned her head, their eyes locked and time came to a screeching halt. Later she wouldn't remember who moved first. But suddenly she was tightly held in his arms, the umbrella carelessly tossed aside as they wrapped one another in a feverish embrace. The kiss that followed was the most beautiful she had ever received, filled with some unnamable emotion, deep, tender, sweet, and all-consuming.

Rain bombarded them, drenching her hair until it hung in wet ringlets. He looked down at her, his breathing uneven and hoarse. Gently he smiled, wiping the moisture from her face. With a laugh, he tugged her hand, and together they ran back to the safety and warmth of the house.

It was the memory of his kiss and that night that sustained Ashley through the long, silent days that followed. Every night she hurried home from work hoping Cooper would contact her in some way. Each day led to bitter disillusionment. When her mother phoned Wednesday afternoon, Ashley already knew what she was going to say.

"Mr. Masters thanked me for the Thanksgiving dinner you brought him. Why didn't you say he was the friend you were going to see?" Her tone hinted of disapproval.

"Because I knew what you would have said if I did," Ashley countered honestly.

"I had no idea you've been seeing Mr. Masters."

"We've only gone out once."

A short, stilted silence followed. "He's too old for you, dear. He's forty, you know."

Closing her eyes, Ashley successfully controlled

the desire to argue. "I don't think you need to worry, Mother," she said soothingly. "I doubt that I'll be seeing him again."

"I just don't want to see you get hurt," her mother added on a gentler note.

"I know you don't."

They chatted for a few minutes longer and ended the conversation on a happy note, talking about Marsha and the coming baby, her mother's first grandchild.

Replacing the phone, Ashley released a long, slow breath. Cooper's image returned to trouble her again. Everything about him only served as a confirmation of her mother's unspoken warning. He wore expensively tailored suits, his hair was professionally styled, and he seemed to be stamped with an unmistakable look of refinement. Something she would never have. And he was almost fourteen years older than she was, but why should that bother him or her parents when it had never mattered to her? At least she didn't need an explanation for why he hadn't contacted her. After talking to her mother, he had undoubtedly been reminded of their differences. Once again he would shut himself off from her, and who knew how long it would be before she could break through the thick wall of his pride?

Sunday morning during church the pastor lit the first candle of the Advent wreath. Ashley listened attentively as the man of God explained that the first candle represented prophecy. Then he read Scripture from the Old Testament that foretold the birth of a Savior.

Ashley left church feeling more uplifted than she had the entire week. How could she be depressed and miserable at the happiest time of the year? Claudia, Seth and the boys were coming, and Cooper wouldn't be able to avoid seeing her. Perhaps then she could find a way to prove that their obvious differences weren't all that significant.

An email from Claudia was waiting for her after work Monday afternoon. It read:

Ashley,

I'm sorry it's taken me so long to write. I can't believe how busy my boys manage to keep me. I've got some wonderful news! No, I'm not pregnant again, although I don't think Seth would mind. Cooper either, for that matter. He's surprised both of us the way he loves the boys. The good news is that we'll be arriving at Sea/Tac Airport, Saturday, December 12th at 10 A.M. and plan to stay with Cooper through to the first of the year. That first week Seth will be involved in a series of meetings, but the remainder of the time will be the vacation we didn't get the chance to take this summer.

I can't tell you how excited I am to be seeing you again. I've missed you so much. You've always been closer to me than any sister. You'll hardly recognize John. At three, he's taller than most four-year-olds, but then what can we expect, with Seth being almost six-six? There's so much I want to tell you that it seems impossible to put in a letter or speak about over the phone. Promise to block out the holidays on your calendar, because I'm dying to see you again. The Lord's been good to me, and I have so much to tell you.

Scotty just woke from his nap and he never has been one to wake in a happy mood. Take care. I'm counting the days until the 12th.

Love,

Claudia, Seth, John and Scott

Ashley read the message several times. Of course, Claudia didn't realize that she already knew they were coming. Again the hurt washed over her that Cooper had pretended she wasn't there when Claudia had phoned on Thanksgiving Day.

She circled the day on her calendar and stepped back wistfully. When Scott had been born that spring, Cooper had flown up to Nome to spend time with Claudia, Seth and John. Ashley had yet to see the newest Lessinger. Cooper had said it earlier, and now Ashley added her own affirmation. This was going to be the most wonderful Christmas yet.

Ashley's alarm buzzed early the morning of the twelfth. She groaned defiantly until she remembered that she would have to hurry and shower if she was going to meet Claudia's plane as she intended.

A little while later, wearing jeans and a red cable knit sweater, she tucked her pant legs into her boots. Thank goodness it wasn't raining.

She parked Milligan in the multistory circular parking garage, then hurried down to baggage claim, her heels clicking against the tiled surface.

Cooper was already waiting when she arrived. He didn't notice her, and for a moment she enjoyed just watching him. He looked fresh and vital. It hardly seemed like more than two weeks since she'd last seen him, and yet they'd been the longest weeks of her life.

The morning sunlight filtered unrestrained through the large plate glass windows, glinting on his dark hair. He was tall and broad shouldered. Seeing him again allowed all her pent up feelings to spill over. It took more restraint than she cared to admit not to run into his arms. Instead she adjusted her purse strap over her shoulder, stuffed her hands in her pockets and approached him with a dignified air.

"Good morning, Cooper." She gave him a bright smile, although the muscles at the corners of her mouth trembled with the effort. "It's a beautiful day, isn't it?"

If he was surprised to see her, he hid the shock well. "Ashley," he said, and stood. "Did you bring Madigan with you?" Concern laced his voice.

"Milligan," she corrected and laughed. "You never give up, do you?"

"Not if I can help it." He seemed to struggle with himself for a moment. "How have you been?"

"Sick," she lied unmercifully. "I was in the hospital for several days, doctors said I could have died. But I'm fine now. How about you?" she asked with a flippant air.

"Don't taunt me, Ashley," he warned thickly.

She was deliberately provoking him, but she didn't care. "For all you know it could be true. It's been more than two weeks since I've heard from you."

Turning his gaze to the window, he stood stiffly, watching the sky. "It seems longer," he murmured so low she had to strain to hear.

"Why?" she challenged, standing directly beside him, her own gaze cast toward the heavens.

"How's Webber?" He answered her question with one of his own.

"Webber?" she repeated, her face twisted into a puzzled frown. "You mean Webb?"

"Whoever." He shrugged.

"How do you know about Webb? Oh, wait. Mom." She answered her own question before he had the chance. "Webb and I are friends, nothing more." So this was the way her mother had handled the situation. For a moment fiery resentment burned in her eyes. She loved her mother, but there were times when Sarah Robbins's actions incensed her.

"Your mother mentioned that you and he see a lot of one another." His words were spoken without emotion, as if the subject bored him.

"Friends often do," she returned defensively. "But then, I doubt you'd know that."

She could feel the anger exude from him as he bristled.

"I'm sorry," she whispered, her tone contrite. "I didn't mean that the way it sounded." When she turned her head to look at him, she saw the cold fury leave his eyes. She placed her hand gently on his forearm, drawing his attention to her. "I don't want to argue. Seth and Claudia will know something's wrong, we won't be able to hide it."

He placed his hand on top of hers and squeezed it momentarily. "I don't want to argue, either," he finished. "According to the notice board, their flight has landed."

Ashley's heart fluttered with excitement. "Cooper," she mouthed softly. "My school is having a Christmas party next weekend. Would you…" Her tongue stumbled over the words. "I mean, could you…would you consider going with me?"

His shocked look cut through her hopes. "Next weekend?"

"The nineteenth…it's a Friday night. A dinner party, I don't think it'll be all that formal, just a faculty get together. It's the last day of school, and the dinner is a small celebration."

"Will you be wearing your red cowboy boots?"

"No, I was going to borrow Dad's fishing rubbers," she shot back, then immediately relented. "All right, for you, I'll wear a dress, pantyhose, the whole bit."

Unbuttoning his coat, Cooper took out his cell phone from inside his suit pocket. He punched a few buttons. A frown brought thick brows together. "It seems I've already got plans that night."

Disappointment settled over Ashley. Somehow she'd known he wouldn't accept, that he would find an excuse not to attend.

"I understand," she murmured, but her voice wobbled dangerously.

The silence between them lasted until she saw Claudia, Seth and the boys descending the escalator. As soon as they reached the bottom John broke loose from his father's hand and ran into Cooper's waiting arms.

"Uncle Coop, Uncle Coop!" he cried with childish delight and looped his arms around Cooper's neck. John didn't seem to remember Ashley at first until she offered him a bright smile. "Auntie Ash?" he questioned, holding out his arms to her.

She held out her own arms, and Cooper handed the boy to her. Immediately John spread moist kisses over her cheek. When she glanced over she noticed that Seth and Cooper were enthusiastically shaking hands.

"Ashley," Claudia chimed happily. "I didn't know whether you'd make it to the airport or not. I love your hair."

"So does Webb," she laughed, and had the satisfaction of seeing Cooper's eyes narrow angrily. "And this little angel must be Scott." With John's legs wrapped around her waist, Ashley leaned over to examine the eight-month-old baby in Claudia's arms. "And I bet John's a wonderful big brother, aren't you, John?"

The boy's head bobbed up and down. Both of the Lessinger boys had Seth's dark looks, but their eyes were as blue as a cloudless sky. Claudia's eyes.

Ashley didn't get a chance to talk to her friend until later that afternoon. Both boys were down for a nap, Seth and Cooper were concentrating on a game of chess in Cooper's den, while Ashley and Claudia sat enjoying the view from a bay window in the formal dining room.

"I can't get over how good you look," Claudia said, blowing into a steaming coffee mug. "Your hair really is great."

"The easiest style I've ever had." Ashley ran her fingers through the bouncing curls and shook her head, and her blond locks fell naturally into place.

"Do you see much of Cooper?" Claudia delivered the question with deceptive casualness.

"Hardly at all," Ashley replied truthfully. "Why do you ask?"

"I don't know. You two were giving one another odd looks at the airport. I could tell he wasn't pleased with your riding that moped. I thought maybe something was going on between the two of you."

Ashley dismissed Claudia's words with a short shake of her hand. "I'm sure you're mistaken. Can you imagine Cooper Masters being interested in anyone like me?"

"In some ways I can," Claudia insisted. "You two balance one another. He takes everything so seriously, while you finagle your way in and out of anything. I know one thing," she said. "He thinks very highly of you. He has for years."

"You're kidding!"

"I'm not. I don't know that he would have been as happy about me marrying Seth if it hadn't been for you."

"Nonsense," Ashley countered quickly. "I knew you and Seth were right for one another from the first moment I saw you with him. I don't know of any couple who belong together more than you two. And it shows, Claudia, it shows. Your face is radiant. That kind of inner happiness only comes with the deep love of a man."

Claudia's face flushed with color. "I know it sounds crazy, but I'm more in love with Seth now than when I married him four years ago. I never thought that would be possible. I don't understand how I could have doubted our love and that God wanted us together. My priorities are so different now."

"What about your degree? Do you think you'll ever go back to school?"

"I don't know. Maybe someday, but my life is so full now with the boys I can't imagine squeezing another thing in. I wouldn't want to. John and Scott need me. I suppose when they're older and in school full time I might think about finishing my doctorate, but that's years down the road. I do know that Seth will do whatever he can to help me if I decide to go ahead and get my degree." Pausing, she took another drink from her mug. "What about you? Any man in your life?"

"Several," Ashley teased, without looking at her friend. "None I'm serious about, though."

"What about Webb? You've written about him."

Before Ashley could assure Claudia her relationship with Webb didn't extend beyond a convenient friendship, a dark shadow fell into the room, diverting their attention to the two men who had just entered.

Seth's smile rested on his wife as he crossed the

room and placed a loving arm across her shoulders. Cooper remained framed in the archway.

"As usual, Cooper beat the socks off me. I don't know why I bother to play. I can't recall ever beating him."

"What about you, Claudia?" Cooper asked. "You used to play a mean, if a bit unorthodox, game of chess."

Standing, Claudia looped her arm around her husband's waist. "Not me, I'm too tired to concentrate. If everyone will excuse me, I think I'll join the boys and take a nap."

Clenching her mug with both hands, Ashley stood. "I'd better rev up Milligan and get home before the weather—"

"No," Claudia interrupted. "You play Cooper, Ash. You always were a better chess player than me."

Ashley threw a speculative glance toward Cooper, awaiting his reaction. He arched his thick brows in challenge. "Would you care for a game, Miss Robbins?" he asked formally.

Wickedly fluttering her eyelashes, she placed both hands over her heart. "Just what are you suggesting, Mr. Masters?"

Claudia giggled. "You know, suddenly I'm not the least bit tired."

"Yes, you are," Seth murmured, tightening his grip on his wife's waist. "You and I are going to rest and leave these two to a game of chess."

Claudia didn't object when Seth led her from the room.

"Shall we?" Cooper asked, long strides carrying

him to her side. He extended his elbow, and when Ashley placed her arm in his, he gave her a curt nod.

The thought of playing chess with Cooper was an opportunity too good to miss. She was an excellent player and had been the assistant coach for the school's team the year before.

The two leather chairs were pushed opposite one another with a mahogany table standing between. An inlaid board with ivory figures sat atop the table.

"I would like to suggest a friendly wager." The words were offered as a clear challenge.

"Just what are you suggesting?" she asked.

"I'm saying that if I win the match, then you'll accept the new car."

"Honestly, Cooper, you don't give up, do you?"

"Accept the car without any obligation to reimburse me," he continued undaunted, "plus the promise that you'll faithfully drive it to and from work daily."

"And just what do I get if *I* win?" she countered.

"That's up to you."

She released a weary sigh. "I don't think you can give me what I want," she mumbled, lowering her gaze to her hands, laced tightly together in her lap.

"I think I can."

"All right," she added, straightening slightly. "If I win, you must promise never to speak derogatorily of Milligan again, or in any way insinuate that riding my moped is unsafe." He opened and closed his mouth in mute protest. "And in addition I would ask that a generous donation be made to the school's scholarship fund. Agreed?" She could tell he wasn't pleased.

"Agreed." The teasing light left his eyes as he viewed the chess board with a serious look. Taking both a black and a white pawn, he placed them behind his back, then extended his clenched fists for her to choose.

She mumbled a silent prayer, knowing she would have the advantage if she were lucky enough to pick white. Lightly, she tapped his right hand.

Cooper relaxed his fist and revealed the white pawn.

Her spirits soared. He would now be on the defensive.

Neither spoke as they positioned the pieces on the board. A strained, tense air filled the den, and the only sound was the occasional crackle from the fireplace.

Her first move was a standard opening, pawn to king four, which he countered with an identical play. She immediately responded with a gambit, pawn to king's bishop four.

It didn't take her long to impress him with her ability. A smug smile lightly brushed her mouth as she viewed his shock as she gained momentum and dominated the game.

Bending forward, he rubbed a hand across his forehead and then his eyes. Ashley was forced to restrain another smile when he glanced up at her.

"Claudia was right, you *are* a good player."

"Thank you," she responded, hoping to hide the pleasure his acknowledgement gave her.

He made his next move, and she paused to study the board.

"Claudia was right about something else, too," he said softly.

"What's that?" she asked absently, pinching her bottom lip between her thumb and index finger, her concentration centered on the chess board.

"I don't think I've ever told you what an attractive woman you are."

His husky tone seemed to reach out and wrap itself around her. "What'd you say?" Her concentration faltered, and she lifted her gaze to his.

His eyes were narrowed on her mouth. "I said you're beautiful."

The current of awareness between them was so strong that she would gladly have surrendered the game right then and there. She felt close to Cooper, closer than she had to any other person. They had so little in common, and yet they shared the most basic, the strongest, emotion of all. If he had moved or in any way indicated that he wanted her, she would have tossed the chess game aside and wrapped herself in his arms. As it was, her will to win, the determination to prove herself, was quickly lost in the power of his gaze.

"It's your move."

Her eyes darkened with anger as she seethed inwardly. He was playing another game with her, a psychological game in which he had proved to be the clear winner with the first move. Using the attraction she felt for him, he'd hope to derail her concentration. His game read Cooper one, Ashley zilch.

She jumped to her feet and jogged around the room.

Pausing to take a series of deep breaths, she took in his cynical look with amusement.

"I hate to appear ignorant here, but just what are you doing?"

"What does it look like?" she countered sarcastically.

"Either you're training for the Olympics or you're sorely testing my limited patience."

"Guess again," she returned impudently, beginning a series of jumping jacks.

"I thought we were playing chess, not twenty questions."

Hands resting challengingly on her hips, she paused and tossed him a brazen glare. "It was either vent my anger physically or punch you out, Cooper Masters."

"Punch me out?" he echoed in disbelief. "What did I do?"

"You know, so don't try to deny it." The anger had dissipated from her blue eyes as she returned to her chair and resumed her study of the board. As the blood pounded in her ears, she knew she'd made a mistake the minute she lifted her hand from the pawn. But would Cooper recognize her error and gain the advantage?

"Cooper?" she whispered.

"Hmm," he answered absently.

"Do you remember the last time I was here?"

He lifted his gaze to hers. "I'm not likely to forget it. After the cold I caught, I coughed for a week."

"Sometimes doing something crazy and irrational

has a price." She leaned forward, her chin supported by the palm of her hand.

"Not this time, Ashley Robbins," he gloated, making the one move that would cost her the game. "Check."

Chapter 4

Ashley stared at the chess board with a sense of unreality. There was only one move she could make, and she knew what would happen when she took it.

"Checkmate."

She stared at him for a long moment, unable to speak or move. Cooper stood and crossed the room to a huge oak desk that dominated one corner. She watched as he opened a drawer and took out some papers. When he returned to her side, he gave her the car keys.

Her hand was shaking so badly she nearly dropped them.

"This is the registration," he told her, handing her a piece of paper. "After what happened not so long ago, I suggest you keep it in the glove compartment."

Unable to respond with anything more than a nod, she avoided his eyes, which were sure to be sparkling with triumph.

"These are the insurance forms, made out in your name. I believe there's a space for you to sign at the bottom of the policy." He pointed to the large "X" marking the spot, then handed her a pen.

Mutely Ashley complied, but her signature was barely recognizable. She returned the pen.

"I believe that's everything."

"No," she protested, unable to recognize the thin, high voice as her own. "I insist upon paying for the car."

"That wasn't part of our agreement."

"Nonetheless, I insist." She had to struggle to speak clearly.

"No, Ashley," he insisted, "the car is yours."

"But I can't accept something so valuable, not over a silly chess game." She raised her eyes to meet his. Their gazes held, his proud and determined, hers wary and unsure. A muscle moved convulsively at the side of his jaw, and she realized she had lost.

"The car is a gift from me to you. There isn't any way on this earth that I'll accept payment. You were aware of the terms before you agreed to the game."

A painful lump filled her throat, and when she spoke her voice was hoarse. "You have so much," she murmured, her voice cracking. "Must you take my pride, too?" Tears shimmered in the clear depths of her eyes. Wordlessly she left the den, took her coat and walked out the front door. Without a backward glance she climbed aboard Milligan and rode home.

Her mood hadn't improved the next morning as she dressed for church. The sky was dark and threatening, mirroring her temper. How could she love someone as headstrong and narrow minded as Cooper Masters? No wonder his business had grown and prospered over the years. He was ruthless, determined and obstinate.

After tucking her Bible into her backpack, she stepped outside to lock her apartment door. A patch of red in the parking lot caught her attention and she noted that a shiny new car was parked beside Milligan in front of her apartment. As she seethed inwardly, it took great restraint not to vent her anger by kicking the gleaming new car.

The first drops of rain fell lazily to the ground. Even God seemed to be on Cooper's side, she thought, as she heaved a troubled sigh. Either she had to change into her rain gear or drive the car. She chose the latter. Pulling out of the parking lot, she was forced to admit the car handled like a dream. Ashley was prepared to hate the car, but it didn't even take the full five miles to church for her to acknowledge she was going to love this car. Just as much as she loved the man who had given it to her.

As the Sunday School teacher for the three-year-olds, she was excited that John Lessinger would be in her class.

Claudia dropped him off at the classroom, Scotty resting on her hip, the diaper bag dangling from her arm.

"Morning." Ashley beamed warmly. "How's Johnny?" She directed her attention to the small boy who hid behind Claudia's skirts.

"He's playing shy today," Claudia warned.

"I don't blame him," Ashley whispered in return. "A lot's happened in the last couple of days."

"I'll drop Scotty off at the nursery and come back to see how John does."

"He'll be fine," Ashley assured her. "Did you see the playdough, Johnny?" she asked, directing his attention to the low table where several other children were busy playing. "Come over here and I'll introduce you to some of my friends."

John's look was unsure, and he glanced over his shoulder at his retreating mother. His lower lip began to quiver as tears welled in his blue eyes. Kneeling down to his level, Ashley placed her hands on his small shoulders. "Johnny, it's Auntie Ash. You remember me, don't you? There's nothing to frighten you here. Come over and meet Joseph and Matthew. You can tell them all about Alaska."

John was playing nicely with the other children when Claudia returned. She sighed in relief. "Now I can relax," she whispered. "I don't know what it is about men and Sunday mornings, but it takes Seth twice as long as me to get ready. Then I'm left to carry Scott, steer John, haul the diaper bag, the Bibles and my purse, while Seth can't manage anything more than his car keys."

Ashley stifled a giggle. She allowed the children to play for several more minutes, chatting with Claudia, who insisted on staying for the first part of Sunday school to be sure John was really all right.

Ashley gathered the children in a circle and had them sit on the patch of carpet in the middle of the floor. As she sat cross-legged on the floor with them, one of the shyer children came over and seated herself in Ashley's lap. "I'm glad we're all together, together, together," the little girl sang in a sweet, melodious voice. "Because Jesus is here, and teacher's here, and—"

"Cooper's here," Claudia chimed in softly.

The song died on the girl's lips as everyone looked over at the tall, compelling figure standing in the open door. His attention was centered on Ashley and the little girl in her lap. For a moment he seemed to go pale, and the muscles in his jaw jerked, and Ashley wondered what she had done now to anger him. Without a word, he pivoted and left the room.

"I'd better see what he wanted," Claudia said, following him out of the room.

Ashley didn't see either of them again until it was time for the morning worship service. The four adults sat together, Claudia between her and Cooper. A hundred questions whirled in her mind. How had Claudia gotten Cooper to attend church? It wasn't all that long ago that he had scoffed at her friend's newfound faith. She wondered if Seth had some influence on Cooper's decision to attend church. More than likely John had said something, and Cooper had been unable to refuse.

Just as the pastor stepped in front of the congregation to light the third candle of the Advent wreath, a loud cry came from the nursery.

Claudia emitted a low groan. "Scotty." She leaned over and whispered to Ashley, "I wasn't sure I'd be able to leave him this long." She stood and made her way out of the pew. Cooper closed the space separating them.

Never had Ashley been more aware of a man's presence. As his thigh lightly touched hers, she closed her eyes at the potency of the contact. Nervously she scooted away, putting some space between them. When he turned and looked at her an unfamiliar quality had entered his eyes. He smiled, one of those rare smiles that came from his heart and nearly stopped hers. Its overwhelming force left her exposed and completely vulnerable. Undoubtedly he would be able to read the effect he had on her and know her thoughts. Quickly turning her face away, she squeezed her eyes closed, and then the pastor, the service, everything, everyone, was lost as Cooper closed his hand firmly over hers.

In all the years she had loved Cooper, Ashley had never dared to dream that he would sit beside her in church or share her strong faith. The intense sensations of having him near touched her so dramatically that for a moment she was sure her heart would burst with unrestrained happiness.

His grip remained tight and firm until Claudia returned to the pew and sat beside Seth. Immediately Cooper released Ashley's hand. The happiness that had filled her so briefly was gone. He seemed content to hold her hand only as long as no one knew. The minute someone came, he let her go.

Once again she was forcefully reminded of the huge differences that separated them. He was a corporate manager, a powerful, wealthy man. She was a financially struggling schoolteacher. In some ways she was certain he cared for her, but not enough to admit it openly. She sometimes feared she was an embarrassment to him, a fear that had dogged her from the beginning.

"Did you win the Irish Sweepstakes?" Webb asked Ashley as she pulled into the school parking lot and climbed out of the shining new car.

"No," she said and sighed unhappily. "I lost a chess game."

He gave her a funny look. "Let me make certain I've got this straight. You *lost* the chess game and won the car?"

"You got it."

Rubbing the side of his chin with one hand, he stared at her with confused eyes. "I know there's logic in this someplace, but for the moment it's escaped me."

"I wouldn't doubt it," she said, and nodded a friendly greeting to the school secretary as she walked through the door.

"What would you have gotten if you'd *won?*" Webb asked as he followed on her heels.

"Milligan and my pride."

"That's another one of those answers that seems to have gone right over my head." He waved his hand over the top of his blond head in illustration. Confusion clouded his eyes. "All I really want to know is whether this person likes chess and plays often? It wouldn't be hard for me to lose. I don't even like the game."

"You wouldn't want to play this person," she mumbled under her breath, heading toward the faculty room.

"Don't be hasty, Ashley," he countered quickly. "Let me be the judge of that."

Tossing him a look she usually reserved for rowdy students was enough to quell his curiosity.

"We're going to the Christmas party Friday night, aren't we?" he asked, steering clear of the former topic of discussion.

Releasing a slow breath, Ashley cupped a coffee mug with both hands. Her enthusiasm for the party had disappeared with Cooper's excuse not to attend. Probably because she believed that the previous appointment he claimed to have was merely a pretext to avoid refusing her outright.

"I don't know, I have a friend visiting from Alaska," she said before sipping. "We may be doing something that night."

"Sure, no problem," he said with a smile. "Let me know if you change your mind."

No pleading, no hesitation, no regrets. The least he could do was show some remorse over her missing the party. As she watched him saunter out of the faculty room, she threw imaginary daggers at his back. Unhappy and more than a little depressed, she finished her coffee and went to her homeroom.

* * *

"Is there something drastically wrong with me?" Ashley asked Claudia later that afternoon. She'd stopped by after school for a short visit with Claudia and the boys before Cooper returned from his office.

When Claudia looked up from bouncing Scotty on her knee, her eyes showed surprise. "Heavens, no. What makes you ask?"

"I mean, you'd tell me if I had bad breath or something, wouldn't you?"

"You know me well enough to answer that."

As Johnny weaved a toy truck around the chair legs, then pushed it under the table to the far side of the room, Ashley's eyes followed the movement of her godson. Lowering her face, she took a deep breath, afraid she might do something stupid like cry. "I want to get married and have children. I'm twenty-six and not getting any younger."

"I'm sure there are plenty of men out there who'd be interested. Only yesterday Seth was saying how pretty you've gotten. Surely there's someone—"

"That's just it," Ashley interrupted, knowing she couldn't mention Cooper. "There isn't, and I found a gray hair the other day. I'm getting scared."

"You and Cooper both. Have you noticed how he's getting gray along his sideburns? It really makes him look distinguished, doesn't it?"

Ashley agreed with a smile, but her eyes refused to meet her friend's, afraid she wouldn't be able to disguise her feelings for Cooper.

"Oh, before I forget, Seth and I have been invited to a dinner party this Friday night, and we were wondering if you could watch the boys. If you have plans just say so, because I think your mother might be able to do it."

Some devilish impulse made her ask, "What about Cooper?"

"He's got some appointment he can't get out of."

For a startled second the oxygen seemed trapped in Ashley's lungs. He had been telling the truth. He *did* have an appointment. In that brief second the sun took on a brighter intensity; it was as if the birds began to chirp.

"I'd love to stay with John and Scott," she returned enthusiastically. "We'll have a wonderful time, won't we, boys?" Neither one looked especially pleased. Glancing at her watch, Ashley quickly stood. "I've gotta scoot, I'll see you Friday. What time do you want me?"

"Is six too early? I'll try to get the boys fed and dressed."

"Don't do that," Ashley admonished with a laugh. "It'll be good practice for me. I need to learn all this motherhood stuff, you know."

"Don't rush off," Claudia said. "Cooper will be home any minute."

"I can't stay. Tell him I said hello—no, don't," she added abruptly. He might have been telling the truth about being busy Friday night, but it didn't lessen the hurt of his rejection. "Mid-year reports go home this Friday, and I want to get a head start."

Claudia regarded her quizzically as she walked her to the door. "Thanks again for Friday. I don't like to leave the boys with strangers. It's bad enough for them to be away from home."

"Happy to help," Ashley said sincerely. Giving a tiny wave to both boys, she smiled when Scotty raised his chubby hand to her. Johnny ran to the front window to look out, and Ashley played peek-a-boo with him. The small head had just bobbed out from behind the drapes when Cooper spoke from behind her.

"Hello, Ashley."

She stiffened at the sound of his voice, her heartbeat racing double time. Last Sunday at church had been the last time she'd seen him.

"Hello." Her voice was devoid of any warmth or welcome. He looked dignified in his suit and silk tie. Childishly she was upset at him all the more for it.

"Is something the matter?" he asked in a quiet voice.

"No," she answered, her gaze stern and unyielding. "I'm just surprised that you'd taint your image by being seen with me."

"What are you talking about?"

"If you don't know, then I'm not going to tell you."

His gaze narrowed. "What's wrong? Obviously something's troubling you."

"The man's a genius," she replied flippantly. "Now, if you'll excuse me, I'll be on my way."

Cooper's eyes contained a hard gleam she had never

seen. His hand shot out and gripped her upper arm. "Tell me what's going on in that unpredictable mind of yours."

Defiance flared from her as she stared pointedly at his hand until he relaxed his hold. Breaking free, she took a few steps in retreat, creating the breathing space she needed to vent her frustration. "I'll have you know, Cooper Masters, I'm not the least bit ashamed of who or what I am. My mother may be your house-keeper, but she has served you well all these years. My father's a skilled sheet metal worker, and I'm proud of them both. I don't have a thing to be ashamed about. Not in front of you or anyone." Having finished her tirade, she avoided looking at him and walked straight to her car.

She never made it. A strong hand on her shoulder swung her around, pinning her against the side of the car. "What are you implying?" The tone of his voice made Ashley shudder. His nostrils flared with barely restrained fury.

Tears shimmered in her eyes until his face was swimming before her. She bit her bottom lip. Suddenly she could feel the anger drain out of him.

"What's the matter with us?" he demanded hoarsely, then expelled an impatient breath.

"Everything!" she cried, her voice trembling. "Everything," she repeated. When she struggled, he re-leased her and didn't try to stop her again. He stepped back as she climbed inside the car, revved the engine, and drove away.

*   *   *

If Ashley was miserable then, it was nothing compared to the way she felt later. To soothe away her emotional turmoil and frustration, she filled the bathtub with hot water and bubble bath, and soaked in it until the water became tepid. In an attempt to pray, she tried the conversational approach that had come so naturally to her in the past, but even that was impossible in her present state of mind.

Sleep was a long time coming that night. She couldn't seem to find a comfortable position, and when she did drift off she found herself trapped in a dream of hopelessness. Waking early the next morning, she rose before the alarm sounded, put on the coffee and sat in the dark, shadow-filled room waiting for the first light.

Lackadaisically, she reached for her devotional and discovered the suggested reading for the day was the famous love chapter in First Corinthians, Chapter Thirteen. *Love is very patient and kind*, verse four stated.

Had she been patient? Ten years seemed a long time to her, and that was how long it had been since she first realized she'd loved Cooper. Since the tender age of sixteen. Glancing back to her Bible, she continued reading. *Love doesn't demand its own way. It isn't irritable or touchy. It doesn't hold grudges and will hardly notice when others do wrong.... If you love someone you will always believe in him, always expect the best of him, and always stand your ground in defending him.*

Closing her Bible, Ashley released an uneven breath. It looked as though she had a long way to go to achieve the standards God had set.

When it came time for her to pray, she got down on her knees, meditating first on the words she had read. Ever since Sunday she'd expected the worst from Cooper, thought the worst of him. She'd wanted to explain how hurt she was, but it sounded so petty to accuse him of being ashamed of her because he'd quit holding her hand. In voicing her thoughts, the whole incident sounded ludicrous. It seemed she was building things in her own mind because she was insecure. The same thoughts had come to her the night he'd taken her to the Italian restaurant, and the night Claudia had phoned from Alaska. She'd never thought of herself as someone with low self-esteem before Cooper.

"Oh, ye of little faith," she said aloud. *No*, her heart countered, *ye of little love*.

Ashley hummed cheerfully as she pulled into the school parking lot. She was proud of the fact that she had worked things out in her own mind—with God's help, of course. The next time she saw Cooper, she would apologize for her behavior and ask that they start again. Poor man, he wouldn't know what to think. One minute she was ranting and raving, and the next she was apologizing.

Today was a special day for her Senior Literature class. They'd been reading and studying the Western classic *The Oxbow Incident* by Walter Van Tilburg Clark. As part of her preparation for their final exam,

Ashley dressed up as one of the characters in the book. Portraying the part as believably as possible, she was usually able to draw out heated discussions and points that might otherwise have been glossed over.

Today she was dressing as Donald Martin, one of the three men accused of cattle rustling in the powerful narrative. This was always Ashley's favorite part of the quarter, and her classroom antics were well known.

Her afternoon students were buzzing with speculation when the bell rang. She waited until everyone was seated before she came through the door to be greeted by laughter and cheers. She was wearing a ten gallon hat. Her cowboy boots had silver spurs, and her long, slim legs were disguised by leather chaps. Two toy six-shooters were holstered at her hips. With her hair tucked under the hat, she'd made a token attempt toward realism by smearing dirt over her creamy smooth cheeks and pasting a long black mustache across her upper lip.

The class loved it, and immediate speculation arose about what character she was portraying.

"I'm here today to talk about mob justice," she began, sitting on the corner of her desk and dangling one foot over the edge.

"She's Gil," one of the boys in the back row called out.

"Good guess, David," she said, pointing to him. "But I'm no drifter. I own my own spread at Pike's Hole. Me and the Missus are building up our herd."

"It's Mex," someone else shouted.

"No way," Diana Crosby corrected. "Mex wasn't married."

"Good girl, Diana." She twirled both six-shooters around a couple of times and by pure luck happened to place them in the holsters right side up. When her class applauded she bowed, her hat falling off her head. As she bent to pick it up she noticed a face staring at her from the small glass portion of the class door. The face was lovingly familiar. Cooper.

"If you'll excuse me a minute, I have to check my horse," she said, quickly making up a pretense to escape into the hallway.

"What are you doing here?" she demanded in a low tone.

A smile danced in his eyes as he attempted to hide his grin by rubbing his thumb across the angular line of his jaw. "Butch Cassidy, I presume."

"Cooper, I'm in the middle of class," she muttered with an exaggerated sigh, both hands gripping his arms. "But I'm so glad to see you. I feel terrible about the way I acted yesterday. I was wrong, terribly wrong."

The laughter faded from his features as he regarded her seriously. "I had no idea the dinner party meant so much to you."

"What dinner party?" He was talking in riddles.

"The one you asked me to attend with you. I assumed that was what upset you yesterday."

She shook her head in wry dismay. "No...that wasn't it."

"Then what was?"

Casting an apprehensive glare over her shoulder, she turned pleading eyes to him. "I can't talk now."

He rubbed a weary hand over his face. "Ashley, I rearranged my schedule. I'll be happy to take you to the school Christmas party."

She groaned softly. "But I can't go now."

"What do you mean, you can't go?" His dark, steely eyes narrowed.

He didn't need to say another word for her to know how much it had inconvenienced him to readjust his schedule.

"Cooper, I'm sorry, but I..."

"Invited someone else," he finished for her, his eyes as cold as a blast of arctic wind. "That Webber fellow, I imagine."

"I haven't got time to stand in the hall and argue with you. My class is waiting."

"And so, I imagine, is Webber."

Fury blazed in her eyes as she slashed him a cutting look. "You do that on purpose."

"Do what?" His voice was barely civil.

"Call Webb 'Webber,' the same way you call Milligan 'Madigan.' I find the whole denial thing rather childish," she snapped resentfully. By now she was too incensed to care if she was making sense.

"I find that statement unworthy of comment."

"You would." She spun away and stalked back into the classroom, restraining the impulse to slam the door.

Claudia was dressed in a mauve-colored chiffon evening gown that was a stunning complement to her auburn hair and cream coloring. Seth, too, looked remarkably attractive in his suit and tie.

"Okay, I showed you where everything is in the bedroom, and here's the phone number of the restaurant." Claudia laid the pad near the phone in the kitchen. "I've left a baby bottle in the refrigerator, but I've already nursed Scotty, so he probably won't need it."

"Okay," Ashley said, following Claudia out of the kitchen.

"Both boys are dressed for bed, and don't let either of them stay up past eight-thirty. You may need to rock Scotty to sleep."

"No problem, I got my degree in rocking chair."

Checking her reflection in the hallway mirror, Claudia tucked a stray hair back into her coiled French coiffure. "You didn't happen to have an argument with Cooper, did you?" The question came out of the blue.

Ashley could feel the blood rush from her face, then just as quickly flood back. "What makes you ask?"

"Seth and I have hardly seen him the last couple of days, and he's been in the foulest mood. It's not like him to behave like this. I can't understand it."

"What makes you think I have anything to do with it?" she asked, doing her best to conceal her reaction.

"I know it sounds crazy, and I wouldn't want to offend you, Ash, but I still think something's stirring between you two. I may be an old married fuddy-duddy, but I recognize the looks he's been giving you. What I can't understand is why the two of you work so hard at hiding it. As far as I'm concerned, you're perfect for one another."

"Ha," Ashley said harshly. "We can't spend two minutes together lately without going for each other's jugular."

Seth took Claudia's wrap from the hall closet and placed it over her shoulders. "Sounds like the way it was with us a few times, doesn't it, Honey?" he asked, and tenderly kissed the creamy smooth slope of Claudia's neck.

"Call if you have any problems, won't you?" Claudia said, suddenly sounding worried. "Scotty will cry the first few minutes after we've left, but he should quiet down in a little bit, so don't panic."

"I never panic," Ashley assured her with a cheeky grin.

True to his mother's word, Scott gave a hearty cry the minute the door was closed.

"It's all right. Look, here's your teddy."

Scotty took the stuffed animal, threw it across the room and cried all the louder.

Ten minutes passed and nothing seemed to calm his frantic cries. Even John looked as if he was ready to give way and start howling.

"Come on, sweetie, not you, too."

"I want my mommy."

"Let's pretend I'm your mommy," Ashley offered, "and then you can tell me how to make Scotty happy."

"Will you hold me like my mommy?" Johnny asked, a tear running down his pale face.

"Sure, join the crowd," Ashley laughed, lifting him

so that she had a baby on each hip. Johnny cried in small whimpering sounds and Scott in large howling sobs.

Pacing the floor, she glanced up to find Cooper standing in the entryway watching her, a stunned look on his face.

Chapter 5

"Look, Johnny, Scott," Ashley said cheerfully. "Uncle Cooper's here."

Both boys cried harder. Scotty buried his face in her neck, his stubby hands tangled in her blond hair. When he pulled a long strand, she cried out involuntarily, "Ouch."

The small protest spurred Cooper into action. He hung his overcoat in the hall closet and entered the living room, taking John from Ashley.

"What's the matter, fella?" he asked in a reassuring tone.

"I want my mommy!" John wailed.

"They went out for the evening," Ashley explained, both hands supporting Scott as she paced the floor, making cooing sounds in his ear. But nothing seemed to comfort the baby, who continued to cry pitifully.

"What about Webber and your party?" Cooper asked stiffly.

"I tried to tell you that I wasn't going," she explained, and breathed in deeply. "I didn't say a thing about attending the party with Webb. You assumed I was."

"Are you telling me the reason you didn't go tonight is because you'd promised to baby-sit John and Scotty?"

Ashley silently confirmed the statement with a weak nod. His dark eyes narrowed with self-directed anger.

"Why do you put up with me?" he asked.

She didn't get the opportunity to answer, because Scotty began bellowing even louder.

A troubled frown broke across Cooper's expression. "Is he sick? I've never heard him cry like that."

"No, just unhappy. Claudia said she'd left a bottle for him. Maybe we should heat it up."

All four moved into the kitchen. With Scotty balanced on her hip, Ashley took the baby bottle out of the refrigerator. "It needs to be heated." She held it out to him.

"If you say so," he said, shrugging his broad shoulders. "How does your mommy do it?" he asked Johnny, who seemed more secure now that his uncle had arrived.

"She nurses Scotty."

Slowly Cooper's dark eyes met hers, amusement flickering across his face. She giggled, and soon they were both laughing. Scotty cried all the harder, clinging to Ashley.

The humor broke the terrible tension that had existed between them for days.

Cooper smiled warmly into her eyes, trying to hold back his laughter. He walked across the room and took a large pan out of the bottom cupboard, then filled it with hot water. "I don't want to chance the microwave. What if I melt the bottle? It's plastic, after all." By the time he'd set the pan on the stove and turned on the burner, he'd regained his composure.

Ashley placed the baby bottle in the water. "Is it supposed to float?"

"I don't know." He shook his head briefly, the look in his eyes unbelievably tender.

"Oh well, we'll experiment, won't we, boys?"

"What's an experiment?" Johnny asked. He was sitting on top of the counter, his short legs dangling over the edge.

"It's a process by which we examine the validity of a hypothesis and determine the nature of something as yet unknown."

"Cooper..." Ashley laughed at the way the three-year-old's mouth and eyes rounded as he tried to understand what Cooper was saying. "Honestly! Let me explain." She turned to Johnny. "An experiment is trying something you've never done before."

"Oh!" Johnny's clouded expression brightened, and he eagerly shook his head. "Mommy does that a lot with dinner."

"That's right." Ashley beamed.

"Smart aleck," Cooper whispered under his breath, his gaze lingering on her for a heart-stopping moment.

Ashley found herself drowning in the dark depths of his eyes and quickly averted her head. The water in the pan was coming to a boil, the baby bottle tossing back and forth in the bubbling liquid.

"It must be ready by now," she commented as she turned off the burner.

Cooper went out to the back porch and returned with a huge pair of barbeque tongs. He quickly lifted the bottle from the hot water, setting it upright on the counter.

"Nicely done," she commented, and waited a few minutes before testing the milk's temperature. Once she was sure it wouldn't burn Scotty's tender mouth, she led the way into the living room.

Remembering what Claudia had said about rocking the baby, Ashley sat in the polished wooden rocker and gently tipped back and forth. Scotty reached for the bottle and held it himself, sucking greedily. Her eyes filled with tenderness. She brushed the fine hair from his face and cupped his ear. The room was blissfully silent as John and Cooper sat across from her.

Johnny crawled into Cooper's lap and handed him a book that he wanted read. Cooper complied, his voice and face expressive as he turned page after page, reading quietly.

Ashley found her attention drawn again and again to the man and the young boy. A surge of love filled her, so strong and overpowering that tears formed in her eyes. Hurriedly she looked away, batting her eyelashes to forestall the moisture.

Losing interest in the bottle, Scotty began chewing the nipple and watching Ashley. His round eyes held a fascinated expression as he studied her hair and reached out to grab her blond curls.

Carefully, she brushed her hair back. As she did her eyes met Cooper's. His gaze had centered on her mouth with a disturbing intensity. The power he had over her produced an aching tightness in her throat.

"You'll make a good mother someday." His voice was low and husky.

"I was just thinking the same thing about you," she murmured, then realizing what she'd said and hastened to correct herself. "I mean a good father."

"I know what you meant."

"Uncle Cooper." Johnny tugged at Cooper's arm. "You're supposed to be reading."

"So I am," he agreed in a lazy drawl. "So I am."

Finished now, Scotty tossed the bottle aside, then struggled to sit up. "I know I should burp him," Ashley said, "but I'm not sure of the best way to hold him."

Cooper stood. "Claudia left a baby book lying around here somewhere. Maybe it would be best to look it up."

The small party moved into Cooper's den. Ashley carried Scotty on her hip. He didn't make a sound, having apparently become accustomed to her, and that pleased her.

Cooper found the book and set it on his desk, flipping the pages. As soon as Ashley bent over next to him to read a paragraph, Scotty burped loudly.

"Well I guess that answers that, doesn't it?" she said, laughing.

"Uncle Coop, can I have a piggy back ride?" Johnny climbed onto the chair and held out his hands entreatingly.

Cooper looked unsure for a moment but agreed with a good-natured nod. "Okay, partner."

Johnny climbed onto Cooper's back, looped his legs around his uncle's waist and clung tightly with his chubby arms. "Gitty-up, horsey," he commanded happily.

Cooper grinned. "How come this is called a piggy-back ride and you say 'Gitty-up, horsey'?"

Johnny chuckled. "It's an experiment."

"He's got you there." Ashley flashed him a cheeky grin.

Cooper mumbled something unintelligible and trotted into the next room.

Ashley followed, enjoying the sight of Cooper looking so relaxed. Scotty clapped his hands gleefully, and Ashley trotted after the others.

After a moment Cooper paused. "I smell something."

"Not..." She didn't finish.

"I think it must be."

Three pairs of eyes centered on the baby. Dramatically, Johnny plugged his nose. "Scotty has a messy diaper," he announced with the formality of a judge.

"Well, he's still a baby, and they're expected to do that sort of thing. Isn't that right, Scotty?"

Unconcerned, Scotty cooed happily, chewing on his pajama sleeve.

"Claudia showed me where everything is, this shouldn't take long."

"Ashley." Cooper stopped her, his face tight. "I think I should probably be the one to change him."

"You? Why? Are you saying it's the proper thing to do, since he's a boy?"

"I'm saying it's not a lot of fun and I've done it before, so..."

Unsuccessfully disguising a grateful smile, she handed him the baby. Scotty protested loudly as Cooper supported him with his hands under the baby's armpits, holding him as far away as possible.

"Call me if you need help."

Johnny led the way up the stairs, the large wooden steps almost more than he could manage. Cooper glanced down, his brow marred by a frown, then followed his nephew down the hall.

Ashley waited at the foot of the stairs, one shoe positioned on the bottom step, in case Cooper called.

"Auntie Ash." Johnny came running down the wide hallway and stopped at the top of the stairs. "Uncle Cooper says he needs you."

A tiny smile formed lines at the edges of her mouth. Somehow the words sounded exceedingly beautiful. She yearned to hear them from Cooper himself, though not exactly in this context.

She entered the bedroom and saw that his frown had deepened. He extended a hand to stop her as she entered the nursery. "I need a washcloth or something...you can give it to John."

Ashley ran the water in the bathroom sink until it was warm and soaked the washcloth in it. After wringing out most of the moisture, she handed it to Johnny, who ran full speed into the bedroom.

Loitering outside the room, Ashley impatiently stuck her head inside the door. "Cooper, this is silly."

"I'm almost finished," he mumbled. "This was just a little...more than I'm used to dealing with." His expensive silk tie was loosened, and the long sleeves of his crisp business shirt had been rolled up to his elbows.

Ashley watched from the doorway, highly amused.

"Voilà," he said, pleased with himself, as he stood Scotty up on the table.

Ashley dissolved into fits of laughter. The disposable diaper stuck out at odd angles in every direction. Had he really done this before, or had he just been trying to spare her an unpleasant task? As she was giggling, the diaper began to slide down Scotty's legs, stopping at knee level. She laughed so hard that her shoulders shook.

"Here, let me try," she insisted after a moment, swallowing her amusement as best she could.

Cooper looked almost grateful when she took the baby and laid him back onto the changing table. She did the best she could, but her efforts weren't much better than Cooper's. He was kind enough not to comment.

When she had finished, she paused to look around the room for the first time. Claudia had told her about the bedroom Cooper had decorated for the boys, but she hadn't had a chance to take it all in earlier. Now she could stand back and marvel. The walls were painted blue, with cotton candy clouds floating past and a huge multicolored rainbow with a pot of gold.

Johnny, who had apparently noticed her appreciation, tugged at her hand. "Come look."

Obligingly, Ashley followed.

He closed the door, and flipped the light switch, casting the room into darkness. "See," he said, pointing to the ceiling.

Ashley looked up and noticed a hundred glittering stars illuminated on the huge ceiling. What had been an attractive, whimsical room with the light on became a land of fantasy with the light off.

"It's great," she murmured, her voice slightly thick. Over and over again Claudia had commented on how much Cooper loved the boys. Ashley had seen it herself. He wasn't lofty or untouchable when he was with John and Scott. His affinity for children showed he could be human and vulnerable. He was so warm and loving with the boys that it was all she could do to keep from running into his arms.

Cooper made a show of checking his wristwatch. "Isn't it about time for you boys to go to bed?"

"Can I wear your watch again?" Johnny asked eagerly.

Cooper didn't hesitate, slipping the gold band from his wrist and placing it on his godson's arm.

Ashley couldn't help but wonder at the ease with which Cooper relinquished a timepiece that must have cost thousands of dollars.

Scotty cried when she placed him in the crib. She stayed for several minutes, attempting to comfort him, but to no avail. She would just get him to lie down and tuck him under the blanket when he would pull himself upright, hold onto the bars and look at her with those pleading blue eyes. She couldn't refuse, and finally gave in and lifted him out of the crib.

"Claudia said something about rocking him to sleep."

"No problem," Cooper said with a sly grin. He left and returned a minute later with the wooden rocker from downstairs.

"Will you pray with me, Uncle Cooper?" Johnny— who was also still wide awake—requested, kneeling at his bedside.

Cooper joined the little boy on the plush navy blue carpet.

For the second time that night Ashley was emotionally stirred by the sight of this man with a child.

"God bless Mommy, Daddy and Scotty," John prayed, his head bowed reverently, his small hands folded. "And God bless Uncle Cooper, Auntie Ash and all the angels. And I love you, Jesus, and amen."

"Amen," Cooper echoed softly.

Scotty had his eyes closed as he lay securely in Ashley's arms. Gently she stood to lay him in the crib, but both eyes flew open anxiously and he struggled to sit up. With a short sigh of acquiescence, she sat back down and began to rock again. Content, Scotty watched her, but with every minute his eyes closed a little more. She wouldn't make the mistake of getting up too early a second time. Gently, she brushed the wisps of hair from his brow.

Cooper was sitting on the mattress beside Johnny, who was playing with the wristwatch, his gaze fixed on the lighted digits. Cooper pushed a variety of buttons, which delighted the boy. After a few minutes, Cooper tucked Johnny between the sheets and leaned over to kiss his brow.

"Night, night, Auntie Ash," Johnny whispered.

She blew him a kiss. Johnny pretended to catch it, then tucked his stuffed animal under his arm and rolled over.

The moment was serene and peaceful. Finally sure that Scotty was asleep, she stood and gently put him into the crib. Cooper came to stand at her side, a hand cupping her shoulder as they looked down on the sleeping baby.

Neither spoke, afraid of destroying the tranquility. When they finally stepped back, he removed his hand. Immediately, Ashley missed the warmth of his touch as they headed back downstairs.

He paused at the bottom of the stairs, a step ahead of her. He turned, halting her descent.

"Ashley," he whispered on a soft trembling breath, his look dark and troubled.

A tremor ran through her at the perplexing expression she saw in his eyes. Spontaneously she slipped her arms around his neck without even being aware of what she was doing.

"Ashley," he repeated, the husky sound a gentle caress. He crushed her to him, his arms hugging her waist as his lips sought hers. The kiss was like it had always been between them. That jolt of awareness so strong it seemed to catch them both off guard. When his mouth broke from hers, she could hear his labored breathing and the heavy thud of his heart.

He loosened his hold, bringing his hands up to her neck, weaving long fingers through her hair. His lips soothed her chin and temple, and she gloried in the tingling sensations that spread through her. She continued to lean against him, needing his support, because her legs felt weak and wobbly.

"I'm sorry about the party tonight," he murmured, and she couldn't doubt the sincerity in his voice.

"No, I'm the one who should be sorry. I said so many terrible things to you." Tipping her head back so she could gaze into his impassioned eyes, she spoke again. "I'm amazed you put up with me." Lovingly, she traced the proud line of his jaw, a finger paused to investigate the tiny cleft in his chin. Unable to resist, she kissed him there and loved the sound of his groan.

"Ashley," he warned, "please, it's hard enough keeping my hands off you."

"It is? Really? Oh, Cooper, really?"

"Yes, so don't tease."

"I think that's the nicest thing you've ever said to me."

His hand curved around her waist as he brought her down the last step. "Have you eaten dinner?"

"No, I didn't have time. You?"

"I'm starved. Maybe we can dig up something in the kitchen."

She couldn't see why they needed to look for anything. Her mother did the cooking for him, and there were bound to be leftovers. "Mom—"

"I gave her the rest of the month off," he explained before she could finish.

"Well, in that case, I vote for pizza."

"Pizza?" He glanced at her, aghast.

"All right, you choose." She placed an arm around him and smiled deeply into his dark eyes.

"Let's look." Together they rounded the corner that led to the kitchen. He checked the refrigerator and turned, shaking his head. "I don't know how we'd manage to make pizza from any of this."

"Not make," she corrected. "Order. All we need to do is phone and wait for the delivery guy."

"Amazing." He tilted his head at an inquiring angle. "Is this something you and this Webber fellow do often?"

A denial rose automatically to her lips, but she successfully swallowed it back. "Sometimes. And his name is Dennis Webb."

The corner of his mouth lifted in a half-smile. "Sorry." But he didn't look the least bit repentant.

"Do you want me to order?"

He straightened and leaned against the kitchen counter. "Sure, whatever you want."

"Canadian bacon, pineapple and olives."

His dark eyes widened questioningly, but he nodded his agreement.

She couldn't help laughing. "It tastes great, trust me."

"I'm afraid I'll have to."

She used the phone in the kitchen. Cooper regarded her suspiciously when she punched in the number without looking it up in the directory.

"You know the number by heart? Just how often do you do this?"

"I'm good with numbers."

After placing their order, she turned and smiled seductively. "Shall we play a game of chess while we're waiting?"

His look was faintly mocking. "I have a feeling I'd better not."

"Why?" she asked, batting her long lashes.

"If I say yes, then no wagers," he insisted.

"You take all the fun out of it," she said, and feigned a pout. "But I'll manage to whip you anyway."

He chuckled and took her hand, leading them into his den.

While she set up the game board, Cooper lit the logs in the fireplace. Within minutes flickering shadows played across the walls.

His eyes were serious as he sat down opposite her. As before, each move was measured and thought-filled. At mid-game the advantage was Ashley's. Then the doorbell chimed, interrupting their concentration.

Cooper answered and returned with a huge flat box, his look slightly abashed. "You ordered enough for a family of five," he chastised her.

"You said you were hungry," she argued, not lifting her gaze from the game. Her eyes brightened as she moved and captured his knight, lifting it from the board.

"How'd you do that?" His expression turned serious as he set the pizza on the hearth to keep warm. "I don't want to stop now. We can eat later."

"I'm hungry," she insisted slyly.

He waved her away with the flick of his hand, his attention centered on the board. "You go ahead and eat, then."

She left the room and returned a minute later with a plate and napkin, sitting on the floor in front of the fire. The aroma of melted cheese and Canadian bacon filled the room when she lifted the lid. "Yumm, this is delicious," she said after swallowing her first bite.

A frown drove three wide creases into his brow as he glanced up. "You're eating in here," he said, as if noticing her for the first time.

"I'm not supposed to?" Color invaded her face until her cheeks felt hot. She was always doing something she shouldn't where Cooper was concerned. Her actions had probably shocked him. No doubt he had never in his entire life eaten any place but on a table with a linen cloth. Pizza on the floor made her look childish and gauche.

His expression softened. "It's fine, I'm sure. It's just that I never have."

"Oh." She felt ridiculously close to tears and bowed her head. The pizza suddenly tasted like glue. She closed the lid, then set her plate aside. "The carpet is probably worth a fortune. I wouldn't want to ruin it," she said with total sincerity.

He put a finger under her chin and raised her eyes to his. "Shh," he whispered, and gently laid his mouth over hers.

His kiss had been unexpected, catching her off guard, but quickly she became a willing victim.

"You're right," Cooper murmured, then chuckled. "The pizza does taste good." He lowered himself onto the floor beside her and helped himself to a piece. "Delicious," he agreed, his eyes smiling.

"Can I have a taste?" she asked, a faint smile curving her mouth.

He held out the triangular wedge. She leaned forward and carefully took a bite.

"Thank you," she told him seriously.

With slow, deliberate movements, he placed the pizza box, plates and napkins aside, and reached for her.

Ashley moved willingly into his arms. Sliding her hands around his neck, she raised her face, eager for his attention. Her mouth was trembling in anticipation when he claimed it. A feeling of warmth wove its way through her and seemed to touch Cooper as the kiss deepened.

Somewhere, a long way in the distance, a bell began

to chime. Fleetingly, she wondered why it had taken so long to hear bells when Cooper kissed her.

Abruptly, he broke away, grumbling something unintelligible. He briefly touched his mouth to her cheek before he stood and answered the phone.

Chapter 6

"It's Claudia," Cooper said, holding out the receiver.

Ashley stood, her movements awkward as the lingering effects of Cooper's kiss continued to stir her senses. "Hello."

"Ash, I'm sorry," Claudia began. "I didn't know Cooper was going to show up. Is everything okay?"

"Wonderful."

"You two aren't arguing, are you?"

"Quite the contrary," Ashley murmured, closing her eyes as Cooper cupped her cheek with his hand. A kaleidoscope of emotions rippled through her.

"Are the boys down?" Claudia inquired.

"The boys?" Ashley jerked her eyes open and straightened. "Yes, they're both asleep."

"Seth and I may be several hours yet. If everything's peaceful, then don't feel like you need to stay. I'm sure Cooper can handle things if the boys wake up. But they probably won't."

"Okay," she agreed. "I'll talk to you later. Don't worry about anything."

The sound of Claudia's soft laugh came over the line. "I don't think I need to. Take care."

"Bye," Ashley said, and replaced the phone. "That was Claudia checking on the boys," she explained unnecessarily.

"I thought it might be," he said, and nuzzled the top of her head. "Let's finish our dinner," he suggested, taking her by the hand and leading her back to the fireplace.

They ate in contented silence. His look was thoughtful as he paused once to ask, "Do you pray?"

The question was completely unexpected.

"Yes," she responded simply. "What makes you ask?"

He shrugged indifferently, and she had the impression he was far more interested than he wanted to admit. "This is the first time I've eaten pizza on the floor with a beautiful woman."

"Beautiful woman?" she teased. "Where?"

His eyes were more serious than she had ever seen them. "You," he answered, and looked away. The steady tone of his voice revealed how sincere he was.

"There are a lot of things I haven't done in my life. Prayer is one of them. Tonight when Johnny had me get down on my knees with him…" He let the rest of what he was going to say fade. "It felt right." He glanced back at her. "Do you kneel down, too, or is that just something for children?"

"I do on occasion, but it certainly isn't necessary."

Cooper straightened, leaning back against the ottoman. "How do you pray?"

Ashley was surprised by the directness of his question. "Whole books have been written on the subject. I don't know if I'm qualified to answer."

"I didn't ask about anyone else, only you," he countered.

"Well," she began, unsure on how best to answer him. "I don't know that anyone else does it like me."

"I've noted on several occasions that you're a free spirit," he muttered, doing his best to hide his amusement. "Okay, let's go at this from a different angle. When do you pray?"

Answering questions was easier for her. "Mostly in the morning, but any time throughout the day. I pray for little things, parking places at the grocery store, and before I pay bills, and over the mail, and also for the big ones, like everyone in my life staying healthy and happy."

"Why mostly in the morning?" He regarded her steadily.

"That's when I do my devotions," she explained patiently.

"What are devotions?"

"Bible reading and praying," she told him. "My private time with the Lord. My day goes better when I've had a chance to discuss things with Jesus."

"You talk to Him as if He were a regular person?"

"He is," she said, more forcefully than she intended.

He paused and appeared to consider her words thoughtfully. "Do you speak to Him conversationally, then?"

"Yes and no."

"You don't like talking about this, do you?"

"It isn't that," she tried to explain, a soft catch in her voice. "If I tell you…I guess I'm afraid you'll think it's silly."

"I won't." The wealth of tenderness in his voice assured her he wouldn't.

"Usually I set aside a formal time for reading my Bible, other devotional books and praying. After I do my Bible reading, I get down on my knees, close my eyes and picture myself on a beautiful beach." She glanced up hesitantly, and Cooper nodded. The warmth in his look seemed to caress her, and she continued. "The scene is perfectly set in my mind. The waves are crashing against the sandy shore and easing back into the sea. I envision the tiny bubbles popping against the sand as the water ebbs out. This is where I meet Christ."

"Does He talk to you?"

"Not with words." She looked away uneasily. "I don't know how to explain this part. I know He hears me, and I know He answers my prayers. I see the evidence of that every day. But as for Him verbally speaking to me, I'd have to say no, though I hear His voice in other ways."

"I don't understand."

"I'm not sure I can explain, I just *do*."

Cooper seemed to accept that. "Then all you do is talk. You make it sound too easy." He seemed unsure, and she hastened to arrest his doubts.

"No, I spend part of the time thanking Him or… praising Him would be a better description, I guess. Another part is spent going over the previous day and asking His forgiveness for any wrongs I've done."

"That shouldn't take a lot of time," he teased.

"Longer than I care to admit," she informed him sheepishly and mentally added that the time had increased since she'd been seeing Cooper. "I also keep a list of requests that I pray about regularly and go down each one."

"Am I on your list?" The question was asked so softly that she wasn't sure he'd even spoken.

"Yes," she answered. "I pray for you every day," she admitted, her voice gaining intensity. She didn't add that all the people she loved were on her list. To avoid other questions she continued speaking. "For a while I wrote out my prayers. That was years ago, and it became a journal of God's faithfulness. But I can't write as fast as I can think, so I found that often I'd lose my train of thought. But I've saved those journals and sometimes read over them. When I do, I'm amazed again at God's goodness to me."

A baby's frantic cry broke into their conversation. "Scotty," Ashley said, bounding to her feet. "I'll go see what's wrong."

Scotty was standing in the crib, holding onto the sides. His crying grew louder and more desperate as she hurried into the room.

"What's wrong, Scotty?" she asked soothingly. Soft light from the hallway illuminated the dark recess of the bedroom. She lifted him out of the crib and hugged him close. Checking his diaper, she noted that he didn't seem to be wet. Probably he'd been frightened by a nightmare. Settling him in her arms, she sat in the rocking chair and rocked until she was sure he was back to sleep. With a kiss on the top of his head, she placed him back in his crib.

Cooper was waiting for her at the bottom of the stairs.

"He's asleep again," she whispered.

"I made coffee, would you like a cup?"

She smiled her appreciation. He curved an arm around her narrow waist, bringing her close to his side as he led her back into the den. A silver tea service was set on his desk. She saw that the remains of their dinner had been cleared away, along with their chess game. Biting into her bottom lip to contain her amusement, she decided not to comment on what a neat-freak he was.

He poured the steaming liquid into the china cups, then offered her one. Her hand shook momentarily as she accepted it. Dainty pieces of delicate china made her nervous, and she would have much preferred a ceramic mug.

"This set is lovely," she said, holding the cup in one hand. Tiny pink rosebuds, faded with age, decorated the teacup. She balanced the matching saucer in the palm of her other hand.

"It was my grandmother's," he said proudly. "There are only a few of the original pieces left."

"Oh." Her index finger tightened around the porcelain handle. In her nervousness, her hand wobbled and the boiling hot coffee sloshed over the side onto her hand and her lap, immediately soaking through her thin corduroy jeans. With a gasp of pain, she jumped to her feet. The saucer flew out of her lap and smashed against the leg of the desk, shattering into a thousand pieces.

"Ashley, are you all right?" Cooper bounded to his feet beside her.

Stunned, she couldn't move, her eyes fixed on the broken china as despair filled her. "I'm so sorry," she mumbled. Her voice cracked, and she swallowed past the huge lump building in her throat.

"Forget the china," he said, and took the teacup out of her hand. "It doesn't matter, none of it matters."

"It does matter!" she cried, her voice wobbling uncontrollably. "It matters very much."

"You've got to get that hand in ice water. What about your leg? Is it badly burned?" He tugged at her elbow, almost dragging her into the kitchen. He brought her to the sink and stuck her hand under the cold water. She looked down to see an angry red patch on the back of her left hand, where the coffee had spilled. Funny, she didn't feel any pain. Nothing. Only a horrible deep regret.

"Cooper, please, listen to me. I'm so sorry...your grandmother's china is ruined because of me."

"Keep that hand under the water," he said, ignoring

her words. Then he went to get ice from the automatic dispenser on the refrigerator door.

Ashley looked away rather than face him. She heard the water splash as he dumped the ice into the sink.

"What about your leg?" he demanded.

"It's fine." She tilted her chin upward and closed her eyes to forestall the tears. The burns didn't hurt; if anything, her hand was growing numb with cold. How could she have been so stupid? His grandmother's china...only a few pieces left. His earlier words echoed in her ears until they were nearly deafening.

"Ashley," he whispered, a hand on her shoulder. "Are you all right? You've gone pale. Is the pain very bad? Should I take you to a doctor?"

Talking was impossible, because her throat felt raw and painful, so she shook her head. "Your grandmother's china," she said at last, her voice barely above a tortured whisper.

"Would you quit acting like it's some great tragedy? You've been burned, and that's far more important than some stupid china."

"Do you know what my mother uses for fancy dinners?" she asked in a hoarse voice, then didn't wait for him to answer. "Dishes she picked up at the grocery store. With every ten dollar purchase she could buy another plate at a discount price."

"What has that go to do with anything?" he demanded irritably.

"Nothing. Everything. I swear I'll replace the saucer. I'll contact an antique dealer, I promise...."

"Ashley, stop." His firm hands squeezed her shoulders. "Stop right now. I don't care about a stupid saucer. But I do care about you." His grip tightened. "The saucer means nothing. Nothing," he repeated. "Do you understand?"

Her throat muscles had constricted so that she couldn't speak. Miserably, she hung her head, and her soft curls fell forward, wreathing her face.

She started to tremble, and with a muted groan Cooper hauled her into his arms.

"Honey, it doesn't matter. Please believe me when I tell you that."

She held on to him hard, because only the warmth of his touch was capable of easing the cold that pierced her heart. A lone tear squeezed past her lashes. She loved Cooper Masters so much it had become a physical pain. Never before had she realized how wrong she was for him. He needed someone who...

She wasn't allowed to complete the thought as Cooper's hand touched her face, turning her to meet his gaze. Her tortured eyes tried to avoid him, but he held her steady.

"Ashley, look at me." He sounded gruff, impatient.

But she was determined, and she shook herself loose, then swayed against him, her fingers spread against his shirt. He found her lips and kissed her with a desperation she hadn't experienced from him. It was as if he needed to confirm what he was saying, to comfort her, reassure her. She knew she shouldn't accept any of it. But one minute in Cooper's arms and it didn't matter. All she could do was feel.

His hands roamed her back as he buried his face in the hair at the side of her face. "Let's sit down."

He took her into the living room and set her down in the soft comfort of the large sofa. Next he opened the drapes and revealed the same view of Puget Sound that they'd enjoyed on Thanksgiving Day, when they'd walked on his property in the rain.

Hands in his pockets, he paused to admire the beauty. "Sometimes in the evening I sit here, staring into the sky, counting the stars." He spoke absently, standing at the far corner of the window, gazing into the still night. "Looking at all that magnificence makes me feel small and very insignificant. One man, alone." His back was to her. "It's times like this that make me regret not having a wife and family. I've worked hard, and what do I have to show for it? An expensive home and no one to share it with." He stopped and turned, their eyes meeting. For a breathless moment they stared at one another. Then he dropped his gaze and turned slowly back to the window.

Confused for a moment, she watched as he turned away from her, as if trying to block her out of his mind. His action troubled her. He stood alone, across the room, a solitary figure silhouetted against the night. What was he telling her? She didn't understand, but she did realize that he had revealed a part of himself others didn't see.

Unfolding her long legs from the sofa, she joined him at the window. Standing at his side, she slipped an arm around his waist as if she'd done it a thousand times.

He smiled at her then, and she couldn't remember ever seeing anything transform a face more. His dark eyes seemed to spark with something she couldn't define. Happiness? Contentment? Pleasure? His smile widened as he looped his arm over her shoulders, and then he brushed her temple with a light kiss.

"Do you have your Christmas tree up yet?"

"No," she whispered, afraid talking normally would destroy the wonderful mood. "I thought I'd put it up tomorrow."

"Would you like some help?"

The offer shocked her. "I'd...I'd love some."

"What time?"

"Probably afternoon." Her sigh was filled with a sense of dread. "I've got to get some shopping done. There are only a few days left, and I've hardly started."

"Me either, and I still need to get something for the boys."

"I'm afraid I haven't had the chance to shop. The last days of school were so hectic. I hate leaving everything to the last minute like this."

"Why don't we make a day of it?" he suggested. "I'll pick you up, say around ten. We can do the shopping, go for lunch and decorate your tree afterward."

"That sounds wonderful. I'd like that. I'd like it very much."

"And, Ashley..." Cooper said, looking away uncomfortably.

"Yes?"

"I was thinking about buying myself a pair of cowboy boots and wanted to ask your advice about the best place to go."

"I know just the store, in the Pavilion near Southcenter. But be warned, they're expensive." As soon as the words were out, she regretted them. Cooper didn't need to worry about money.

He chuckled and gave her a tiny squeeze. "I wish other people were as reluctant to spend my money."

"We'll see how reluctant I am tomorrow," she murmured with a small laugh.

Chapter 7

Ashley changed clothes three times before the doorbell chimed, announcing Cooper's arrival. Her final choice had been a soft gray wool skirt and a white bouclé-knit sweater. The outfit, with knee-high black leather boots, was one she usually reserved for church, but she wanted everything to be perfect for Cooper.

A warm smile lit up her face as she opened the door. "Morning, you're right on…" She didn't finish; the words died on her lips. Cooper in jeans! Levis so new and stiff they looked as if they would stand up on their own. Her lashes fluttered downward to disguise her shock.

"Morning. You look as beautiful as ever."

"Thank you," she whispered, somewhat bewildered. "Do you want a cup of coffee or something before we go?"

"No, I think we'd better get started before the crowds get too bad."

She lounged back in her seat, content to let him drive. He flipped a switch, and immediately the interior was filled with classical music. She savored the gentle sounds of the string section and glanced up, surprised when the music abruptly changed to a top forty station.

"Why'd you do that?" she asked, her blue gaze sweeping toward him, searching his profile.

"I thought this would probably be more to your liking." His gaze remained on the freeway, the traffic surprisingly heavy for early morning.

"It's not," she murmured, a little of her earlier happiness dissipating with the thought that Cooper assumed she preferred more popular music to the classics. *But don't you?* her mind countered.

They took the exit for Southcenter, a huge shopping complex south of Seattle, but didn't stop there. The area's largest toy store was situated nearby, and they had decided earlier that it would be the best place to start.

The parking lot was already full, so Cooper had to drive around a couple of times before locating a spot at the far end.

His hand cupped her elbow as they hurried inside. Only a few shopping carts were left, and she glanced around, doing her best to squelch a growing sense of panic. The store had barely opened, and already there was hardly room to move through the aisles.

"My goodness," she murmured impatiently. They were forced to wait to move past the throng of shoppers entering the first aisle. "Do you want to come back later?" she asked, glancing at him anxiously.

"I don't think it's going to get any better," he muttered darkly.

"I don't think it will, either. Maybe we should decide now what we want to buy the boys. That would at least streamline the process. We're going together, aren't we?" At Cooper's questioning glance, she added, "I mean, we'll split the cost."

"I'll pay," he insisted.

"Cooper," she groaned. "Either we divide the cost or forget it."

His mouth thinned slightly. "All right, I should know better. You and that pride of yours."

He looked as if he wanted to add something more, but the crowd moved, and she pushed the cart forward.

"Okay, what should we get Johnny?" Her eyes followed the floor-to-ceiling display of computer games. On the other side of the aisle were more traditional games and puzzles.

"I've thought of something perfect," Cooper announced proudly. "I'm sure you'll agree."

"What?"

"A computer chess game. I saw one advertised the other day."

"He's too young for that," Ashley declared. She hated to stifle Cooper's enthusiasm, but Johnny wasn't interested in chess.

"He's not," Cooper shot back. "I've been teaching him a few moves. It's the perfect gift—educational, too."

"Good," she said emphatically. "Then you get him that, but I want to buy him something he'll enjoy."

Cooper's soft chuckle caught her unaware. "What's so funny?" she asked.

"You." He paused and looked around before lightly kissing her cheek. "I can't think of a thing in the world that you and I will ever agree on. Our tastes are too different." His gaze seemed to be fixed on her softly parted lips. "Do men often have to restrain themselves from kissing you?"

A happy light shimmered from her deep blue eyes. "Hundreds," she teased. Immediately she realized it had been the wrong thing to say. She could almost visualize the wall that was going up between them.

He straightened and pretended an interest in one of the displays.

"Cooper," she whispered, and laid her hand across his forearm. "That was a dumb joke."

"I imagine it was closer to the truth than you realize."

"Oh, hardly," she denied with a light laugh.

An hour and a half later, their packages stored in the booth beside them, Ashley exhaled a long sigh.

"Coffee," Cooper told the waitress, who quickly returned and filled their mugs.

"I can't remember a time when I needed this more," Ashley murmured and took an appreciative sip.

"Me, either. Could you believe that checkout line?"

"But Johnny's going to love his fire truck and hat."

"And his computer chess game."

"Of course," she agreed, grinning.

"At least we agreed on Scotty's gift. That wasn't so difficult, was it?"

Ashley's gaze skipped from Cooper to the stuffed animal beside him, and she burst into peals of laughter. "Oh, Cooper, if only your friends could see you now with that gorilla next to you."

"Yes, I guess that would be cause for amusement."

Digging through her purse, Ashley brought out her Bible, flipping through the worn pages.

"What are you doing now?" he asked in a hushed whisper.

"Don't worry, I'm not going to stand on the seat and start a crusade. I want to find something."

"What?"

"A verse." She paused, a finger marking the place. "Here it is. First Peter 1:4."

"Honestly, you've got to be the only woman in the world who whips out her Bible in a restaurant."

Unaffected by his teasing tone, she laid the book open on the tabletop, turned it sideways and pointed to the passage she wanted him to read. "After what we just went through, I decided I wanted to be sure heaven has reserved seating. It does, look." Aloud she read a portion of the text. "'To obtain an inheritance which is reserved in heaven for you.'"

A hint of a smile quivered at the edges of his mouth. "You're serious, aren't you?"

"Sure I am. I've seen pictures of riots that looked more organized than that mess we were in."

He laughed loudly then, attracting the curious glances of others. "Ashley Robbins, I find you delightful."

Pleased, she beamed and placed the small Bible back inside her purse.

"Where do you want to go next?" he asked as he glanced at his wristwatch.

"Do you need to be back for something?"

He raised his eyes to meet hers. "No," he said, and shook his head to emphasize his denial.

"If you feel like you could brave the maddening crowd a second time, we could tackle the mall."

He looked unsure for a moment. She couldn't blame him. The thought of facing thousands of last-minute shoppers wasn't an appealing one, but she did still have gifts to buy—and he wanted those boots.

"Sure, why not?" he agreed.

Ashley could think of forty thousand hectic reasons why not, but she didn't voice a single one, content simply being with Cooper.

"However, I hope you don't object if we store Tarzan's friend in the trunk of the car," he added, and glanced wryly at the stuffed animal.

The crowds at the mall proved to be even worse than the toy store, but a couple of hours later, their arms loaded with packages, they finally retreated to the car.

Even Cooper, who was normally so calm and reserved, looked a bit ashen after fighting the chaos.

They hadn't even stopped for lunch, eating caramel apples instead as they walked from one end of the mall to the other.

"Do you think Claudia will like the necklace?" he asked as he joined her in the front seat and inserted the key into the ignition.

"Of course." Ashley had picked out the turquoise necklace and knew her friend would love it, but he was still skeptical. "Trust me."

"There's something about that phrase that makes me nervous."

"But you didn't buy two. Now I'm curious," she ventured, not paying attention to what he'd said.

"Two? Two what?"

"Necklaces." She gave him an impatient look. Sometimes they seemed to be speaking at complete cross purposes.

"Do you think Claudia would want two?" He gave her a curious glance.

"Of course not," she said with a sigh. "But you always buy me the same thing as Claudia." She didn't add that it had been perfume for the past three Christmases.

"Not this year."

"Really?" Her interested piqued, she asked, "What are you getting me?"

"Like John and Scott, you'll have to wait until Christmas morning."

She was more pleased than she dared show. Not that she would be forced to wait until Christmas, but that she'd moved beyond the same safe category as Claudia. It thrilled her to know that their relationship had evolved to the point that he wanted to get her something different this year.

Cooper played with the radio until he found some Christmas music.

Again Ashley could feel the comforting music float around her, soothing her tattered nerves. "Doesn't that make you want to sing?"

"Every time you say that we have a storm," he complained.

"Killjoy," she muttered under her breath.

A large hand reached over and squeezed hers. "Ready to decorate the tree?"

"More than ready," she agreed. Much of her shopping remained to be done, but she'd promised Claudia that they would head out early Monday morning so there would be plenty of time to finish.

The remainder of the short drive to her apartment was accomplished in a companionable silence. Her mind wandered to the first time Cooper had asked her to dinner after she'd paid off the loan. At the time she would have doubted she could ever sit at his side without being nervous. Now she felt relaxed, content.

Although nothing had ever been openly stated, their relationship had come a long way in the past couple of months. She could only pray that this budding rapport would continue after Claudia, Seth and the boys returned to Alaska.

Ever the gentleman, Cooper took the apartment key away from her and unlocked the door. Men didn't usually do that sort of thing for her, but then again, she probably wouldn't have let anyone but Cooper.

"I put the tree on the lanai until it was time to decorate," she told him, and took his coat, hanging it with hers in the closet. When she turned around Cooper was helping himself to a handful of popcorn.

"I wouldn't eat that if I were you, it's a week old."

He dropped the kernels back into the bowl and wrinkled his nose.

"Quite giving me funny looks like I'm a terrible housekeeper. You're supposed to leave the popcorn out to get stale. It strings easier that way."

"Strings?"

"For the tree."

"Of course, for the tree," he echoed.

She had the uneasy sensation that he didn't know what she meant. Lightly, she shrugged her shoulders. He would learn soon enough.

"Are you hungry?" she asked on her way into the kitchen. "I can make us pastrami sandwiches with dill pickles and potato chips."

"That sounds good, except I'll have my potato chips on the side."

"Cute," she murmured, sticking her head around the corner.

"With you I never know," he complained with a full smile.

While she made lunch, Cooper brought the Christmas tree inside. Since it was already in the stand, all he had to do was find a place to set it in the living room. When he'd finished he joined her in the compact kitchen.

Working contentedly with her back to him, she hummed softly and cut thin slices of pickle.

"You can have one of the chocolates I bought if you like," she told him, as she spread a thick layer of mustard across the bread.

"I thought you said chocolates weren't meant to be shared."

She laughed softly. "I was only teasing."

"Ashley…"

Just the way he spoke her name caused her to pause and turn around.

"I think we should do this before we eat."

"Do what?" Her heart was chugging like a locomotive at the look he was giving her.

"This." He took the knife out of her hand and laid it on the counter. His gaze centered on her mouth.

She gave a soft welcoming moan as his lips fit over hers. All day she'd yearned for his touch. It was torture to be so close to him and maintain the friendly facade, when in her heart all she wanted was to be held and loved by him.

When he dragged his mouth from hers, she knew he felt as unsatisfied as she did. Kissing was quickly becoming insufficient to satisfy either of them. His hands roamed possessively over her back, arching her closer. Again his mouth dipped to drink from the sweetness of hers. With a shuddering breath he released her.

Sensation after sensation swirled through her.

These feelings he stirred within her were what God had intended her to feel toward the man she loved, and she couldn't doubt the rightness of them. But what was *he* feeling? Certainly he wasn't immune to all this.

His smile was gentle when he asked, "Did you say something about lunch?"

"Lunch," she repeated like a robot, then lightly shook her head, irritated that she was reacting like a lovesick teenager. No, she mused, Cooper couldn't help but be aware of the powerful physical attraction between them. He was simply much more in control of himself than she was.

A few minutes later she carried their meal into the living room on a tray. He was sorting through her ornaments and looked up. A frown was creasing his brow.

"What's wrong?" she asked, setting their plates on the coffee table and glancing over at him.

"There's something written across these glass ornaments."

"I know," she answered simply.

"But what is it and why?"

A soft smile touched her mouth as she lifted half of her sandwich and prepared to take the first bite. "Remember how I mentioned that I dated the man who sold me Milligan a couple of times?"

"I remember."

The tightness in his voice sent her searching gaze to him a second time. "Unfortunately, Jim was decidedly not a Christian. We saw one another a couple of times in December, and he couldn't understand why I didn't want to do certain things."

"What things?" Cooper's tone had taken on an arctic chill.

"It doesn't matter," she said, and smiled, dismissing his curiosity. The past was over, and she didn't want to review it with him. "But one thing I *am* grateful for is the fact Jim told me the Christmas tree is a pagan custom. He found it interesting that I professed this deep faith in Christ yet chose to allow a pagan ritual to desecrate my home." She set the sandwich aside and knelt beside Cooper on the carpet. "You know, he's right. I was shocked, so I decided to make my Christmas tree Christ centered."

"But how?"

"It wasn't that difficult. The tree is an evergreen, constant, never changing, just as my faith in Christ is meant to be. And Christ died upon a tree. The lights were the easiest part. Jesus asks that each one of us be the light of the world. But when it came to the ornaments, I had to be a little inventive, so I took glitter glue—"

"Glitter glue?" he interrupted.

"Glue that has glitter already in it. It's much easier to write out the fruits of the Holy Spirit that way."

"Hold on, you've lost me."

"Here." She stood and retrieved her Bible from the oak end table. Flipping the pages, she located the verses she wanted. "Paul wrote in his epistle to the Galatians about the fruits of the Christian life."

"Love, joy, peace," he read from each of the pink glass ornaments. "I get it now."

"Exactly," she stated excitedly.

"Clever girl." His thick brows arched expressively.

"Thank you."

"I'm very curious now about how you tie in the popcorn."

"Yes, well…" Frantically, her mind searched for a plausible reason. She hadn't thought about the decorative strings she added each year.

"I've got it," he said. "White and spotless like the Christ child."

"Very good," she congratulated him.

There was a disconcerted look in his eyes as they met hers. "Your commitment to Christ is important to you, isn't it?"

"Vital," she confirmed. "One's relationship with God is a personal thing. But Christ is the most important person in my life. He has been for several years."

"You stopped seeing Madigan because he didn't have the same belief system as you."

"More or less. In some ways we hit it off immediately. I liked Jim, I still do. But our relationship was headed for a dead end, so I cut it off before either one of us got serious."

"Because he didn't believe the same way as you? Isn't that narrow minded?"

"To me it isn't, and that wasn't the only reason. Cooper…" She paused and held her breath when she saw his troubled look. "Why all the questions? Do you think I'm wrong in the way I believe?"

"It doesn't matter what I think."

"Of course, it matters." *Because you do,* she added silently.

He rose and walked to the far side of the room. "I don't believe the same way you do. Oh, I acknowledge there's a God. I couldn't look at the heavens and examine our world and not believe in a Supreme Being. I accept that Christ was born, but I never have understood salvation, justification and all the rest of it. Everyone talks about the free gift, but—"

A loud knock on her door interrupted him.

She glanced at him and shrugged. She wasn't expecting anyone. She got to her feet, crossed the room and checked the peephole.

"It's Webb," she told Cooper before opening the door.

"Hello, Sweet Thing. How's your day been?" He sauntered into the room whistling "White Christmas" and paused long enough to brush his lips across her cheek. The song died on his lips when he spotted Cooper.

"Webb," Ashley said stiffly, folding her hands tightly together in front of her. "This is Cooper Masters. I believe I've mentioned him."

She watched as the two men exchanged handshakes. "Cooper, this is Dennis Webb."

Ashley wanted to shout at her friend. Webb couldn't have picked a worse time to pop in for one of his spontaneous visits.

"No, I can't say that I recall you mentioning him," Webb announced as he glanced back to Ashley.

She seethed silently and somehow managed a weak smile.

"I can't say the same about you," Cooper muttered in the stiff, formal tone she'd come to hate.

"Would you like to sit down, Webb?" She motioned toward the sofa and glared at him, desperately hoping he would get the message and leave.

"Thanks." He plopped down on the couch and crossed his legs. "You missed a great party last night. Hardly seemed right without you there, Ash. Next time I won't take no for an answer."

Cooper lowered himself onto the far end of the sofa. His back remained rigid.

"I'll make coffee," Ashley volunteered as she left the room, thinking the atmosphere back there was so thick she could taste it.

"I'll see if I can help in the kitchen," she heard Webb say, and a second later he was at her side.

"Who is this guy?" he hissed.

"What do you mean?" she demanded in a hushed whisper, then didn't wait for an answer. "He's my best friend's uncle, and what do you mean I've never mentioned him? I talk about him all the time."

"You haven't," Webb insisted. "Unless he's the one you played chess with and lost?"

"That's him." Her fingers refused to work properly, and coffee grounds spilled across the counter. "Darn, darn, darn."

"I don't care who he is, if he calls me Webber one more time, I'm going to punch him."

"Webb," she expelled her breath and noticed that

Cooper was watching her intently from the doorway. She stopped talking and forced a beguiling smile onto her face. Her teeth were clenched so tight her jaw hurt. "Can't you see it's not a good time?" she hissed beneath her breath.

"Are you saying you want me to leave?"

"Yes." She nearly shouted the one word.

Cooper stepped closer. "Is everything all right, Ashley?" he asked in a formal tone, but his burning gaze was focused on Webb.

The look was searing. She had never seen such disapproval illuminated so clearly on anyone's features. Cooper's mouth was pinched, his eyes narrowed. For a crazy second she wanted to laugh. The two men were eyeing one another like bears who had encroached on each other's territory.

"I'm fine. Webb was just saying that he has to go."

"I do?" he said. "Oh, yes, I guess I do." He walked out of the kitchen with Ashley on his heels. "I'll talk to you soon," he told her, his gaze full of meaning.

"Right." She held open the door for him. "Sorry you have to leave so soon."

The look Webb gave her nearly sent her into peals of laughter. "I'll phone you soon," she promised.

"Nice meeting you, Cooper," Webb said graciously. "Now that I recall, Ash *has* mentioned you. I understand you play a mean game of chess."

"I play," Cooper admitted with a look of indifference.

"I dabble in the game myself," Webb said, tossing Ashley a teasing glance.

"See you later, Webb," she said firmly, and closed the door. The lock clicked shut, and she paused, her eyes closed, and released a long, slow, breath.

"Nice fellow, Webber," Cooper said from behind her.

"He's a friend." She had to be certain Cooper understood that her relationship with Webb didn't go any further than that of congenial co-workers.

"I imagine he's the kind of Christian who fits right into that cozy picture you have built in your mind." His tone was almost harsh.

Ashley did her best to ignore it. "Webb's a wonderful Christian man."

"You probably should marry someone like him," he stated with a sharp edge. His gaze narrowed on her. It wasn't difficult to tell that he was angry, but she didn't know why.

"You're upset, aren't you?" she asked, confronting him. Her back was against the door, her hands clenched at her side.

Cooper's long strides carried him to the far side of the room. He tried to ram his hands in his pockets, apparently forgetting he was wearing jeans. That seemed to irritate him all the more.

"We never did eat our lunch," she said shakily.

He glared at the thick sandwich and then back to her. "I'm not hungry."

"Let's decorate the tree, then." She hugged her middle to ward off the cold she felt beginning to surround her. Cooper was freezing her out, and she didn't know what to say or do to prevent him from doing that.

He stared at her blankly, as if he hadn't heard a word she'd said. Helplessly, she watched as he opened the closet door and took out his coat.

"Cooper?" she whispered, but he didn't hesitate, slipping his arms into the sleeves and starting on the buttons.

She was still standing in front of the door, and she decided she wouldn't move, wouldn't let him walk out as if she wasn't there. What had happened? Everything had been so beautiful last night and today, and now, for no apparent reason, he was pushing her away. She felt as if their relationship had taken a giant step backward.

His drawn expression didn't alter as he came to stand directly in front of her. His hand brushed a blond curl off her face and lingered a second to trace a finger across her cheek.

"You really should marry someone like Webber."

"No." The sound was barely audible. "I won't." How could she marry Webb when she loved Cooper?

"Funny how we never seem to do the things we should," he muttered cryptically.

"Cooper?" Her voice throbbed with a feeling she couldn't identify. Agony? Need? Desperation? "What's wrong?" she tried again.

"Other than the fact you and I are as different as night and day?"

"We've always been different, why should it matter now?"

"I don't know," he told her honestly.

"I had a wonderful time today," she whispered, and

hung her head to avoid his searching look. Her lashes fluttered wearily. She knew she was losing, but not why. "I don't want it to end like this. I didn't know Webb was coming."

"It isn't Webber," Cooper admitted harshly. "It's everything." An ominous silence followed his announcement. "I like to pretend with you."

"Pretend?" She lifted her gaze, uncertain of what he was admitting.

"You're warm and alive, and you make me yearn for things that were never meant to be."

"Now you're talking in riddles. And I hate riddles, because I can never understand them. I don't understand *you*."

"No," he murmured, and rubbed a hand across his face. "I don't suppose that's possible."

Ashley didn't know what directed her, perhaps instinct. Of their own volition her arms slipped around his neck. At first he held himself stiff and unyielding against her, but she refused to be deterred. Her exploring fingers toyed with the dark hair at the back of his head. She applied a gentle pressure, urging his mouth to hers. His resistance grew stronger, forcing her to stand on her tip toes and mold herself to him. Gradually, she eased her mouth over his.

He didn't want her kiss, but she could feel the part of him that unwillingly reached out to her.

Abruptly he broke the contact and pulled himself away. Both hands cupped her face, tilting it up at an angle. A smoldering light of something she couldn't decipher burned in his eyes.

"Ashley." The husky tone of his voice betrayed his desire, yet she marveled at his control.

"Hmm?" she answered with a contented whisper.

"Next time I start acting like a jerk, promise me you'll bring me out of my ill temper just like this."

She gave a glad cry and kissed him again. "I promise," she said after a long while.

Chapter 8

"Was Cooper with you Saturday?" Claudia asked as she laid the menu aside.

Most of Monday morning and half the afternoon had been spent finishing up their Christmas shopping. For the past two hours Ashley had dragged Claudia to every antique store she could find.

Her index finger made a lazy circle around the rim of her water glass. "What makes you ask?" A peculiar pain knotted her stomach. It happened every time she suspected Cooper didn't want anyone to know they were seeing one another. She had spent the entire day with him. After decorating the tree they'd gone out to dinner and a movie. It was midnight before he kissed her good night. Yet he hadn't told Claudia anything.

"What makes me ask?" Claudia repeated incredulously. "You mean besides the fact that he mysteriously disappeared for the entire day? Then he saunters in about midnight with a sheepish look. Gets up early Sunday morning whistling. Cooper. Whistling. He even went to church with us again, which surprised both Seth and me."

"What makes you think I had anything to do with it?"

"What is it with you two? You'd think you were ashamed to be seen with one another."

"You're being ridiculous."

"I'm not. Look at how elusive you're being. Were you or were you not with Cooper Sunday?"

"Yes, I was with him."

"Just part of the time?"

"No," she admitted and breathed in heavily. "All day."

"Ash?" Claudia hesitated as if searching for the right words. "I know you're probably going to say this is none of my business, but I've never seen you act like this."

"Act like what?" she returned defensively.

"All our lives you were the fearless one. There didn't seem to be anything you weren't willing to try. I've never seen you so reticent."

Ashley shrugged one shoulder slightly.

"You're in love with Cooper, aren't you?"

A small smile played over Ashley's mouth. "Yes." It felt good to finally verbalize her feelings. "Very much."

Claudia's eyes glinted with an inner glow of happiness. "Who would ever have guessed you'd fall in love with Cooper?"

"I don't know. Probably no one."

"Has he told you he loves you yet?" Claudia asked, obviously doing her best to contain her excitement.

"No, but then I'm not exactly an 'uptown girl,' am I?" The words slipped out more flippantly than she'd intended.

"Ashley," Claudia snapped, "I can't believe you'd say something like that. You're closer to me than any sister could ever—"

"It's not you," Ashley interrupted, lowering her gaze to her half-full water glass. "Cooper's ashamed to be seen with me."

"That's pure nonsense," Claudia insisted.

"I wish it was," Ashley said in a serious tone.

Any additional discussion was interrupted by the waitress, who arrived to take their order.

"Promise me one thing," Claudia asked as soon as the woman was gone, her eyes pleading.

"What?"

"That you won't drag me to any more antique shops. Cooper doesn't care about that saucer, so I don't see why you should."

"But I do," Ashley said forcefully. "I'm going to replace it if I have to look for the rest of my life."

"Honestly, Ash, it's not that big a deal. Cooper would feel terrible if he knew the trouble you're putting yourself through.

"Don't you dare tell him."

Their Cobb salads arrived, and the flow of conversation came to a halt as they began to eat.

"You're planning to come with us Wednesday, aren't you?" Claudia asked, looking up from her salad.

"Is that the day you're taking the boys to Seattle Center Enchanted Forest?" Every Christmas the Food Circus inside the Center created a fantasyland for young children. The large open area was filled with tall trees and a train that enthralled the youngsters. Clowns performed and handed out balloons. "That's Christmas Eve day."

"Brilliant deduction," Claudia teased. "Cooper's going," she added, as if Ashley needed an inducement.

Ashley's blond curls bounced as she laughed. "I'd be excited about it even if Cooper wasn't coming along. We're going to have a wonderful time. The boys will love it."

"Cooper's been asking Seth a lot of questions," Claudia announced unexpectedly.

"Questions? About what?"

"The Bible." Claudia placed her fork beside her plate. "They spent almost the entire afternoon on Sunday discussing things. When I talked to Seth about it later, he told me that he felt inadequate because some of Cooper's questions were so complicated. Personally, I don't know where Cooper stands with the Lord, but he seems to be having a difficult time with some of the basic concepts." She paused, then added, "He can't seem to accept that salvation is not something we can earn with donations or good works."

"I can understand that," Ashley defended him.

"Cooper has worked hard all his life. Nothing's been free. I can see that the concept would be more difficult for him to accept than for others."

Claudia lounged back, a smile twinkling in her eyes. "You really *do* love him, don't you?"

"I'll tell you something else that'll shock you." Ashley nervously smoothed her pant leg. "I've loved him from the time I was sixteen. It's just been…harder to hide lately."

Claudia's expression softened knowingly. "I think I guessed how you felt almost as soon as I saw the two of you together at the airport when Seth and I arrived with the boys. And then, when I thought back, I realized how long it had been going on, at least for you."

"How did you know?" Ashley's eyes narrowed thoughtfully.

"From the time we were teens, it was you who defended Cooper when he did something to irritate me. You were always ready to leap to his defense."

"Was I so obvious?"

"Not at all," Claudia assured her. "Now, are you ready for something else?" She didn't wait for a response. "Cooper's been in love with you since before I married Seth."

"That I don't believe," Ashley argued. She picked up her fork and put it back down twice before finally setting it aside.

"Think about it," Claudia challenged, a determined lift to her chin. "Seth asked me to marry him, and I was so undecided. I knew I loved him, but moving to Alaska, leaving school and all my dreams of becoming a doctor, made the decision difficult. You were telling me to follow my heart, and at the same time Cooper was unconditionally opposed to the whole idea."

"I remember how miserable you were."

"I was more than miserable. I was at the airport wanting to die, I loved him so much, yet I felt it would never work for Seth and me. You told me if I loved him to go after him." Her blue eyes glimmered with the memory, and a soft smile played at the corners of her mouth. "Still, I was undecided, and I looked to Cooper, wanting him to make up my mind for me. It's funny how clearly I can recall that scene now. Cooper glanced from me to you. At the time I didn't recognize the look in his eyes, but I do now. After so many bitter arguments, Cooper looked at you and told me the decision was mine."

"I think you've blown the whole thing out of proportion." Ashley felt safer in denying what her friend thought than placing any faith in it.

"Don't you see?" Claudia persisted. "Cooper changed his mind because, for the first time in his life, he knew what it was to be in love with someone."

"I wish it were true," Ashley murmured sadly, "but if he felt that way four years ago, why didn't he make an effort to go out with me?"

A wayward lock of auburn hair fell across Claudia's cheek. "Knowing Cooper, that isn't so difficult to understand."

"I wish I could believe it, I really do."

Claudia reached across the small table and squeezed Ashley's forearm. "I've been waiting four years to give you the kind of advice you gave me. Go for him, Ash. Cooper needs you."

Ashley's eyes were filled with determination. "I have no intention of letting him go."

Claudia's laugh was almost musical. "In some ways I almost pity my uncle."

Ashley was sitting on the floor with Scott on her lap when Johnny crawled in beside him. "Can we play a game, Auntie Ash?"

Ashley looked into his round blue eyes, unsure. She'd told Claudia she'd watch the boys while her friends wrapped Christmas presents, and she didn't want to get Johnny all wound up.

"What kind of game?"

"Horsey. Uncle Cooper let me ride him, and Scotty and Daddy were the other horsey."

The picture that flashed into her mind produced a warm smile. "But I wouldn't be a good horse for both you *and* Scotty," she told him gently.

A disappointed look clouded his expressive face, but he accepted her decision. "Can you read?" he asked next, and handed her a book.

"Sure." With her natural flair for theatrics, she began to read from the *Bible Story Book*.

"How many days until Jesus's birthday?" Johnny asked when she'd finished.

"Only a few now. Are you excited to open all your presents?"

Eagerly he shook his head. "If Jesus hadn't been

born, would we have Christmas?" He cocked his head at a curious angle so he could look at her.

"No. We wouldn't have any churches or Sunday School, either."

"What else wouldn't we have?"

"If Jesus hadn't come, our world would be a very sad place. Because Jesus wouldn't live in people's hearts, and they wouldn't love one another the way they should."

"We wouldn't have a Christmas tree," Johnny added.

"Or presents, or Easter."

The young boy's eyes grew wide. "Not even Easter?"

"Nope."

Johnny sat quietly for a minute. "Then the best gift of all at Christmas is Jesus."

A rush of tenderness warmed Ashley's heart. "You said it beautifully."

Scotty squirmed out of her arms and onto the thick carpet, crawling with all his might toward the Christmas tree. Ashley hurriedly intercepted him and, with a laugh, swept him from the carpet and into the air high above her head.

Scotty gurgled with delight. "You like this funny looking tree, don't you?" she asked him, laughing. "I bet if you got the opportunity, every present here would be torn to shreds."

The front door closed, and she turned with Scotty in her arms to find Cooper shaking the rain from his hat.

"Hi."

He didn't see her immediately, and as he turned a surprised look crossed his dark features. Almost as quickly the look was replaced with one of welcome that sent her heart beating at an erratic pace.

"Claudia and Seth left you to the mercies of these two again?"

"No, they're wrapping presents. My duty is to keep the boys out of trouble."

He hung his coat in the hall closet and joined her, lifting Johnny into his arms. The boy squeezed Cooper's neck and gave him a moist kiss on the cheek.

"You know what Auntie Ash said?" John leaned back to look at his uncle.

"I can only guess," Cooper replied, his eyes brightening with a smile. Lovingly he searched her face.

"She said if Jesus hadn't been born, we wouldn't have Christmas."

"No, we wouldn't," Cooper agreed.

"I know something else we wouldn't have," she murmured and moistened her lips.

Johnny's gaze followed hers, and he shouted excitedly, "Mistletoe."

Cooper's eyes hadn't left hers, although his narrowed slightly as if he couldn't take them off her.

"Mistletoe," she repeated, her invitation blatant.

Motionless, Cooper held her look, but gave her no indication of what he was thinking.

Two quick strides carried him to her side. Her senses whirled as he placed Johnny on the ground and gathered her in his arms. Half of her pleasure came from the fact that he didn't look around to see if anyone was watching.

Cooper's gaze skidded to the baby she was still holding between them, and he let out a long exaggerated sigh. "No help for this. I can't kiss you properly while you're holding the baby."

"I'll take a rain check," she teased.

"But I won't," he announced, then removed Scotty from her arms and gently set him on the floor.

Ashley started to protest, but before she could utter a sound, Cooper's mouth was over hers. Winding her arms around his neck, she reveled in the feel of him as his hands gripped her narrow waist.

The sound of someone clearing their throat had barely registered with her when he abruptly broke off the kiss and breathed in deeply.

"You two forget something?" Claudia demanded, hands on her hips as she watched them with a teasing smile.

"Forget?" Ashley was still caught in the rapture; clear thinking was almost impossible. Cooper's warm breath continued to caress her cheek, and she knew he was as affected as she was.

"Like Scotty and John?"

"Oh." Ashley gasped and looked around, remembering how the baby had been enthralled with the Christmas tree.

Seth had lifted the baby by the seat of his pants and was holding him several inches off the ground.

"I think we've been found out," Ashley whispered to Cooper.

"Looks that way," he said releasing her.

Seth handed his wife the baby, who cooed happily, and the two men left the room.

"I've been meaning to ask you all day what you're wearing tomorrow," Claudia said, tucking her son close to her side.

"Wearing tomorrow?" Ashley echoed. "I don't understand?"

"To the party." Claudia looked at her as if she had suddenly developed amnesia.

"The party?"

"Cooper's dinner party tomorrow night, of course," Claudia said, laughing lightly.

The world suddenly seemed to come to an abrupt stop. Ashley's heart pounded frantically; the blood rushed to her face. In that instant she knew what it must feel like to be hit in the stomach. Claudia continued to elaborate, giving her the details of the formal dinner party. But Ashley was only half listening; the words drifted off into nothingness. The only sound that penetrated the cloud of hurt and disappointment were the words *family...friends.* She was neither. She was the cook's daughter, nothing more.

She heard footsteps, and her breathing became actively painful as her gaze shifted to meet Cooper's eyes. Standing there, Ashley prayed she would find something in his look that could explain why she had been excluded from the party. But all she saw was regret. He hadn't wanted her to know.

"Ashley, are those tears?" Claudia asked in a shocked whisper. "What did I say? What's wrong?"

In a haze, Ashley looked beyond the concerned face of her friend. Seth was standing with Johnny at his side, a troubled look on his face. Everyone she loved was there to witness her humiliation. Without a word, she turned and walked out of the house.

"Ashley." There was a pleading quality in Cooper's voice as he followed her out of the house. She quickened her pace, ignoring his demand that she wait. By the time he reached her, she was inside her car, the key in the ignition.

"Will you stop?" he shouted, his mouth tight. "At least give me the chance to explain."

Nothing was worth her staying and listening; he'd said everything without having uttered a word. She wanted to tell him that, but it was all she could do to swallow back the tears.

When she started the engine, Cooper tried to yank open the car door, but she was quicker and hit the lock. Jerking the car into reverse, she pulled out of the driveway. One last glance in Cooper's direction showed him standing alone, watching her leave. His shoulders were hunched in defeat.

Her cell phone was ringing even before she reached her small apartment. She knew without looking that it was Cooper. She also knew he would refuse to give up, so finally, in exasperation, she answered.

"Yes," she snapped.

A slight pause followed. "Miss Robbins?"

"Yes?" Some of the impatience left her voice.

"This is Larry Marshall, of Marshall's Antiques.

You talked to me this morning about that china saucer you were looking for."

"Did you find one?"

"A friend of mine has the piece you're looking for," he told her.

"How soon can I pick it up?"

"Tomorrow, if you like. There's only one problem," he continued.

"What's that?"

"My friend's shop is in Victoria, Canada."

Ashley wouldn't have cared if it was in Alaska. Replacing Cooper's china saucer was of the utmost importance. He need never know it had come from her. She could give it to Claudia. After writing down the dealer's name and address, she thanked the man and told him she would put a check in the mail to cover his finder's fee.

Immediately after she replaced the receiver, the phone rang again. She stared at it dumbfounded, unable to move as Cooper's name came up on the screen. She stared at it for a long moment, unwilling to deal with him. After several rings she muted the phone and stuck it back inside her purse.

Silence followed, and she exhaled, unaware until then that she'd been holding her breath. Her palms hurt, and she turned her hand over and saw that her long nails had made deep indentations in the sensitive skin of her palm.

For weeks she'd tried to convince herself that Cooper wasn't ashamed to be seen with her, but the love she felt had blinded her to the truth. Even what Claudia had explained to her over lunch couldn't refute the fact that he hadn't invited her to the dinner party.

Twenty minutes later the doorbell chimed.

"Ashley!" Cooper shouted and pounded on the door. "At least let me explain."

What could he possibly say that hadn't already been said more clearly by his action?

Her heart was crying out, demanding that she listen, but she'd been foolish in the past and had learned from her mistakes. She'd been too easily swayed by her love, but not again.

"Please don't do this," he said.

Her resolve weakened. Cooper had never sounded more sincere. She jerked open the hall closet door and whipped her faux fur jacket off the hanger, put it on and zipped it up all the way to her neck. Then she threw open the front door, crossed her arms and stared at a shocked Cooper with defiance flashing from her blue eyes.

"You have three minutes." Unable to look at him, she held up her wrist and pretended an acute interest in her watch.

"Where are you going?" he demanded.

"Two minutes and fifty seconds," she answered stiffly. "But if you must know, I'm going to see Webber. He happens to like me. It doesn't matter to him that my mother's some rich man's cook, or that my father's a laborer."

"It's Webb."

"Dear heaven," she said, and laughed almost hysterically. "You've got me doing it now."

"Ashley," he said, his voice softening. "It doesn't matter to me who your mother is or where your father works. I'm sorry about the party. I wouldn't want to hurt you for the world."

She bit into the soft skin of her inner lip to keep from letting herself be affected by his words. Her back rigid, she glared at the face of the watch, her body frozen. "Two minutes even," she murmured.

"I didn't think you'd want to come," he began again. "Mostly it's business associates—"

"Don't make excuses. I understand, believe me," she interrupted.

"I'm sure you don't," he countered sharply.

"But I do. I'm the kind of girl who enjoys pizza on the floor in front of a fireplace. I wouldn't fit in, that's what you're saying isn't it? It would be terribly embarrassing for all involved if I showed up wearing red cowboy boots. I might even break a piece of china or, worse yet, use the wrong spoon. No, I understand. I understand all too well." Her eyes and throat burned with the effort of suppressing tears. "Your time's up. Now, if you'll excuse me…" She stepped outside and closed the door.

"I want you to be there tomorrow night," he told her as she turned her key in the lock.

"I don't see any reason to make an issue over it. I couldn't have come anyway, I'm working tomorrow night."

"That's not true," he said harshly.

"You don't stop, do you? Does it give you pleasure to say these things to me…to call me a liar?"

she whispered. "I suppose I should have learned how stubborn you are when I was forced to accept the car." She turned her stricken eyes to his. "I'm not lying."

"You told me school's out," he said with calculated anger.

"It is," she said. "This is my second job, the menial one. I'm a waitress, remember?"

Frustration marked his features as he followed her into the parking lot. "Ashley..."

"I'd like to stay and chat, but I have to be on my way." She paused and laughed mirthlessly. "I appreciate what you're trying to do, but you're the last person on God's green earth I ever want to see again. Goodbye, Cooper."

"Try to understand." The glimpse of pain she witnessed in his eyes couldn't be disguised. Despite what he'd done, she hadn't meant to hurt him, but in her own anguish she had lashed back at him. It was better that she leave now, before they said more hurtful things to one another.

A tight smile lingered on her mouth as she stared into his hard features. "I do understand," she whispered in defeat.

"I doubt that," he mumbled, as he opened the car door for her and stepped back.

She could see him in the side mirror, standing stiff and proud, his look angry, arrogant. He almost fooled her, until he lifted a hand and wiped it across his face. When he dropped his arm, she noted the pain and frustration that glittered from his eyes. The sight made her ache inside, but she wouldn't let herself be influenced, not after what he'd done.

Ashley pulled out of the parking lot, intent on doing as she'd said. Webb would know what to say to comfort her. He was her friend, and she needed him. Tears blinded her vision, and she had to wipe them aside at every traffic signal. Tears would shock Webb; he'd never seen her cry.

Webb's car was in the driveway as she pulled in. He must have seen her arrive, because he opened the front door before she'd had time to ring the bell.

"Ashley." He sounded surprised, but his amazement quickly turned to apprehension. "Are you all right? You look upset. You're not crying, are you?"

All she could do was nod. "Oh, Webb," she sobbed, and walked into his arms.

He hugged her and patted her back like a comforting big brother, which was just what she needed. "I don't suppose this has anything to do with that Cooper character, does it?"

Miserably, she nodded. "How'd you know?"

He led her into the house and closed the door. "Because he just pulled up and parked across the street."

Ashley's head snapped up. "You're kidding! You mean he followed me here?" She took a tissue from her purse and blew her nose. "He probably followed me to find out if I was telling the truth."

"The truth?"

"I told him I was coming to see you. Do you mind?" She glanced up at him anxiously.

"Of course I don't mind." Webb's enthusiasm

sounded forced. "Cooper's only four inches taller than I am and outweighs me by fifty pounds. Do you think he'll give me a choice of weapons?"

"You're being silly." She laughed, and then, to her supreme embarrassment, she hiccupped.

"Hang on," he said, and disappeared into the kitchen. A moment later he was back. "Here, drink this." He handed her a bottle of water.

She accepted because it gave her something to do with her hands. Tipping her head back, she took a large swallow.

"You're in love with him, aren't you?"

"Don't be ridiculous. I thoroughly dislike the man," she countered quickly.

"Now that's a sure sign. I wasn't positive before, but that clinched it."

"Webb, don't tease," she pleaded.

"Who's joking?" He led her to a chair, then sat across the room from her. "I've seen it coming on for the last couple of weeks. Other than the fact that he thinks I'm his arch rival and can't seem to get my name right, I like your Cooper."

"He's not mine," she said, more forcefully than she'd meant to.

"Okay, I won't argue. But if you love each other and really want things to work out, then whatever's wrong can be cleared up. If it doesn't, then you have to believe God has other plans for you."

Ashley closed her eyes for a long moment, then opened them and released a weary sigh. "You know, one of the worst things about you is that you're so darn logical. I can't stand it. I've always said an organized desk is the sign of a sick mind."

"And that, my friend, is one of the nicest things you've ever said to me."

They talked for a bit longer, and Webb did his best to raise her spirits. He joked with her, coaxing her to smile. Later they ordered pizza and played a game of Scrabble. He won royally and refused to discount the fact that her mind wasn't on the game. When he walked her to the car, he kissed her lightly and waved as she backed out of the driveway.

Ashley slept fitfully, her heart heavy. The alarm went off at four-thirty, and she doubted that she'd gotten any rest. Cold water took the sleep out of her eyes, but she looked wan and felt worse. Connecting with the early ferry still meant a five-hour ride across Puget Sound to Victoria, British Columbia. The schedule gave her an hour to locate the antique shop, buy the saucer and connect with the ferry home. The trip would be tiring, and she would barely have enough time to shower and change clothes before leaving for her job at Lindo's Mexican Restaurant.

She had visited the Victorian seaport many times, and its beauty had never failed to enthrall her. Usually she came in summer when the Butchart Gardens were in full bloom. She found it amazing how a city tucked in the corner of the Pacific Northwest could have the feel, the flavor and the flair of England. Even the accent was decidedly British.

Without difficulty she located the small antique

shop off one of the many side streets that catered to the tourists. When Larry Marshall phoned she'd been so pleased to have found the saucer that she'd forgotten to ask about the price. She paled visibly when the proprietor cheerfully informed her how fortunate she was to have found this rare piece and she read the sticker. Her mind balked, but her pride made two hundred dollars for one small saucer sound like a bargain.

On the return trip, she stood at the rail. A demon wind whipped her hair across her face and numbed her with its cold. But she didn't leave, her eyes following the narrow strip of land until it gradually disappeared. Only when a freezing rain began to pelt the deck did she move inside. Surprisingly, she fell asleep until the foghorn blast of the ferry woke her as they eased into the dock in Seattle.

An hour later she smiled at Manuel, Lindo's manager, as she stepped in the back door. After hanging her coat on a hook in the kitchen, she paused long enough to tie an apron around her waist.

"There's someone to see you," Manuel told her in a heavy Spanish accent.

She looked up, perplexed.

"Out front," he added.

She peered around the corner to see a stern-faced Cooper sitting alone at a table. His steel-hard eyes met and trapped her as effectively as a vice.

Chapter 9

Carrying ice water and the menu, Ashley approached Cooper. What was he doing here? What about the party?

Dark, angry sparks flashed from his gaze, and a muscle twitched along the side of his jaw as his eyes followed her. "Where have you been all day?" he asked coldly.

Ashley ignored the question. "The daily special is chili verde." She pointed it out on the menu with the tip of her pencil. "I'll be back to take your order in a few minutes." Her voice contained a breathless tremor that betrayed what seeing him was doing to her. She hated herself for the weakness.

"Don't walk away from me," he warned. The lack of emotion in his voice was almost frightening.

"Are you ready to order now?" She took out the

small pad from the apron pocket. Her fingers trembled slightly as she paused, ready to write down his choice.

"Ashley." His look was tight and grim. "Where were you?"

"I could say I was with Webb," she said, and swallowed tightly at the implication she was trying to give.

"Then you'd be lying," he added flatly.

"Yes, I would."

"Okay, we'll do this your way. It doesn't matter where you were or what sick game you've been playing with me...."

"Sick game?" she echoed, remarkably calm. A sad smile touched her mouth as she averted her gaze.

"I didn't mean that," he muttered.

"It doesn't matter." She lowered her chin. "You'd think by now that we could accept the fact that we're wrong for one another. Forcing the issue is only going to hurt us." She paused and swallowed past the growing tightness in her throat. "I'm not willing to be hurt anymore."

His narrowed eyes searched hers. "I want you to come to the party with me."

Sadly, she hung her head. "No."

"I've already talked to the manager. He says he doesn't think tonight's going to be all that busy anyway."

"I won't go," she repeated insistently.

"Then I'm not leaving. I'll sit here all night if that's what it takes." The tight set of his mouth convinced her the threat wasn't idle.

"But you can't, your guests..." She stopped, angry

at how easily she'd fallen into his plan. "I won't be blackmailed, Cooper. Sit here all night if you like." Her pulse raced wildly.

"All right." His head shifted slightly to one side as he studied the menu. "I'll take a plate of nachos and the special you mentioned."

Furiously, she wrote down the order.

"You stay?" Manuel asked after she called Cooper's order into the kitchen. "I already call my cousin to come in and work for you. You can go to this important party."

"I'm here to work, Manuel," she explained in a patient tone. "I'm sure there will be enough work for both your cousin and me."

Nothing seemed to be going right. Cooper watched her every action like a hawk studying its prey before the kill. By seven o'clock Manuel's cousin had served nearly every customer. Only two customers were seated in her section. Ashley was convinced Cooper had somehow arranged that. She wanted to cry in frustration.

"Cooper," she pleaded, "won't you please leave? It's almost seven."

"I won't go without you," he told her calmly.

"Talk about sick games," she lashed back, and to her consternation a sensuous smile curved his mouth.

"I'm not playing games," he stated firmly.

"Then if you miss your own party it's your problem." She tried to sound nonchalant.

By seven-fifteen she was pacing the floor, her resolve weakening. Cooper couldn't offend his associates this way. It could hurt him and his business.

Using the need to refill his coffee cup as an excuse, she avoided his gaze as she said, "I don't have anything to wear."

"Cowboy boots are fine. I'll wear mine, if you like." Her hand was suddenly captured between his. "Nothing in the world means more to me than having you at my side tonight."

"Oh, Cooper," she moaned. "I don't know. I don't belong there."

He studied her slowly, his eyes focused on her soft mouth. "You belong with me."

She felt the determination to defy him drain out of her. "All right," she whispered in defeat.

"Thank God." As he hurried out of the booth he added, "I'll meet you at your place."

Numbly she nodded. As it worked out, he pulled into the apartment parking lot directly behind her.

"While you change, I'll phone Claudia."

Ashley wanted to kick herself for being so weak. Examining the contents of her closet, she pulled out a wool blend dress with a Victorian flair. The antique lace inserts around the neck, bodice and cuffs gave the white dress a formal look. The glittering gold belt matched the high heels she chose.

Her fingers shook as she applied a light layer of makeup. After a moment of hurried effort, she gripped the edge of the small bathroom sink as she stopped to pray. It wasn't the first time today that she'd turned to God. She'd tried to pray standing on the deck of the ferry, the wind whipping at her, but somehow the words wouldn't come. The pain of Cooper's rejection had been too sharp to voice, even to God. Now, having finished, she lifted her head and released a shuddering breath. More confident, she added a dab of perfume to the pulse points at her wrists and neck, and stepped out to meet Cooper.

He turned around as she entered the room. A shocked look entered his eyes. "You're beautiful."

"Don't sound so surprised. I can dress up every now and then."

"You're a little pale. Come here, I can change that." Before she was aware of what he was doing, he pulled her into his arms and kissed her. The demand of his mouth tilted her head back. His hand pressed against her back, arching her against him.

Ashley's breath caught in her lungs at the unexpectedness of his action. Her hands were poised on the broad expanse of his chest, his heartbeat hammering against her palm.

"There." He tilted his face to study her. "Plenty of color now." Releasing her, he held her coat open so she could easily slip her arms inside. "I'm afraid we're going to make something of a grand entrance. Everyone's arrived. Claudia sounded frantic. She said the hors d'oeuvres ran out fifteen minutes ago."

"Is my mother...?" She let the rest of the question fade, sure Cooper would know what she was asking.

"No, it's being catered." With a hand at the back of her waist, he urged her out the door.

"Oh, Cooper." She hurried back inside. "I almost

forgot." Her heels made funny little noises against the floor as she rushed into her bedroom and came out with the wrapped package. "Here." She gave it to him.

"Do I have to wait for Christmas?"

"No. It's a replacement for the saucer I broke, the one from your grandmother's service."

"I can't believe... Where did you ever find it?"

"Don't ask."

"Ashley..." He set his hands on her shoulders and turned her around so she was facing him. "Is this what you were up to today?"

She nodded silently.

His mouth thinned as his look became distant. "I think I went a little crazy looking for you." He slipped an arm around her waist. "We'll talk about that later. If we keep Claudia waiting another minute, she's likely to disown us both."

The street and driveway outside Cooper's house looked like a high performance car showroom. Ashley felt her nerves tense as she clenched her hands in her lap.

"Ashley, stop."

"Stop?"

"I can feel you tightening up like a coiled spring. Every man here is going to be envious of me. Just be yourself."

The front door flew open before they were halfway up the walk. Claudia stood there like an avenging warlord, waving her arms and glaring at them.

"Thank goodness you're here!" she exclaimed forcefully. "If you ever do this to me again, I swear

I'll..." Her voice drifted away. "Don't stand out here listening to me, get inside. Everyone's waiting." Her gaze narrowed on Cooper. "And I do mean everyone."

Ashley didn't need to be reminded that some of the most important people in Seattle would be there.

Claudia gave her an encouraging smile, winked and took her coat.

His hand at her elbow, Cooper led Ashley into the living room. The low conversational hum rose as a few guests called out his name. Apparently the champagne had been flowing freely, because no one seemed to mind that Cooper was late to his own party.

He introduced her to several couples, though she knew she couldn't hope to remember all the names. After twenty minutes the smile felt frozen on her face. Someone handed her a glass of what she assumed was wine, but she didn't drink it. Tonight she would need to keep her wits about her in a room full of intimidating people. There was hardly room to maneuver, and she felt as if the walls were closing in around her.

"Is this the little lady who kept us waiting?" A distinguished, middle-aged man with silver streaks at his temples asked Cooper for an introduction.

"I am," she admitted with a weak smile. "I hope you'll forgive me."

"I find it very easy to forgive someone as pretty as you. Maybe we could get together later, so I can listen to your excuse."

"Whoa, Tom," Cooper teased, but his voice contained an underlying warning. "The lady's with me."

With a good-natured chuckle, Tom slapped him across the shoulder. "Anything you say."

Ashley spotted Claudia at the far side of the room. "If you'll both excuse me a minute...?" she whispered.

Claudia caught her eye and arched her delicate brows.

"Boy, am I glad to see a familiar face," Ashley said, and released a slow sigh as she leaned against the wall for support.

"What took you two so long?" Claudia demanded. "I was frantic. You wouldn't believe some of the excuses I gave. Dear heavens, Ash, where were you today? I thought Cooper was going to go mad."

"Canada."

"Canada?" Claudia shot back. "Well, I must admit, that was one place he didn't look. Have you talked to your mother yet? I don't know what he said to her, but he was closed up in his den for an hour afterward. Believe me, he didn't look happy. No one, not even the boys, could get near him."

"I know he feels miserable about the whole thing, but I understand better than he realizes. I wouldn't have invited me to this party, either. Look at me. I stick out like a sore thumb."

"If you do, it's because you're the prettiest woman here."

Ashley's light laugh was forced. "You're a better friend than I thought."

"I *am* your friend, but don't underestimate yourself." A hush came over the room as someone in a caterer's apron made the announcement that dinner was ready. "I don't know why Cooper wouldn't invite you tonight. He wasn't overly pleased with me for letting the cat out of the bag, I can tell you that."

"No, I imagine he wasn't." How much simpler things would have been if she'd stayed innocently unaware. "But I'm glad you did," she murmured, and hung her head. "Very glad." When she glanced up she saw the object of their conversation weaving his way toward her. Progress was slow, as people stopped to chat or ask him a question. Although he smiled and chatted, his probing gaze didn't leave her for more than a moment.

"I don't want you hiding in a corner," he muttered when he finally got to her, and gripped her elbow, then led her toward the huge dining room.

"I'm not hiding," she defended herself. "I just wanted to talk to Claudia for a minute."

"It was far longer than a minute," he said between clenched teeth.

"Honestly, Cooper, are you going to start an argument now? I'm here under protest as it is."

"You're here because I want you here. It's where you belong." His control over his temper seemed fragile.

Rather than say anything she would regret later, Ashley pinched her mouth tightly closed.

The dining room table had been extended to accommodate forty guests. Ashley looked at the china and sparkling crystal, and the fir and candle centerpiece that extended the full length of the table. Everything was exquisite, and she was filled with a sense of awe. She didn't belong here. What was she doing fooling herself?

Cooper sat at the head of the table, with Ashley at his right side. Under normal circumstances she would have enjoyed the meal. The caterers had also supplied four waitresses, and she found herself watching their movements instead of involving herself in idle conversation with Cooper or the white-haired man on her right. Once the salad plates were removed, they were served prime rib, fresh green beans and new potatoes. Every bite and swallow was calculated, measured, to be sure she would do nothing that would call attention to herself. For dessert a cake in the shape of a yule log was carried into the room. She only took one bite, afraid she would end up spilling frosting on her white dress. Once, when she glanced up, she found Cooper watching her, his look both foreboding and thoughtful. If this was a test, she was certain she was failing miserably, and his look did nothing to boost her confidence.

When the meal was finished, she couldn't recall ever being more relieved.

Cooper's hand was pressed to her waist, keeping her at his side, as they moved into the living room. She didn't join the conversation, only smiled and nodded at the appropriate times. An hour later, her face felt frozen into a permanent smile.

A few people started to leave. Grateful for the opportunity to slip away, she murmured a friendly farewell and left Cooper to deal with his guests.

"I don't know how much more of this I can take," she whispered to Claudia.

"Don't worry, you're doing great. Not much longer now."

"Where's Seth?"

"Checking the boys. He's not much for this kind of thing, either. Haven't you noticed the way he keeps loosening his tie? By the time the evening's over, the whole thing will be missing."

"What time is it?" Ashley muttered.

"Just after eleven."

"How much longer?"

"I don't know. Don't look now, but Cooper's headed our way."

His stern expression hadn't relaxed. He was obviously displeased about something. "I want to talk to you in my den when everyone's gone." His look was ominous as he turned and left.

Primly, Ashley clasped her hands together in front of her. "Heavens, what did I do now?" she asked Claudia.

Claudia shrugged. "I don't know, but for heaven's sake, humor him. Another day like today, and Seth and I are packing our bags and finding a hotel."

By the time the last couple had left, Ashley's stomach was coiled into a hard lump.

The caterers were clearing away glasses and the last of the dishes from the living room when Cooper found her in the corner talking to Seth and Claudia. As Claudia had predicted, Seth's tie had mysteriously disappeared. His arm was draped across his wife's shoulders.

Seth looked over to Cooper. "You don't mind if we head upstairs, do you?"

"No, no, go ahead." Cooper's answer sounded preoccupied. He gestured toward his den. "We'll be more comfortable in there," he said to Ashley.

She tossed Claudia a puzzled look. Cooper didn't look upset anymore, and she didn't know what to think. His face was tight and drawn, but not with anger. She couldn't recall ever seeing him quite like this.

"Oh!" Claudia paused halfway up the stairs and turned around. "Don't forget tomorrow morning. We'll pick you up around ten. The boys are looking forward to it."

"I am, too," Ashley replied.

They entered the familiar den, and he closed the door, leaning against the heavy wood momentarily. He gestured toward a chair, and she sat down, her back straight.

Again he paused. He rubbed the back of his neck, and when he glanced up, it struck Ashley couldn't remember ever having seen him look more tired.

"Cooper, are you feeling all right? You're not sick, are you?"

"Sick?" he repeated slowly. "No."

"What's wrong, then? You look like you've lost your best friend."

"In some ways, I think I have." He moved across

the room to his desk, rearranging the few items that littered the top.

Impatiently, Ashley watched him. He'd said he wanted to talk to her, yet he seemed hesitant.

"How do you feel about the way things went tonight?" he asked finally.

"What do you mean? Was the food good? It was excellent. Do I like your friends? I found them to be cordial, if a bit overwhelming. Cooper, you have to remember I'm just an ordinary schoolteacher."

The pencil he'd just picked up snapped in two. "You know, I think I'm sick of hearing how ordinary you are."

"What do you mean?" She watched as his mouth formed a brittle line.

"You ran to a corner to hide every chance you got. You wouldn't so much as lift a fork until you'd examined the way three other people were holding theirs to be sure you did it the same way."

"Is that so bad?" she flared. "I felt safe in a corner."

"And not with me?"

"No!"

"I think that tells me everything I want to know."

"You forced me into coming tonight," she accused him.

"It was a no-win situation. You understand that, don't you?"

She stood and moved to the far side of the room. Cooper was talking down to her as if she was a disobedient child, and she hated it. "No, I don't. But there's very little I understand about you anymore."

"I didn't invite you tonight for a reason!" he shouted.

"Do you think I don't already know that?" she flashed bitterly. "I don't fit in with this crowd."

"That's not why," he insisted loudly.

"If you raise your voice to me one more time, I'm leaving." Tears welled in her eyes. How she hated to cry. Her eyes stung, and her throat ached. "It's not the first time, either, is it?"

"What are you talking about?" He tossed her a puzzled look.

"For a while I thought it was just my overactive imagination. That I was thinking like an insecure schoolgirl. But it's true."

"What are you talking about?" What little patience he had was quickly evaporating.

"The first time we went out, you chose a small Italian restaurant, and I thought you didn't want to be seen with me."

"You can't honestly believe that?" His eyes filled with disbelief.

"Then Claudia phoned on Thanksgiving Day and I was there, but you didn't say a word." She paused long enough to swallow back a sob. "I knew you didn't want Claudia or Seth or anyone else to know I was with you. Even in church when you held my hand, it was done secretively and only when there wasn't a possibility of anyone seeing us."

A tense silence enclosed them.

"You've thought that all this time?" The dark, troubled look was back on his face.

She nodded. "I don't know about you, but I'm tired. I want to go home."

His dark eyes searched her face. She noted the weariness that wrinkled his brow and the indomitable pride in his stern jaw.

He opened the door wordlessly and retrieved her coat. He didn't say a word until he pulled up in front of her apartment building. "I find it amazing that you could think all those things, yet continue to see me."

"Now that you mention it, so do I," she returned bitterly.

His mouth thinned, but he didn't retaliate.

She handed him her apartment key, and he unlocked the door. She held out her hand, waiting for him to return the key. He didn't seem to notice, his look a thousand miles away.

When he did glance up, their eyes met and held. The troubled look remained, but with flecks of something she couldn't quite decipher. A softness entered as he lowered his gaze to her soft mouth. "It's not true, Ashley, none of it." With that he turned and left.

Stunned, she stood watching him until he was out of sight.

Her room was dark and still when she turned out the light. She hadn't behaved well tonight. That was what had originally upset Cooper. But she'd been frightened, out of her element. Those people were important, and she was nothing. The four walls surrounding her seemed to close in. Why had he left that way? For once, couldn't he have stayed and explained himself? Tomorrow she would make sure everything was cleared up between them. No more misunderstandings, her heart couldn't take it.

"Are you ready, Auntie Ash?" Johnny asked as he bounded into her apartment excitedly the next morning.

"You bet." She bent over to give her godson a big hug.

"You should hurry, cause Daddy's driving Uncle Cooper's car," John added.

Ashley straightened. "Where's Cooper?"

"He decided at the last minute not to come. What happened with you two last night?" Claudia asked.

"Why?"

Claudia glanced at her son, who was impatiently pacing the floor. "We'll talk about it later."

"Uncle Cooper bought the car seat just for Scotty," Johnny told her proudly when she climbed in the back seat. "He said I was a big boy and could use a special one with a real seat belt. Watch." He pulled the belt across his small body, and after several tries the lock clicked into place. "See? I can do it all by myself."

"Good for you." Ashley looped an arm around his shoulders.

"You should put yours on, too," Johnny insisted. "Uncle Cooper does."

"I think you're right," she agreed with a wry smile.

It was all Ashley could do not to quiz her friend about Cooper's absence as Seth maneuvered in and out of the heavy traffic.

"Christmas Eve Day," Johnny said as he looked

around eagerly. "It's Jesus's birthday tomorrow, and we get to open all our gifts. Scotty's never opened presents."

"I don't think he'll have any problem getting the hang of it," Seth teased from the front seat.

"You're coming tonight, aren't you, Ash?" Claudia half turned to glance into the rear seat.

"I don't know," Ashley said, trying to ignore the heaviness that weighted her heart.

"But I thought it was already settled. Christmas Eve with us and Christmas with your parents."

Ashley pretended an inordinate amount of interest in the scenery flashing past outside her window. "I thought it was, too." Cooper was saying several things with his absence today. One of them was crystal clear. "Maybe I'll come for a little while. I want to see the boys open the presents from Cooper and me."

"Do I get to open a present tonight?" Johnny demanded.

Claudia threw Ashley a disgruntled look. "We'll see," she answered her son.

The downtown Seattle area was crowded with last minute shoppers. Amazingly, Seth found a parking place on the street. While Ashley and Claudia dug through the bottoms of their purses for the correct change for the meter, Seth opened the trunk and retrieved the stroller for Scotty.

"Can I put the money in?" Johnny wanted to know.

Ashley handed him the coins and lifted him up so he could insert them into the slot.

"Good boy," Ashley said, and he beamed proudly.

"Now tell me what happened," Claudia insisted in a low voice. "I'm dying to know."

"Nothing, really. He wasn't pleased with the way the party turned out. Mainly, he was disappointed in me."

"In *you*?" Claudia looked surprised. "What did you do? I thought you were fine."

"I don't understand him, Claudia." She couldn't conceal a sigh of regret. "First, he pointedly doesn't invite me and openly admits he didn't want me there. Then he forcefully insists that I attend. And to make matters worse, he doesn't approve of the way I acted."

"If you ask me, I think he's got a lot of nerve," Claudia admitted. "I hardly spoke to him this morning. But something's wrong. He's miserable. He loves you, I'd bet my life on it. It would be a terrible shame if you two didn't get together."

"I suppose."

"You suppose?" Claudia drawled the word slowly. "If you love one another, then nothing should keep you apart."

"Spoken like a true optimist. But I'm not right for Cooper," Ashley announced sadly. "He needs someone with a little more—I hate to use this word, but... finesse."

"And you need someone more easy-going and fun-loving. Like Webb," Claudia finished for her.

"No, not at all." Ashley's cool blue eyes turned questioningly toward her friend. "I'm surprised you'd even suggest that. Webb's a friend, nothing more."

Clearly pleased, Claudia shook her head knowingly.

"I don't think you realize that you bring out the best in Cooper, or that he does the same for you. I don't think I've seen a couple who belong together more than you two."

"Oh, Claudia, I hope we do, because I love him so much."

"Have you ever thought about letting *him* know that?"

A blustery wind whipped Ashley's coat around her, preventing her from answering.

"I think we should catch the monorail," Seth suggested. "It's getting windy out here. Agreed?"

The two women had been so caught up in their conversation they'd hardly noticed.

"Fine." Ashley shook her head.

"Sure," Claudia said, looking a little guilty as Seth handled both boys so she could talk.

For a nominal fee they were able to catch the transport that had been built as part of the Seattle World's Fair in 1962. The rail delivered them to the heart of the Seattle Center, only a few blocks from the Food Circus.

The boys squealed with delight the minute they spied the Enchanted Forest. Scotty clapped his hands gleefully and pointed to the kiddy size train that traveled between artificial trees.

"Are you hungry?" Seth wanted to know.

"Not me." Ashley's thoughts were on other things.

"I wouldn't object to cotton candy," Claudia confessed.

"I had to ask," Seth teased, and lovingly brushed his lips over his wife's cheek.

Ashley viewed the tender scene with building despair. Someday, she wanted Cooper to look at her like that. More than anything else, she wanted to share her life with him, have his children.

"Ash, are you all right?" Claudia asked.

Quickly, she shook her head. "Of course. What made you ask?"

"You looked so sad."

"I am, I…"

"My goodness, Ash, look, Cooper's here."

"Cooper?" Her spirits soared. "Where?"

"Across the room." Claudia pointed, then waved when he saw them.

His level gaze crossed the crowded room to hold Ashley's, his look discouraging.

"I'm going to do it," Ashley said, straightening. Claudia gave her a funny look, but didn't question her as she started toward him.

They met halfway. He looked tired, but just as determined as she felt.

"Ashley."

"I want to talk to you," she said sternly.

"I want to talk to *you*, too."

"Wonderful. Let me go first."

He looked at her blankly. "All right," he agreed.

"You asked me last night why I continued to see you if I believed all those things I confessed. I'll tell you why. Simply. Honestly. I love you, Cooper Masters, and if you don't love me, I think I'll die."

Chapter 10

"That's not the kind of thing you say to a man in a public place." He studied her face for a tantalizing moment, gradually softening.

"I know, and I apologize, but I couldn't hold it in any longer."

"Why couldn't you have told me that last night?"

Oblivious to the crowds milling around, they stared at one another with only a small space separating them.

"Because I was afraid, and you were so…"

Cooper rubbed a hand across his eyes. "Don't say it. I know how I was."

"When you weren't with Claudia this morning, I didn't know what to think."

"I couldn't come. Not when you believed that I

didn't want to be seen with you—that I was ashamed of you. You've carried that inside all these weeks, and not once did you question me."

Her teeth bit tightly into her lower lip. "I was afraid. Sounds silly, doesn't it?" She didn't wait for him to answer. "Afraid if I brought my fears into the open and forced you to admit it, that I wouldn't see you again. I couldn't face the truth if it meant losing you."

"The day you started ranting about your mother being my cook and your father being a steelworker... Was that the reason?"

She looked away and nodded.

Slowly he shook his head. "I can understand how you came to that conclusion, but you couldn't be more wrong. I love you, Ashley, I—"

"Cooper, oh, Cooper," she cried excitedly and threw her arms around him, spreading happy kisses over his face.

His mouth intercepted her as he hungrily devoured her lips. Although she could hear the people around them, she wouldn't have cared if they were in New York City at Grand Central Station. Cooper loved her. She'd prayed to hear those words, and nothing, not even a Christmas crowd in a public place, was going to ruin her pleasure.

When he dragged his mouth from hers, his husky voice breathed against her ear, "Do you promise to do that every time I admit I love you."

"Yes, oh, yes," she said with a joyous smile.

He cleared his throat self-consciously. "In case you hadn't noticed, we have an audience."

She was too contented to care. A searing happiness was bubbling within her. "I want the whole world to know how I feel."

"You seem to have gotten a good start," he teased with an easy laugh, and kissed the top of her head. "Don't look now, but Claudia and company are headed our way."

Reluctantly, Ashley dropped her arms and stepped back. Cooper pulled her close to his side, cradling her waist.

"Is everything okay with you two, or do you need more time?" Claudia's gaze went from one of them to the other. "If that embrace was anything to go by, I'd say things are looking much better."

"You could say that," Cooper agreed, his eyes holding Ashley's. The look he gave her was so warm and loving that it seemed to burst free and touch her heart and soul.

"But there are several things we need to discuss," Cooper continued. "If you don't mind, I'm going to take Ashley with me. We'll all meet back at the house later."

Claudia and Seth exchanged knowing looks. "We don't mind," Seth answered for them.

"But…Seth has your car," Ashley said, confused. "How will we…?"

He smiled. "I have a second car, since I can't afford to be without transportation. We'll be fine."

"Do I still get to open a present tonight? Because Auntie Ash said we could," Johnny quizzed anxiously, not the least bit interested in the logistics of the grown-ups' plans.

Cooper's eyes met Claudia's, and she shrugged.

"I think that will be fine, if that's what your Auntie Ash said," Seth interrupted.

"Uncle Cooper?" John's head tilted up at an inquiring angle.

"Yes?" He squatted down so that he was eye level with his godson.

"Is there mistletoe here, too?"

Briefly Cooper scanned the interior of the huge building. "I don't see any, why?"

"Cause you were kissing Auntie Ash again."

"Sometime I like to kiss her even when there isn't any reason."

"You mean like Daddy and Mommy?"

"Exactly," he said, and smiled as his eyes caught Ashley's.

"I think it's time we left and let these two talk. We'll meet you later," Seth announced. Claudia lifted Johnny into her arms and turned around, then looked back and winked.

"Are you hungry?" Cooper asked.

She hadn't eaten all day. "Starved. I hardly touched dinner last night."

"I noticed." His tone was dry.

She ignored it. "And then this morning I was too miserable to think about food. But now I could eat a cow."

"We're at the right place. Choose what you want, and while you find us a table, I'll go get it."

The Food Circus had a large variety of booths that sold every imaginable cuisine. The toughest decision was making a choice from everything that was available.

They hardly spoke as they ate their chicken. Ashley licked her fingers. Cooper carefully unfolded one of the moistened towelettes that had been provided with their meal and carefully cleaned his own hands.

He glanced up and found her watching him. A tiny smile twitched at the corner of her mouth. "What's so funny?" he asked.

"Us." She opened her own towelette and followed his example. "Claudia told me she didn't know any two people more meant for one another."

Cooper acknowledged the statement with a curt nod. "I know I love you, whether we're right or wrong for one another doesn't seem to be the question." He reached across the table and captured her hand. "But then, you're an easy person to love. You're warm and alive, and so unique you make my heart sing just watching you."

"And you're so calm and dignified. Nothing rattles you, and so many times I've wished I could be like that."

"We balance one another." His eyes searched hers in a room that seemed filled with only them.

A burst of applause diverted Cooper's attention to the antics of a clown. "Let's get out of here."

Ashley happily agreed.

They stood, dumped their garbage in the proper receptacles, and linked their arms around one another's waists as they strolled outside.

A chill raced over her forearms, and she shivered.

Cooper brought her closer to his side. "Cold?"

"Only when you close me out," she whispered truthfully. "If you hadn't admitted to loving me, I don't know that I could have withstood the cold."

He drank deeply from her eyes, perhaps realizing for the first time how strong her emotions rang. "We need to talk," he murmured, and quickened his pace.

A half hour later he pulled into the driveway of his home.

"Coffee?" he suggested as he hung her coat in the hall closet.

"Yes." She nodded eagerly. "But, Cooper, could I have it in a mug? I'd feel safer."

His mouth thinned slightly, and she knew her request had troubled him. "I'm not the dainty teacup type," she said more forcefully than she wanted to. "What I mean is…"

"I know what you mean." Lightly he pressed a kiss on her cheek, then against the hollow of her throat. "Do you have any idea how difficult it's been this week to keep my hands off you?"

"Not half as difficult as it's been not to encourage you to touch me," she admitted, and felt color suffuse her cheeks.

A few minutes later he carried two ceramic mugs into the den on a silver platter.

A soft smile danced from Ashley's eyes. "Compromise?"

"Compromise," he agreed, handing her one of the mugs.

She held it with both hands and stared into its

depths. "I have a feeling I know what you're going to say."

"I doubt that very much, but go ahead."

"No." She shook her head, then nervously tugged a strand of hair around her ear. "I've put my foot in my mouth so many times that for once I'm content to let you do the talking."

"We seem to have a penchant for saying the wrong things to each other, don't we?" His gaze searched hers, and the silence was broken only by an occasional snap and pop from the logs in the fireplace.

His look was thoughtful as he straightened in his chair. Nervously, she glanced around the den she had come to love—the books and desk, the chess set. One of the most ostentatious rooms in the house and, strangely, the one in which she felt the most comfortable. Maybe it was because this was the room Cooper used most often.

"I think it's important to clear away any misunderstandings, especially about the party. Ashley, when I saw how hurt you were to be excluded, well…I can't remember ever feeling worse. Believe this, because it's the truth. I wanted you there from the first. But I felt you would be uncomfortable. Those people are a lot like me."

"But I love you," she said, keeping her gaze on her coffee.

"I didn't know that at the time. I didn't want to do anything that was going to make you feel ill-at-ease. Thrusting you into my world could have destroyed our promising relationship, and that was far more important to me. Now I realize what a terrible mistake that was."

"And the other things?" She had to know, had to clear away any reasons for doubt.

"Thinking over everything you've told me, your point of view makes perfect sense." He set his cup aside and sat on the ottoman in front of her chair. Holding her face with both hands, he tilted her gaze to meet his. Ashley couldn't doubt the sincerity of his look. "I did those things because I thought you wouldn't want to be associated with me. I didn't let Claudia know you were here on Thanksgiving when she phoned to protect you from speculation and embarrassing questions. The same with what happened in church."

"Oh, Cooper..." She groaned at her own stupidity. "I was so miserable. I know it was stupid not to say anything, but I was afraid of the truth."

His kiss was sweet and filled with the awe of the discovery of her love. "Things being what they are, maybe you should open your Christmas gift now."

"Oh, could I?"

"I think you'd better." He opened the closet and brought out a large, beautifully wrapped box.

Much bigger than an engagement ring, Ashley mused thoughtfully, fighting to overcome her disappointment. Cowboy boots? She'd tried on a couple of pairs when they'd bought his, but she'd decided against them because of the expense. But if her present was cowboy boots, why would Cooper feel it was important to give it to her now?

He placed it on her lap, and she untied the red velvet bow, then hesitated. "My gift to you is at home." It was important that he know he'd meant enough to her to buy him something special. "But I'm making you wait until Christmas."

"Maybe I should make *you* wait, too," he teased, ready to take back the gaily wrapped present.

"No you don't," she objected, and gripped the package tightly.

"Actually," he said, and the teasing light left his eyes, "it's important that you open this now." He smiled huskily and kissed her. His lips were a light caress across her brow.

Ashley's fingers shook as she pulled back the paper and lifted the lid of the box. Inside, nestled in white tissue, was a large family Bible. Her heart was thumping so loudly she could barely hear Cooper speaking above the hammering beat.

"A Bible," she murmured and looked up at him, her gaze probing his.

"I've thought about what you said about your relationship with Christ, and how important it was to you. I wanted to have a strong faith for you, because of my love. But that wasn't good enough. There were so many things I didn't understand. If Christ paid the price for my salvation with His life, then how can my faith be of value if all I have to do is ask for it?" He stood and walked across the room, pausing once to run his hand through his hair. "I talked to Seth about it several times. He always had the answers, but I wasn't convinced. Last Sunday I was in church, sitting in the sanctuary waiting for the service to begin, and I asked God to help me. On the way out of church after the service I saw the car I had given you in the parking lot. Suddenly I knew."

Ashley had been at church, but she had taught Sunday School and then helped in the nursery during the worship service. She had talked only briefly to Claudia and hadn't seen Cooper at all.

"My car? How did my car help?"

"It sounds crazy, I know," he admitted wryly. "But I gave it to you because I love you. Freely, without seeking reimbursement, knowing that you couldn't afford a car. It was my gift to you, because I love you. It suddenly occurred to me that was exactly why Christ died for me. He paid the price because I couldn't."

Unabashed tears of happiness clouded her eyes as her hands lovingly traced the gilded print on the cover of the Bible.

"I've made my commitment to Christ," he told her, his voice rich and vibrant. "He's my Savior."

"Oh, Cooper." She wiped a tear from her cheek and smiled up at him.

"That's not all."

An overwhelming happiness stole through her. She couldn't imagine anything more wonderful than what he'd just finished explaining.

"Do you recall the first Sunday Claudia and Seth arrived?"

Ashley nodded.

"I stepped into your Sunday school class." He looked away as a glossy shine came over his dark eyes. "You were on the floor with a little girl sitting in your lap."

"I remember. You turned around and walked out. I thought I'd done something to upset you."

"Upset me?" he repeated incredulously. "No. Never that. You looked up, and your blue eyes softened, and in that moment I imagined you holding another child. Ours. Never have I felt an emotion so strong. It nearly choked me, I could hardly think. If I hadn't turned around and walked away, I don't know what I would have done."

Ashley thought her heart would burst with unrestrained joy. "Our child."

"Yes." Cooper knelt on the floor beside her, took the Bible out of its box and set the box on the floor. Reverently, he opened the first pages of the holy book. "I got this one for a reason. I've written our names here, and I'm asking that we fill the rest out together."

Ashley looked down at the page, which had been set aside to record a family history. Both their names were entered under "Marriage," the date left blank.

"Will you marry me, Ashley?" he asked, an unfamiliar humble quality in his voice.

The lump of joy in her throat prevented her from doing anything but nodding her head. "Yes," she finally managed. "Yes, Cooper, yes." She flung her arms around his neck and spread kisses over his face. She laughed with breathless joy as the tears slid down her cheeks.

His arms went around her as he pulled her closer.

His mouth found hers in a lingering kiss that cast away all doubts and misgivings.

She lovingly caressed the side of his face. "I don't know how you can love me. I always seem to think the worst of you."

"Not anymore you won't," he whispered against her temple as he continued to stroke her back. "I won't ever give you reason to doubt again. I love you, Ashley."

She linked her hands behind his neck and smiled contentedly into his eyes. "I do want children. Just being with Johnny and Scott has shown me how much I want babies of my own."

"We'll fill the house. I can't wait to tuck them into bed at night and listen to their prayers."

"What about horsey rides?"

"Those too."

"Cooper…" She paused and swallowed tightly. "Why were you so angry with me after the party?" She wanted everything to be right and needed to know what she'd done to displease him.

Some of the happiness left his face. "I love you so much, Ashley. It hurt me to see you so uncomfortable, afraid to make a move. Your fun-loving, outgoing nature had been completely squelched. I wanted you to be yourself. Later—" He sat on the ottoman and took both her hands in his. "—I had already gotten the Bible with the hope of asking you to marry me, and you listed off all the things I had done to make you believe I was ashamed to be seen with you. I don't mind telling you that it shook me up. I was on the verge of asking you to be my wife, and you didn't even know how much I loved you."

"I won't have that problem again," she told him softly.

"I know you won't, because you'll never have reason to doubt again. I promise you that, my love."

The sound of footsteps in the hall brought their attention to the world outside the door.

Cooper stood, and extended a hand toward her. "I don't think either Claudia or Seth will be surprised by our announcement. Or your family, for that matter."

"My family?"

"I talked to your mother and father yesterday. They've given us their blessing. I was determined to have you, Ash. I wouldn't want to live my life without you now." He hugged her tightly and curved an arm around her waist. "Christmas. It's almost too wonderful to believe. God gave His Son in love. And now He's given me you."

* * * * *

Dear Reader,

It is such a pleasure to see the reissue of one of my first novels, *In the Spirit of…Christmas*. As with all my books, this one began as seeds in my subconscious—a snippet of overheard conversation and an incident that happened to someone I know. Like the pines on Lindsey's tree farm, the seeds took root and grew into a young woman whose heart was broken by a cheating fiancé and a man who lost his wife at Christmas. Two people with issues of trust. One feared trusting God. The other feared trusting man. But a little girl, a big dog and a Christmas miracle just may bring the healing they both require.

I love hearing from readers. You can connect with me on Facebook and Twitter, or sign up for my newsletter, read my blog or send an email through my website: www.lindagoodnight.com.

Wishing you a joyous Christmas season,

Linda Goodnight

IN THE SPIRIT OF...
CHRISTMAS

Linda Goodnight

Dedicated with love to my aunts and uncle: Pat, Carmie, Robert and my late Aunt Bonnie. I'll never forget how you stood, a wall of family support at my first book-signing. Your loving enthusiasm touches my heart. Daddy would be so proud.

Chapter 1

Leaning over the steering wheel of his blue-and-gray Silverado, Jesse Slater squinted toward the distant farmhouse and waited. Just before daybreak the lights had come on inside, pats of butter against the dark frame of green shutters. Still he waited, wanting to be certain the woman was up and dressed before he made his move. She had an eventful day ahead of her, though she didn't know it.

Aware suddenly of the encroaching autumn chill, he pulled on his jacket and tucked the covers around the child sleeping on the seat beside him, something he'd done a dozen times throughout the night. Sleeping in a pickup truck in the woods might be peaceful, but it lacked a certain homey comfort. None of that mattered this morning, for no matter how soul-weary he might be, he was finally back home. *Home*—a funny word after all these years of rambling. Even though he'd lived here only six years after his mother had inherited the farm, they were formative years in the life of a boy. These remote mountains of southeastern Oklahoma had been the only real home he'd ever known.

Peace. The other reason he'd come here. He remembered the peace of lazy childhood days wading in the creek or fishing the ponds, of rambling the forests to watch deer and squirrel and on a really lucky day to spot a bald eagle soaring wild and regal overhead.

He wanted to absorb this peace, hold it and share it with Jade. Neither of them had experienced anything resembling tranquility for a long time.

The old frame house, picturesque in its setting in the pine-drenched foothills of Oklahoma's Kiamichi Mountains, was as it had always been—surrounded by green pastures and a dappling of scattered outbuildings. Somewhere a rooster heralded the sun and the sound sent a quiver of memory into Jesse's consciousness.

But his memory, good as it was, hadn't done justice to the spectacular display of beauty. Reds, golds and oranges flamed from the hills rising around the little farm like a fortress, and the earthy scent of pines and fresh air hovered beneath a blue sky.

"Daddy?"

Jesse turned his attention to the child whose sleepy green eyes and tangled black hair said she'd had a rough night too.

It was a sorry excuse of a father whose child slept

in a pickup truck. And he was even sorrier that she didn't find it unusual. His stomach knotted in that familiar mix of pain and joy that was Jade, his six-year-old daughter.

"Hey, Butterbean. You're awake."

Reaching two thin arms in his direction, she stretched like a kitten and yawned widely. "I'm hungry."

Jesse welcomed the warm little body against his, hugging close his only reason to keep trying.

"Okay, darlin'. Breakfast coming right up." With one eye on the farmhouse, Jesse climbed out of the truck and went around to the back. From a red-and-white ice chest he took a small carton of milk and carefully poured the contents into a miniature box of cereal.

Returning to the cab, he handed the little box to Jade, consoling his conscience with the thought that cereal was good for her. He didn't know much about that kind of thing, but the box listed a slew of vitamins, and any idiot, no matter how inept, knew a kid needs milk.

When she'd eaten all she wanted, he downed the remaining milk, then dug out a comb and wet wipes for their morning ablutions. Living out of his truck had become second nature for him during fifteen years on the rodeo circuit, but in the two years since Erin had died, he'd discovered that roaming from town to town was no life for a little girl. She'd been in and out of so many schools only her natural aptitude for learning kept her abreast of other children her age. At least, he assumed she was up to speed academically. Nobody had told him different, and he knew for a fact she was smart as a tack.

But she needed stability. She deserved a home. And he meant for her to have one. He lifted his eyes to the farmhouse. This one.

A door slammed, resounding like a gunshot in the vast open country. A blond woman came out on the long wooden porch. Of medium height, she wore jeans and boots and a red plaid flannel jacket that flapped open in the morning air as she strode toward one of the outbuildings with lithe, relaxed steps. No hurry. Unaware she was being watched from the woods a hundred yards away.

So that was her. That was Lindsey Mitchell, the modern-day pioneer woman who chose to live alone and raise Christmas trees on Winding Stair Mountain.

Well, not completely alone. His gaze drifted to a monstrous German shepherd trotting along beside her. The animal gave him pause. He glanced over at Jade who was dutifully brushing her teeth beside the truck. She hadn't seen the shepherd, but when she did there would be trouble. Jade was terrified of dogs. And for good reason.

Running a comb through his unruly hair, he breathed a weary sigh. Dog or not, he had to have this job. Not just any job, but *this* one.

When his daughter had finished and climbed back into the cab, he cranked the engine. The noise seemed obscenely loud against the quiet noises of a country morning.

"Time to say hello." He winked at the child, extracting an easy grin, and his heart took a dip. This little girl was his sunshine. And no matter how rough their days together had been, she was a trooper, never complaining as she took in the world through solemn, too-old eyes. His baby girl had learned to accept whatever curves life threw her because it had thrown so many.

Putting the truck into gear he drove up the long driveway. Red and gold leaves swirled beneath his tires, making him wonder how long it had been since anyone had driven down this lane.

The woman heard the motor and turned, shading her eyes with one hand. The people in the nearby town of Winding Stair had warned him that she generally greeted strangers with a shotgun at her side. Not to worry, though, they'd said. Lindsey was a sweetheart, a Christian woman who wouldn't hurt a flea unless she had to. But she wasn't fool enough to live alone without knowing how to fire a rifle.

He saw no sign of a weapon, though it mattered little. A rifle wouldn't protect her against the kind of danger he presented. Still, he'd rather Jade not be frightened by a gun. The dog would be bad enough.

He glanced to where the child lay curled in the seat once again, long dark eyelashes sweeping her smooth cheeks. Guilt tugged at him. He'd been a lousy husband and now he was a lousy father.

As he drew closer to the house, the woman tilted her head, watching. Her hair, gleaming gold in the sun, lifted on a breeze and blew back from her shoulders so that she reminded him of one of those shampoo commercials—though he doubted any Hollywood type ever looked this earthy or so at home in the country setting. The dog stood sentry at her side, ears erect, expression watchful.

Bucking over some chug holes that needed filling, Jesse pulled the pickup to a stop next to the woman and rolled down the window.

"Morning," he offered.

Resting one hand atop the shepherd's head, Lindsey Mitchell didn't approach the truck, but remained several feet away. Beneath the country-style clothes she looked slim and delicate, though he'd bet a rodeo entry fee she was stronger than her appearance suggested.

Her expression, while friendly, remained wary. "Are you lost?"

He blinked. Lost? Yes, he was lost. He'd been lost for as long as he could remember. Since the Christmas his mother had died and his step-daddy had decided he didn't need a fourteen-year-old kid around anymore.

"No, ma'am. Not if you're Lindsey Mitchell."

A pair of amber-colored eyes in a gentle face registered surprise. "I am. And who are you?"

"Jesse Slater." He could see the name held no meaning for her, and for that he was grateful. Time enough to spring that little surprise on her. "Calvin Perrymore sent me out here. Said you were looking for someone to help out on your tree farm."

He'd hardly been able to believe his luck when he'd inquired about work at the local diner last night and an old farmer had mentioned Lindsey Mitchell. He hadn't been lucky in a long time, but nothing would suit his plan better than to work on the very farm he'd come looking for. Never mind that Lindsey Mitchell raised Christmas trees and he abhorred any mention of the holiday. Work was work. Especially here on the land he intended to possess.

"You know anything about Christmas-tree farming?"

"I know about trees. And I know farming. Shouldn't be too hard to put the two together."

Amusement lit her eyes and lifted the corners of her mouth. "Don't forget the Christmas part."

As if he could ever forget the day that had changed the direction of his life—not once, but twice.

Fortunately, he was spared a response when Jade raised up in the seat and leaned against his chest. She smelled of sleep and milk and cereal. "Where are we, Daddy?"

The sight of the child brought Lindsey Mitchell closer to the truck.

"You're at the Christmas-tree farm." She offered a smile that changed her whole face.

Though she probably wasn't much younger than his own thirty-two, in the early-morning light her skin glowed as fresh as a teenager's. Lindsey Mitchell was not a beautiful woman in the Hollywood sense, but she had a clean, wholesome, uncomplicated quality that drew him.

Something turned over inside his chest. Indigestion, he hoped. No woman's face had stirred him since Erin's death. Nothing stirred him much, to tell the truth, except the beautiful little girl whose body heat warmed his side just as her presence warmed the awful chill in his soul.

"A Christmas-tree farm. For real?" Jade's eyes widened in interest, but she looked to him for approval. "Is it okay if we're here, Daddy?"

The familiar twinge of guilt pinched him. Jade knew how her daddy felt about Christmas. "Sure, Butterbean. It's okay."

In fact, he was anxious to be here, to find out about the farm and about how Lindsey Mitchell had come to possess it.

"Can I get out and look?"

Before he had the opportunity to remember just why Jade shouldn't get out of the truck, Lindsey Mitchell answered for him. "Of course you can. That's what this place is all about."

Jade scooted across the seat to the passenger-side door so fast Jesse had no time to think. She opened the door, jumped down and bounded around the pickup. Her scream ripped the morning peace like a five-alarm fire.

With a sharp sense of responsibility and a healthy dose of anxiety, Jesse shot out of the truck and ran to her, yanking her shaking body up into his arms. "Hush, Jade. It's okay. The dog won't hurt you."

"Oh, my goodness." Lindsey Mitchell was all sympathy and compassion. "I am so very sorry. I didn't know Sushi would frighten her like that."

"It's my fault. I'd forgotten about the dog. Jade is terrified of them."

"Sushi would never hurt anyone."

"We were told the same thing by the owner of the rottweiler that mauled her when she was four." Jade's sobs grew louder at the reminder.

"How horrible. Was she badly hurt?"

"Yes," he said tersely, wanting to drop the subject while he calmed Jade. The child clung to his neck, sobbing and trembling enough to break his heart.

"Why don't you bring her inside. I'll leave Sushi out here for now."

Grateful, Jesse followed the woman across the long front porch and into the farmhouse. Once inside the living room, she motioned with one hand.

"Sit down. Please. Do you think a drink of water or maybe a cool cloth on her forehead would help?"

"Yes to both." He sank onto a large brown couch that had seen better days, but someone's artistic hand had crocheted a blue-and-yellow afghan as a cover to brighten the faded upholstery. Jade plastered her face against his chest, her tears spotting his chambray shirt a dark blue.

Lindsey returned almost immediately, placed the water glass on a wooden coffee table and, going down on one knee in front of the couch, took the liberty of smoothing the damp cloth over Jade's tear-soaked face. The woman was impossibly near. The clean scent of her hair and skin blended with the sweaty heat of his daughter's tears. He swallowed hard, forcing back the unwelcome rush of yearning for the world to be normal again. Life was not normal, would never be normal, and he could not be distracted by Lindsey Mitchell's kind nature and sweet face.

"Shh," Lindsey whispered to Jade, her warm, smoky voice raising gooseflesh on his arms. "It's okay, sugar. The dog is gone. You're okay."

The sweet motherly actions set off another torrent of reactions inside Jesse. Resentment. Delight. Anger. Gratitude. And finally relief because his child began to settle down as her sobs dwindled to quivering hiccups.

"There now." Adding to Jesse's relief, Lindsey handed him the cloth and stood, moving back a pace or two. She motioned toward the water glass. "Would you like a drink?"

Jade, her cheek still pressed hard against Jesse's chest, shook her head in refusal.

"She'll be all right now," Jesse said, pushing a few stray strands of damp hair away from the child's face. "Won't you, Butterbean?"

Like the trooper she was, Jade sat up, sniffed a couple of times for good measure, and nodded. "I need a tissue."

"Tissue coming right up." Red plaid jacket flapping open, Lindsey whipped across the room to an end table and returned with the tissue. "How about some juice instead of that water?"

Jade's green eyes looked to Jesse for permission.

He nodded. "If it wouldn't be too much trouble."

"No trouble at all." Lindsey started toward a country-kitchen area opening off one end of the living room. At the doorway, she turned. "How about you? Coffee?"

The woman behaved as if he were a guest instead of a total stranger looking for work. The notion made him uncomfortable as all get out, especially considering why he was here. He didn't want her to be nice. He couldn't afford to like her.

Fortunately, he'd never developed a taste for coffee, not even the fancy kind that Erin enjoyed. "No thanks."

"I have some Cokes if you'd rather."

He sighed in defeat. He'd give a ten-dollar bill this morning for a sharp jolt of cold carbonated caffeine.

"A Coke sounds good." He shifted Jade onto the couch. Her hair was a mess and he realized he'd been in such a hurry to get here this morning, he hadn't even noticed. Normally, a headband was the best he could do, but today he'd even forgotten that. So much for first impressions. Using his fingers, he smoothed the dark locks as much as possible. Jade aimed a wobbly grin at him and shrugged. She'd grown accustomed to his awkward attempts to make her look like a little girl.

He glanced toward the kitchen, saw that Lindsey's back was turned. With one hand holding his daughter's, he took the few moments when Lindsey wasn't in sight to let his gaze drift around the house. It had changed—either that or his perception was different. Eighteen years was a long time.

The wood floors, polished to a rich, honeyed glow, looked the same. And the house still bore the warm, inviting feel of a country farmhouse. But now, the rooms seemed lighter, brighter. Where he remembered a certain dreariness brought on by his mother's illness, someone—Lindsey Mitchell, he supposed—had drenched the rooms in light and color—warm colors of polished oak and yellow-flowered curtains.

The house looked simple, uncluttered and sparkling clean—a lot like Lindsey Mitchell herself.

"Here we go." Lindsey's smoky voice yanked him around. He hoped she hadn't noticed his intense interest. No point in raising her suspicions. He had no intention of letting her know the real reason he was here until he had the proof in his hands.

"Yum, Juicy Juice." Jade came alive at the sight of a cartoon-decorated box of apple juice. "Thank you."

Lindsey favored her with another of those smiles that set Jesse's stomach churning. "I have some gummy fruits in there too if you'd like some—the kind with smiley faces."

Jade paused in the process of stabbing the straw into the top of her juice carton. "Do you have a little girl?"

Jesse was wondering the same thing, though the townspeople claimed she lived alone up here. Why would a single woman keep kid foods on hand?

If he hadn't been watching her closely to hear the answer to Jade's questions, he'd have missed the cloud that passed briefly over Lindsey's face. But he had seen it and wondered.

"No." She handed him a drippy can of Coke wrapped in a paper towel. "No little girls of my own, but I teach a Sunday-school class, and the kids like to come out here pretty often."

Great. A Sunday-school teacher. Just what he didn't

need—a Bible-thumping church lady who raised Christmas trees.

"What do they come to your house for?" Jade asked with interest. "Do you gots toys?"

"Better than toys." Lindsey eased down into a big brown easy chair, set her coffee cup on an end table and leaned toward Jade. Her shoulder-length hair swept forward across her full mouth. She hooked it behind one ear. "We play games, have picnics or hayrides, go hiking. Lots of fun activities. And," she smiled, pausing for effect, "I have Christmas trees year-round."

Christmas trees. Jesse suppressed a shiver of dread. Could he really work among the constant reminders of all he'd lost?

Jade smoothly sidestepped a discussion of the trees, though he saw the wariness leap into her eyes. "I used to go to Sunday school."

"Maybe you can go with me some time. We have great fun and learn about Jesus."

Jesse noticed some things he'd missed before. A Bible lay open on an end table near the television, and a plain silver cross hung on one wall flanked by a decorative candle on each side. Stifling an inner sigh, he swallowed a hefty swig of cola and felt the fire burn all the way down his throat. He could work for a card-carrying Christian. He had to. Jade deserved this one last chance.

"We don't go anymore since Mama died."

Jesse grew uncomfortably warm as Lindsey turned her eyes on him. Was she judging him? Finding him

unfit as a father because he didn't want his child growing up with false hopes about a God who'd let you
down when you needed Him most?

He tried to shrug it off. No way he wanted to offend
this woman and blow the chance of working here. As
much as he hated making excuses, he had to. "We've
moved a lot lately."

"Are you planning to be in Winding Stair long?"

"Permanently," he said. And he hoped that was true.
He hadn't stayed in one spot since leaving this mountain as a scared and angry teenager. Even during his
marriage, he'd roamed like a wild maverick following the rodeo or traveling with an electric-line crew,
while Erin remained in Enid to raise Jade. "But first
I need a job."

"Okay. Let's talk about that. I know everyone
within twenty miles of Winding Stair, but I don't know
you. Tell me about yourself."

He sat back, trying to hide his expression behind
another long, burning pull of the soda. He hadn't expected her to ask that. He thought she might ask for
references or about his experience, but not about him
specifically. And given the situation, the less she knew
the better.

"Not much to tell. I'm a widower with a little girl
to support. I'm dependable. I'll work hard and do a
good job." He stopped short of saying she wouldn't
regret hiring him. Eventually, she would.

Lindsey studied him with a serene expression and
a slight curve of a full lower lip. He wondered if she
was always so calm.

"Where are you from?"

"Enid mostly," he answered, naming the small town west of Oklahoma City that had been more Erin's home than his.

"I went to a rodeo there once when I was in college."

"Yeah?" He'd made plenty of rodeos there himself.

With a nod, she folded her arms. "What did you do in Enid? I know they don't raise trees in those parts."

He allowed a smile at that one. The opening to the Great Plains, the land around Enid was as flat as a piece of toast.

"Worked lineman crews most of the time and some occasional rodeo. But I've done a little of everything."

"Lineman? As in electricity?"

"Yes, ma'am. I've helped string half the power lines between Texas and Arkansas."

His answer seemed to please her, though he had no idea what electricity had to do with raising Christmas trees.

"How soon could you begin working?"

"Today."

She blinked and sat back, taking her coffee with her. "Don't you even want to know what the job will entail?"

"I need work, Miss Mitchell. I can do about anything and I'm not picky."

"People are generally surprised to discover that growing Christmas trees takes a lot of hard work and know-how. I have the know-how, but I want to expand. To do that I need help. Good, dependable help."

"You'll have that with me. I don't mind long hours, hard work or getting dirty."

"The pay isn't great." She named a sum barely above minimum wage. He wanted to react but didn't. He'd made do on less. Neither the job nor the money was the important issue here.

"The hours are long. And I can be a slave driver."

Jesse couldn't hold back a grin. Somehow he couldn't imagine Lindsey as much of a slave driver. "Are you offering me the job or trying to scare me off?"

She laughed and the sound sent a shiver of warmth into the cold recesses of Jesse's heart. "Maybe both. I don't want to hire someone today and have him gone next week."

"I'm not going anywhere. Jade's already been in two schools this year, and it's only October."

Her eyes rested on Jade as she thought that one over. One foot tapping to a silent tune while she munched gummy faces, his daughter paid little attention to the adults.

"I have about twenty acres of trees now but plan to expand by at least another ten by next year. Would you like to have a look at the tree lot?"

"Not now." Not at all, ever, but he knew that was out of the question. Once he took possession the Christmas trees would disappear. "Just tell me what I'll be doing."

For the next five minutes, she discussed pruning and replanting, spraying and cutting, bagging and shipping. All of which he could do. No problem. He'd just pretend they were ordinary trees.

"I'll need character references before I make a final decision."

Jesse reached in his jacket pocket and pulled out a folded paper. He'd been prepared for that question. "Any of these people will tell you that I'm not a serial killer."

"Well, that's a relief. I'd hate to have to shoot you."

He must have looked as startled as he felt because she laughed. "That was a joke. A bad one, I'll admit, but I can shoot and I do have a gun."

Was she warning him to tread lightly? "Interesting hobby for a woman."

"The rifle was my granddad's. He had quite a collection."

"Is he the one who taught you to shoot?"

"Mostly. But don't worry about safety." She glanced at his adorable little girl with the missing front tooth. "I have a double-locked gun safe to protect the kids who come out here. Owning a firearm is a huge responsibility that I don't take lightly."

Rising from the overstuffed armchair, she took the sheet of references from his outstretched fingers. The clean scent of soap mixed with the subtle remnants of coffee drifted around her. The combination reminded him way too much of Erin.

"I'll give some of these folks a call and let you know something this afternoon. Will that be all right?"

"Sure."

"I'll need your telephone number. Where can I reach you?"

Jesse rubbed a hand over the back of his neck. "Hmm. That could be a problem. No phone yet."

"Where are you living? Maybe I know someone close by and could have them bring you a message."

"That's another problem. No house yet either."

She paused, a tiny frown appearing between a pair of naturally arched eyebrows. Funny that he'd notice a thing like a woman's eyebrows. "You don't have a place to live?"

Jade, who'd been as quiet as a mouse, happily sipping her juice and munching green and purple smiley faces, suddenly decided to enter the conversation. "We live in Daddy's truck."

Great. Now he'd probably be reported to child welfare.

But if Lindsey considered him a poor parent, she didn't let on in front of Jade. "That must be an adventure. Like camping out."

"Daddy says we're getting a house of our own pretty soon."

Jesse was glad he hadn't told the child that he'd been talking about *this* house.

Lindsey's eyes flickered from Jade to him. "Have you found anything yet?"

Oh, yes. He'd found exactly the right place.

"Not yet. First a job, then Jade and I have a date with the school principal. While she's in school I'll find a place to stay."

"Rental property is scarce around here, but you

might check at the Caboose. It's an old railroad car turned into a diner on the north end of town across from the Dollar Store. Ask for Debbie. If there is any place for rent in the area, she'll know about it."

"Thanks." He stood, took Jade's empty juice carton and looked around for a trash can.

"I'll take that." Lindsey stretched out a palm, accepting the carton. No long fancy nails on those hands, but the short-clipped nails were as clean as a Sunday morning.

"Come on, Jade. Time to roll." Jade hopped off the couch, tugging at the too-short tail of her T-shirt. The kid was growing faster than he could buy clothes.

Stuffing the last of the gummy fruits into her mouth, she handed the empty wrapper to Lindsey with a shy thank-you smile, then slipped her warm little fingers into his.

"How about if I give you a call later this afternoon," Jesse asked. "After you've had a chance to check those references?"

"That will work." She followed him to the door.

Jade tugged at him, reaching upward. "Carry me, Daddy."

He followed the direction of her suddenly nervous gaze. From the front porch the affronted German shepherd peered in through the storm door, tail thumping hopefully against the wooden planks.

Jesse swept his daughter into his arms and out the door, leaving behind a dog that terrified his daughter, a house he coveted and a woman who disturbed him a little too much with her kindness.

He had a very strong feeling that he'd just compounded his already considerable problems.

Chapter 2

Uncertainty crowding her thoughts, Lindsey pushed the storm door open with one hand to let the dog inside though her attention remained on the man. He sauntered with a loose-limbed gait across the sunlit yard, his little girl tossed easily over one strong shoulder like a blanket.

Jesse Slater. The name sounded familiar somehow, but she was certain they'd never met. Even for someone as cautious of the opposite sex as she was, the man's dark good looks would be hard to forget. Mysterious silver-blue eyes with sadness hovering at the crinkled corners, dark cropped hair above a face that somehow looked even more attractive because he hadn't yet shaved this morning, and a trim athletic physique dressed in faded jeans and denim jacket over a Western shirt. Oh, yes, he was a handsome one all right. But looks did not impress Lindsey. Not anymore.

Still, she couldn't get the questions out of her head. Why would a man with no job and a child to raise come to the small rural town of Winding Stair? It would be different if he had relatives here, but he'd mentioned none. Something about him didn't quite ring true, but she was loath to turn him away. After all, if the Christmas Tree Farm was to survive, she needed help—immediately. And Jesse Slater needed a job. And she'd bet this broad-shouldered man was a hard worker.

The child, Jade, hair hanging down her father's back like black fringe, looked up and saw that Sushi was now inside, then wiggled against her father to be let down. She slid down the side of his body then skipped toward the late-model pickup.

At the driver's-side door, Jesse boosted the little girl into the cab and slid inside behind her. Then for the first time he looked up and saw Lindsey standing inside the storm door, watching his departure. He lifted a hand in farewell, though no smile accompanied the gesture. Lindsey, who smiled—and laughed—a lot, wondered if the darkly solemn Jesse had experienced much joy in his life.

The pickup roared to life, then backed out and disappeared down the long dirt drive, swirling leaves and dust into the morning air.

Lindsey, who preferred to think the best of others, tried to shrug off the nagging disquiet. After months of seeking help, she should be thankful, not suspicious, to have a strong, healthy man apply for the job. But the fact that she'd almost given up hope that anyone would be willing to work for the small salary she could afford to pay was part of what raised her suspicions.

She wrestled with her conscience. After all, the poor man had lost his wife and was raising a small daughter alone. Couldn't that account for his air of mysterious sadness? Couldn't he be seeking the solitude of the mountains and the quiet serenity of a small town to help him heal? Even though she knew from experience that only time and the Lord could ease the burden of losing someone you love, the beautiful surroundings were a comfort. She knew that from experience too.

Stepping back from the doorway, she stroked one hand across Sushi's thick fur. "What do you think, girl?"

But she knew the answer to that. Sushi was a very fine judge of character and she hadn't even barked at the stranger. Nor had she protested when the man had come inside the house while she was relegated to the front porch.

Looking down at the sheet of paper still clutched in one hand, Lindsey studied the names and numbers, then started for the telephone.

"If his references check out, I have to hire him. We need help too badly to send him away just because he's too good-looking."

Later that afternoon, Lindsey was kneeling in the tree lot, elbow-deep in Virginia pine trimmings, when

Sushi suddenly leaped to her feet and yipped once in the direction of the house.

A car door slammed.

Pushing back her wind-blown hair with a forearm, Lindsey stood, shears in hand and strained her eyes toward the house. A blue Silverado once more sat in her driveway and Jesse Slater strode toward her front door.

Quickly, she laid aside the shears and scrambled out of the rows of pine trees.

Hadn't the man said he'd call for her decision? What was he doing out here again? Her misgivings rushed to the fore.

"Hello," she called, once she'd managed to breech the small rise bordering the tree lot. The house was only about fifty yards from the trees, and Sushi trotted on ahead.

Jesse spun on his boot heel, caught sight of her and lifted a hand in greeting.

"No wonder you didn't answer your phone," he said when she'd come within speaking distance.

With chagrin, Lindsey realized that it had happened again. While working in the trees, she frequently lost track of time, forgot to eat, forgot about everything except talking to the Lord and caring for the trees. Maybe that's why she loved the tree farm so much and why she'd been so reluctant to take on a hired hand. While among the trees, she carried on a running conversation with God, feeling closer to Him there than she did anywhere—even in church.

"I'm sorry. I didn't realize it was so late." Holding

her dirty hands out to her sides, she said, "Why don't you come on in while I wash up? Then we can talk."

Jesse, who'd managed to shave somewhere since she'd seen him last, hesitated. "I hate to ask this, but would you mind putting the dog up again? My daughter is with me."

Lindsey pivoted toward the truck, aware for the first time that a small, worried face pressed against the driver's-side window. "I don't mind, but that is something else we need to discuss. If you're going to work for me, we have to find a way for Jade and Sushi to get along."

A ghost of a grin lit the man's face. "Does that mean none of my references revealed my sinister past?"

"Something like that." In fact, his references had been glowing. One woman had gone beyond character references though, and had told Lindsey about Jesse's wife, about the tragic accident that had made him a widower, and about his raw and terrible grief. Her sympathy had driven her to pray for the man and his little girl—and to decide to hire him.

"If you'll carry Jade inside again, I'll hold Sushi and leave her outside while we talk."

Jesse did as she asked, galloping across the lawn with the child on his back, her dark hair streaming out behind like a pony's tail. Dog forgotten in the fun, Jade's giggle filled the quiet countryside.

"Would you like some tea? Or a Coke?" Lindsey asked once the child and man were seated inside on the old brown sofa. "I've been in the trees so long I'm parched as well as dirty."

"A Coke sounds great, although we don't intend to continue imposing on your hospitality this way."

"Why not?"

He blinked at her, confused, then gave a short laugh. "I don't know. Doesn't seem polite, I suppose."

She started into the kitchen, then stopped and turned around. "If you're going to work for me, we can't stand on ceremony. You'll get hungry and thirsty, so you have to be able to come up here or into the office down at the tree patch and help yourself."

"So I have the job." With Jade glued to his pants leg, he followed Lindsey into the kitchen, moving with a kind of easy, athletic grace.

Lindsey stopped at the sink to scrub her hands. The smell of lemon dishwashing liquid mingled with the pungent pine scent emanating from her skin and clothes. It was a good thing she loved the smell of Christmas because it permeated every area of her life. Even when she dressed up for church and wore perfume, the scent lingered.

"If you want it. The hours are long. The work is not grueling, but it is physical labor. You can choose your days off, but between now and Christmas, things start hopping."

An odd look of apprehension passed over Jesse's face. He leaned against the counter running alongside the sink. "What do you mean, *hopping?*"

"Jesse, this is a Christmas tree farm. Though I'm mostly a choose-and-cut operation, I also harvest and transport a certain number of trees to area city lots, grocery stores, etc., about mid-November." She dried her hands on the yellow dishtowel hanging over the oven rail.

"Do you do that yourself or have someone truck them?" He followed her to the refrigerator where she handed him two colas. He popped the lids and gave one to Jade, then took a long pull on the other, his silver eyes watching her over the rim.

"Right now I'm delivering them myself, but long-range I want a large enough clientele to ship them all over the country." Her shoulders sagged. "But that takes advertising and advertising takes money—which I do not have at present." Taking a cola for herself, she waved a hand. "But I'm getting off topic here. Let's go sit down and discuss your job. Jade," she said, glancing down toward the child, "I have some crayons and a coloring book around here somewhere if you'd like to color while your dad and I talk."

The child's eyes lit up, so Lindsey gathered the materials she kept stashed in a kitchen drawer and spread them on the table.

The child eyed the table doubtfully and clung tighter to her father's leg. She pointed toward the living room, not ten feet away. "Can I go in there with you and Daddy?"

The poor little lamb was a nervous wreck without her daddy.

"Of course, you can." Lindsey swept up the crayons and book and proceeded into the living room, settling Jade at the coffee table.

All the while, she was aware of the handsome stranger's eyes on her. His references were excellent.

She could trust him. She *did* trust him. She even felt a certain comfort in his presence, but something about him still bothered her.

Was it because he was too good-looking? She had been susceptible to good looks once before and gotten her heart broken.

No. That had happened a long time ago and, with the Lord's help, she had put that pain behind her.

Hadn't she?

The sharp tang of Coke burned Jesse's throat as he watched the play of interesting emotions across Lindsey's face. She was not a woman who hid her feelings particularly well. If he was to pull this off, he would have to win her confidence. And right now, from the looks of her, she was worried about hiring him.

"I'm a hard worker, Miss Mitchell. I'll do a good job."

"Lindsey, please. There can't be that much difference in our ages."

"Okay. And I'm Jesse. And this lovely creature is Jade." He poked a gentle finger at Jade's tummy.

His little girl beamed at him as though he'd given her a golden crown and, as usual, his heart turned over when she smiled. That one missing front tooth never failed to charm him. "Daddy's silly sometimes."

"I guess I'll have to learn to put up with that if he's going to work out here. What about you? What are we going to do about you and my dog?"

"I don't like dogs. They're mean." When Jade drew back against the couch, green eyes wide, Jesse sighed.

What in the world was he going to do about this stand-off between dog lover and dog hater? He'd give anything to see Jade get over her terrible fear of dogs, but the trauma ran so deep, he wondered if she ever would. In fact, since Erin's death, her fear had worsened, and other fears had taken root as well. She didn't want him out of her sight, she was terrified of the dark, and her nightmares grew in intensity.

He took a sip of cola, thinking. "Could we just play it by ear for a while and see how things go? Jade will be in school most of the time anyway."

"I work long, sometimes irregular hours, especially this time of year."

"I don't mind that." The more hours he worked the more money he'd make. And the more time he'd have to question Lindsey and check out the farm.

"Then I have a suggestion. The school bus runs right by my driveway. Why not have Jade catch the bus here in the morning and come back here after school?"

Jesse breathed an inward sigh of relief. He'd hoped she'd say that. Otherwise he would have to take off work twice a day to chauffeur his child to and from school.

"That would be a big help."

"Yes, but coming here will also put her in contact with Sushi morning and night."

"Hmm. I see your point." Pinching his bottom lip between finger and thumb, he considered, but came away empty. "Any ideas?"

"Yes, but fears like that don't disappear overnight. We'll need some time for Jade to acclimate and to realize that Sushi is one of the good guys." She smiled one of those sunshine smiles that made him feel as though anything was possible—even Jade accepting the dog.

"In the meantime, while Jade is here, Sushi can remain outdoors or in one of the bedrooms with the door closed. When we're working in the field, sometimes she hangs out in the office anyway. She won't like being left out, but it will only be until Jade feels more comfortable with her around."

There she went again, tossing kindness around like party confetti. He had to stop setting himself up this way. Liking Lindsey Mitchell could not be part of the deal. "I'm sorry about this. Sorry to be so much trouble."

"Don't worry about it. Jade's fear isn't your fault, and she certainly can't help it." She shot a wink toward Jade who looked up, green eyes wide and solemn. "Not yet, anyway."

The child was poised over a drawing of the Sermon on the Mount, red crayon at the ready. Jesse swallowed hard.

"Daddy, I want to see the Christmas trees."

The knot tightened in Jesse's chest. Pictures of Jesus. Christmas trees. What was next? "How about tomorrow?"

Jade didn't fuss, but disappointment clouded her angelic face. She resumed coloring, trading the red crayon for a purple one.

"Come on, Jesse." Lindsey rose from the armchair. "You may as well see where you'll be spending most of your time. While we're down there, I'll show you the little office where I keep the equipment and explain my plans for this Christmas season."

He'd have to do it sooner or later. Feeling as if he were being led to the gallows, Jesse swigged down the remainder of his Coke and stood.

"Where are the Christmas trees?" Gripping Jesse's hand, Jade took in rows and rows of evergreens, swiveling her head from side to side plainly searching for something more traditionally Christmas.

She might be disappointed, but Jesse inhaled in relief, feeling the pungent pine-scented coolness in his nostrils. They were just trees. Plain ordinary pine trees, no more Christmassy than the thousands of evergreens lining the woods and roads everywhere in this part of Oklahoma. The only differences were the neat rows and carefully tended conical shapes of a specific variety. Nothing to get all worked up over.

"Where are the decorations? And the presents?" Jade was as bewildered as she was disappointed.

Kneeling in the rich dirt, Lindsey clasped one of Jade's small hands in hers. "Listen, sweetie, don't fret. Right now, the lot doesn't look like anything but green pine trees, but just you wait another month. See that little building over there?"

After turning to look, Jade nodded. "Are the Christmas trees in there?"

Lindsey laughed, that warm, smoky sound that made Jesse's stomach clench. "Not yet. But the decorations are in there. Lights, and Santas, and angels. Even a nativity set and a sleigh."

"Yeah?" Jade asked in wonder.

"Yeah. And with your daddy to help me this year, we'll set out all of the decorations, string lights up and down these rows, hook up a sound system to pipe in Christmas carols. Maybe you and I can even decorate one special tree up near the entrance where cars pull in. Then every night and day we'll have a Christmas party. People will come to choose a tree and we'll give them wagon rides from the parking area through the tree lot."

The woman fairly glowed with excitement and the effect was rubbing off on Jade. Pulling away from her dad for the first time, she clapped her hands and spun in a circle.

"Let's do it now."

"Whoa, Butterbean, not so fast." He laid a quieting hand on her shoulder. "Lindsey already told you that part comes later." The later the better as far as he was concerned.

"But soon, though, sweetie." Lindsey couldn't seem to bear seeing Jade disappointed. She motioned toward an open field where a large brown horse grazed on the last of the green grass. "See that horse down there? He loves to pull a wagon, does it all the time for hayrides—but at Christmas he gives visitors rides from the parking area through the tree lot."

"What's his name?"

"Puddin'. Don't you think he looks like chocolate pudding?"

Jade giggled. "No. He's big."

"Big, but very gentle. He likes kids, especially little girls with green eyes."

"I have green eyes."

Lindsey bent low, peering into Jade's face. "Well, how about that? You sure do. You'll be his favorite."

Jesse watched in amazement as Lindsey completely captivated his usually quiet daughter. If he wasn't very careful, he'd fall under her spell of genuine decency too. Given his mission, he'd better step easy. Common sense said he should discourage Jade from this fast-forming friendship, but she'd had so little fun lately, he didn't have the heart to say a word.

"Can I go see the Christmas in your building?"

"Sure you can." Popping up, Lindsey dusted her knees and looked at Jesse. His reluctance must have shown because she said, "If we can convince your daddy there are no monsters in there."

Mentally shaking himself, Jesse forced a smile he didn't feel. Santas and angels and horse-drawn wagons. Great. Just great. He wanted no part of any of it. But he wanted this job. And he wanted this farm. To get them both he'd have to struggle through a couple of months of having Christmas shoved down his throat at every turn. It was more than he'd bargained for, but he'd have to do it.

Somehow.

Chapter 3

Delighted to see Jade so excited and to find a fellow Christmas lover, Lindsey clasped her small hand and started toward the storage building. Jesse's voice stopped her.

"You two go ahead. I'll get busy here in the trees."

Lindsey turned back. A crisp October breeze had picked up earlier in the afternoon, but the autumn sun made the wind as warm as a puppy's breath. "Work can wait until tomorrow."

"You have plenty of trimmings here to get rid of. I'll start loading them in the wheelbarrow."

If reluctance needed a pictorial representation, Jesse Slater had the job. Hands fisted at his side, the muscles along his jawbone flexed repeatedly. Lindsey's medical training flashed through her head. Fight or flight—the adrenaline rush that comes when a man is threatened. But why did Jesse Slater feel threatened? And by what? She was the woman alone, hiring a virtual stranger to spend every day in her company. And she didn't feel the least bit threatened.

"Don't you want to see all my Christmas goodies?"

His expression was somewhere between a grimace and a forced smile. "Some other time."

He turned abruptly away and began gathering trimmed pine branches, tossing them into the wheelbarrow. Lindsey stood for a moment, observing the strong flex of muscle beneath the denim jacket. His movements were jerky, as though he controlled some deep emotion hammering to get loose.

Regardless of his good looks and his easy manner, something was sorely missing in his life. Whether he realized it or not, Jesse was a lost and lonely soul in need of God's love.

Ever since coming to live on her grandparents' farm at the age of fifteen, Lindsey had brought home strays, both animal and human. She'd been a stray herself, healed by the love and faith she'd found here in the mountains. But there was something other than loneliness in Jesse. Something puzzling. Maybe even dangerous.

Then why didn't she send him packing?

"Could we go now?" A tug from Jade pulled her attention away from the man and back to the child.

"Sure, sweetie. Want to race?"

The storage and office buildings, which looked more like old-time outhouses than business buildings, were less than fifty feet from the field. Lindsey gave the child a galloping head start, her short, pink-capri-clad legs churning the grass and leaves. When enough distance separated them, Lindsey thundered after her, staying just far enough behind to enjoy the squeals and giggles.

When Lindsey and Jade returned sometime later, Jesse had shed his jacket and rolled back his shirt-sleeves. The work felt good, cleansing somehow, and he wanted to stay right here until nightfall.

"That was fun, Daddy." Jade pranced toward him with a strand of shiny silver garland thrown around her neck like a boa. "Lindsey let me bring this to decorate a tree."

"Little early for that isn't it?" He tried not to react, tried to pretend the sight of anything Christmassy didn't send a spear right through his heart. But visions of gaily-wrapped gifts spilled out around a crushed blue car still haunted him.

Lindsey shrugged. "It's never too early for Christmas. Looks like you've been busy."

He'd filled and emptied the wheelbarrow several times, clearing all the rows she'd trimmed today.

"Impressed?"

She rested her hands on her hipbones and smiled. "As a matter of fact, I am."

"Good." Yanking off his gloves, he resisted returning the smile. "What's next?"

"Nothing for now. It will be dark soon."

She was right. Already the sun bled onto the trees

atop the mountain. Darkness would fall like a rock, hard and fast. He'd run away once into the woods behind the farm and darkness had caught him unaware. He'd spent that night curled beneath a tree, praying for help that never came.

"Guess Jade and I should be heading home then."

Knocking the dust off his gloves, he stuffed them into a back pocket, letting the cloth fingers dangle against his jeans.

"Did you find a house to rent today?"

"Your friend Debbie hooked me up. Sent me to the mobile-home park on the edge of town."

She picked up his jacket, swatted the pine needles away and handed him the faded denim. "Is it a nice place?"

He repressed a bitter laugh and tossed the jacket over one shoulder. Anything was nice after living in your truck. When Jade had seen the tiny space, she'd been ecstatic.

"The trailer will do until something better comes along." He couldn't tell her that the something better was the farm she called home.

By mutual consent they fell in step and left the tree lot, Jade scampering along between them, deliberately crunching as many leaves as possible.

Before they reached his truck, Lindsey said, "I have extra linens, dishes and such if you could use them."

Don't be so nice. Don't make me like you.

He opened the door and boosted Jade into the cab. "We're all right for now."

"But you will let me know if you discover something you need, won't you?"

Grabbing the door frame, he swung himself into
the driver's seat.

"Sure." Not in a hundred years. What he needed
was somewhere in the courthouse in Winding Stair
and she didn't need to know a thing about it—yet. He'd
planned to start his investigation today, but finding a
place to live had eaten up all his time. Soon though.
Very soon he would have the farm he'd coveted for
the past eighteen years.

Lindsey wiped the sticky smear of Jade's maple
syrup off the table, trying her best not to laugh at the
father-and-daughter exchange going on in her kitchen.
In the week since she'd hired Jesse Slater, he and Jade
had become a comfortable part of her morning routine. As many times as she'd offered, Jesse refused to
take his meals with her, but he hadn't objected when
she'd taken to preparing breakfast for his little girl.

Now, as she cleaned away the last of Jade's pan-
cakes, Jesse sat on the edge of a chair with his daughter perched between his knees. Every morning he
made an endearingly clumsy attempt to fix the child's
beautiful raven hair. And every day Lindsey itched to
do it for him. But she said nothing. Jade was, after all,
Jesse's child. Just like all the other children she loved
and nurtured, Jade was not hers. Never hers.

Normally, he smoothed her hair with the brush,
shoved a headband in place, and that was that. This
morning, however, Jesse had reached his limit when

Jade announced she wanted to wear a ponytail like her new best friend, Lacy. Lindsey suppressed a smile. From the expression on his face, Jesse considered the task right next to having his fingernails ripped out with fencing pliers.

A pink scrunchie gritted between his teeth, he battled the long hair into one hand, holding it in a stranglehold. He'd once let slip that he'd ridden saddle broncs on the rodeo circuit and, Lindsey thought with a hidden smile, that he must have done so with this same intense determination.

Finally, with an audible exhale, he dropped back against the chair. "There. All done."

"Jess…" Lindsey started, then hushed. As much as she longed to see the little girl gussied up like the princess she could be, she wouldn't interfere.

Jade touched a hand tentatively to her head. The lopsided ponytail resided just behind her left ear. A long strand of unbound hair tumbled over the opposite shoulder and the top of her head had enough bumps and waves to qualify as an amusement-park ride.

"Daddy, I don't think Lacy wears her ponytail like this."

Lindsey couldn't hold back the laughter bubbling up inside her. Dropping the dishtowel over the back of a chair, she covered her face and giggled.

Jesse heaved an exasperated moan and rolled his silver eyes. "What? You don't appreciate my talent?"

Lindsey could barely get her breath. "It isn't that— It's just, just—" She took one look at the child's hair and started up again.

Jesse had never joked with her before, didn't smile much either, but this time a reluctant half smile tugged at one corner of his mouth and kicked up, setting off laugh crinkles around his eyes. "If I were a hairdresser in LA, this would be all the rage."

"If you were a hairdresser in LA, I'd stay in Oklahoma."

"All right, boss lady, if you think you can do better—" He bowed toward Jade, extending his arm with a flourish. "She's all yours."

"I thought you'd never ask. I have been itching to get my hands on that gorgeous hair." She grabbed the hairbrush and guided the grinning child back into the chair, then stood behind her. As she'd suspected, the dark hair drifted through her fingers like thick silk. In minutes she had the ponytail slicked neatly into place.

"Impressive," Jesse admitted, standing with his head tilted and both hands fisted on his hips.

"I love playing hairdresser."

"No kidding?" His gaze filtered over her usual flannel and denim. "You don't seem the type."

"I think I should be insulted." She smoothed her hand down Jade's silky ponytail. "Just because I dress simply and get my hands dirty for a living doesn't mean I'm not a girl, Jesse."

He held up both hands in surrender. "Hey, no offense meant. You are definitely a girl. Just not frilly like some."

Like your wife? she wondered. Was she frilly? Is that the type you prefer?

As soon as the thoughts bounded through her head,

Lindsey caught them, shocked to even think such things. Once she'd dreamed of marrying a wonderful man and having a houseful of children, but after her fiancé's betrayal, trusting a man with her heart wasn't easy. Add to that the remote, sparsely populated area where she'd chosen to live, and she'd practically given up hope of ever marrying. Besides, she had a farm to run. She didn't want to be interested in Jesse romantically. He was her hired hand and nothing more.

She turned her attention to Jade, handing the child a mirror. "There, sweetie. See what you think."

Jade touched her hair again. Then a smile bright enough to light a room stretched across her pretty face. "I'm perfect!"

Both adults laughed.

Jade flopped her head from side to side, sending the ponytail into a dance. "How did you make me so pretty?"

"My Sunday-school girls come out for dress-up parties sometimes. We do hair and makeup and wear fancy play clothes. It's fun."

"Can I come sometime?"

"Sure. If it's okay with your dad. In fact, tonight is kid's night at church if you'd like to come and meet some of my Sunday-school students."

"Daddy?" Jade asked hopefully, her eyebrows knitted together in an expression of worry that made no sense given the harmless request.

Some odd emotion flickered over Jesse, but his response was light and easy. He pecked the end of her nose with one finger. "Not this time, Butterbean. You and I have to work on those addition facts."

The child's happiness faded, but she didn't argue. Head down, ponytail forgotten, she trudged to the couch and slid a pink backpack onto her shoulders. Her posture was so resigned, so forlorn that Lindsey could hardly bear it.

"Hey, sweetie, don't worry. My Sunday-school class comes out here pretty often. Maybe you can come another time."

The child gave a ragged sigh. "Okay." She hugged her father's knees. "Bye, Daddy."

He went down in front of her, drawing her against his chest.

Lindsey's throat clogged with emotion. The man was a wonderful dad, the kind of father she'd always dreamed of having for her own children someday. But someday had never come.

"I'll get the dog," she said, going to the door in front of Jade as she had every morning this week. She brought Sushi inside, watching through the glass storm door as the little girl headed to the bus stop, a small splash of pink and white against the flaming autumn morning. In the distance, Lindsey heard the grinding gears of the school bus.

As a teenager she'd ridden that bus to high school and home again, and in the years since she'd watched it come and go year after year carrying other people's children. But this morning she watched a child make the journey down her driveway to the bus stop, and, for the first time, felt a bittersweet ache in her throat because that child was not her own.

By noon the damp October morning had given way to blue skies and the kind of clouds Jade called marshmallows. A bit of breeze swirled down from the north, promising a frost soon, but Jesse wasn't the least bit cool. As he sat on the top step, leaning backward onto the front porch, he enjoyed what had become his usual lunch, a Coke and a ham sandwich, and pondered how one little woman had ever done all this work by herself.

Besides the routine weeding and spraying, he'd helped her clear several acres of land in preparation for planting another thousand or so trees next week. And from her description of November's chores, October was a vacation.

He had to admit, however reluctantly, that he admired Lindsey Mitchell. She never complained, never expected him to do anything she wasn't willing to do herself. As a result he worked twice as hard trying to lift some of the load off her slim shoulders, and her gratitude for every little thing he did only made him want to do more.

She was a disconcerting woman.

Twisting to the left so he could see her, he said, "Mind if I ask you a question?"

Wearing the red flannel and denim that seemed so much a part of her, Lindsey sat in an old-fashioned wooden porch swing sipping her cola. A partially eaten ham sandwich rested at her side. Sushi lay in front of her, exercising mammoth restraint as she eyed the sandwich longingly.

"Ask away." With dainty movements, Lindsey tore off a piece of ham and tossed it to the dog.

"What would entice a pretty young woman to live out here all alone and become a Christmas-tree farmer?"

The corners of her eyes crinkled in amusement as she wiped her fingers on her jeans. Jesse's stomach did that clenching thing again.

"I didn't exactly plan to be a Christmas-tree farmer. It just happened. Or maybe the Lord led me in this direction." One hand gripping the chain support, she tapped a foot against the porch and set the swing in motion. "My parents are in the military so we moved around a lot. When I was fourteen—" she paused to allow a wry grin. "Let's just say I was not an easy teenager."

Surprised, Jesse swiveled all the way around, bringing one boot up to the top step. Lindsey was always so serene, so at peace. "I can't see you causing anyone any trouble."

"Believe me, I did. Dad and Mom finally sent me here to live with my grandparents. They thought stability, the same school, the country atmosphere and my grandparents' influence would be good for me. They were right."

"So you didn't grow up here?" Now he was very interested.

Lindsey shook her head, honey-colored hair bouncing against her shoulders, catching bits of light that spun it into gold. Odd that he would notice such a thing.

"Actually none of my family is originally from around here. My grandparents bought this farm after they retired. Gramps began the Christmas Tree Farm as a hobby because he loved Christmas and enjoyed sharing it with others."

Jesse decided to steer the conversation toward her grandparents and their purchase of the farm, feeling somewhat better to know Lindsey had not been involved in what had happened eighteen years ago.

"How long did your grandparents own this place?"

"Hmm." Her forehead wrinkled in thought. "I'm not sure. They'd probably been here three or four years when I came. I've lived here nearly fifteen years."

Jesse did the math in his head. The time frame fit perfectly. He rotated the Coke can between his palms then tapped it against his upraised knee. So her grandfather had been the one.

"Did you have any idea who your grandfather bought this place from?" As soon as he asked, Jesse wanted his words back. The question was too suspicious, too far off the conversation, but if Lindsey noticed she said nothing.

"I haven't a clue. All I know is after Granny passed away, Gramps put the farm and everything on it into my name. By then, I wanted to live here forever, so other than bringing me to a faith in Jesus, this was the greatest gift they could have given me."

The too-familiar tug of guilt irritated Jesse. He had no reason to feel bad for her. She'd enjoyed the benefit of living here for years while he'd wandered around like a lost sheep. Only during his too-short time with Erin had he ever found any of the peace that hovered over Lindsey like a sweet perfume. And he was counting on this farm to help him find that feeling again.

"So you became a tree farmer like your grandfather."

Stretching backward, Lindsey ran both hands through the top of her hair, lifted the sides, and let them drift back down again. Jesse found the motion as natural and appealing as the woman herself.

"I tried other things. Went to college. Became a lab tech. Then Sean and I—" She paused, and two spots of color stained her cheekbones. "Let's just say something happened in my personal life. So, when Gramps passed away three years ago, I couldn't bring myself to let the tree farm go. After that first year of doing all the things he'd taught me and of watching families bond as they chose that perfect Christmas tree, I understood that this was where my heart is."

Though curious about the man she'd mentioned, Jesse decided to leave the subject alone. Knowing about her love life would only make his task more difficult. "So you gave up your job to dedicate all your time to the farm."

"I still take an occasional shift at the hospital and fill in for vacations in the summer to keep my skills sharp or to put a little extra money in the bank. But this is my life. This is what I love. And unless economics drive me out of business, I'll raise Christmas trees right here on Gramps' farm forever."

Though she couldn't possibly know his thoughts, to Jesse the announcement seemed like a challenge. Averting his eyes, he ripped off a piece of sandwich and tossed the bit of bread and ham to the dog.

Sushi thumped her tail in thanks.

"You spoil her more than I do."

"Yeah." He pointed his soda can toward the north. "We have visitors."

A flock of geese carved a lopsided V against the sky, honking loudly enough to rival a rush-hour traffic jam.

"They're headed to my pond."

"And then to a vacation in Florida."

Lindsey laughed and drew her knees up under her chin. "Watching them makes me feel lazy."

"What's on for this afternoon now that we've cleared that new plot of land?"

"Tomorrow we'll need to go over to Mena and pick up the saplings I've ordered. So this afternoon I thought we'd get ready for the wienie roast."

"Who's having a wienie roast?"

"I am. Well, my church actually, but since I have such a great place for it, complete with a horse to give wagon rides, I host the party out here every fall. I hope you and Jade will come."

"I wouldn't want to impose." In truth, the idea of hanging out with a bunch of church people made him sweat. He'd played that scene before, for all the good it had done him in the end.

"Trust me, after you drag brush for the campfire, whittle a mountain of roasting sticks and set up tables, chairs and hay bales, you will have earned a special place at this function."

"I don't know, Lindsey. I'm not sure I would fit in."

Dropping her feet to the porch floor, Lindsey leaned forward, face earnest, hair swinging forward, as she reached out to touch his arm.

"Please, Jesse. Jade would have so much fun. And having a little fun now and then wouldn't hurt you either."

He was beginning to weaken. A wienie roast was not the same as going to church. And Jade would love roasting marshmallows over a campfire. More than that, it was high time he got moving on his mission.

Lindsey's words echoed his thoughts. "Winding Stair is full of good people. The party would be a great opportunity for you to get acquainted with some of them."

She was right about that. He needed to get friendly with the townsfolk. But not for the reasons she had in mind. He gulped the rest of his cola, taking the burn all the way to his stomach.

Somebody in this town had to know what had happened eighteen years ago. The more people trusted him, the sooner he could have his answers—and the sooner he and Jade could take possession of this farm.

Likely no one would remember him. Les Finch had not been a friendly man, and they'd kept to themselves up here in the mountains. As a boy, Jesse had been a quiet loner, preferring the woods to school activities. And his name was different from his mom and stepdad. His secret was, he believed, safe from the unsuspecting folk of Winding Stair.

He didn't like playing the bad guy, but right was right. This was his home…and he intended to claim it.

Chapter 4

"Think this will be enough?"

At Jesse's question, Lindsey dumped an armload of firewood into a huge oval depression in the ground. Dusting bark and leaves from the front of her jacket, she evaluated the stack of roasting sticks Jesse had piled next to a long folding table.

"How many do you have there? Fifty, maybe?"

He hitched one shoulder, distant and preoccupied as if whittling enough roasting sticks was the last thing on his mind. "Close."

"That should do it." She knelt beside the campfire pit and began to arrange the wood. "Some of the older boys like to make their own—especially when they have a girlfriend to impress."

"It's a man thing." Jesse tossed the last stick onto

the pile and snapped shut a pocketknife, which he then shimmied into his front jeans' pocket. "I think we're about set. What time will the guests arrive?"

"Sevenish. Some will meet at the church and bring the bus. Others will drift in at will throughout the evening." Leaning back on her heels, she gazed up at him. The look on his face said he wanted to be a thousand miles away by then. "It'll be fun, Jesse."

Jade, who resided less than five feet from her daddy at all times, sat on a bale of hay munching an apple with childish contentment. One tennis-shoed foot was curled beneath her while the other beat a steady rhythm against the tight rectangle of baled grass.

"I never went to a wienie roast before," she said.

She'd been ecstatic, hopping and dancing around her father like a puppy when he'd told her of the plans. Lindsey wished Jesse showed half that much enthusiasm.

"You'll like it. We'll play games and take a ride in the wagon and roast marshmallows." Playfully bumping the child's hip with her own, Lindsey sat down next to her. "You'll need your coat. The temperature gets pretty cool after the sun goes down."

Jesse propped a booted foot on the end of the bale next to Jade. He rubbed at his bottom lip, pensive. "We better head home and get cleaned up."

Jade frowned at one palm and then the other. Apple juice glistened on her fingers. "I'm clean."

Jesse shot Lindsey a wry glance. "Well, I'm not." Scooping his daughter up into strong arms, he rubbed her nose with his. "And we'll stop by the store for some marshmallows."

The gap-toothed smile appeared. "Okay!"

He tossed Jade over his shoulder the way Lindsey had seen him do a dozen times. After a thoughtful pause, he said, "I guess we'll see ya at seven then."

Watching the enigmatic man and his child cross the yard, Lindsey experienced an uncomfortable sense of loss and loneliness. Given the number of times she'd asked him or Jade to church functions, she'd been pleasantly surprised when Jesse had agreed to come to the party. He'd been more than clear on a number of occasions that spiritual issues were on his no-call list.

Still, she had a funny feeling about Jesse's decision to join tonight's festivities. He'd been almost grim all afternoon while they'd made the preparations, as if the party was a nasty medicine to take instead of a pleasure to be enjoyed.

Going to release a resentful Sushi from her office confinement, Lindsey heard the roar of Jesse's pickup truck fading into the distance and wondered if he would return at all.

By seven-thirty, friends of every age milled around the clearing along the back side of Lindsey's farm, but there was no sign of Jesse and Jade. Disappointment settled over Lindsey like morning fog on a pond as she watched the driveway for the familiar silver-and-blue truck. The party would have been good for father and daughter. That's why her disappointment was so keen, not because she missed their company, although she was too honest to deny that fact completely. Still, she had plenty of other friends around, and the party, as always, was off to a roaring start.

Beneath a full and perfect hunter's moon, the scent of hickory smoke and roasting hotdogs circled over a crackling campfire. The night air, cool and crisp, meant jackets and hooded sweatshirts, many of which lay scattered about on hay bales or on the short browning grass as their owners worked up a sweat in various games.

A rambunctious group of teenagers and young adults played a game of volleyball at the nets she and Jesse had strung up. Smaller children played tag by lantern light or crawled over the wagonload of hay parked at an angle on the north end of the clearing. Most of the adults chatted and laughed together around the food table and a huge cattle tank filled with iced-down soda pop and bottled water.

"Where's that hired hand of yours, Lindsey?" Pastor Cliff Wilson, standing with a meaty arm draped over the shoulder of his diminutive wife, was only a few years older than Lindsey. She still had difficulty believing that this gentle giant had once spent more time in the county jail for drinking and disturbing the peace than he did in church. Just looking at him reminded Lindsey and everyone else of the amazing redemptive power of Jesus' love. "I thought we'd get to meet him tonight."

"I did, too, Cliff," she said. "But it looks like he backed out on coming. Jade will be so disappointed." So was she. Jade needed the interaction, and though

Jesse held himself aloof, he needed to mingle with people who loved and served God.

"Jade?" Cliff's wife, Karen, spoke up. "What a pretty name. Is that his little girl?"

Karen and Cliff had yet to conceive and every child held special interest for the pastor's wife.

"Yes. She's adorable. A little shy at first, so if they do come, give her some time to warm up." Lindsey took a handful of potato chips from a bag on one of the long folding tables and nibbled the salt from one. "Aren't you two going to eat a hotdog?"

Karen laughed and hugged her husband's thick shoulder. "Cliff's already had three."

The pastor rubbed his belly. "Just getting started."

Downing a sizeable portion of cola, the minister slid two franks onto the point of a stick and poked it into the flames. "One for me, and one for my lady friend here."

Lindsey smiled, admiring the open affection between the pastor and his wife.

"Come on, Lindsey." Debbie Castor, the waitress at the Caboose Diner and one of Lindsey's closest friends, had joined the volleyball game. "We need someone who can spike the ball. Tom's team is waxing us."

Tom was Debbie's husband, and they loved competing against each other in good-natured rivalries.

"Okay. One game. I still haven't had my hotdog yet." To shake off her disappointment at Jesse's absence, Lindsey trotted to the makeshift court. She was in good shape from the physical aspect of her job and was generally a good athlete, but tonight her mind wasn't on the game. Up to now, Jesse had always kept his word, and she experienced a strange unease that something was amiss.

When Tom's team easily defeated Debbie's, she stood with hands on her knees catching her breath. "Sorry, guys. I wasn't much help tonight. I must be losing my touch."

"Maybe after you eat you'll regain your former glorious form, and we'll play another game."

With a laugh, she said, "No deal, Tom. You just want to beat us again."

"Right on, sister," Tom teased, bringing his arms forward to flex like a body builder. Balding and bespectacled, the fireman fooled everyone with his small stature and mischievous nature. Only those who knew him understood how strong and athletic he really was.

Still grinning, Lindsey fell in step beside Debbie and headed back to the campfire. "Have you eaten yet?"

"Half a bag of Oreos," Debbie admitted. "All I want lately is chocolate." Leaning closer she whispered, "I think I'm pregnant again."

Lindsey's squeal was silenced by Debbie's, "Shh. I don't want Karen to hear until I'm sure. I wouldn't want to hurt her."

"Ah, Deb. She's not like that. Karen will be happy for you."

"But to see someone like me have an unplanned pregnancy when she can't even have an intentional one must be difficult for her."

Lindsey knew the pain of wanting, but never having children, and yet her joy for her friends was genuine.

"Does Tom know yet?"

Debbie nodded, her orange pumpkin earrings dancing in the firelight. "He's still a little shell-shocked, I'm afraid. Finances are so tight already with the three we have, but he'll come around."

"You and Tom are such great parents. This baby will be the darling of the bunch, you wait and see. God always knows what He's doing."

"You're right, I know, but it's still a shock." Looking around, she spotted Tom across the way. "I think I'll go over and let the daddy-to-be pamper me awhile."

Lindsey watched her friend snag another cookie as she sashayed around to the opposite side of the campfire where her husband waited. A twinge of envy pinched at her as she gazed at the group gathered on her farm. They were mostly couples and families, people who shared their lives with someone else. Even the teenagers paired up or hung together in mixed groups going through the age-old ritual of finding a partner.

Lindsey loved these people, liked attending functions with them, but times such as these made her more aware than ever of how alone she was.

To shake off the unusual sense of melancholy, Lindsey found a roasting stick and went in search of a frankfurter to roast. She had too much to be thankful for to feel sorry for herself. She'd chosen to live in this remote place away from her family where there were few unattached men her age. If the Lord intended for her to have a mate, He'd send one her way.

An unexpected voice intruded on her thoughts.

"Could you spare two of those for a couple of fashionably late strangers?"

A pair of solemn silver eyes, aglow in the flickering firelight, met hers.

Her heart gave a strange and altogether inappropriate lurch of pleasure.

Jesse was here.

Jesse stared into Lindsey's delighted eyes and wished he was anywhere but here. From the minute he'd left the farm, he had struggled with a rising desire not to return. Except for his promise to Jade, he wouldn't have. He no more belonged with Lindsey and her holy church friends than he belonged in Buckingham Palace with the queen.

Jade gripped his leg, eyes wide as she watched children running in wild circles outside the perimeter of the firelight.

"You didn't think we were coming, did you?" he said to Lindsey.

She handed him a roasting stick, eyebrows lifted in an unspoken question. "I was beginning to wonder if something had happened."

The open-ended statement gave him the opportunity to explain, but he let the moment pass. His life was his business. Lindsey's gentle way of pulling him in, including him, was already giving him enough trouble.

"We brought marshmallows." Jade's announcement

filled the gap in conversation. She thrust the bag toward Lindsey.

"Cool. Let's eat a hotdog first and then we'll dig into these." Lindsey placed the bag on the table and took a wiener from a pack. "Do you want to roast your own?"

Jade pulled back, shaking her head. "Uh-uh. The fire might burn me."

"How about if I help you?" Lindsey slid the hotdog onto the stick and held it out.

Jesse could feel the tension in his child's small fingers. Her anxiety over every new experience worried him. He squatted down in front of her. "It's okay. Lindsey won't let you get hurt."

Indecision laced with worry played over his daughter's face. Lindsey, with her innate kindness, saw the dilemma. Jade wanted the fun of roasting the hotdog, but couldn't bring herself to trust anyone other than him. Jesse hid a sigh.

"This hotdog will taste better if Daddy cooks it. Isn't that right, sugar?" Lindsey said, handing him the loaded stick. "I'll grab another."

Squatting beside Lindsey with Jade balanced between his knees, Jesse thrust the franks into the flames. Jade rested a tentative hand just behind his.

More than anything Jesse longed to see Jade as confident and fearless as other six-year-olds. Deep inside, he was convinced that regaining his inheritance, giving her a stable home environment and surrounding her with familiar people and places would solve

Jade's problem. Tonight he hoped to take another step in that direction.

Letting his gaze drift around the campfire, Jesse studied the unfamiliar faces. Somebody here must have known Lindsey's grandparents and probably even his stepfather. Some self-righteous churchgoer standing out there in the half darkness sucking down a hot-dog might have even been involved in the shady deal that had left him a homeless orphan.

"Everyone here is anxious to meet you," Lindsey said, her voice as smoky and warm as the hickory fire.

Given the train of his thoughts, Jesse shifted uncomfortably. "Checking out the new guy to make sure you're safe with me?"

The remark came out harsher, more defensive than he'd planned.

Serene brown eyes probing, Lindsey said, "Don't take offense, Jesse. This is a small town. They only want to get acquainted, to be neighborly."

He blamed the fire and not his pinch of guilt for the sudden warmth in his face. She was too kind and he wished he'd followed his gut instinct and stayed at the cramped little trailer.

"Here you go, Butterbean." Taking the hotdog from the flames, he went to the table for buns and mustard. Lindsey and Jade followed.

One of the biggest men he'd ever seen handed him a paper plate. "You must be Jesse."

Lindsey made the introductions. "This is my pastor, Cliff Wilson."

Jesse's surprise must have shown because the clergyman bellowed a cheerful laugh. "If you were out killing preachers, you'd pass me right up, wouldn't you?"

Cliff looked more like a pro wrestler than a preacher. A blond lumberjack of a man in casual work clothes and tennis shoes with blue eyes as gentle and guileless as a child's and a face filled with laughter.

"Good to meet you, sir," Jesse said stiffly, not sure how to react to the unorthodox minister.

"Everyone calls me Pastor Cliff or just plain Cliff." The preacher offered a beefy hand which Jesse shook. "You from around this area?"

"Enid." Giving his stock answer, Jesse concentrated on squirting mustard onto Jade's hotdog. No way he'd tell any of them the truth—that he'd roamed this very land as a youth.

"Lindsey says you're heaven-sent, a real help to her."

"I'm glad for the work." He handed the hotdog to Jade, along with a napkin. "Lindsey's a fair boss."

By now at least a half dozen other men had sidled up to the table for introductions and food refills. Jesse felt like a bug under a magnifying glass, but if he allowed his prickly feelings to show, people might get suspicious. He needed their trust, though he didn't want to consider how he'd eventually use that trust against one of their own.

"A fair boss? Now that's a good 'un." A short, round older man in a camouflage jacket offered the joking comment. "That girl works herself into the ground just like her grandpa did. I figure she expects the same from her hired help."

Jesse stilled, attention riveted. This fellow knew Lindsey's grandparents and was old enough to have been around Winding Stair for some time. He just might know the details Jesse needed to begin searching the courthouse records.

"Now Clarence." Eyes twinkling a becoming gold in the flickering light, Lindsey pointed a potato chip at the speaker. "You stop that before you scare off the only steady worker I've ever had."

"Ah, he knows I'm only kidding." Clarence aimed a grin toward Jesse. "Don't you, son?" Before Jesse could respond, the man stuck out his hand. "Name's Clarence Stone. I live back up the mountain a ways. If you ever need anything, give me a holler."

A chuckle came from the man in a cowboy hat standing next to Clarence. His black mustache quivered on the corners. "That's right, Jesse. Give Clarence a holler. He'll come down and talk your ears off while you do all the work."

Clarence didn't seem the least bit offended. He grinned widely.

"This here wise guy is Mick Thompson," he said with affection. "Mick has a ranch east of town, though if it wasn't for that sweet little wife of his, he'd have gone under a long time ago."

Mick laughed, teeth white in his dark face. "I have to agree with you there, Clarence, even if Clare is your daughter. I wouldn't be much without her."

Jesse's mind registered the relationship along with

the fact that Mick owned a ranch. Now that was something Jesse understood.

"You raise horses on that ranch of yours?" he asked, making casual conversation while hoping to turn the conversation back to Lindsey's grandparents.

"Sure do. You know horses?" Mick sipped at his plastic cup.

"I've done a little rodeo. Bronc-riding mostly."

"No kidding?" Mick's eyebrows lifted in interest. "Ever break any colts?"

"Used to do a lot of that sort of work." Before Erin died. But he wouldn't share that with Mick.

"Would you like to do it again?"

"I wouldn't mind it." He missed working with rough stock, and breaking horses on the side would put some much-needed extra money in his pocket.

"Don't be trying to hire him away from Lindsey, Mick," the jovial Clarence put in. "She'll shoot you. And I'll be left to support your wife and kids."

"You'd shoot me yourself if you thought Clare and the kids would move back up in those woods with you and Loraine."

Both men chuckled, and despite himself, Jesse enjoyed their good-natured ribbing.

Lindsey, having drifted off in conversation with a red-haired woman, missed the teasing remark. Without her present, Jesse wanted to turn the conversation back to her grandfather, but wasn't sure how to go about it without causing suspicion.

"Tell you what, Jesse," Mick said, stroking his mustache with thumb and forefinger. "When you have some time, give me a call. I have a couple of young geldings that need breaking, and I can't do it anymore. Bad back."

Were all the people of Winding Stair this trusting that they'd offer a man a job without ever seeing him work?

"How do you know I can handle the job?"

Mick's mustache quirked. "Figure you'd say so if you didn't think you could."

"I can."

"See?" Mick clapped him on the back and clasped his hand in a brief squeeze. "My number's in the book. And I pay the going rate."

"Appreciate the offer, but I doubt I can get loose from here until after the holidays."

The familiar sense of dread crawled through his belly. He'd much rather be tossed in the dirt by a bucking horse than spend one minute in Lindsey's tree lot. He'd counted on the old adage that familiarity breeds indifference. So far, that hadn't proven true. If anything, he dreaded the coming weeks more than ever.

Mick sipped at his soda before saying, "After Christmas is fine with me. Those colts aren't going anywhere. Meantime, if you need help hauling these trees, let me know. I got a flatbed settin' over there in my barn rustin'."

"He sure does," Clarence teased. "And it would do him good to put in a full day's work for a change."

An unbidden warmth crept through Jesse. Offers of help from friends didn't come too often, but this offhand generosity of strangers was downright unsettling.

"Jade, Jade." Two little girls about Jade's age came running up and interrupted the conversation. One on each side, they grabbed her hands and pulled. "Come play tag."

She looked to Jesse for approval. "Can I, Daddy?"

"Don't you want to finish your hotdog?"

"I'm full." She handed him the last bite of the squeezed and flattened sandwich.

He downed the remains and wiped the mustard off her face. "Go on and play."

She grabbed his hand and tugged. "Come with me."

Jesse shook his head, standing his ground for once. "I haven't finished my own hotdog. I'll be here when you get back. Promise."

After a moment of uncertainty, the desire to play with her friends won out.

Jesse's heart gladdened to see his little girl race away with the other children for once instead of clinging to his leg like a barnacle.

Biting into his smoky hotdog, Jesse watched and listened, hoping for an opportunity to casually probe for information. His attention strayed to the gregarious preacher.

Pastor Cliff seemed to be everywhere, laughing, joking and making sure everyone had a great time. The teenagers flocked around him as though he was some football star, begging him to join their games, occasionally pelting him with a marshmallow to gain his attention. Punctuating the air with a few too many "praise the Lords" for Jesse's comfort, the preacher nonetheless came across like a regular guy. He'd even overheard Cliff promise to help repair someone's leaky roof next week. The big man sure wasn't like any minister Jesse had ever encountered.

"When are we taking that wagon ride, Lindsey?" Cliff bellowed, indicating a small boy perched on his shoulders. "Nathaniel says he's ready when you are."

"Do you kids want the tractor or the horse to pull us?" Lindsey called back.

"The horse. The horse," came a chorus of replies from all but the preacher.

Jesse knew the big, powerful horse stood nearby inside a fenced lot, his oversized head hanging over the rails, waiting his opportunity. The animal liked people and was gentle as a baby.

"How about you, Cliff? What's your preference?" a man called, his face wreathed in mischief.

The oversized preacher waved his upraised hands in mock terror. "Now, Tom, you know I don't mess with any creature that's bigger than me."

"Which wouldn't be too many, Cliff," came the teasing answer.

Everyone laughed, including Cliff, though the joke was on him. Grudgingly, Jesse admired that. The minister he'd known would have seen the joke as an offense to his lofty position.

"You're out-voted, preacher," Lindsey called, starting toward the gate. "I'll get Puddin'."

Shoving his hands into the pockets of his jean jacket, Jesse fell into step beside her. Though mingling with the church crowd provided opportunities to gather information, he needed some distance. He hadn't expected their friendliness, the ease with which they accepted him, and most of all, he'd not expected them to be such everyday, normal people. Lindsey's church family, as she called them, was fast destroying his long-held view of Christians as either stiff and distant or pushy and judgmental.

"Need any help?" he asked.

She withdrew a small flashlight from inside her jacket, aimed the beam toward the gate, and whistled softly. "I put his harness on earlier. All I need to do is hook the traces to the wagon."

Jesse stepped into the light and raised the latch. In seconds the big horse lumbered up to nuzzle at his owner while she snapped a lead rope onto his halter. Together they led him toward the waiting wagon.

"He's a nice animal." Jesse ran a hand over the smooth, warm horseflesh, enjoying the feel again after too much time away from the rodeo. "What breed is he?"

"Percheron mostly." She smiled at the horse with affection. "Although I'm not sure he's a full-blood since I have no papers on him, but he has the sweet temperament and muscular body the breed is known for. And he loves to work."

"Percheron." Jesse rolled the word over in his head. He knew enough about horses to know the name, but that was about it. "Different from the quarter horses I'm used to."

"Certainly different from the wild broncs. Puddin' doesn't have a buck anywhere in him." One on each side of the massive horse, they headed back toward the heat and light of the bonfire. "Every kid within a ten-mile radius has ridden him, walked under him, crawled over him, and he doesn't mind at all." She turned toward him, her face shadowed and pale in the bright moonlight. "What about you? Do you still have horses?"

He shook his head. "No. After Erin died, I—" He stopped, not wanting to revisit the horrible devastation when he'd sold everything and hit the road, trying to run from the pain and guilt. He'd told Lindsey more about his past than he'd ever intended to, but talking about Erin was taboo. "I'd better find Jade."

He stalked off toward the circle of squealing children, aware that he'd been abrupt with Lindsey and trying not to let that bother him. He'd intentionally sought her company, and now he was walking away.

Ruefully, he shook his head. What a guy.

In the distance he spotted Jade, her long hair flying out behind her as she ran, laughing. With a hitch beneath his rib cage, he watched his daughter, grateful for the rare display of playful abandon. Letting the shadows absorb him, he stood along the perimeter of children, hoping this place would ultimately heal them both.

"Hey, Jesse." A hand bigger than Puddin's hoof landed on his shoulder. The preacher. "Great party, huh?"

"Yeah." Though he didn't belong here, he had to admit the party was a success. Just seeing Jade carefree was worth a few hours discomfort on his part.

"Lindsey's a great gal."

Jesse followed the minister's gaze to where Lindsey, surrounded by too many youthful helpers, attached the patient horse to the wagon. Silently, he agreed with Cliff's assertion. Lindsey *was* a good woman. Her decency was giving his conscience fits. "You known her long?"

"A few years. Ever since coming here to minister." Cliff nodded at the rowdy crowd around the fire. "Most of these folks have known her and each other much longer, but God really blessed me when he sent me to Winding Stair. I feel as if Lindsey and all the others out there are my family now."

Clarence approached, this time accompanied by a small, gray-haired woman with rosy cheeks who carried a plate of homemade cookies. "That's the way it's supposed to be, ain't it, preacher?"

Cliff reached for the cookies. "Yep."

"How about you, Jesse?" Clarence motioned toward the plate.

Out of courtesy Jesse accepted the dessert, taking a bite. He liked the mildly sweet flavor of the old-fashioned cookie. "These are good."

"Course they are," Clarence said. "Loraine makes the best oatmeal cookies in the county. And if you don't believe me, just ask her."

"Oh, Clarence, you old goof." The smiling little woman flapped a hand at him. "Jesse, don't pay any mind to my husband. This isn't my recipe and he knows it. Lindsey's grandma gave it to me. Now that woman could cook."

Blood quickening, Jesse saw the opportunity and took it. "You knew Lindsey's grandparents?"

"Sure did. Better folks never walked the earth, as far as I'm concerned." She paused long enough to dole out more cookies to passers-by. Jesse kept his mouth shut, waiting for her to go on, blood humming with the hope that he was about to learn something.

"Betty Jean—that was her grandma—could do about anything domestic. A country version of Martha Stewart, I guess you'd say." She chuckled softly at her own joke. "And she wasn't stingy about it either. Would share a jar of pickles or a recipe without batting an eye. A fine neighbor, she was. A real fine neighbor."

She looked a little sad and Jesse shifted uncomfortably. He needed to keep Loraine and Clarence talking but he didn't want to think of the Mitchells as decent folks. There was nothing decent about stealing from an orphan.

Keeping his tone casual, Jesse said, "Lindsey's a good cook too."

"Betty Jean would have made sure of that." Loraine thrust the nearly empty plate toward him. "Another cookie?"

"Might as well take one, Jesse," Clarence put in with a chortle. "She ain't happy unless she's feeding someone."

Jesse hid a smile. It was hard not to like Loraine and Clarence Stone. "Thanks."

He accepted the cookie, mind searching for a way to gain more information. He'd suffered through an hour of stilted conversation to get this far. He wasn't about to let this chance slip away.

"What about Lindsey's grandpa? I guess he's the one who taught her to use that rifle...."

"Yep," Clarence said. "That was Charlie, all right. Me and him used to hunt and fish together, and he liked to brag about Lindsey's shooting. Called her his little Annie Oakley."

Jesse's stomach leaped.

Charlie.

His patience had paid off. At last, he had someone to blame along with his stepfather. Lindsey's grandfather, the man who'd stolen this eighty-acre farm from a teenage boy, was named Charlie Mitchell.

In the shadowy distance, snatches of conversation and laughter floated on the night air. One particular laugh—a throaty, warm sound that sent shivers down his spine—stood out from the rest.

Lindsey.

He wanted to put his hands over his ears, to block out the sound. He'd finally discovered some information, and nobody, no matter how sweet and kind, was going to stop him from using it.

Chapter 5

Lindsey draped her jacket over the back of a kitchen chair and went to the sink. She'd had a long afternoon without Jesse there to help, but she couldn't complain. In the weeks he'd worked on the farm, this was the first time he'd asked for time off. So she had spent the afternoon marking the trees they'd soon cut and bale for delivery.

Ever since the night of the cookout, she'd noticed a shift in him. He worked harder than ever on the farm, putting in long hours and cutting himself no slack. But he seemed to be bothered by something—not that there was anything new about that—but this was a subtle mulling as though he had something heavy on his mind.

With a sigh, Lindsey acknowledged how much

she'd come to depend upon the mysterious Jesse. She needed him, and regardless of his inner demons, she liked him. He was a good man with a heavy burden. If only she could find a way to help him past that burden—whatever it was.

Two or three times today she'd turned to ask Jesse's advice about something before remembering he was gone. Funny how she'd never needed anyone before other than Sushi and the Lord, but Jesse had changed all that. And she wasn't sure becoming dependent on her hired hand was such a good idea.

Turning the water tap, she filled a glass and drank deeply, thirsty even though the early November weather was cloudy and cool with the promise of rain hanging like a gray veil over the land. In the back of her mind, she faintly registered a rumbling in the distance but paid little mind. After washing and drying her hands, she headed to the refrigerator.

She had one hand on last night's chicken and rice when the screaming began.

An adrenaline rush more powerful than an electric shock propelled her into action. Faster than she thought possible, Lindsey bounded into the bedroom, unlocked the gun case, removed her rifle and rushed out into the yard, loading the weapon as she moved. An occasional mountain lion roamed these hills.

Peering in the direction of the screams, Lindsey stopped...and lowered the gun.

Jade stood halfway down the gravel driveway, frozen in fear, screaming her head off. Directly in front of her, Sushi lay on her back, feet in the air, groveling for all she was worth.

With a feeling somewhere between relief and exasperation, Lindsey stashed the rifle on the porch and loped down the driveway.

What was Jade doing here? Where was Jesse? And when would the child realize that Sushi was her friend?

"Sushi, come," she called. The German shepherd leaped to her feet, shook off the dust and leaves and trotted to Lindsey's side. Pointing to a spot several yards away from the terrified child, she commanded, "Stay."

The dog obeyed, plopping her bottom onto the dirt, tongue lolling, while she watched Jade with worried eyes.

Jade's screaming subsided, but the harsh sobs continued as Lindsey went down on her knees and took the little girl into her arms. She had a dozen questions, but now was not the time to ask them. Soon enough she could discover why Jesse had not picked up Jade at school as he'd planned.

"Jade, listen to me." Pushing the tangled hair, damp with tears, back from Jade's face she said gently, "Stop crying and listen. We need to talk like big girls."

Jade gave several shuddering sobs, scrubbing at her eyes with her fingertips. "The dog was going to get me."

"That's what we have to talk about. Sushi will not hurt you. Look at her. She's sitting down there begging for you to like her, but she won't even come near you unless I tell her to."

"She ran at me. I saw her teeth."

"She was smiling at you. You're part of her family now and she was excited to see you. That's how she behaves when I come home from someplace, too."

"It is?" Wary and unconvinced, Jade glanced from Lindsey to Sushi and back again.

"Sure. Every time you come home, she whines to be let out so she can play with you. It makes her very sad that you don't like her."

Jade's expression said she was thinking that over, but still she clung tightly to Lindsey.

"Where's my daddy?"

"I'm not sure, sweetie. He was supposed to pick you up at school."

The little girl's small shoulders slumped. "He's probably dead." And she burst out crying again.

"No, Jade, no." Please God, let me be right. Don't let anything else happen to this child. The loss of her mother had completely destroyed her sense of safety. "Your daddy is running late and didn't get back in time. He'll be here soon, and while we wait, you and I can have a dress-up tea party."

Lindsey could see she scored some points with the idea so she pressed the advantage. "Sushi wants to come, too. She even has some dress-up clothes."

Jade found that amusing. A hesitant smile teetered around her mouth. "Really?"

"Absolutely. All my Sunday-school kids invite

Sushi to their tea parties because she's such a nice dog, so she has a hat, a boa and a fancy vest to wear."

"She might bite me."

"No," Lindsey said firmly. "She will not." Sliding Jade to the ground, she took the child's hand. "Come on. I'll show you."

Sushi waited right where she'd been told to stay, eagerly thumping her tail at the first sign of movement in her direction.

Jade pulled back. "Uh-uh."

Lindsey sighed, but relented and swept the little girl into her arms. "Okay, then. I have another idea."

She carried Jade to the house. A bewildered Sushi remained in the driveway as commanded.

"Stand here inside the house where you can see Sushi and me through the glass door." Lindsey took a piece of leftover chicken from the fridge. She'd planned to have the meat for supper, but helping Jade begin the process of overcoming this phobia was far more important. "Watch what a good girl Sushi is and how she loves to play, but she always minds me when I tell her to do something. Okay?"

Nodding and wide-eyed, Jade stood inside the door, her face pressed to the glass while Lindsey stepped onto the porch and called the dog. When Sushi arrived, skidding to a stop at her owner's command, Lindsey spent several minutes putting the animal through all her obedience commands. Extremely well disciplined, Sushi even resisted the piece of baked chicken, though Lindsey knew the meat was her favorite treat.

Then she played with Sushi, petting her, tossing sticks that the dog retrieved, scratching her belly.

Finally, Lindsey lay down on the porch to show her total trust of the dog. Sushi responded by plopping her big head onto Lindsey's chest with a delighted sigh that made Jade laugh.

Sitting up, Lindsey rotated toward Jade. "See what a good girl she is?"

"Uh-huh."

"Would you like to pet her?"

"Uh-uh." But Lindsey could see that, for once, she wanted to.

Confident they'd made progress, Lindsey relented. "Maybe next time?"

Leaving Sushi on the porch, Lindsey dusted her clothes and came inside. She peeked at the yellow tea-pot clock hanging over the cook stove. Jade had been here at least thirty minutes and still no sign of Jesse. Refusing to worry, she internalized a little prayer, and turned her attention to occupying Jade. The little girl didn't need to fret about her daddy even if Lindsey was.

"I'm starved."

"Me, too."

Using her best imitation of an English lady, Lindsey said, "Shall we prepare tea and dine?"

Jade giggled. "Can we dress up too? And you can be the princess and I'll be the queen?"

"Lovely idea, my queen. Right this way, please." Nose in the air as befit royalty, she led the way to the huge plastic storage bin in her bedroom closet where she kept a variety of thrift-shop and novelty-store play clothes. Jade, getting into the spirit of the game, followed suit. She fell upon the container, carefully lifting out one garment after another, exclaiming over each one as if the clothes came from Rodeo Drive.

In no time, she'd chosen outfits for both of them and they traipsed on plastic high heels, boas trailing, into the kitchen to prepare the Oklahoma version of high tea.

"Let's make fancy sandwiches first. Later, we'll do cookies."

"Do you have Christmas cookie cutters?" Jade shoved at her sun hat, repositioning the monstrosity on her head. Bedecked with more flowers than Monet had ever painted, the hat tied with a wide scarf under the child's chin. Lindsey thought she looked adorable.

"A bunch of them. We can use them on the sandwiches if you want to."

"Cool. Do you gots sprinkles too?"

"Oh, yeah. I have tons of sprinkles. All colors. But let's not put those on the sandwiches."

Jade giggled. "For the cookies, silly. I want to make Daddy a big red cookie." Her face fell. "I wish my daddy would come. I'll bet he's getting hungry."

"He'll be here soon," Lindsey said with more confidence than she felt as she spread the sandwich fixings on the table. "Tell you what. Let's say a little prayer asking Jesus to take care of him and bring him safely home."

She hardly noticed that she'd referred to her own

house as home for Jesse and Jade. Semantics didn't matter right now.

"Okay." To Lindsey's surprise, Jade closed her eyes and folded her little hands beneath her chin. Even though Jesse shied away at the mention of God, someone had taught this child to pray.

Closing her own eyes, Lindsey said a short but heartfelt prayer.

"Amen."

Jade's shoulders relaxed. "Jesus will take care of Daddy, won't He?"

"Yes, He will. And He'll take care of you too." She smeared mayo on a slice of bread, handing it to Jade to layer on the meat and cheese. "Did you know you have a guardian angel who is always with you?"

Shaking her head, Jade licked the mayo off one finger.

"Well, you do. Everybody does. But God has very special guardian angels that take care of children. Jesus loves you so much He tells your very own angel to keep watch over you day and night."

"Even when I'm asleep?"

"Yes." She chose an angel from the pile of cookie cutters. "That's why you don't need to be afraid of anything—ever. Your angel is always here, looking after you."

Jade took the metal angel, studied it, and then pressed the shape into a sandwich. "Does Daddy have a guarding angel?"

Lindsey smiled at the mispronunciation. "He sure does."

"Can I save this angel sandwich for my daddy?"

"Of course you can. We'll make enough of everything so he can eat, too, when he gets here."

That seemed to satisfy Jade, and Lindsey wished she were as easily comforted. Where was Jesse? Leaving Jade alone was so uncharacteristic of him. Had something happened? In the weeks of their acquaintance she'd grown fond of him, fonder than was comfortable, and the thought of something happening to him was unspeakable.

Agitated and filled with self-recriminations, Jesse stormed across Lindsey's yard, hoping with everything in him that Jade was here. He couldn't believe he'd gotten so busy, so deeply enmeshed in the stacks of court records that the time had slipped away and he'd forgotten to pick Jade up from school until she was long gone. What kind of lousy father was he anyway?

Sushi bounded out to meet him, a good sign. His spirits lifted somewhat, though he'd feel better if the German shepherd bit him. He deserved to be punished. For all his searching, he hadn't found a bit of useful information; not one single reference to any transaction between Charles Mitchell and Les Finch.

The day as gray as his mood, Jesse mounted the porch—and heard singing. A husky adult voice that sent an unexpected shiver of pleasure dancing along his nerve endings blended sweetly with a higher, childish melody.

Relief flooded him. Jade was here. Pausing at the

open door, he could see the two through the glass. They were in the kitchen at the table, their backs turned, singing "Mary Had a Little Lamb" while they worked at something.

He squinted, leaning closer. What kind of get-ups were they wearing?

With an inner smile, he waited until they finished their song before pecking lightly on the door. Two heads swiveled in his direction.

"Daddy!" Jade dropped something onto the table and clambered off her chair. She ran toward him, nearly tripping over a long, white dress that looked suspiciously like a well-used wedding gown. Taking a moment to hike the yards of wrinkled satin and lace into one hand, she stumbled onward, lime-green high heels clunking against the wooden floor.

Mood elevating with every step his baby took, Jesse opened the door and stepped inside the living room.

"My, don't you look beautiful," he said.

But Jade was having none of his compliments. She got right to the point. "The teacher made me ride the bus 'cause you didn't come."

"I'm sorry I was late, Butterbean. Your teacher did the right thing sending you to Lindsey where you would be safe and happy."

"Where were you? I got scared. I thought you were dead like Mommy."

A searing pain cut off Jesse's windpipe. Of course, she'd think that. That's why he always made a point of being exactly where she expected—to allay her well-founded fears.

Lindsey appeared in the living room. "Your daddy is here now, Jade, and he's just fine."

"Jesus took care of him the way you said."

A serene smile lit Lindsey's eyes. "Yes, He did."

Jesse didn't know what was going on with their talk of Jesus and decided not to ask. He looked to Lindsey, grateful for her care of Jade, but not wanting to tell her where he'd been. Wearing a hat with peacock feathers sticking out the top, and a rather bedraggled fake fur stole over someone's old red prom dress, she looked ridiculously cute. If he hadn't felt so guilty, he would have laughed.

"I'm sorry for putting you out this way."

"Jade is no problem. But we were a little concerned about you."

Exactly what he didn't need—Lindsey's concern, although he knew it was there, felt it day in and day out as she carefully avoided subjects she'd discovered were painful or taboo. Always, that gentle aura of peace and inner joy reached out to him.

"I had some personal business to handle which took much longer than I'd planned. Somehow the time got away from me, and by the time I rushed over to the school..." He lifted his hands and let them fall.

"Well, you're here now." Lindsey smiled that sweet, tranquil smile that changed her face to a thing of beauty. Jesse tried, but failed, to resist the pleasure that one motion gave him.

And then she made things worse by asking, "Are you hungry?"

An unbidden rush of warmth filled him from the

inside out. Coming to this house and this woman was starting to feel far too natural and way too good.

"Come on, Daddy. Come see. We're making a tea party, and I'm the queen." Skirts sweeping the floor, Jade led the way into the kitchen and lifted an odd-shaped bit of bread from the table, thrusting it at him. "I made this guarding angel for you."

"Tea, huh? And an angel sandwich." He took the offering, examining the small figure with all due seriousness. "Sounds delicious. Anything I can do to help?"

Lindsey nodded toward a plate of fresh fruit. "You could slice up the apples if you'd like."

"Lindsey." Jade's plaintiff protest drew both adults' attention. She eyed her father skeptically. "He can't come to the tea party without dress-up clothes."

An ornery gleam flashed in Lindsey's brown eyes. "She's right, Dad. Tea requires formal attire."

Before he could object on purely masculine grounds, Jade rushed off, returning with a purple boa, a tarnished tiara, and a yellow-and-black satin cape. "Here, Daddy, you can be king."

Lindsey laughed at the pained expression on Jesse's face and in return, received his fiercest glare of wry humor.

"I'll get you for this," he muttered under his breath as Jade dressed him, carefully twining the boa around his neck before placing the crown on his head with a triumphant—if somewhat crooked—flourish.

Lindsey wrinkled her nose at him and adjusted her stole with a haughty toss of her head. "Mess with me, mister, and I'll find you a pair of purple plastic high heels to go with that dashing feather boa."

Jesse surprised himself by tickling her nose with the aforementioned boa. "I'm the king, remember. Off with your head."

She laughed up at him, and he realized how much smaller she was than he, and how feminine she looked in a dress, even a silly outfit like this one. Out of her usual uniform of jeans and flannel, she unsettled him. Lindsey was a pretty woman as well as a nice one.

One more reason he needed to find the answer to his questions and get out of here. He couldn't get attached to a woman he'd eventually have to hurt.

For all his searching today, he'd found no record of this farm or the transaction between his stepfather, Les Finch, and Charles Mitchell. If he didn't find something next time, he'd be forced to ask the clerk for information, a risk he hadn't wanted to take. Asking questions stirred up suspicion. Someone was bound to want to know what he was up to. Sooner or later, word would filter back to Lindsey and he'd be out of a job and out of luck. Discretion made for a slow, but safer, search.

Lindsey whacked his shoulder with her boa. "Are you going to slice that fruit or stand there and stare at my glorious hat?"

Her humor delighted him. "The hat does catch a man's eye."

Lindsey and Jade both giggled at his silliness. Even he wondered where the lightheartedness came from. He'd had a rotten afternoon, but the warmth of this house and the company of these two females lifted his spirits.

Taking up the stainless-steel knife, he sliced an apple into quarters. "What kind of sandwiches are we making?"

"Baloney and cheese."

"Ah, a gourmet's delight." Placing the apple slices on a plate in as fancy a design as he could manage, he plucked a few grapes and arranged them in the center.

Lindsey clapped a slice of wheat bread on top of the meat and cheese. "And afterwards, we'll make sugar cookies."

"With sprinkles," Jade chimed in, her face a study in concentration as she pushed the metal cutters into the sandwiches.

"Jesse, why don't you arrange the fancy sandwiches on this plate while Jade finishes cutting them. Then we'll be ready to eat."

They were only sandwiches. Bread, baloney, cheese and mayonnaise. He could do this. Looking at his beaming child instead of the Christmas shapes, Jesse made a circle of sandwiches on the platter.

"What about the tea?" Jade asked.

"Oh. The tea!" Lindsey clattered across the floor in her high heels, opened a cabinet and removed a quart fruit jar. "I hope the two of you like spiced tea."

"Hot tea?" Jesse asked doubtfully.

She dumped a healthy amount of the mixture into a blue ceramic teapot. With a twinkle in her eye, she admitted, "Spiced tea tastes a lot like apple cider. Grandma taught me to make it. It's a conglomeration of tea, orange drink mix, lemonade and a bunch of yummy spices."

"Sounds better than hot tea," he admitted, pointing an apple slice at her before popping it into his mouth. "Maybe I can stand it."

Lindsey sailed across the floor and tapped his hand with the spoon. "Even the king has to wait until we all sit down together."

"Meanie." He snatched a grape. At her look of playful outrage, he laughed and snitched another.

She stopped dead, spoon in one hand, silly hat tilted to one side in rapt attention. "Jesse," she said, her smoky voice breathy and soft.

"What? Am I drooling grape juice?"

"You laughed."

He opened his mouth once, closed it and tried again. Sure he laughed. People laughed when they were happy. The realization astonished him. He'd laughed because he was happy. When was the last time he'd felt anything even close to happiness?

"I won't do it again."

"Oh, yes you will." All business and smiles, she shouldered him out of the way. "Go get that little card table in the laundry room and set it up. Jade will put on the table cloth and centerpiece while I finish our tea fixin's."

"Yes, ma'am." He saluted, slung his cape over his face in a super-hero imitation and did as he was told.

By the time the table was ready and they'd sat down to dine on the odd little meal, Jesse had gotten into the swing of the tea party. Wearing a get-up that would make his rodeo buddies howl, knees up to his chin, he reached for one of Jade's raggedy cookie-cutter sandwiches.

"Let's bless the food," Lindsey said, folding her hands in front of her.

A worried expression replaced the glow on Jade's face, and nearly broke Jesse's heart. Seated across from him at the small square table, she looked from Lindsey to him, waiting. Jesse did the only thing he could. He bowed his head, closed his eyes, and listened to Lindsey's simple prayer. When he looked back into his daughter's face, he knew he'd done the right thing. Playing the hypocrite for fifteen seconds hadn't killed him.

Stunned to realize he not only hadn't been bothered by the prayer or the other Christian references, Jesse chewed thoughtfully on the most delicious baloney and cheese sandwich he'd ever tasted and watched Lindsey do the same. He wondered at how time spent with her had changed him, easing the prickly sensation that usually came at the mention of God. Most of all he wondered at how easily Lindsey Mitchell, the lone pioneer woman, had become a part of his and Jade's lives. Considering how dangerous that was for him, he should toss down his Santa sandwich and run. But he knew he wouldn't. Lindsey's gentle female influence was so good for Jade. He tried to be a decent dad, but there were things a little girl needed that a man never even thought of.

"Tea, your highness?" Lindsey said to Jade, holding the pretty teapot over a dainty cup.

"Yes, your princess-ness. Tea, please." Pinky finger pointed up—he didn't know where she'd learned that—Jade lifted the poured tea and sipped carefully. "Delicious. Try it, Daddy."

"That's 'your daddy-ness' to you, queenie." Taking a sip of the surprisingly tasty tea, Jesse relished the sound of his child's giggle.

Yes, Lindsey was good for her. And as disturbing as the thought was, she was good for him, too.

Taking a sandwich from the serving dish, Jade said, "I think Sushi wants this one." She handed the food to Lindsey. "Will you give it to her so she won't be sad?"

Jesse couldn't believe his ears. Jade was worried about upsetting the dog? Capturing Lindsey's glance, he asked a silent question with his eyes.

Brown eyes happy, Lindsey only shrugged and said, "We're gaining ground." Getting up from her chair, she started toward the door. "Come with me, Jade. You can watch from inside."

When Jade followed, Jesse couldn't be left behind. He had to see this with his own eyes—if he could keep his tiara from falling down over them. Sure enough, Jade stood inside the glass door, a tentative smile on her face, while Lindsey stepped out on the porch and fed the dog.

If Jade overcame her fear of dogs, he'd almost believe in miracles.

Lindsey must have noticed his bewildered expression because she laughed.

"Doubting Thomas," she said to him, then leaned

toward Jade. "Did you see the way Sushi wagged her tail? That means thank you."

Holding on to her flowered hat, Jade pressed against the glass and whispered to the dog. "You're welcome."

When Sushi licked the door, Jade jumped back, almost stumbling over her skirts, but at least she didn't scream.

"Sushi gave you a kiss, Butterbean," Jesse offered after he'd swallowed the thickness in his throat.

"Uh-huh. I saw her, but I didn't want a doggy kiss. I'm the queen." Resuming her air of royalty, she lifted the tail of her dress and clomped to the kitchen. "Can we make cookies now? It's almost Christmas."

Lindsey, satin skirts rustling, peacock feather flopping, followed behind Jade like a cartoonist's version of a royal lady-in-waiting. "You're right. Christmas will be here before we know it. Guess what your daddy and I are doing tomorrow?"

Jesse had a sneaky feeling he didn't want to know.

The gap in Jade's mouth flashed. "What?"

"We're going to put up the decorations and get the Christmas-tree lot ready for visitors."

"Yay! Can I help? Can I decorate a tree? Can I put up the angel?" Jade wrapped her arms around Lindsey's red-satin-covered knees and hopped up and down. "Please, please, please."

Jesse's stomach sank into his boots. The day he'd dreaded had come. The Christmas season was upon him.

Chapter 6

"It Came Upon a Midnight Clear" blared from a loudspeaker positioned over the gate that opened into the Christmas-tree lot. The smell of pine mingled with the musty scent of Christmas decorations brought out of storage this morning. Though the temperature was in the high thirties, Jesse stripped away his jean jacket and hung the worn garment on the fence next to Lindsey's red plaid one.

He didn't have to look around to find the jacket's owner. Every cell in his body knew she was near—a sensation he found singularly disconcerting, to be sure. Last night, in the midst of a costumed tea party, some subtle shift in their boss/employee relationship had occurred. And Jesse didn't know if the change was a good thing or a very dangerous one.

From his spot stringing lights on staked poles, he turned to find her just inside the entrance, rubbing dust from a large wooden nativity scene. She'd shared her plans with him for the lot, and though the overwhelming dose of Christmas wasn't his idea of a good time, Lindsey's customers would come for this very atmosphere of holiday cheer.

Shoppers would park outside the gate then ride in the horse-drawn wagon down a lane aglow with Christmas lights and dotted with various lighted holiday ornaments: the nativity, a sleigh with reindeer, angels, snowmen. Jesse couldn't imagine anything she'd forgotten.

Chest tight, whether from watching Lindsey or thinking too much, he turned his concentration to the electrical part of his job. Electricity he knew. Lights he knew. The rest he'd ignore. And as soon as the opportunity arose, he'd kill that music.

"Jesse, could you put more speakers along the drive and down into the lot? I'm not sure we can hear the music all the way."

His shoulders slumped. So much for killing the tunes. After twisting two wires together, he rose from his haunches and asked, "Wouldn't my time be better spent cutting and baling those trees we marked this morning?"

She paused, pushed back her hair with one hand and studied him. When those eyes of hers lasered into him he couldn't do anything but wait until she finished speaking. She had pretty eyes, golden-brown and warm and slightly tilted at the edges like almonds.

"Why do you dislike Christmas?"

He blinked, squeezing hard on the pliers in his fist. "Never said I didn't like Christmas."

"Okay, then," She gave a saucy toss of her head. "Why do you dislike Christmas *decorations?*"

If the subject weren't so problematic, he'd have smiled. Lindsey's way of injecting humor into everything could lift anybody's mood.

Sushi chose that moment to insinuate her furry self against his legs, almost knocking him into the row of linked-together stakes.

Squatting, he took refuge in the dog, scuffing her ears with both hands. "Did I remember to thank you last night?"

"You just changed the subject."

He gave a little shrug. "So I did."

"Okay, I'll let you off the hook—for now." She lifted the hair off her neck, a habit of hers that Jesse liked. The movement was so utterly female. Erin had done that. Jade did it sometimes too.

"What are you thanking me for? Or was that just a ruse you use to avoid answering my question?"

He shook his head. "No ruse. I owe you big-time."

"For what?"

She really didn't know?

"About a dozen things. Looking after Jade until I got here. For supper."

"Such as it was." She laughed, letting her hair tumble down. Even without the sunlight, her hair looked shiny and clean.

"I've eaten worse than baloney sandwiches and sugar cookies."

"Don't forget the fruit." She tilted a wise man backwards and washed his ancient face. "Last night was fun, Jesse."

"Yeah." No point in denying the truth. Rising, he gave Sushi one final stroke. "Most of all, I appreciate your patience with Jade about the dog. I know leaving her outside is a pain."

Lindsey captured him with her gaze. "I don't want thanks for that, Jesse. I just want to see Jade confident and unafraid."

Taking up the next strand of lights waiting to be hung, he sighed. "Me, too."

"She'll get there." The wise man satisfactorily cleaned, she left him and the rest of the nativity. Coming up beside Jesse, she took one end of the lights, holding them in place while he secured them to the poles. "She's already less fearful than when she first came."

"I noticed. She didn't even fuss when I put her to bed last night. She said her guarding angel would watch her sleep." He glanced toward her, noticed the curve of her cheek and the tilt of her lips, then quickly looked away. "She talked a lot about that."

"I hope you didn't mind me telling her."

He hitched a shoulder, not wanting to go there. "It's okay. Whatever works."

Lindsey laid a hand on his arm. "The Bible works because it's true, Jesse," she said, her smoky voice soft. "Aren't you comforted knowing your own special angel watches over you?"

The warmth of her fingers spread through his shirt sleeve. He tried to concentrate on twisting plastic fasteners.

"Can't say I've given it much thought."

"Maybe you should." She dropped her hand and went back to straightening the tangle of lights, but her touch stayed with him like a promise made.

Could Lindsey be right? Was there more to this Christian thing than he'd ever realized? Being around her and her church friends, witnessing her steadfast faith and the way she handled the bumps in her life with a certain assurance had him thinking about God with a fresh perspective. As a boy he'd believed, had even accepted Jesus as his savior at church camp when he was twelve. And then life had turned him upside down, and the God of the universe had seemed so far away.

But why would a caring God, a God who assigned each person an angel, take a man's wife and leave a little girl motherless? Why would He allow a vicious drunk to steal a boy's home and toss him out on the streets to fend for himself? Where was God in that?

He didn't know. But more and more lately, he wanted to reconcile Lindsey's God with the one in his head.

"Silent Night" drifted into his awareness. Lindsey moved away, back to the nativity. Other than the floodlights she'd asked him to rig up, the set looked ready to him. As she adjusted the sheep and fluffed the hay inside the manger, joy practically oozed from her.

Sure she was happy. Why shouldn't she be? Other than losing her elderly grandparents, Lindsey had probably never had a moment's heartache in her life. Loving God and exuding tranquility was easy for her.

Frustrated at his line of depressive thinking, he yanked hard on a tangled cord, and turned his mind to more important matters—his search.

They had trees to haul this week which would give him the time and opportunity to ask questions in town. Yesterday at the courthouse he'd slipped up once, expressing to the clerk his interest in the transaction that gave Lindsey's grandfather ownership of the Christmas Tree Farm. When the woman had looked at him curiously, he'd covered his tracks with vague remarks about Lindsey's plans for expansion. If only he could talk freely with someone like Clarence or Loraine Stone, the couple who claimed to have known Charlie Mitchell so well. Sooner or later, by biding his time and listening, he'd have his opportunity.

After dusting and organizing the main pieces of the nativity, Lindsey went back to the storage shed for the final figure—the eight-foot-tall animated camel who blinked long-lashed eyes and mooed. She tugged and pulled, careful not to damage the heavy object in the journey across the rough field. Stopping to readjust, she saw Jesse leap the fence and trot in her direction.

"Why didn't you say something?"

"I can get it."

With a look of exasperation, he hoisted the camel into his strong arms. "You shouldn't have to. That's why you hired me."

Oddly touched and feeling more like a helpless female than she'd ever felt in her life, Lindsey traipsed along beside him. How could she not admire this man? Every time she turned around, he was lifting work from her shoulders, both literally and figuratively. She'd never seen anyone work so hard for so little pay. And for all his silences and secrets, Jesse had a way of making her feel special.

Lindsey wasn't sure if that was such a good idea, given the spiritual differences between them, but she liked Jesse Slater. And she loved his little girl.

As if he'd heard her thoughts of Jade, Jesse spoke. His voice came from the opposite side of the camel's hump.

"Jade will be excited when she sees all this."

"You don't think she'll be disappointed that we did so much without her?" She'd worried about that all day. After the way Jade had begged to take part, Lindsey didn't want her hurt. But setting up the farm for Christmas took time.

"I explained to her last night that we'd have to do most of the work today. She was okay with it as long as she gets to do something."

A jingle bell came loose from the saddle and Lindsey ducked beneath the camel's neck to retrieve it.

"I promised to save the 'best stuff' until she gets here. She and I are going to put up the wreaths and decorate that tree up front." She pointed toward the entrance, the bell in hand jingling merrily. "And she can flip on the lights as soon as the sun sets. I hope that's enough."

Jesse's silver eyes, lit by an inner smile, slanted toward her. "You're amazing with her, you know it?"

Buoyed by the compliment, Lindsey shook the bell at him and grinned. "I cheat. I use Christmas."

The teasing admission moved the smile from Jesse's eyes to his lips, changing his rugged, bad-boy expression into a breathtaking sight. That solitary action shot a thrill stronger than adrenaline through Lindsey. Someday, she'd break all the way through the ice he'd built around himself and make him smile all the time.

Startled at such thinking, Lindsey rushed ahead to open the gate. Where had that come from? Jesse was her employee and maybe her friend. But that was all he could be.

Heart thudding in consternation, she analyzed the thought. As a Christian, she wanted to see him happy. She wasn't falling for him. Was she? She'd been in love with a man like Jesse before—a devastatingly handsome man filled with secrets. And Sean had betrayed her so completely she'd come home to the farm and promised never to fall for a pretty face again.

Jesse eased the camel into place alongside the rough wooden building that sheltered the baby Jesus and his earthly parents. He'd already positioned bales of hay around the site and spread straw on the ground. Later, he'd rig up the spotlights and the Star of Bethlehem to bring the scene to life.

In minutes, he had the camel bellowing and blinking.

With a grimace, he shut off the mechanism. "Jade will love that monstrosity."

With laughter and a clap of her hands, Lindsey put aside her troubled thoughts. "I thought as much. We'll let her turn it on as soon as she gets home from school."

Jesse dusted his hands down the sides of his jeans, one corner of his mouth quirking ever-so-slightly. "What's next? Singing Santas? Yodeling elves?"

"Nothing quite that fun. We'd better begin cutting and baling. I'd like to haul the first load tomorrow if we have enough ready."

"So soon?"

"The rush begins on Thanksgiving. That's only a week away. Stores and lots like to have their trees ready to sell."

Switching off the last strains of "Silent Night," he gestured in the direction of the trees. "Lead on, boss lady."

Though disappointed to lose the beautiful music, Lindsey hummed Christmas carols as they began the process of cutting the marked and graded trees. Jesse manned the chain saw and as each tree toppled, Lindsey slid a rolling sled-like device beneath the pine and pulled it to the waiting baler.

Accustomed to lifting the heavy trees, Lindsey manhandled each one into the cone-shaped baler to be compressed into a tight bundle and secured with netting.

Saw in one gloved hand, Jesse poked his head around a tree. "Leave those for me to lift and bale."

"We'd never get finished that way. I'm used to the work, Jesse. Stop fretting."

But pleasure raced through her blood when he laid aside the saw long enough to lift the baled tree onto the flatbed truck. She might be accustomed to heavy work, but being treated like a girl was a novel and somewhat pleasant, if misguided, occurrence.

Following him back into the wide row, and lost in thought, Lindsey never saw the danger coming. One minute, she was examining a hole in her glove and the next she heard the crack and whine of falling timber.

"Lindsey, look out!"

She looked, but all she saw was green blocking the gray-blue sky and rapidly closing in on her.

Then all the air whooshed from her lungs as Jesse came flying and knocked her to the ground, taking the brunt of the felled pine across his back and head.

She tasted dust and pine sap. Prickly needles poked over Jesse's shoulders and scratched the side of her face. Her pulse pounded and her knees trembled as if she'd done jumping jacks for the last hour.

One arm flung protectively over her head, his chest lying across her back, Jesse's warm breath puffed against her ear. "Are you okay?"

He sounded scared.

"Fine." She struggled to draw air into her lungs. "You?"

"Yeah." Jesse's heart raced wildly against her shoulder blades. The situation was anything but intimate, and yet Lindsey was aware of him in an entirely new way.

"You're crushing me," she managed.

"Sorry." He shoved the tree to one side before rolling to a sitting position.

Offering a hand, he pulled Lindsey up to sit beside him. Breath coming in rapid puffs, his concerned gaze checked her over.

With a tenderness usually reserved for Jade, he stroked one calloused finger down her cheek. "You have a scratch."

She studied his face, but resisted the urge to touch him. Already her skin tingled from his simple gesture, and her insides were too rattled from the accident to think straight. Her throat felt tight and thick. "So do you."

He flicked one shoulder, tossing off her concern like an unwanted gum wrapper.

"I'll heal." He took a deep breath and blew out a gusty sigh. "Man, that scared me. I can't believe I let that tree get away from me."

"Not your fault. I heard the saw. I knew you were harvesting, but I was…distracted." She wasn't about to tell him that he'd been the distracting element. And now she was more discombobulated than ever. Jesse had put himself in harm's way to protect her. And she liked the feeling of having a man—of having Jesse— look after her.

Oh, dear. She could be in real trouble here if she

didn't watch her step. There was no denying Jesse's attractiveness, but the idea of letting another handsome face turn her head was worrisome. Jesse's secretiveness and his resistance to the Lord bothered her, too. But as a Christian, she wanted to provide a shining example of Christ's love; to share the incomprehensible peace of mind the Lord had given her.

Somewhere there had to be a midway point between being Jesse's friend in Christ and falling for him.

She only wished she knew how to find it.

Chapter 7

"Are you sure you don't mind?" Jesse asked the moment he and Jade arrived on Thanksgiving Day. "We can still head down to the Caboose and grab a bite to eat."

A sharp wind, the likes of which rip and tear across Oklahoma with the energy of wild, vicious dogs, swept a draught of cold air into the farmhouse.

Though the oven had warmed the place considerably, Lindsey wasn't one to fritter away expensive heating fuel. She plucked at the quilted sleeve of Jesse's coat and pulled him inside.

"And waste this feast I've been cooking all morning? Not a chance, mister. You are stuck with my home cooking. No arguments."

Ducking beneath her daddy's arms, Jade slipped

into the house and started shedding her outerwear. She wore a red wool coat Lindsey had never seen before over a plaid jumper, black tights and patent-leather shoes. Lindsey's heart did a funny stutter-step. Jesse had dressed her up for Thanksgiving dinner.

"You guys toss your coats in the bedroom. I need to check on the dressing and sweet potatoes."

Hands on the snaps of his jacket, Jesse stood in the kitchen doorway sniffing the air. "Candied sweet potatoes?"

She nodded. "With marshmallows and brown sugar."

He let out a low groan. "Forget the Caboose. I wouldn't leave now even if you chased me with that shotgun of yours."

Lindsey couldn't hold back the rush of pleasure. She knew she was blushing and quickly bent over the oven door to blame her increased color on the heat.

Asking Jesse and Jade to Thanksgiving dinner made perfect sense. They had no other place to go, and she had no family living close enough to cook for. In fact, she'd been as energetic as that silly bunny for the three days since Jesse had agreed to share the holiday with her.

"So," Jesse said, coming back into the kitchen from putting away his wraps. "What can we do to help?"

The foil-covered turkey was nicely basted and already out of the oven. The dressing and sweet potatoes were almost ready as were the hot rolls. Though she didn't want to admit as much to Jesse, she'd gotten up earlier than normal to bake everything the way her grandmother always had.

"We'll be ready to eat soon." She turned with a smile, wiping her hands on her bib apron. "You could set the table if you'd like."

"Come on, Butterbean," he said to Jade. "The slave driver is putting us to work."

He was in high spirits today, a rare occurrence to Lindsey's way of thinking. And she liked seeing him this way, without the load of care he usually wore like an anvil around his neck.

Jade's dress shoes clicked on the kitchen floor as she helped her daddy spread the white lacy tablecloth and set out three of Granny's best Blue Willow place settings.

After carefully positioning a knife and fork on top of paper napkins, she looked up. A small frown puckered her brow. "Where's Sushi going to eat?"

"Sushi?" Lindsey hesitated, a potholder in one hand. "I put her in the extra bedroom."

"Oh." Turning back to her job, Jade said nothing more about the dog. The adults exchanged glances.

Jesse mouthed, "Don't ask me."

Jade seemed unmindful that she'd raised adult eyebrows with her concern for a dog she supposedly despised. Letting the subject drop, Lindsey returned to the task of getting the food on the table. In her peripheral vision, she caught the red flash of Jade's plaid jumper and gleaming shoes.

"You sure look pretty today," she said.

"Well, thank you, ma'am." Jesse's teasing voice had her spinning toward him. "You look pretty, too."

Jade burst into giggles. "Daddy! She meant me. I'm pretty."

On tiptoes, the little girl twirled in a circle.

Jesse slapped a hand against one cheek in mock embarrassment. "Do you mean to tell me that I don't look pretty?"

Gap-tooth smile bigger than Dallas, Jade fell against him, hugging his legs. "You're always pretty."

Lindsey had to concur, even though she'd never before seen Jesse in anything but work clothes. Seeing him in polished loafers, starched jeans, and a light blue dress shirt that drew attention to his silvery eyes took her breath away.

Considering how decked-out the Slaters were, she was glad she'd taken the time to dress up a bit herself. Though her clothes were still casual, she'd chosen dark brown slacks instead of jeans and a mauve pullover sweater. And she'd put on earrings, something usually reserved for church. They were only small filigree crosses, but wearing them made her feel dressed-up.

With a wry wince of remembrance, she glanced down. If only she'd exchanged her fluffy house shoes for a snazzy pair of slides... Ah, well, she was who she was. As Granny used to say, you can't make a silk purse out of a sow's ear.

Delighted to have guests on Thanksgiving Day, she didn't much care what anyone wore. Just having them here was enough.

After sliding a fragrant pan of yeast rolls from the

oven, she slathered on melted butter, and dumped the rolls into a cloth-covered basket.

Without waiting to be told, Jesse put ice in the glasses and poured sweet tea from the pitcher Lindsey had already prepared.

"What's next?" he asked, coming to stand beside her at the counter. He brought with him the scent of a morning shower and a manly cologne that reminded Lindsey of an ocean breeze at sunrise.

She, on the other hand, probably smelled like turkey and dressing with a lingering touch of pine.

"I think we're about ready." She handed a bowl of cranberry sauce to Jade. "If you'll put this beside the butter, your daddy and I will bring the hot stuff."

Jade took the bowl in both her small palms, carefully transferring the dish to the table. Jesse and Lindsey followed with the rest and settled into their places.

The trio sat in a triangle with Jesse taking the head of the table and the two ladies on either side of him. Lindsey, out of long habit, stretched out a hand to each of them.

Jade reacted instantly, placing her fingers atop Lindsey's. After a brief, but noticeable interval, Jesse did the same, and then joined his other hand to his daughter's.

The moment Jesse's hand touched hers, Lindsey recognized her error. She hoped with all her might that the Lord would forgive her, because she was having a hard time concentrating on the prayer with Jesse's rough, masculine skin pressing against hers.

Somehow she mumbled her way through, remembering to thank God for her many blessings during the past year, including the blessing of Jesse and Jade.

Jesse tensed at the mention of his name. At the closing "amen," he cleared his throat and shifted uncomfortably. Jade, on the other hand, beamed like the ray of sunshine she was.

"Guess what?" she offered, with the usual scattered thought processes of a six-year-old. "I have a loose tooth."

"Let's see." Lindsey leaned forward, pretending great interest as Jade wiggled a loosening incisor. "Maybe it will fall out while you're eating today."

Jade's eyes widened in horror. "What if I swallow it?"

The poor little child was afraid of everything.

"Well, if you do," Jesse said, helping himself to the sweet potato casserole, "it won't hurt you."

"But I can't swallow it. I have to show it to my teacher so she can put my name on the tooth chart."

Doing her best to suppress a laugh, Lindsey placed a hot roll on her plate and passed the basket to Jesse. His eyes twinkled with his own amused reaction. Swallowing the tooth wasn't the problem. Jade was afraid of being left out, a perfectly healthy, normal worry for a first-grader.

"I don't think you'll swallow the tooth, Jade, but if you do, the teacher will still put your name on the chart."

Green eyes blinked doubtfully. "How will she know?"

"She can look at the new empty place in your mouth."

The little girl's face lit up. She wiggled the tooth again. "Maybe it will come out today."

"We have corn on the cob. That's been known to do the trick."

"Okay." Jade reached eagerly for the corn Lindsey offered. "Eat one, Daddy."

Jesse quirked an eyebrow in teasing doubt. "I don't know, Butterbean. Your old dad can't afford to lose any of his teeth."

"Oh, Daddy." She pushed the platter of steaming corn in his direction. "It's good."

"Okay, then. I just hope you don't have to go home with a toothless daddy."

Jade grinned around a huge bite of corn as her daddy filled his plate.

"This all looks terrific, Lindsey." Jesse added a hearty helping of turkey and dressing. "You've worked hard."

"Cooking was fun. I haven't had a real Thanksgiving dinner since Gramps died."

He spread butter on the golden corn, his surprised attention focused on Lindsey. "Why not? Don't you usually visit your family for holidays?"

"Some holidays, but not this one. I can't. Thanksgiving begins my peak season, and lots of families want their tree the weekend after Thanksgiving."

"Then your family should come here."

"Oh," she gestured vaguely, then scooped up a bite of green bean casserole. "They're all pretty busy with their own lives. Kim, my sister, is expecting a baby early next year. She's in Colorado near her husband's family so naturally, they have their holidays there."

Chewing the creamy casserole, Lindsey had to admit the food tasted incredible. Could she credit the home cooking? Or the company?

Jesse absently handed Jade a napkin. With a sweet smile filled with yellow corn, she swiped at her buttery face.

Having a child—and a man—at her dinner table gave Lindsey an unexpected sense of fulfillment.

"What about your parents?" Jesse asked, coming right back to the conversation.

"Like Kim, they want me to come to them. Right now they're in Korea, so that wasn't possible this year."

"You wouldn't leave the trees anyway."

"I might sometime if I could find the right person to run the place for a couple of days."

He chewed thoughtfully, swallowed and took a drink of tea before saying, "I would have done it this year if you'd said something."

Lindsey's insides filled, not with the sumptuous Thanksgiving meal, but with the pleasure of knowing Jesse meant exactly what he'd said. She mulled over the statement as she watched him eat with hearty male abandon.

"I never would have considered asking you."

Fork in hand, he stiffened. His silver eyes frosted over. "You don't trust me to do a good job?"

"Of course, I trust you." Almost too much, given

how little she knew about him. "I only meant that leaving you to do all the work while I vacationed would be a huge imposition."

His tense jaw relaxed. "Oh."

He studied the rapidly disappearing food on his plate, some thought process that Lindsey couldn't read running amok inside his head.

A vague unease put a damper on Lindsey's celebratory mood. Why had Jesse reacted so oddly?

She bit into the tart cranberry-and-sage-flavored dressing, pondering. Had she offended him? Or was the problem deeper than that?

Jade, who'd been busily doing damage to the ear of corn, stopped long enough to take a huge helping of turkey.

"You won't eat that," Jesse said, reaching for the meat.

Jade slid the plate out of his reach. "It's for Sushi. She's hungry and lonely. She might be crying."

Lindsey couldn't believe her ears. Jade worried about the dog without any encouragement from the adults? Was this the break she'd been praying for?

Jesse seemed to recognize the moment, too, for he tossed down his napkin and said, "Can't have Sushi crying." Chunk of dark meat in hand, he pushed back from his chair. "Let's take her this."

Lindsey thrilled when Jade slipped down from her chair to follow her dad. She took his outstretched hand, her own tiny one swallowed up in the protective size of her father's.

Unable to avoid the parallel, Lindsey thought of her

heavenly Father, of how His huge, all-powerful hand is always outstretched in protection and care. The comparison brought a lump to her throat. She'd messed up a lot in her life, but the Father had never let her down. Even when she'd sequestered herself here on Winding Stair to hide from the hurts of this world, He'd come along with her, loving her back to joy, giving her this farm in place of the things she'd lost.

Jesse and his daughter took three steps across the sun-drenched kitchen before Jade stopped and turned. She stretched out a hand.

"Come on," she said simply as though Lindsey was an expected presence, a part of her life.

The lump in Lindsey's throat threatened to choke her. How long had she hungered for a child? A family? And now, on this Thanksgiving Day she felt as if she had one—if only for today.

Dabbing at her mouth with a napkin, she rose and joined the pair, asking tentatively, "Would you like Sushi to come out and play?"

"I don't want to play."

Before Lindsey had time to express her disappointment, Jade went on. "But she can come out and sit by you."

At the bedroom door, Lindsey went down in front of the child. "You are such a big girl. I'm so proud of you for being nice to Sushi. She *is* lonely in there all by herself and she doesn't understand why she's locked up."

Dark hair bouncing, Jade nodded. "I know."

"We'll give her this turkey." She indicated the meat

in Jesse's hand. "And then I'll pet her a little before letting her out. She might be excited and jump because she's happy to see us."

Jade reached both arms toward her father. "Hold me up, Daddy."

With a sigh that said he didn't consider this progress, he hoisted his daughter. Lindsey opened the door and commanded, "Sushi, stay."

The German shepherd, already spring-loaded, wilted in disappointment, but she followed her owner's command. Tail swishing madly, ears flicking, she waited while Lindsey stroked and murmured encouragements. Once convinced that Sushi's self-control was intact, she gazed up at Jade.

"She's all ready for that turkey. Hold it by your fingertips and give it to her."

Heart thudding with hope, Lindsey told the dog to sit and be gentle.

Worried green eyes shifting from the dog to Lindsey, Jade gathered her courage. When she looked to Jesse, he winked and gave her an encouraging nudge. "Go ahead."

Taking the poultry, Jade strained forward. Jesse held on tight, face as tense and hopeful as Lindsey's heart.

As if she understood the child's dilemma, Sushi waited patiently, and then daintily took the meat between her front teeth.

Jade's nervous laugh broke the anxious moment. Lindsey hadn't realized she was holding her breath. As casually as she could while rejoicing over this huge step, she turned back to the kitchen. Sushi's toenails tapped the floor as she followed. She pointed to a spot far away from Jade, and the dog collapsed in ecstasy.

To her delight, Jade slithered out of Jesse's arms, unafraid to be on even ground with the animal.

"How about some pecan pie?" Lindsey asked, tilting the pie in their direction.

Jade shook her head. "Can I play with your playhouse?"

She indicated the extra room where Lindsey kept toys and games for her Sunday-school girls.

"Sure. Go ahead."

As Jade skipped off into the other room, Lindsey lifted an eyebrow toward Jesse. "Pie?"

Jesse patted his flat, muscled stomach. "Too full right now. Later maybe?"

"Later sounds better to me, too. I'm sure there are plenty of football games on if you'd like to watch television while I clean the kitchen."

"No deal. You cook. I wash."

Lindsey was shocked at the idea. "You're my guest. You can't wash dishes."

Already rolling up his shirtsleeves, Jesse argued. "Watch me."

"Then I'm helping, too." She tossed him an apron, the least frilly one she owned.

He tied it around his slender middle, and in minutes they had the table cleared and water steaming in the old-fashioned porcelain sink.

As Lindsey stacked the dishes on the counter, Jesse washed them. The sight of his strong dark arms plunged into a sink full of white soapsuds did funny things to her insides.

They were down to the turkey roaster when the crunch of tires on gravel turned their attention to visitors.

"Who could that be?" Lindsey asked, placing a dried plate into the cabinet before pushing back the yellow window curtain. "I don't recognize the vehicle."

Jesse came up beside her. A hum of awareness prickled the skin on Lindsey's arms.

"I'll go out and check." Her breath made tiny clouds on the cool window. "Could be an early customer."

Her prediction proved true, and though she normally didn't open until the day after Thanksgiving, she was too kindhearted to turn them away.

Upon hearing their story, she was glad they'd come.

"Thank you for letting us interrupt your holiday," the woman said as she watched her children traipse happily through the thick green pines. "We thought decorating the tree before their dad shipped out for the Middle East tomorrow would help the kids. They've never had Christmas without him."

Lindsey placed a hand on the woman's arm. "It's us who owe you—and your husband—thanks."

As they went from tree to tree, discussing the perfect shape and size, Lindsey realized that Jesse and Jade had disappeared. In moments, she knew why. Red and green lights, dim in the bright November sun, flicked on all over the lot. Then the gentle strains of

"Away in a Manger" filtered from the stereo speakers Jesse had stretched from the gate into the trees.

When he returned, coming up beside Lindsey with Jade in tow, she couldn't hold back her gratitude. "Thank you for thinking of that."

He shrugged off the compliment. "Some people like this stuff."

But you don't. What could have happened to turn Jesse into such a Scrooge? She wanted to ask why again, to press him for information, but now, with a customer present, was not the moment.

The family found the perfect tree and Jesse set to work. In no time, the tree was cut, baled, and carefully secured on top of the family's car. Three exuberant children piled inside the four-door sedan, faces rosy with excitement and cold. The soldier reached for his wallet, but Lindsey held out a hand to stop him.

"No way. The tree is a gift. Enjoy it."

The man argued briefly, but seeing Lindsey's stubborn stance, finally gave in. "This means a lot to my family."

He got inside the car and started the engine.

"Merry Christmas," Lindsey said, leaning down into the open window. "You'll be in my prayers."

With more thanks and calls of Merry Christmas, the family drove away, the Virginia pine waving in the wind.

"That was a real nice thing you did," Jesse said, his arm resting against hers as they watched the car jounce down the driveway.

"I love to give trees to people like that. What a blessing."

"You don't make money giving them away."

"No, but you create joy, and that's worth so much more."

Jade, who'd been listening, rubbed her hand across the needles of a nearby pine and spoke in a wistful voice. "I wish I could have a Christmas tree."

"What a grand idea!" Lindsey clapped her hands. The sound startled several blackbirds into flight. "Let's pick one right now. You and your daddy can decorate it tonight."

Beside her, Jesse stiffened. A warning sounded in Lindsey's head, but she pushed it away, intent upon this latest happy project.

"Come on." She gestured toward the smaller trees. "You can choose your very own tree. Any one you want."

Jade held back, her face a contrast of longing and reluctance.

The warning sound grew louder. "What's wrong, sweetie? Don't you want a tree?"

Small shoulders slumping with the weight, Jade wagged her head, dejected. "Daddy won't let me."

"Sure he will."

But one look at Jesse told her she was wrong.

"Jesse?" With a sinking feeling, she searched his face. What she found there unnerved her.

"Leave it alone, Lindsey," he growled, jaw clenching and unclenching.

"Daddy hates Christmas." Tears shimmered in Jade's green eyes. "Mommy—"

"Jade!" Jesse's tortured voice stopped her from saying more. He stared at his daughter, broken and forlorn.

Jade's eyes grew round and moist. Biting her lower lip, she flung her arms around Jesse's knees.

Expression bereft, Jesse stroked his daughter's hair, holding her close to him.

Heart pounding in consternation, Lindsey prayed for wisdom. Whatever had happened was still hurting Jesse and this precious little girl. And avoiding the issue would not make the pain go away.

She touched him, lightly, tentatively. "Let me help, Jesse. Talk to me. Tell me what's wrong."

"Talking doesn't change anything." His face was as hard as stone, but his eyes begged for release.

She hesitated, not wanting to toss around platitudes, but knowing the real answer to Jesse's need. "I don't know if you want to hear this, but there's nothing too big for the Lord. Jesus will heal all our sorrows if we let Him."

"I wish I could believe that. I wish…" With a weary sigh, he lifted Jade into his arms and went to the little bench along the edge of the grove and sat down. With a deep, shivering sigh, he stared over Jade's shoulder into the distance, seeing something there that no one else could.

Unsure how to proceed, but knowing she had to help this man who'd come to mean too much to her,

Lindsey settled on the bench beside him and waited, praying hard that God would give her the words.

Something terrible had broken Jesse's heart and her own heart broke from observing his pain.

After an interminable length of silence disrupted only by the whisper of wind through pine boughs, Jade climbed down from her daddy's lap.

Her dark brows knit together. "Daddy?"

"I'm okay, Butterbean." He clearly was not. "Go play. I want to talk to Lindsey."

"About Mommy?"

Jesse dragged a hand over his mouth. "Yeah."

Lindsey saw the child hesitate as though she felt responsible for her father's sorrow. Finally, she drifted away, going to the parked wagon where she sat anxiously watching the adults.

When Jesse finally began to speak, the words came out with a soft ache, choppy and disconnected.

"Erin looked a lot like Jade. Black hair and green eyes. Pale skin. She was a good woman, a Christian like you." He hunched down into his jacket, though the afternoon air wasn't cold. "I tried to be one, too, when she was alive."

So that explained how Jade had learned to pray and why she knew bits and pieces about Jesus. Jesse and his wife had known the Lord, but something had driven him away from his faith.

"Christmas was a very big deal to her. She loved to shop, especially for Jade and me. We didn't have a lot of money." He kicked at a dirt clod, disintegrating the clump into loose soil. "My fault, but Erin made the best of it. We always had a good Christmas because of her. She could make a ten-dollar gift seem worth a million."

Something deep inside told Lindsey to be quiet and let him talk. Letting the pain out was the first step to healing, and the cleansing would give the Lord an opportunity to move in. Granny had taught her that when she'd wanted to curl into a ball and disappear from the pain of Sean's betrayal.

"Two years ago—" He stopped, sat up straight and tilted his head backward, looking into the sky.

"What happened?" she urged gently.

"Christmas Eve. Erin had a few last-minute gifts to buy. One present she'd had in layaway for a while, though I didn't know it at the time. She'd been waiting to have enough money to pick up that one gift." He swallowed hard and scrubbed a hand across his eyes. "Jade and I stayed at the house, watching Christmas cartoons and munching popcorn balls. We were waiting for Erin to get home before we hung the stockings. We never hung them because Erin never came home."

Biting at her lower lip, Lindsey closed her eyes and prayed for guidance.

"Oh, Jesse," she whispered, not knowing what else to say. "I'm so sorry."

He shifted around to look at her. "I'm not telling you this for sympathy."

But sympathy wasn't the only emotion rushing through her veins.

She was starting to care about Jesse. Not only the way a Christian should care about all people, but on a personal level too. Every day she looked forward to the minute the blue-and-silver truck rumbled into her yard, and he swung down from the cab and ambled in that cowboy gait of his up to the front porch. She relished their working side by side. She enjoyed looking into his silvery eyes and listening to the low rumble of his manly voice. She appreciated his strength and his kindness.

She cared, and the admission unsettled her. He was too wounded, too broken, and too much in love with a dead wife for her to chance caring too much. She could be a friend and a shoulder to cry on, but that was all she could let herself be.

Jesse gripped the edge of the bench, needing Lindsey's compassion and afraid of flying apart if he accepted it. Now that he'd begun the awful telling, there was no way he could stop. Like blood from a gaping wound, the words flowed out.

"Three blocks from our house a drunk driver hit her, head-on."

He'd been sitting in his recliner, Jade curled against him watching Rudolph when the sirens had broken the silent night. He'd never forget the fleeting bit of sympathy he'd felt for any poor soul who needed an ambulance on Christmas Eve. Safe and warm in his living room, he had no way of knowing the holiday had chosen him—again—for heartache.

"A neighbor came, pounding on the door and yelling. She'd seen the wreck, knew it was Erin's car. I ran." He didn't know why he'd done that. A perfectly good truck sat in the driveway, but he hadn't even thought of driving to the scene. "Like a fool, I ran those three blocks, thinking I could stop anything bad from happening to my family."

He relived that helpless moment when he'd pushed past policemen, screaming that Erin was his wife. He recalled the feel of their hands on him, trying to stop him, not wanting him to see.

"She was gone." Stomach sick from the memory, he shoved up from the bench, unable to share the rest. Lindsey was perceptive. She'd understand that he'd witnessed a sight no man should have to see. His beautiful wife crushed and mangled, the Christmas gifts she'd given her life for scattered along the highway, a testament to the violence of the impact.

Back turned, he clenched his fists and told the part that haunted him still.

"The present she'd gone after was mine." He'd wanted the fancy Western belt with his name engraved on the back, had hoped she'd order it for him. Now the belt remained in its original box, unused, a reminder that Erin had died because of him.

"Now you know why I feel the way I do about Christmas." He spoke to the rows and rows of evergreens, though he knew Lindsey listened. He could feel her behind him, full of compassion and care. When she laid a consoling hand on his back, he was glad. He needed her touch. "Jade and I both have too many bad memories of Christmas to celebrate anything."

Jesse looked toward the wagon which had already

been outfitted for hauling visitors through the grove. Jade had crawled beneath the down quilt and lay softly singing along with the music, waving her hands in the air like a conductor. He'd somehow tuned out the carols until then.

Lindsey's hand soothed him, making small circles on his back. "Don't you want Jade to remember her mother?"

"Of course I do. How could you ask me that?"

"You said Erin loved Christmas and wanted the holiday to be special for you and Jade. Those times with her mother are important to Jade, and Christmas is one of the best memories of all."

Not for him. And not for Jade either.

"I'd never take away her memories of Erin," he said gruffly.

"When you refuse to let her have a Christmas tree, you're telling her child's mind to forget her mother and to forget all those wonderful times with her."

"That's not true," he denied vehemently. "I'm protecting her. I don't want her to relive that terrible night every Christmas."

"Are you talking about Jade? Or yourself?"

He opened his mouth to refute the very idea that he was protecting himself instead of Jade. But words wouldn't come.

"You can't allow your own pain to keep Jade from having a normal childhood." Her warm, throaty voice implored him.

"I'd never do that," he said, but the denial sounded weak. With growing angst, he realized Lindsey could be right. In his self-focused pain, he'd hurt his little girl, denying her the right to remember her mother laughing beneath the tree on Christmas morning, the three of them dancing to "Jingle Bell Rock."

He squeezed his eyes closed as memories washed over him.

"Not intentionally, but don't you realize that she reads everything you do or don't do, interpreting your actions in her childish understanding? She wants to have Christmas, but she worries about you."

A great blue heron winged past, headed to the pond. Out in the pasture, the black horse grazed on an enormous round bale of hay, summer's green grass a memory.

"I don't want her worrying about me."

"You can't stop her. She wants you to be happy. She loves you. God loves you, too, Jesse, and He wants to help you get past this."

"I don't know how." And even if he did, he wondered if "getting past" Erin's death wouldn't somehow be disloyal.

"Erin's death wasn't your fault. Start there."

"I can't help thinking she would be alive if she hadn't gone shopping."

"Those are futile thoughts, Jesse. You would be better served to wonder how you can honor her life."

He turned toward her then. She'd hit upon the very thing he longed for. "I don't know how to do that either."

"You already are in one way. You're raising Jade to be a lovely child. But God has more for you. He wants you to have a life free of guilt and anger. Full of peace."

Jesse felt the tug of that peace emanating from his boss lady. A fierce longing to pray, something he hadn't done in two years, gnawed at him.

"Let's go choose a tree," Lindsey urged, holding out a hand. "For Jade."

He took a breath of clean mountain air and blew it out, his chest heavy and aching. He could do this for his baby. A Christmas tree wasn't that big a deal, was it? He'd worked in the things for a couple of months now without dying.

His eyes drifted over the acres of pines, noting one major difference. These were bare. If he took a Christmas tree back to the trailer, Jade would want to decorate it.

He turned his attention to the wagon where his brave little trooper no longer sang and conducted. Huddled down into the quilt, her black hair tousled, she lay sleeping.

Last Christmas, the first anniversary of Erin's death, he'd done his best to ignore the holiday altogether. Erin's family, far away in Kentucky had sent gifts, but he'd tossed them in the garbage before Jade had seen them. The few times she'd mentioned presents, he'd reacted so harshly she'd quickly gotten the message that the subject of Christmas was off limits.

But she'd cried, too. And that forgotten memory of her tears tormented him.

Fighting down a rising sense of dread, Jesse took Lindsey's hand. "Let's go wake her."

Lindsey's quiet eyes studied him. "Are you okay with this?"

Though uncertain, he nodded.

They went to the wagon where Jade lay sleeping like an angel, her black hair a dark halo around her face. Sooty lashes curved upon her weather-rosy cheeks. One arm hugged the covers, rising and falling with the rhythm of her silent breath.

"Look at her, Jesse. You have so much to be thankful for. I know people who'd give anything to have a child like Jade." Her voice grew wistful. "Including me."

Her soft-looking lips turned down, one of the rare times he'd seen her unhappy. He didn't like seeing her sad.

"I thought you were perfectly content up here alone." They spoke in hushed tones so as not to startle the sleeping child. But the quiet created an intimacy that made him feel closer to Lindsey than he had to anyone in a long time.

"I'm learning to be content in the Lord, but that doesn't mean I don't think about having a family someday."

Something stirred inside Jesse. Lindsey would make a great mother—and a good wife to the right man. Someday one of those holy churchgoers who'd never committed a sin in his life would marry her.

Already miserable with the forthcoming Christmas tree, he didn't want to think about Lindsey with some other man.

Fighting off the uncomfortable thoughts, he stroked

a knuckle down Jade's cheek. "Hey, Butterbean. Wake up. Ready to get that Christmas tree?"

His little girl blinked, her green eyes sleepy and confused, but filled with a hope that seared him. "Really?"

With a nod, he swallowed hard and helped her down from the wagon. As if she expected the offer to be rescinded at any moment, Jade wasted no time. She grabbed each adult by the hand and pulled them toward the grove.

An hour later, laden with lights and tinsel and lacy white angel ornaments Lindsey had given Jade from a box in her Christmas building, they'd headed back to the trailer. Jade had been ecstatic over the three-foot tree, raising the level of Jesse's guilt as well as his anxiety. All the way into town he'd wondered if he could actually go through with it, if he could spend a month staring at a reminder of all he'd lost.

In the end he'd been a coward, placing the small, shining tree in Jade's bedroom where he wouldn't have to see it. His child had been so thrilled with the thing, she hadn't questioned the reason. He'd nearly broken, though, when she'd crawled exhausted beneath her covers, the sweetest smile on earth lifting her bow mouth. "Is it okay if I say a prayer and thank Jesus for my tree and all my guarding angels?"

"Sure, baby, sure."

Long after she'd fallen asleep, he'd sat in the trailer's tiny living room, staring blindly at the paneled wall.

What had he gotten himself into? Lindsey Mitchell

with her sweetness and overwhelming decency was
tearing him apart. His frozen heart had begun to thaw.
And like blood-flow returning to frost-bitten fingers,
the sensation was pure torture.

Chapter 8

Jesse was tired, bone-weary. A basket of laundry at his feet, he sat on the plastic couch in his mobile home folding clothes. Jade was in her tiny excuse of a bedroom playing with a small dollhouse borrowed from Lindsey.

After the busy Thanksgiving weekend, he'd worked half of last night, and even though the tree farm was jumping this morning, he'd knocked off at noon. He felt bad about leaving Lindsey alone with the customers, but he had business to attend to.

Then he'd spent hours in the courthouse and on the telephone, leaking out bits of himself to strangers in exchange for information about his stepfather. One conversation had given him the name of a backwoods lawyer who'd been around eighteen years ago.

A lawyer with a drinking problem who'd been known to do "buddy deals." Trouble was, no one remembered where the man had gone when he'd left Winding Stair years ago.

His stomach growled and he tried to remember if he'd eaten today. Probably not. Lindsey usually forced lunch on him, but he'd left too early for that.

He needed answers worse than he needed food. Day after day in Lindsey's company was starting to scare him. And for all the good she'd done his child, Jade was getting too attached. He had to bring this situation to an end soon.

A sudden knock rattled the entire trailer. Tossing aside a worn towel, he went to answer the door, bristling at the sight of his oversized visitor. Preacher Cliff whatever-his-name-was. No wonder the trailer had shaken under the pounding. So Lindsey had betrayed his confidence and sicced her minister on him. Preparing for an onslaught of unwanted advice, pat answers and sympathy for his loss, he opened the door.

"Hey, Jesse, how are you doing?"

Jesse accepted the warm handshake and exchanged greetings. "Come on in."

Not that he really wanted the preacher in his house, but he didn't want to upset Lindsey either.

"No, no. I can't stay. The men are working on the church Christmas display tonight, and Karen threatened not to feed me if I was late to supper." He gave a hearty laugh and tapped his belly. "Can't be starving the skinny little preacher."

In spite of himself, Jesse smiled. It was hard not to like Lindsey's pastor.

"I hate to bother you with this," Cliff went on, "but Lindsey tells me you're a whiz with electrical hookups. Brags to everyone about you. We're having a bit of trouble at the church getting our display to work right, and she thought you might be willing to have a look."

Jesse's first impulse was to say no and slam the door, but the preacher's words soaked through first. Lindsey bragged about him to other people?

In spite of himself he asked, "Any idea what's gone wrong?"

"Aw, I don't know. Clarence and Mick seemed to think the problem is in the breaker box, but we can't fix it."

Jesse squinted in contemplation. "Clarence and Mick will be there?"

"They're at the church right now. That's why I came by to talk to you. They're at their wits' end with this thing."

Clarence Stone was a man who'd been around a while, a man who might know more about the lawyer, Stuart Hardwick. Spending time in his company, even at a church, could be worth the effort. And he'd seen Mick Thompson several times since the cookout weeks ago and liked the guy. He wasn't one of those preachy kind of Christians who didn't know how to get his hands dirty. And their common interest in horses might someday lead to friendship. He'd need a friend when he regained the land that Lindsey now called home.

Ignoring the pinch of regret that grew worse each time he thought of Lindsey's reaction to losing the farm, he looked at his watch. "I'll head over there now, see what I can do."

Cliff clapped Jesse on the shoulder. "Great. I'll meet you in the parking lot."

Jesse knew where Winding Stair Chapel was located and, after collecting Jade and her dolls and making sure his tools were in the truck, drove to the church.

Three other pickups were parked outside the native-rock building. Their owners were scattered around the outside of the church at various projects. They'd set up a life-sized nativity and lined the railed walkway from the parking area to the entrance with luminaries. The two huge evergreens standing sentry on each corner of the lot had been draped with lights, and the outline of an enormous star rose high over the chapel. A man wearing a leather tool belt balanced on the roof, labored over the star.

The men had gone to a lot of trouble, and from the looks of things, they were far from finished.

He was surprised to find himself here, at a church. Not that he didn't believe in God, but part of him wondered if God believed in him. He'd felt empty for such a long time.

"Man, are we glad to see you," Mick Thompson called as soon as Jesse and Jade exited the pickup. "Help's on the way, boys," he bellowed to the remaining men. "Lindsey's expert is here."

Lindsey's expert? The friendly greeting buoyed

Jesse. As tired as he was, he wanted to help if possible. "I'll do what I can. What's the main trouble?"

Clarence Stone waved his arms at a latticework of electrical circuitry spread over the churchyard. "Everything. We're all hooked up, cords and wires are run, but the angels won't flutter and Baby Jesus won't shine."

Jesse squelched his amusement at the old man's joking manner.

"Show me your electrical setup and where all the breakers are. I have my tester and tool pouch in the truck. Maybe we can find the source of the problem and work from there."

Boots crunching across the gravel drive, Mick motioned toward the lighted building. "My wife is in the Sunday school preparing next week's lesson. Your little girl can play with my kids if she wants to. Clare will keep an eye on her while you're busy."

Jade jumped at the chance and was taken inside by the giant preacher who'd wheeled in behind Jesse. It did Jesse's heart good to see Jade willing to be out of his sight for a few minutes.

"Breaker box is in the church office," Clarence said and led Jesse down the long hall to the back of the church. To Jesse, the older man's presence and eager conversation was a stroke of good luck.

"The tree farm hopping yet?" Clarence asked as Jesse stepped up on a ladder to examine the box that housed the breakers. He unscrewed four screws and removed the face plate.

Jesse nodded, concentration riveted more on testing

the voltage to the breakers than on the conversation. "We've been real busy since Thanksgiving."

Clarence peered upward, leaning an arm against the rock wall below Jesse. "I reckon Lindsey's in her element. Never seen a child love Christmas the way she does. Been that way ever since I knew her."

"How long has that been?" Jesse said the words casually, never taking his eyes off the readings. The breakers had power. The problem was likely in the attic.

"Ever since she moved in with Charlie and Betty Jean. Before that really. I'd see her now and again when she and her folks came to visit."

"Lindsey thought a lot of her Grandma and Grandpa Mitchell." He flipped the main breaker to the off position.

"Mitchell?" Clarence stared up at him, puzzled for a moment. "You mean Baker, not Mitchell. Mitchell was the other side of the family. I never knew them. Now Charlie and me, we was good friends. Hauled hay with each other. Things like that."

As Clarence rattled on about his friendship with Lindsey's grandfather, the light came on inside Jesse's head. The volt meter trembled in his fingers as adrenaline zipped through him. No wonder he'd had such a hard time finding data. He'd been looking under the wrong name.

"I suppose the Bakers have owned that farm for generations." He knew better, but figured tossing the idea out in the open would keep Clarence talking.

"Nah. Charlie bought the place when he retired

from the phone company. Let's see..." Clarence squinted at the ceiling, rubbing his chin. "'Bout twenty years ago, I reckon. Before that a man name of Finch owned it, if memory serves. I didn't know him too well. Not a friendly sort. Charlie started the tree farm."

Les Finch. Jesse's gut clenched. No, his stepfather wasn't a friendly sort unless a man had a bottle of whiskey or something else he wanted. And he had never owned the farm, either, but he'd wanted everyone to think he did.

Carefully, he guided the subject away from Les Finch. No use helping Clarence remember the boy who'd lived on that farm with the unfriendly Finch.

"I have an idea what the problem is, but I need to get up in the attic." He looked around, saw the opening and moved the ladder beneath.

Clarence followed along, eager to help and full of chatter, but otherwise basically useless. "Think you can fix it?"

Taking his flashlight from his tool pouch, Jesse shoved the attic door open and poked his head into the dark space above. The problem was right in front of him. "Should have the power up and running in no time."

Clarence clapped his hands. "Lindsey said you would. She sure thinks highly of you, and that means something to us around here. Lindsey's like her grandma. Has a heart of gold and will do about anything for anybody. But she don't trust just everyone. Kinda got a sore spot where that's concerned."

A sore spot? Lindsey? Tilting his face downward

at the old farmer, curiosity piqued, he asked, "Why do you say that?"

"Well, I reckon you'll hear it if you stay around here long enough, though I'm not surprised Lindsey didn't tell you herself. Some things are kinda painful to discuss."

Jesse concentrated on repairing a ground wire that had been chewed in half by some varmint, likely a squirrel, but every fiber of his being was tuned in to Clarence.

"Some college fella without a lick of sense or decency broke her heart a few years back. Poor little thing come crying home all tore up and hasn't left that farm for more than a day or two since. Sometimes I think she's hiding out up there so no one can hurt her again."

Jesse wrestled with the need to punch something but used his energy to splice the line and wrap the ends with insulated tape. His blood boiled to think of Lindsey crying over some snot-nosed college boy.

"I've never noticed anything wrong." But that wasn't exactly true. Hadn't he seen the shadows in her eyes when she talked about wanting a child like Jade? "She seems happy enough."

"Naturally. She's got the Lord. I don't know how folks that don't know the Lord get by when hard times come."

Jesse was beginning to wonder that himself.

"I figure she's over the guy by now." At least, he hoped so. He collected his tools, placing each one in his pouch.

"No doubt about that. She's a strong young woman, but the heartache of having her fiancé get some other girl pregnant while she was away making money for the wedding, won't ever leave her. That's why I say trust don't come easy."

Jesse's pliers clattered to the tile below. He clenched his fists as anger, swift and hot, bubbled up in him. What kind of low-life would do such a thing? Gentle, loving Lindsey, who gave and helped and never asked for anything in return, shouldn't have been treated so cruelly. She must have been crushed at such betrayal from the man she loved and trusted.

Clumping down the ladder, he went to the breaker box, insides raging at the injustice. A good woman like Lindsey deserved better.

As he flipped the breaker switch, illuminating the darkening churchyard, the awful truth hit him like a bolt of electricity. Lindsey trusted him, too. And he was going to hurt her almost as much.

Lindsey was happy enough to sing—and so she did—inside the Snack Shack, as she liked to call the small building where she and Jade served hot apple cider and Christmas cookies to their "guests." Gaily bedecked with holiday cheer, the cozy room boasted a long table where customers could warm up and enjoy the music and atmosphere while Jesse baled their chosen tree and Lindsey rang up their sale.

At present, a family of five occupied the room, admiring Lindsey's miniature Christmas village while they munched and waited. They'd had their ride through the grove, all of them singing at the top of their lungs, the children so full of excited energy they kept hopping off the wagon to run along beside. Their unfettered cheer delighted Lindsey and had even brightened Jesse's usually serious countenance.

Jade, catching the good mood, had agreed to let Sushi roam free as long as Jesse was within sight.

Yes, Lindsey's life was full. Not since before Gramps died had the holidays seemed so merry.

The door flew open and Jesse stepped inside, rubbing his gloveless hands together. A swirl of winter wind followed him. The collar of his fleece-lined jacket turned up, framing his handsome face.

An extra jolt of energy shot through Lindsey. More and more lately, Jesse's presence caused that inexplicable reaction. With a simple act like walking into a room, he made her world brighter.

Two nights ago he'd solved a problem with the electricity at the church, and she'd been so proud of him. He was smart and resourceful and the hardest, most honest worker anyone could ask for.

"Daddy!" Jade charged from behind the homemade counter where she'd been doling out gingerbread men. "Want a cookie?"

Lindsey grinned. Jade had forced the sweets on him every time he'd entered the building. He never stayed long, just grabbed the cookie and ran. Even though he had been busy with a steady stream of customers all night, she suspected that the holiday atmosphere still bothered him.

"I'm stuffed, Butterbean." Absently patting her

head, he said to the eagerly waiting family, "Your tree's ready to go. It's a beauty."

After giving the kids a few more cookies and the man a set of tree-care instructions, she, Jade and Jesse escorted the family out into the clear, cold night. Together they stood, Jade between them, watching the car pull away. For a moment, as cries of "Merry Christmas" echoed across through the crisp air, Lindsey had the fleeting thought that this is what it would be like if the three of them were a family bidding goodbye to friends after a fun-filled visit.

A gust of wind, like an icy hand, slapped against her.

Flights of fancy were uncharacteristic of someone as practical as she. And yet, here she stood, in the nippy, pine-scented night, behaving as if Jesse and Jade belonged to her. The need for family had never weighed as heavy nor had the longing been so great.

Wise enough to recognize the symptoms, Lindsey struggled to hold her emotions in check, to fight down the rising ache of need. She loved the dark-haired child clinging to her hand. And she had feelings for Jesse, though she refused to give those feelings a name.

Jesse was good help, and he was great company, but they were too different. His grief for his late wife, coupled with his ambivalence toward God, were all the roadblocks the Lord needed to put in her way. She had ignored the signs before. She wouldn't let herself be that foolish again.

The evening's pleasure seeped away. Maybe she wasn't meant to have a family. Maybe the Lord intended her to be alone, growing trees for other families to enjoy, and sharing her maternal love with the children from her church. After the foolish mistakes she'd made with Sean, perhaps the Lord didn't trust her to make that kind of decision.

Jesse pulled Jade against him to block the wind and tugged her coat closed, though his mind was on Lindsey. He felt her sudden withdrawal as if she'd turned and walked away. When the customers pulled out of the drive she'd been laughing and happy, but now her shoulders slumped, and she stared into the distance like a lost puppy.

"Are you okay?"

"Tired, I guess." She pulled the hood of her car coat up and snapped the chin strap.

Sure she was tired. Had to be after the long days of hard work they'd been putting in. Though things would settle down after the holidays, this was the busiest time of year for the farm. He knew for a fact she was up every morning with the sun and worked on the books long after he went home. He'd tried to take more of the physical labor on himself, but when he did she added something else to her own chore list. Still, he had a feeling more than exhaustion weighed her down tonight.

"Let's close up. It's nearly ten anyway." They normally locked the gates and cut the lights at ten.

Solemn-faced, she nodded. "I'll unharness Puddin' and get him settled."

As she turned to go, Jesse reached out and caught

her elbow. He had the sudden and troublesome yearning to guide her against his chest and ask what was wrong. Not a smart idea, but an enticing one.

"You and Jade take care of things inside," he said. "I'll tend to Puddin' and the outdoor chores."

The wind whipped a lock of hair from beneath her hood and sent it fluttering across her mouth. Tempted to catch the wayward curl, to feel the silky softness against his skin, Jesse shoved his hands into his pockets.

"Come inside and warm up first," she said, tucking the stray hair back in place. "You've been out in this wind all evening."

So had she for the most part, but he didn't argue. A warm drink and a few minutes of rest wouldn't hurt him and it would please her. Funny how pleasing Lindsey seemed important tonight.

Inside the building, Jesse stood amidst the cheery knickknacks breathing in the scents of cinnamon and pine and apples. The room reeked of Lindsey and the things she enjoyed. If he wanted to stop thinking about her—and he did—here among her decorations was not the place to do it.

Normally, the Snack Shack and all the holiday folderol depressed him, but depression plagued him less and less lately. He'd figured he was just too busy and tired to notice, but now he worried that Lindsey and not fatigue had taken the edge off his sorrow.

To avoid that line of thinking, he gazed around the room at the lighted candles, the holly rings, and all the other festive things that Lindsey loved. Looking at them didn't hurt so much anymore.

"You ought to put a little gift shop in here." He didn't know where that had come from.

"I've thought about it, but never had enough help to handle gifts and the trees." Lindsey was behind the counter helping Jade seal leftover cookies into zip-up bags.

"You should consider the idea."

"Too late this year. Maybe next."

Jesse could see the notion, coming from him, pleased her. He had other ideas that would please her, too. Some he'd shared, like the concept of developing a Web site for the farm and using the Internet for free marketing. He'd even volunteered to start tinkering with designs after the rush season.

Lifting a glass angel, he turned the ornament in his hands. What was happening to him? Why was he thinking such ridiculous, useless thoughts?

Lindsey didn't need a Web site or advertising or even a gift shop. This time next year she and her Christmas trees would be long gone. That's the way it had to be. Justice would be served. He'd have his home...and his revenge.

The tender, loving expression on the angel's face mocked him. Discomfited, he put the ornament back on the shelf.

Lindsey bustled around the counter, carrying a steaming cup. "Cider?"

Her inner light was back on, and he was glad. Taking the warm mug, he smiled his thanks and waited like a child expecting candy for her to return the smile.

His fingers itched to touch her smooth skin, and this time, before he could change his mind, he cupped her cheek. A question sprang to her eyes—a question he couldn't answer because he didn't understand himself.

Dropping his hand, he avoided her gaze and pretended to sip the warm drink. Ever since Clarence had told him of Lindsey's cheating fiancé, he'd struggled against the need to take her in his arms and promise that no one would ever hurt her that way again. The reaction made no sense at all.

A strange energy pulsed in the space between them and he knew she waited for him to say something, to explain his uncharacteristic behavior. But how could he explain what he didn't understand?

He felt her move away, wanted to call her back, wanted to say…what? That he liked her? That he was attracted to her?

He heard her murmuring to Jade, but his head buzzed so much he couldn't make out the conversation. He sipped the sweet cider, hoping to wash away his deranged thoughts. Attracted? No way. Couldn't happen.

He looked up to find Lindsey gathering his drowsy daughter into her arms. Most nights Jade fell asleep long before closing and Lindsey put her to bed on an air mattress behind the counter. Tonight being Friday, Jade had stayed awake as long as possible, but a few moments of quiet stillness had done her in.

His baby girl snuggled into Lindsey's green flannel, eyes drooping as she relaxed, contented and comfortable. Expression tender, his boss lady brushed a kiss onto Jade's peaceful forehead. They looked so right together, this woman and his child.

Something dangerous moved inside Jesse's chest. A thickness lodged in his throat. Lindsey Mitchell was slowly worming her way into his heart.

A war raged within him. He couldn't fall in love with Lindsey. He couldn't even allow attraction. To do so would betray Erin's memory and interfere with his plans for restitution and revenge. He was within arm's reach of everything he'd dreamed of for years. He and Jade deserved this place. No matter how sweet Lindsey Mitchell might be, he would not be distracted.

Once he'd discovered Lindsey's grandfather's real name, he had easily found the information he needed. Sure enough, Stuart Hardwick, the crooked lawyer, had done the deal. When he'd told the court clerk this morning that he'd been searching under the wrong name, she'd curled her lip in reproach. "Coulda told you that if you'd asked."

Now that a clerk knew he was searching Lindsey's farm records, it was only a matter of time before word leaked out and Lindsey knew his intent. He thought about going to the sheriff with what he knew, but a confession from Hardwick would settle matters more quickly. He needed to find Stuart Hardwick first— and fast.

He took one last glance at Lindsey.

He was too close to the truth to let anything—or anyone—stop him now.

Hardening his heart, he went out into the cold night.

Chapter 9

Waving a paper, Jade barreled down the lane, pink backpack thumping against her purple coat.

"Lindsey. Lindsey! Can you make a costume?"

On her knees, clearing away the remains of a tree stump, Lindsey braced as Jade tumbled against her. Mother love too fierce to deny rose inside her. Jade needed her love and attention, regardless of the sorrow Lindsey would someday suffer when the child was gone. She wasn't foolish enough to think a man of Jesse's talents would always work for minimum wage.

"What kind of costume, sweetie?"

"An angel. An angel." Jade's excitement had her fluttering around waving her arms like wings. "I'm the guarding angel for Jesus."

Every year the elementary school put on a Christmas program. The conclusion of the play was traditionally a nativity scene with the singing of "Silent Night" by the entire audience. Once there had been talk of removing the religious scene from the school, but such an outcry arose that the tradition remained. The town loved it, expected it, and turned out en masse to see the little ones dressed in sparkly, colorful costumes. Jade, with her milky skin and black hair, would be a beautiful angel.

Jesse came around the end of a row where he'd been cutting trees for a grocer who had requested a second load.

"What's all the noise about?" he demanded, his expression teasingly fierce. "I can't even hear my chain saw with you two carrying on this way."

Jade threw her arms around his legs and repeated her request for an angel costume. The fun drained out of Jesse's face.

"Lindsey's too busy with the farm," he said shortly.

Jade's happy expression fell, and Lindsey couldn't bear to see her disappointment.

Jesse had behaved strangely all day, his manner brusque and distant. He'd even refused their usual lunch break of sandwiches in the Snack Shack, saying he'd eat later. But there was no reason for him to dim Jade's happiness.

"Making a costume for Jade would be my pleasure. You know that."

"Don't bother yourself." Jesse spun away and started back into the trees.

"Jesse." She caught up to him, touched his arm.

"I'd love to make the costume for Jade. What's wrong with you today?"

"You're not her mother. Stop trying to be."

Stricken to the core, Lindsey cringed and pressed a shaky hand to her lips. Was that what he thought? That she wanted to take Erin's place?

Jesse shoved both hands over his head. "Look. I shouldn't have said that. I'm sorry. It's just that—" His expression went bleak. He squeezed his eyes closed. "No excuses. I'm sorry."

"Daddy." Jade, whom they'd both momentarily forgotten, slipped between them, tears bright in her green eyes. "It's okay. I don't have to be in the play."

Lindsey thought her heart would break—for the child, for herself and even for the troubled man.

Jesse fell to his knees in front of Jade and gripped her fiercely to him, his face a mask of regret. "Daddy didn't mean it, Butterbean. You can be in the play."

Over her dark head, he gazed at Lindsey desolately. "Make the costume. It would mean a lot to both of us."

Throat thick with unshed tears, Lindsey nodded, confused and hurt. She'd never intended to touch a nerve. She'd only wanted to see the little girl happy.

Pushing Jade away a little, Jesse smoothed her dark hair, leaving both hands cupped around her face. "You'll be the prettiest angel in the program. Lindsey will make sure of that." He raised pleading eyes. "Won't you, Lindsey?"

Like the Oklahoma weather, Jesse had changed from anger to remorse. Bewildered and reeling from his sharp accusation, Lindsey's stomach churned. But not wanting Jade to suffer any more disappointment, she swallowed her own hurt and agreed. "Jade and I can shop for materials tomorrow after school if that's okay."

She felt tentative with him in a way she never had before. What had brought on this vicious outburst in the first place?

"Whatever you decide is fine. Anything." Rising, he turned Jade toward the Snack Shack. Lindsey knew their conversation wasn't over, but he didn't want the little girl to hear any more. "Better head up there and do your homework. You and Lindsey can talk about the costume later."

With the resilience of childhood, Jade started toward the building, but froze when the German shepherd bolted from the trees to follow.

"Sushi!" Lindsey commanded. "Come." The disappointed dog obeyed, coming to flop in disgust at Lindsey's feet. Jade was making progress, but not enough to be alone in the building with the animal.

As soon as the door closed behind his daughter, Jesse said, "You have been nothing but good to Jade and me. I had no right to snap at you, to say such an awful thing."

"I'm not trying to replace Erin," she said quietly.

"I know. I'm sorry." Absently, he stroked the adoring dog, his body still stiff with tension. "How can I make it up to you?"

"Forget it ever happened." She smiled, perhaps a bit tremulously, although she felt better knowing he hadn't intended to hurt her. "And I'll do the same."

His jaw tightened. Her forgiveness seemed to anger him. "Don't be so nice all the time, Lindsey. When someone treats you like dirt, take up for yourself."

She wanted to disagree. Arguing over small injustices and taking offense served no good that she could see, but Jesse seemed bent on picking a fight. And she refused to play into his bad mood. "I don't understand you today."

"Welcome to the club." He shoved his hands in his pockets and looked up at the gray-blue sky. "I'm a jerk, Lindsey. You should fire me."

She longed to comfort him, though she was the wounded party. Normally, Jesse was easygoing and pleasant company. More than pleasant company, if she admitted the truth. But something was terribly wrong today, and getting her back up wasn't the solution.

"Your job is safe. I can't get along without you."

The Freudian slip resounded in the chilly afternoon air. She not only couldn't get along without him, she didn't want to. He'd become too important.

Resisting the urge to smooth her fingers over the rigid line of his jaw and tell him that, another wayward notion drifted through her mind. Jesse Slater, even in a bad mood, was a better man than her former fiancé would ever be. Her stomach hurt to make the comparison, but the ache cleared when she realized that no matter what torment beat inside Jesse, he was too honorable to do the kind of things Sean had done. Jesse knew when he was wrong and apologized. Sean never had.

His gaze riveted on the sky, Jesse's quiet voice was

filled with repressed emotion. "Do you think God plays favorites?"

Lindsey blinked. Where had that come from? And what did it have to do with sewing an angel costume? "Do you?"

"Sure seems that way."

"Is that what's bothering you today? You think God doesn't care about you as much as He does other people?"

"I've wondered." A muscle twitched along one cheekbone. "But maybe I don't deserve it."

She ran her fingertips over the soft needles of the closest tree, praying for the right words to help her friend. "Jesus loved us—all of us—so much He died for us."

"I've been giving that a lot of thought lately." He studied the ground as if the Oklahoma dirt held the answers to the mysteries of the universe. "But not everyone is as good as you are, Lindsey. Definitely not me."

Lindsey's pulse did a stutter-step.

"I'm not perfect, Jesse," she said. "I've done things I'm not proud of, too."

Picking up her shears, she clipped at a wayward branch, unable to look at Jesse but compelled to share. "I was engaged once."

Snip. Snip. She swallowed, nervous. "And I did things I regret. I trusted the wrong man, telling myself that love made our actions all right." She snipped again, saw the shears tremble. "But that was a mistake. He was a mistake."

Jesse's work-hardened hand closed over hers, gently taking the clippers. "Lindsey."

Her gaze flew to his face.

She wondered if she had disappointed him, but Jesse needed to understand that she had made her share of wrong choices—and yet God loved her.

Fire flashed in Jesse's silvery eyes. "The man," he said, "was a moron."

Sweet relief washed through Lindsey. Jesse wasn't angry *at* her. He was angry *for* her.

"So was I. Then. But God forgave me, and eventually I forgave myself." She reached for the cutters, her fingers grazing his. "He'll do the same for you."

"Yeah. Well…" Jesse let the words drift away.

She knew he'd tried to serve God in the past, but had drifted away when Erin died. Understandable, but so backwards. She'd learned the hard way to run *to* the Lord when trouble struck instead of away from Him.

They stood in silence, contemplative for a bit until Jesse bent to retrieve the chain saw.

"Guess we better get back to work if I'm going to haul that load in the morning."

For all the conversation, trouble still brooded over him like a dark cloud.

"Jesse."

He paused.

"Is there anything else bothering you?" she asked, certain that there was. "Anything I can help with?"

Silver eyes studied her for several long seconds. He took her hand and squeezed it. "I'm grateful to you, Lindsey. No matter what happens. Remember that."

Puzzled by the strange declaration, Lindsey waited for him to say more, but before he could, a truck rumbled through the gate, and the moment was gone. As if relieved by the interruption, Jesse hurried to greet the customer.

She'd seen so much change in Jesse since the day he'd first driven into her yard asking for a job. She'd watched him grow more comfortable with her talk of God. He was easier around the Christmas decorations too, and since telling her of Erin's death, he'd opened up some about his feelings of guilt in that department. And he smiled more too.

But today, regardless of his denial, Jesse battled something deep and worrisome. And given his peculiar behavior, she had a bad feeling that his troubles had something to do with her.

Heat from the farmhouse embraced Jesse as he came through the door. The dog, curled beside the living-room furnace, lifted her head, recognized him, and lay down again with a heavy sigh. Jesse stood for a moment in the doorway, taking in the warm, homey comfort of this place. A sense of déjà vu came over him, a subconscious memory of long ago when the world had been right.

The aroma of roast beef tickled his nose and made his hungry stomach growl. The tree patch was quiet, only one buyer since noon, and Lindsey had knocked off early to make Jade's costume and cook supper for them all. After his behavior the other day, he found it hard to refuse her anything.

Jade's giggle blended with Lindsey's rich laugh in a sweet music that had Jesse longing to hear it again and again. They were at the table, happily laboring over some kind of gauzy white material and yards of sparkly gold tinsel.

He'd been wrong to jump on Lindsey about making the costume and even more wrong to accuse her of trying to take Erin's place. No one could do that. But Lindsey's love and motherly care was changing Jade for the better. Only a fool would deny or resent the obvious.

And he'd almost told Lindsey the truth. He'd yearned to admit that her farm was his and that he wanted it back. The torment was eating him alive because, to get what he wanted, he had to break Lindsey's heart. He'd tried praying, as she had suggested, but his prayers bounced off the ceiling and mocked him.

Lindsey spotted him, then, standing in the doorway, watching. Her full mouth lifted. "You look frozen."

He gave a shiver for effect. The temperature had plummeted into the twenties, unusual for this part of the country. Working outside in the Oklahoma wind proved a challenge.

"I thought you could make that costume in an hour?"

"I can. But I'm teaching Jade."

Stripping off his heavy coat, he came on into the kitchen. "Isn't she too little for sewing?"

"Daddy!" Insulted, Jade jammed a saucy hand onto

a hip. "I have to learn sometime. Besides, I'm the tryer-on-er."

Amused, he tilted his head in apology. "I stand corrected."

"We'll have the body of the gown finished in a few minutes. Coffee's on and Cokes are in the fridge. Whichever you want."

No matter how cold the weather, Jesse liked his cola. Going to the refrigerator, he took one, popped the top and turned to watch the womenfolk do their thing.

Patiently, Lindsey held the gauzy fabric beneath the sewing-machine needle, demonstrating how to move the gown without sewing her own fingers. She looked so pretty with her honey hair falling forward, full lips pursed in concentration. He'd been right the first time he'd seen her. Lindsey, beneath her flannel and denim, was very much a woman.

He sipped his cola, wanting to look away, but he couldn't. Watching Lindsey gave him too much pleasure.

When the seam was sewn, Jade took the scissors and proudly clipped the thread.

"There you go, Miss Angel." Lindsey held the white flowing garment against Jade's body. "Perfect fit."

Jade looked doubtful. "Where's the wings?"

"We'll do those after supper. Jesse, if you'll move the machine, we can set the table."

"Anything to hurry the food." He unplugged the old Singer that must have belonged to her grandmother, and hefted it into Lindsey's spare room.

"Tell me your part again," Lindsey was saying as he came back into the kitchen.

"Below the angel's shining light, love was born on Christmas night," Jade recited, slowly and with expression.

"You're going to be the very best speaker." Scooping the remaining materials off the table, Lindsey spoke to Jesse. "Isn't she, Dad?"

"No doubt about it." He hooked an arm around Jade's middle and hoisted her up. Her giggle made him smile. "And the prettiest angel, too."

"Are you going to come watch me?"

The question caught him by surprise. Slowly, he eased her down into a chair. "Well...I don't know, Jade. I'm awfully busy here at the tree farm."

Whipping around, a steaming bowl in one hand, Lindsey refused to let him use that excuse. "We'll be closed that night."

Jade was getting too involved with all this Christmas business. Next thing he knew, she'd be talking about Santa Claus and wanting to hang up stockings.

"I'm not much on Christmas programs. You two can go without me."

Both females looked at him with mild reproach. The room grew deafeningly quiet until only the tick of the furnace was heard.

Finally, Lindsey slapped a loaf of bread onto the table and turned on him. Her golden-brown eyes glowed with a hint of anger. "The program is important to Jade, and you need to be there. You might actually enjoy yourself."

He doubted that, but he didn't want Lindsey upset with him again. He was still battling guilt over the last time.

With a defeated sigh, he followed her to the stove, took the green peas from her and carried the bowl to the table.

"All right, Butterbean," he said, tapping Jade on the nose. "If the tree lot is closed, I'll be there."

"Really, Daddy?" The hope in her eyes did him in.

"Really."

Her beauteous smile lit the room and illuminated his heart.

As he drew his chair up to the table, the familiar gnaw of dread pulled at his stomach. A Christmas program. What had he gotten himself into?

The atmosphere at the Winding Stair Elementary School was one of controlled chaos. After dropping an angelic Jade at her classroom with a gaggle of lambs and ladybugs, Jesse followed Lindsey down the long hall to the auditorium. The noise of a community that knew each other well filled the place with cheer. Everyone they passed spoke to Lindsey and many, recognizing him, stopped to shake his hand and offer greetings.

He hadn't been to a school Christmas program since he was in grade school himself, but the buzz of excitement was the same.

At the door, a teenage girl in a red Santa hat offered him a program and a huge flirtatious smile.

"Hi, Lindsey," she said, though her eyelashes fluttered at him. He ignored her, staring ahead at the milieu of country folks gathered in this one place.

Lindsey greeted the girl warmly, then began the slow process of weaving through the crowd toward the seats. She'd been right. The program was a community event. Everyone was dressed up, the scent of recent showers and cologne a testament to the importance of Winding Stair's Christmas program.

"I think you have an admirer," Lindsey teased when they were seated.

He knew she meant the teenager at the door, but the idea insulted him. "She's a kid."

Lindsey laughed softly. "But she's not blind or stupid."

Surprised, he turned in the squeaky auditorium seat. What had she meant by that? But Lindsey had taken a sudden interest in studying the photocopied program.

"Look here." She pointed. "Jade is on stage for a long time."

"No kidding?" He looked over her shoulder with interest. The sweet scent of jasmine rose up from the vicinity of her elegant neck and tantalized his senses. From the time she'd climbed into his truck, he'd enjoyed the fragrance, but up close this way was even nicer.

She looked pretty tonight, too. He'd never seen her in a real dress and when she'd opened the front door, he'd lost his breath. Surprise, of course, nothing more. In honor of the occasion, she wore red, a smooth, sweater kind of dress that looked pretty with her honey-colored hair.

The lights flickered, a signal he supposed, for the crowd hushed and settled into their seats. The doors on each side of the auditorium closed and the principal stepped out in front of the blue velvet curtain to welcome everyone.

In moments, the curtains swooshed apart, and Jesse waited eagerly for the moment his baby would come on stage.

The program was festive and colorful and full of exuberant good will if not exceptional talent. Most of the children were animals of some sort and each group sang to the accompaniment of a slightly out-of-tune piano.

When two ladybugs bumped heads, entangling their antenna, Jesse laughed along with the rest of the crowd. A teacher scuttled from backstage, parted the antenna and with a smiling shrug, disappeared again. The children seemed unfazed.

Another time, one of the fireflies dropped his flashlight and the batteries came clattering out. To the delight of the audience, the little boy crawled through legs and around various other insects until he'd retrieved all the scattered parts of his illumination.

Despite his hesitancy to come tonight, Jesse was having a good time. None of the awful, tearing agony of loss overtook him as he'd expected. He had to credit Lindsey and his little angel for that.

"There she is," Lindsey whispered and pushed at

his shoulder as if he couldn't see for himself the vision moving onto the stage.

Beneath the spotlight, his angel glittered and glowed in the costume Lindsey had so lovingly created. Her halo of tinsel shimmered against the shining raven hair as she bent to hover over the manger. Even from this distance, he could see her squinting into the crowd, looking for him.

In a sweet, bell-like voice, she spoke her lines, and Jesse reacted as if he hadn't heard them a thousand times in the past two weeks.

"Beneath the angel's shining light, love was born on Christmas night."

Tenderness rose in his throat, enough to choke him.

As he watched Jade, angel wings outstretched, join her class in singing "Silent Night," he thought his heart would burst with pride. Such sweetness. Such beauty. And he'd almost missed it.

Erin should have been here, too.

He waited for the familiar pain to come, and was surprised when it didn't.

Jade caught sight of him somehow and her entire face brightened. Had she thought he wouldn't stay?

With a start, he realized how wrong he'd been to let his own loss and pain affect his child's happiness and well-being. Huddled in his darkness, he'd let two years of Jade's life pass in a blur while he nursed his wounds and felt sorry for himself.

As the program ended and Jade was swept away in the thundering mass of first-graders, Jesse looked down. At some point during the play, he'd taken hold of Lindsey's hand and pulled it against his thigh. How had that happened? And why didn't he turn her loose now that the play was over? But with her small fingers wrapped in his, he was reluctant to let her go.

"She was wonderful," Lindsey said, eyes aglow as she turned to him.

"The best one of all."

"Of course." And they both laughed, knowing every parent in the room thought the same thing about his or her own child.

And even though she wasn't Jade's parent, Jesse knew Lindsey loved his daughter unreservedly.

Still holding her hand, and bewildered by his own actions, Jesse rose and began the shuffle out of the jammed auditorium and down the hall to the classrooms. There they collected Jade from the rambunctious crowd of first-graders and headed out the exit.

"Excuse me." A man about Jesse's age stopped them as they started down the concrete steps. A vague sense of recognition stirred in Jesse's memory. "I saw you earlier and couldn't help thinking that I should know you? Did you ever go to school here?"

Jesse stiffened momentarily before forcing his shoulders to relax. No use getting in a panic. Play it cool. "Sorry. I'm a newcomer. Moved here back in October."

The man tilted his head, frowning. "You sure remind me of a kid I went to junior high with. Aw, but that's a long time ago."

"Well, you know what they say." Jesse shrugged,

hoping he sounded more casual than he felt. "Everybody looks like someone."

"Ain't that the truth? My wife says I'm starting to resemble my hound dog more and more every day."

They all laughed, and then using the excuse of the cold wind, Jesse led the way to the truck. He'd been expecting that to happen. Sooner or later, someone was bound to recognize him from junior high school. He glanced at Lindsey as she slid into the pickup. Still smiling and fussing over Jade, she hadn't seemed to notice anything amiss.

Cranking the engine, he breathed a sigh of relief. That was a close one.

Chapter 10

"Ice cream, Daddy. Pleeease." Jade, who'd begged to keep her costume on, bounced in the seat of the Silverado. She was still hyper, wired up from her very first Christmas program. With every bounce, her angel wings batted against Lindsey's shoulder.

Lindsey awaited Jesse's reply, hoping he'd see how much Jade needed a few more minutes of reveling in the moment.

Jesse shook his head as he turned on the defrosters. "Too cold for ice cream."

The three of them had rushed across the schoolyard to the parking lot, eager to escape the cold wind after the brief, but chill-producing delay by the man who'd thought Jesse looked familiar. The truck was running and heat had begun to blow from the vents, but they still shivered.

"Hot fudge will counter the cold," Lindsey suggested, casting a sideways grin at Jesse. "We gotta celebrate."

"You're no help," he said, rolling his silver eyes. "But if you ladies want ice cream, ice cream you shall have. Let's head to the Dairy Cup."

A quiver of satisfaction moved through Lindsey. Jesse had enjoyed tonight, she was certain. But what had really stunned her was when he'd reached over and grasped her hand. For a second, she'd almost forgotten where she was, though she doubted Jesse had meant anything by it. Most likely, he'd reached for her in reaction to Jade's thrilling grand entrance. Still, those moments of her skin touching his while they shared Jade's triumph lingered sweetly in her mind.

As the truck rumbled slowly down Main Street, her legs began to thaw.

"I'll be glad when the weather warms up again," she said.

Jesse's wrist relaxed over the top of the steering wheel. "Supposed to tomorrow, isn't it?"

"Some. But there's a chance of snow too."

"Snow!" Jade exclaimed and started bouncing again. "Can we make a snowman?"

Lindsey patted the child's knee. "Wouldn't be any fun unless we did."

Jesse glanced her way. "I have a load of trees to haul to Mena tomorrow. I hope we don't get snow before that's done."

"If it snows, you can't haul those trees. These mountain roads can be treacherous in snow or ice."

"Might as well get the job done. I have some other business to take care of in Mena, too."

His personal business intrigued her, though she would never pry. Several times he'd taken off an afternoon for "business reasons." And just last Sunday at church someone had mentioned seeing him at the municipal building several times. What kind of business would require so many visits to the courthouse?

"Well, all right, stubborn. I'll just pray the snow holds off."

She managed to distract the wiggling Jade by pointing out the Christmas decorations visible everywhere. They drove past closed businesses gaily decorated with white stenciled greetings and flashing red and green lights. Fiber-optic trees rotated in some display windows, and attached to the light posts were giant candy canes that caught the reflection of car lights and wobbled with each gust of wind.

Winding Stair looked as lovely and quaint as always at Christmas.

"This town is like a step back in time," Jesse said, as though he'd read her mind.

"I love it."

"The place grows on you, that's for sure."

She wasn't certain what he meant by that, but at least he hadn't criticized her beloved town. Small, provincial and backwoods it might be, but Winding Stair took care of its own.

"There are a lot of good people here. Not fancy, but good to the bone."

He stared at her across Jade's head for so long she feared he'd run a stop sign.

"Yeah," he finally said. "There are."

What was that supposed to mean?

Her pulse was still thudding in consternation when they pulled into the graveled drive of the Dairy Cup and got out. From the number of cars around the café, other playgoers had also experienced a sudden need for celebration.

Jade raced to the door, black hair blowing wildly from beneath her tinsel halo. Her wings sparkled and jostled against her back. Lindsey had wanted to replace the wings with a coat, but Jade had pleaded to wear the costume a while longer. They had compromised by sliding the coat onto her arms—backwards.

The small, independently owned Dairy Cup boasted all of five booths and a short counter with three stools. Jesse took the only empty spot, a back booth next to the jukebox. Lindsey slid onto the green vinyl seat across from him while Jade rushed to the jukebox.

"Can we play a song, Daddy?"

Jesse fished in his pocket and handed over a quarter.

"The menu is up there," Lindsey said, pointing to a signboard above the cash register. "Tell me what you want and I'll go up and order for us."

"My treat," Jesse said. "I owe you for making me go to the play tonight."

She smiled, pleased at his admission. "So you really did have a good time?"

"Yeah. A real good time." He folded his hard-working hands on the tabletop. "So what will you have, Miss Mitchell?"

Jade's quarter clunked in the slot. A slow, romantic love song poured out of the machine.

You, Lindsey wanted to say. And the thought shocked her. She looked up at the menu so that Jesse couldn't read the answer in her eyes.

"Chili sounds good."

"I thought you were all for hot fudge."

She flopped her palms out to each side and grinned. "I'm female. I changed my mind."

"Chili sounds good to me too." He turned in the seat toward his daughter. She was twirling in a circle to the music, the glitter on her wings sparkling beneath the fluorescent lights. "Hey, Butterbean, what do you want?"

She twirled right on over to him and plopped onto the vinyl seat. She took his cheeks between her small hands and smooched him. "A hotdog."

"A hotdog! You wanted ice cream."

She shrugged small shoulders. The gossamer wings rose and fell, and then she scooted out of the booth and began twirling again. "A hotdog."

Lindsey pressed a hand to her mouth, suppressing a giggle.

Jesse shook his head, the edges of his mouth quivering. "Women. I'll never understand them."

Pretending exasperation, he rose and went to order.

Lindsey watched him. In truth, she couldn't keep her eyes off him. Though the notion was ridiculous, she felt as if they were on a date. All evening, there had been small sparks between them. He'd even looked at her differently when she'd opened the door wearing a dress. Something had happened tonight, some subtle change in their relationship. And she knew without a doubt, this was something she'd better pray about.

The next afternoon, Jesse pulled the long flatbed truck next to the curb on a side street in the town of Mena. Lindsey's prayers must have worked because the snow had held off, although the sky had that shiny white glare that usually meant wintry weather. He was loaded down with trees, but the delivery stop would have to wait. This one couldn't.

A row of nicely appointed residences, all with wide lawns and wreaths on the doors, lined the street. He pulled the small scrap of paper from his jacket and read the number for the hundredth time. Yes, this was the place. According to his information, a retired lawyer lived here. Stuart Hardwick.

Heart racing, he strode to the door and knocked. He'd rehearsed his speech all the way from Winding Stair, but when the door opened, the words stuck in his throat.

An old man, with a bulbous nose and a shock of white hair, squinted at him. "Yes?"

"Mr. Hardwick?"

"I'm Hardwick. Who are you?"

"Jesse Slater." Placing a hand on the wooden door

to keep it from being closed in his face, he said, "May I come in? We need to talk."

"I don't know you, Mr. Slater."

Using his free hand, Jesse fumbled for the copied document, drew it out and flipped it open beneath Hardwick's nose. "You knew my stepfather, Les Finch."

The old man peered at the paper, scratching his chin. "Maybe I did and maybe I didn't. I worked for a lot of folks over the years."

"Could we at least discuss it?"

Hardwick considered for a minute before stepping back. "Too cold to stand in the door. Come on in."

Passing through a small entry, they entered a musty-smelling, overheated living room. The man clicked on a lamp and shuffled to a table littered with glasses and papers.

"Care for a drink, Mr. Slater?" He lifted a half-empty whiskey bottle.

"No thanks." After living with Les Finch, strong drink had never tempted Jesse.

"You won't mind if I do then." After filling a glass to the rim, he sipped, then sat down in a chair and waved for Jesse to do the same.

"Now what's this business of yours? Let me see that paper."

Jesse handed over the form his stepfather had signed, making the sale of Jesse's farm valid.

"Eighteen years ago my mother died, leaving her parents' farm to me. My stepfather, Les Finch, somehow managed to sell the place, claiming ownership."

"What's that got to do with me?"

"Someone smarter about legal and business affairs than Les had to do the paperwork."

"And you think I'm that man?"

"I know you are."

"Look, son, I'm an old man. Retired now. Eighteen years is a long time." His tone was soothing, compassionate, and Jesse figured he had perfected this tone in years of making deals. "Why don't you just let this thing go?"

"Because I have a little girl, and she deserves the home I never had. That farm belongs to me, and I want it back—for her."

Studying the paper, the lawyer took another sip of whiskey. "This document looks legal enough to me. How are you planning to prove the place is yours?"

"You. I want you to tell the truth. Confess that you helped Les Finch figure a way to forge my mother's name to forms that gave him ownership."

"Whoa now, boy. You're accusing me of a crime."

The old hypocrite. He *had* committed a crime, probably more than one. Anger hotter than the stifling room temperature rose in Jesse.

"What did he pay you, Hardwick?" he asked through clenched teeth. "Part of the profits? A gallon of Kentucky bourbon?"

Jesse regretted his outburst immediately. Stuart Hardwick's bulbous nose flared in anger while his manner grew cool as the December day.

"I'm afraid I can't help you, Mr. Slater. Now if you will excuse me, it's time for my afternoon nap."

He tossed back the remaining liquor and pushed out of the chair.

Jesse leaped to his feet, unwilling to let the crooked lawyer off the hook. He squeezed his hands tight to keep from grabbing Hardwick by the shirt collar and wringing the truth out of him.

"Listen, old man, Les Finch stole everything I owned, moved me off to an unfamiliar city, and then tossed me out like a stray dog when I was barely fifteen. Scared, alone, heartbroken, hungry. Do you know what that's like?" He slammed his fists together. "That's never going to happen to my little girl. Never."

Hardwick turned away, went to the table and poured another drink. His hand trembled on the glass. "Any man who'd treat a kid so badly isn't worth much."

"No, he's not. He wasn't." The lawyer stood so long with his back turned, leaning on the table with shoulders slumped and the whiskey in front of him, that Jesse softened. "Maybe you didn't know that Finch would abandon me once he had his hands on the sale money. Maybe you would have done things differently if you'd known. Isn't that reason enough to help me now?"

Hardwick slowly shook his head. "I don't know, boy. Like I said, that was a long time ago." He took a deep pull of the liquor, shuddered, and backhanded his mouth. "Tell you what. You write down where you can be contacted. If I remember anything, I'll get in touch."

There was nothing left for Jesse to do short of physical violence, and he wouldn't lower himself to that.

Deflated and disheartened, he scribbled his address on the back of the paper and left the house.

By the time he reached the retailer who'd ordered the extra load of pines, he'd regained a splinter of hope. After all, Hardwick hadn't flatly refused to help him. If the old bird had any conscience left at all, maybe he'd still come through.

"Looks like a nice bunch of trees, Mr. Slater," the lot owner said as he inspected the pines piled high on Lindsey's flatbed.

Pride welled up inside Jesse as he slipped on his leather gloves and loosened the tie-down ropes to unload. "Miss Mitchell takes very good care of her lot. All her trees are in perfect condition like this."

"My customers have sure been happy with that first load you brought in. They sold fast." The owner waved his hand toward the Christmas trees remaining on his lot. "These you see out here now came in from out of state, but they're about gone too. Can't be running low on trees with Christmas still more than a week away."

To Jesse's way of thinking, the out-of-state pines weren't half as green and well-shaped as Lindsey's. The man should have bought all his stock from the Christmas Tree Farm.

The lot owner turned toward his office and bellowed, "Jerry, get out here and help get these trees in place."

A man, presumably Jerry, came out, buttoning his coat against the chill, and began moving the trees onto the lot. In minutes, the three had unloaded the truck.

As Jesse shouldered a final baled pine, an idea

came to him. "Mr. Bailey, have you ever considered ordering all your trees from us? You can't get trees this fresh anywhere else."

The man stopped, thought a minute, then said, "You're right about that, but I like to offer more variety to my customers. You folks have nice trees, but all of them are Virginias."

"Look out there, Mr. Bailey." Jesse gestured to where the new Virginia pines were being erected alongside the less fresh trees. "Which do you think people will buy? Will they care if it's a Virginia instead of a Scotch, or will they want the freshest, prettiest tree available?"

"Got a point there, Slater. Tell you what." He dug in his pocket for a business card. "I own six lots in this part of the country. You have Miss Mitchell give me a call when the season ends, and we'll talk about it. Maybe we can work out a deal for next year."

Jesse's spirits soared. An exclusive sale to six area dealers would be a huge boost to Lindsey's business. They'd need to clear and plant more acres, but that was no problem. He could do it.

With a firm handshake and a hearty thanks, Jesse leaped into the truck and started back up the winding road toward home. He slapped the steering wheel and whistled "Jingle Bells" as the old truck bounced and chugged up the mountain. Visions of Lindsey's golden eyes, her tawny hair and her pretty smile danced before him sweeter than sugar plums.

Man, he couldn't wait to tell her the news and to

feel her smoky laugh wrap around him like a warm hug. She'd be so happy.

And she'd think he was the biggest hero in town.

The cheerful thoughts no sooner filtered through his brain than reality crowded in.

His fingers tightened on the wheel.

For now he had to play the role of Mr. Nice Guy, helping Lindsey's business grow and prosper. For the sake of his child, he had to lie and deceive. He wasn't sure what that made him, but one thing was for sure— he was nobody's hero.

Chapter 11

Fat white flakes of snow began falling about an hour before closing time. The last customer, her tree in the back of an SUV, hurried away before the roads became troublesome.

Standing beneath the dark sky, snow swirling around her in the still cold, Lindsey knew they'd have no more business tonight. She stroked a hand over Sushi's pointed ears, smiling when the dog licked at a snowflake.

Jesse's news about a possible exclusive contract had been especially encouraging, given how slow the farm had been for the last several days. Her big days were always on the weekends, but with an employee's wages to pay, she needed cash coming in.

She'd tried not to worry, trying instead to pray and

let the Lord handle everything. And the possibility of selling more trees locally was surely an answer to those prayers. The lot owner in Mena had paid cash for this last load, too, and that was doubly good news. She lifted her heart in silent gratitude.

Jesse had been, for him, almost animated when he'd arrived home that afternoon. She'd laughed with joy, restraining the urge to throw her arms around him. Lately, she wanted to do that every time she saw her hired hand.

"Might as well shut down for the night," she said, pulse accelerating as he came toward her. Crossing the short, shadowy distance between them, he looked lean and mysterious and incredibly attractive.

"Where's Jade?" His voice raised goose bumps on her arms.

She rubbed at them and hitched her chin toward the Snack Shack. "Inside."

His boots crunched as he twisted toward the building. "Let's get her and take a ride. Puddin's still harnessed."

"Are you serious?" Although she enjoyed driving families through the trees, she'd never taken a ride for her own personal pleasure. Riding alone had held no attraction. But riding with Jesse...

"Come on. It'll be fun." He paused, then frowned down at her in concern. "Unless you're too tired."

"No. No. Not at all." In fact, energy strong enough to run the Christmas lights suddenly zipped through her. "A ride sounds wonderful."

"You know what they say in this part of the country. Enjoy the snow fast." He rubbed his gloved hands together and smiled. "It will be gone tomorrow."

Lindsey's stomach went south. If she'd known a wagon ride would make him smile, she'd have suggested one sooner.

"Race ya to the shack," she said, eager to encourage his cheerful mood. "Last one to tell Jade is a rotten egg."

Before Jesse could react, she grabbed the advantage and took off in a hard run.

"Hey!" His boots thudded against the hard ground, and she watched his long shadow rapidly overtaking hers. Catching up in record time, Jesse nabbed her elbow. As if she'd reached the end of a bungee cord, Lindsey plummeted backward, banging into his chest.

He quickly righted her so that she wouldn't fall, and they stood staring at each other, smiling and panting. His strong, workman's hands held her by the upper arms. Bright Christmas lights around the window of the shack blinked off and on, bathing them in alternating shades of red and green.

Sushi leaped around their legs, barking in excitement.

"Cheater," he said, eyes twinkling an odd shade of blue in the rotating light.

He was inches away, his mouth so close and so tempting. She wanted him to kiss her.

The door to the Snack Shack opened behind them, and Jade called out in a worried voice. "Why is Sushi barking?" And then the child noticed the fluffy white flakes. "It's snowing!"

Coatless, she rushed outside and twirled around, grabbing for snowflakes, fear of the dog forgotten in her excitement.

Jesse dropped his hands and stepped away from Lindsey. A vague, but troubling disappointment crept over her. She had no business wanting more from Jesse than friendship. Crossing her arms, she hugged herself against the sudden cold.

"Get back inside and get your coat on," Jesse called, moving menacingly toward Jade.

The child yelped like a stepped-on pup and, giggling, bolted for the warm building. Jesse growled like a bear and gave chase.

Trying to forget that infinitesimal moment when she'd thought Jesse might kiss her, Lindsey followed them inside.

"Yay! Yay! Yay!" Jade cried, hopping and dancing and squealing in the wagon bed. She opened her mouth, trying to catch snowflakes on her tongue.

"Better get under those covers, Butterbean."

To Lindsey, the child's exuberance was a refreshing change from the frightened little girl of months ago. She still feared the dark and anything unfamiliar, but according to Jesse the nightmares had slowly disappeared, and she seemed so much easier in her own skin.

At her daddy's suggestion, though, Jade settled down and slid beneath the downy covers. She hummed happily.

After a double-check of Puddin's harness, Lindsey

came around to step up into the wagon. Jesse appeared at her side, hand on her elbow, and guided her safely onto the bench. She felt both feminine and foolish, considering the number of times she'd boarded alone.

Sushi stood on the ground a few feet away, tail thumping madly, mouth open and smiling, begging to join the fun.

Lindsey twisted around. "Jade, Sushi wants to ride with us."

She let the suggestion hang in the air, waiting for the little girl to make the decision.

Jade levered up to peer over the side at the begging German shepherd who managed to look so pitiful Lindsey was hard-pressed not to laugh.

"Okay." Jade pointed toward the very end of the wagon. "Down there."

Lindsey rejoiced for the progress.

Jesse gave a quick look of gratitude and squeezed her hand.

Once the dog was safely ensconced, Jesse rattled the reins and Puddin' plodded forward. Jingle bells, attached to the sides, tickled the air and blended with Christmas carols still echoing from the sound system.

Jesse didn't complain about the carols anymore. Could he be healing?

Heart full and happy for reasons she hadn't yet considered, Lindsey clapped her hands and began singing at the top of her lungs.

Jesse laughed.

The beautiful, male sound thrilled her so much that

she sang all the louder, standing in the wagon to throw her hands into the air.

"You're crazy, woman." And he laughed again.

Jade crawled from beneath her covers to join the rowdiness. Jesse shook his head. "Now you're corrupting my daughter."

Lindsey gave him a playful push. "Oh, come on, Scrooge, sing."

"You don't know what you're asking for." He guided the horse along the perimeter of the trees, turning down a wide alleyway. "For all you know, I can't carry a tune."

"You can't be that bad." When he only grinned, she taunted, "Can you?"

As she'd hoped, Jesse rose to the teasing challenge. In the next moment, all three were belting out a loud and energetic version of "Frosty the Snowman" with Jesse providing the "thumpety, thump, thump" at the appropriate time.

At the end of the song, they all laughed so hard, tears welled in Lindsey's eyes. Jade flopped onto the seat between the adults, pointing out every snowflake that landed on the horse's back, asking questions about angels and Jesus and Christmas. While the briskly refreshing air reddened noses and cheeks, the pleasure of a family feeling warmed Lindsey from the inside out. She loved this little girl as if she'd borne her.

At last, Jade's energy was exhausted, and she drooped against her daddy's side. He stopped the wagon.

"Looks like the princess is tuckered out," he said quietly.

Scooping her into his arms, he carried Jade to the wagon bed and gently placed her beneath the quilts.

Lindsey turned on the seat to watch them, heart overflowing as Jesse adjusted his daughter's covers, snugging them securely under her chin. When he bent to kiss the angel face, Lindsey knew what she'd been trying to deny for so long. She not only loved Jade.

She loved Jade's daddy.

She'd been building to this moment since the day he'd arrived. Over the weeks, he'd not only lightened her workload and given her great new ideas for the farm, he'd filled her with a new sense of purpose and joy.

Closing her eyes at the wonder and beauty of so tremendous an emotion, she felt the wagon give as Jesse returned to his seat.

"Ready to head for home?" he asked, his voice muted.

She turned to look at him and knew the light of love was there for him to see.

Snowflakes tumbled down and the ground resembled a sugar-sprinkled spice cake. Tips of tree branches were flocked white. Indeed, they needed to call it a night.

But she was reluctant to leave this cold cocoon that had been spun around them here in the snowy, lighted grove.

"Whenever you are." The words came out in a whisper.

Shifting on the seat, he said, "You're snow-kissed," and rubbed his thumb across her lower lip.

He stared at her for two beats, then bent his head and brushed his lips over hers. Where her mouth was cold, his was warm and subtle and incredibly tender. So tender, tears sprang to her eyes.

When the kiss ended, their gazes held for the longest time.

"You're a very special lady, Lindsey Mitchell," he said at last and leaned his forehead against hers. His warm breath puffed softly against her skin, raising gooseflesh.

Pulse tripping madly, Lindsey caressed his cheek. "No more special than you—and that little girl back there."

Straightening, he took her hand and pulled her close beside him on the wagon seat. "We were both a mess when we met you. But you've changed us. And I'm grateful."

"I love her." She dare not say she loved him, too, though it was true. She'd never expected to trust enough to love again, but even with his faults and moods, Jesse had proven himself a thousand times over to be an honorable man.

She wanted to ask his feelings for her. He cared, yes, but love? She didn't know.

Lord, she thought, I need Your direction. I've waited so long to love someone again. But is Jesse the right one? Or have I been alone too long to see things clearly?

She loved Jesse. There was no doubt in her mind

about that, and real love was always from God. But as much as she loved him, Lindsey loved the Lord more. As long as Jesse had spiritual issues to resolve, she would do what she'd done for so long—wait upon the Lord, and pray that He would renew her strength. Because, if Jesse was wrong for her, it would take all the strength she had to get over him.

"Jade loves you too," Jesse replied. He gazed off into the dark woods. "I don't know what to do about that."

"Do?" His statement bewildered her. "Love is a good thing, Jesse, not a problem you have to fix."

"I don't want her to be hurt anymore. Erin—" He shifted in the seat, putting distance between them as if he'd somehow betrayed his dead wife by kissing Lindsey.

Suddenly, the hurtful words of days ago came back to her. "Are you afraid that if Jade cares for me, she'll forget her mother? That I'll replace Erin in Jade's life?"

He shook his head in denial, but Lindsey felt his withdrawal. Giving her hand a quick squeeze and release, he gathered the reins, shook them, and set the horse plodding forward.

The tinkling bells had lost their cheer.

Jesse had the strongest urge to grab his child, get in his truck and run. Instead, he guided the placid Puddin' out of the Christmas trees toward the barn.

The jingle of harness and the plod of hoofed feet were the only sounds to break the pristine night.

He could never run far enough to forget what had just happened between him and Lindsey.

Lindsey.

"She won't."

Jesse shifted his gaze to the parka-clad woman beside him, mind too scattered to catch the drift of her conversation. "What?"

"Jade will remember Erin. Maybe not specifics, but she'll have memories. Most of all she'll remember the way her mother loved her."

"I hope so."

"She does. We've talked about it."

He blinked in surprise. "You and Jade talked about Erin?"

"She needs to talk about her mother, Jesse, to share her memories, to ask questions."

Discussing Erin had always hurt too much. He'd assumed Jade felt the same.

"What kind of questions could a six-year-old have?"

Lindsey blinked up at him. "Plenty. She asked me where her mama was now and if dying had hurt. Things like that."

"Oh, God." He squeezed his eyes closed. That his baby would worry about such things cut him to the quick.

"Yes. That's exactly what I told her. Because Erin was a Christian, she was with God now, in His big, wonderful house in Heaven."

"Did that upset her? Talking about her mother's death, I mean."

He'd never considered discussing such a horrible

event with a child. And at the time, Jade had barely been four. Surely she couldn't remember that much.

"Just the opposite. She seemed happy, relieved. Her little mind had some things about that day very confused."

Jumping down from the wagon to open the barn door, Jesse frowned. "What kind of things?"

"For some reason, Jade thought she was to blame for her mother's death."

The old wooden door scraped back, clattering against the wall. Snow swirled up from the motion.

"Where would she get such a crazy idea?"

"Who knows? Children don't think like we do. They're egocentric. The world turns because of them. So when something bad happens, it must have been because they were bad."

"That's ridiculous."

"She said you were mad for a long time." She stuck a gloved hand out and caught a giant snowflake. "I tried to explain the difference between mad and sad."

Climbing back onto the cart, Jesse rattled the reins to send the horse into the barn.

"She was right. I was angry."

"That's normal, isn't it?"

"But I never dreamed Jade would take the blame on herself or think I was mad at her. She's my heart. My reason for going on."

"She's very secure in your love, Jesse. You're a good father." The lights from the barn reflected in her guileless eyes. "We're making a memory book. A Mama and Jade memory book."

Something turned over in Jesse's chest. "What's that?"

"Jade is drawing pictures of all the things she remembers about her mother. And I'm helping her write down other memories." She touched his arm. "She won't forget."

No. Jade wouldn't forget. Not with Lindsey around to gently, lovingly preserve those precious memories.

Wonder expanded inside him.

What kind of woman would nurture a dead woman's memory for the sake of a child? A woman she hadn't even known?

He had the overpowering desire to kiss her again. To hold her and tell her all that was in his heart.

Lindsey Mitchell was something special.

She was sweet and good. And loving.

Indecision warred within him. Feelings, long sublimated, rose to the surface. Falling for Lindsey Mitchell was the worst thing that could happen, for both of them. She deserved better. He cared about her. He cared a lot and didn't ever want to see her hurt. And hurting her would be the ultimate end of their relationship.

Part of him wanted to confess everything here and now and beg her forgiveness. But fear held him back. He'd enjoyed their sweet kiss. He'd seen the tenderness in her eyes, and he didn't want to replace that affection with loathing.

Lindsey valued honesty above everything, and he'd lied to her from the beginning. She'd never forgive him for his deceit.

And what about Erin? Being faithful to her was as important to him as remembering was to Jade. He'd made a promise at her funeral to take care of their little girl. Giving her this farm was the only way he knew how to keep that promise.

Oh man. He was in a mess. For weeks, he'd envied Lindsey's easy way of praying, of turning troubles over to the Lord. More than anything, he wished he could do that now.

He'd known for a while that he wanted to kiss her. But tonight, she'd given him back his joy. He'd laughed and sung like a maniac—and enjoyed every crazy second.

Then when he'd looked around and had seen her surrounded by snowflakes, he'd no longer had the will to resist.

Long years from now when she was gone from this place, he'd recall the cold snow dissolving against her skin as he'd warmed her soft lips with his.

He drew the horse to a stop next to a stall, hopped to the ground and reached up for Lindsey. Swinging her down from the wagon, he stood with his hands on her waist. "I had fun."

"Me too." An ornery glint turned her eyes to gold. She poked a gloved finger into his chest. "And now that I know you can sing…"

He quirked a brow, glad they were still comfortable with one another. "Are you threatening blackmail?"

"Of course."

"A good Christian woman like you. What an example," he said mildly.

She whopped him on the arm and turned away to unharness the horse. Puddin' stood patiently waiting for his warm stall and extra feed.

"You didn't mind my talking to Jade about her mother, did you?"

"No. I'm glad." If he'd been a better father, he would have recognized the need.

"Good."

The barn grew silent. Outside, snow filtered down like feathers from angel wings. Jesse crossed to the feed bin. The rich scent of hay and sweet feed filled the shadowy barn.

"Jesse." Lindsey's hushed tone was serious again, warning him. His hand stilled on the galvanized feed bucket.

"Yeah?" He turned his head, but Lindsey stood with her back to him, her hands making absent circles on the horse's neck.

The bells on the harness jingled. Then another moment of silence passed. Jesse got a sinking feeling in the pit of his stomach.

Lindsey's shoulders rose and fell. The horse blew impatiently.

When she finally spoke, her smoky voice flowed out on a sigh. "I have feelings for you."

Jesse drew in a deep, sorrowful breath of horse-scented air and squeezed his eyes shut. He exhaled slowly, trying to control the riot inside his chest.

"I know," he said quietly. Dread, like a lead weight, pressed down on him. The last thing he needed right now was to get emotionally involved with a woman—especially this one. And yet, he was.

She gave a little self-deprecating laugh that hurt his heart. "Just wanted to get it out in the open. It won't affect our working together."

He'd never thought of Lindsey as anything but strong and capable. But she looked small and vulnerable beside the massive horse, her hair bunched around the neck of her coat in a child-like tangle.

What did he say without hurting her? The truth? That he'd come here under false pretenses. That he planned to take away the farm she worked so hard to hold on to? Did he tell her he felt something, too, but old grievances were too deeply engrained to turn back now?

He shook his head ruefully. No, the truth would hurt her most of all.

Pouring the sweet feed into the trough, he waited for the noise to subside and then said the only thing he could. "Not a problem."

Liar, he thought, his insides rattling like hail on the tin roof of his trailer.

Lindsey's feelings were a major problem.

And so were his own.

Chapter 12

Desperation drove Jesse down the curvy mountain road on Sunday morning. Desperation also allowed Jade to attend Sunday school with Lindsey at Winding Stair Chapel. Jesse dare not take Jade where he was going.

The only way to avoid more suffering on the part of everyone involved was to bring the situation to its rightful end. He'd give Stuart Hardwick one more opportunity to come clean and then he'd find his own lawyer and go to the sheriff. The story could break out into the open soon and Lindsey could discover the truth about him.

His chest tightened. Both were bound to happen anyway.

He wished he'd never met Lindsey Mitchell.

No. That wasn't true. He wished she didn't live on the property that belonged to him.

He never should have kissed her. The memory of her sweetness stayed with him like the haunting lyrics of a bittersweet song.

Halfway down the mountain, he passed the turn to Clarence Stone's place and slowed the Silverado, bringing the truck to a stop in the middle of the muddy road. A coyote leaped from the field and loped across in front of him. Jesse watched the wild, wily creature disappear.

He had taken a liking to the old farmer and had the strongest urge to drive up and talk to him.

He glanced at the clock on the dashboard.

"The guy's probably in church already," he muttered.

Just the same, he threw the truck into reverse, backed up and made the turn. All the way up the road, he questioned his own reasoning.

A talk with Stuart Hardwick was pressing. So why was he on his way to see a man he hardly knew? To talk? To somehow reassure himself that taking back the farm was the right thing to do?

The idea scared him. Nobody, but nobody was going to talk him out of that farm.

Mud splattered against the side of the truck as the road narrowed and curved sharply upward. In minutes, the lane dead-ended at a small frame house surrounded by a knee-high white fence. Two dogs of questionable heritage leaped from the front porch to loudly herald his arrival.

The front door, gaily decked with a holiday wreath, opened immediately. Jingle bells swayed merrily with the movement. Loraine Stone's face appeared, then disappeared as Jesse stepped down from the truck and slammed the door.

Clarence shoved the old-fashioned storm door open. "Come in here, boy. Good to see you."

The snow had disappeared almost as quickly as it had come, leaving behind wet, soggy ground.

Jesse picked his way across the spongy yard and carefully wiped his boots on the welcome mat before stepping into the warm living room. The scent of recently fried bacon hung in the air.

"Well, Jesse. What brings you down the mountain this morning?"

He was wondering the same thing himself.

Taking in Clarence's church attire, he shifted uncomfortably. "I guess you're about to leave for church. I don't want to delay you."

"Don't worry about that. Sit down and tell me what's on your mind." Clarence pushed a drowsy cat to one side and joined her in a big flowered easy chair, relaxing as if he had nothing better to do than sit and visit. "A feller doesn't drive back up in here on a muddy day for no reason."

Jesse took the couch opposite him, thinking he should be in Mena by now.

"I don't really know why I stopped by."

One corner of the old man's mouth twitched as if he knew why. The notion irritated Jesse somewhat.

"Anything to do with Lindsey?"

"No." But the denial came too quickly. Leaning his elbows on his thighs, he clarified. "Partly."

Clarence studied him for a minute while scratching the cat behind one ear. His wife appeared in the living room, dressed for church and carrying a shiny black purse.

"You want me to go on, hon?" she asked.

Jesse leaped to his feet. "No, I'll go. We can talk again some other time." Since he had no idea why he'd come here, he might as well leave. And he had no intention of coming back again.

Clarence gestured him down. "You stay put. The Lord has a reason for you showing up on my doorstep on Sunday morning."

The Lord? Not since coming to Winding Stair had Jesse considered that God was interested in anyone's day-to-day activities. But according to Lindsey and her friends, God cared about everything.

Loraine Stone leaned down and pecked her husband on the cheek. "You might take a peek at that roast after a while."

Purse hooked over one elbow and a fabric-covered Bible in her hand, she left, acting neither upset nor surprised that her husband had stayed behind to talk to a virtual stranger. Clarence had once referred to himself as a good listener. Maybe others made this trek up the mountain to seek wisdom from the old guy.

Jesse wanted to laugh. Seeking wisdom sounded a bit too mystical for his comfort.

In minutes, the putter of a car engine sounded and then faded in the distance.

"You want some coffee, son?"

"No, thanks. I really should go. I have some business to attend to in Mena." But he didn't get up.

Clarence rose and got them both a cup of coffee anyway. Setting the mug on the polished coffee table in front of Jesse, he said, "Mind my asking what kind of business a man conducts on Sunday morning?"

As a matter of fact, Jesse did mind. "Personal."

Settling back into the chair, Clarence adjusted the cat before asking the same question again, "Have anything to do with Lindsey?"

"No." Jesse shook his head to clear away the lie. "Yes."

Clarence's grin gleamed in the sunlight that sliced a space between the drapes. "When your mind's made up, you're full of indecision, ain't ya, boy?"

The gentle jab brought a smile. "I have a problem, Clarence. And I don't know what to do about it."

"I don't either. But I know Someone who does."

Jesse knew what was coming. For once, he didn't mind. He was just grateful that Clarence hadn't asked for details about his problem.

"The Lord knows everything." Clarence paused to blow across the top of his coffee and sipped lightly before continuing. "He has the answer to every question and every problem every time."

"You make it sound easy."

"Nothing easy about living right in this crazy world. But letting God direct your path and trusting that He has everything under control is as easy as pie."

"I don't know how to go about that."

"Just start by talking to Him. He's like any other friend. The more you visit, the closer you get."

"I never thought of God as a friend." Jesse took the coffee from the table and studied the warm mug between his palms, pondering God as an approachable being. That wasn't the way he'd been taught, but he'd observed that kind of attitude in Lindsey.

"Well, He is. Jesus is the best friend you'll ever have. And He's always there to listen to your troubles and to help you work out the answers."

"Is that it? Just pray and the answer will come?"

"Most of the time. But remember that God ain't Santa Claus. He'll give you what you need, and that's not always what you want."

To Jesse the words seemed like a warning. A warning he didn't want to hear.

"But doesn't a man have a right to do what he believes is best?" The heat of the room coupled with his heavy jacket increased the pressure building inside him. He clinked the mug onto the table, shoulders bunching forward in tension. "Shouldn't I fight for what I know is rightfully mine?"

He caught himself and stopped, having almost said too much.

"Rights. We sure hear a lot about people's rights these days." Clarence's voice was conversational as if he hadn't noticed the edge in Jesse's words. "But when I get to thinking about Jesus and what He did for us, I know we've become a self-centered world, too stuck on our own desires. Jesus could have demanded His rights—and gotten them. But He chose to do what was best for others instead of what was easy for Himself."

Jesse thought about that, his chest tight with indecision. Clarence had something special in his life just as Lindsey did, but the old man couldn't possibly understand what he'd been through. Clarence had a home and stability and people who cared for him.

A small voice pecked at his conscience. Everyone had heartache. Just because he didn't know about theirs, didn't mean they hadn't suffered too.

"Anything you'd like me to pray with you about, Jesse?"

Jesse declined with a shake of his head. "No, thanks, but I appreciate the offer."

He stood to leave. Clarence pushed the lazy calico cat to one side and followed suit.

"Well, I'll be praying for you anyway. You'll make the right decision. Whatever that may be."

Jesse only hoped Clarence was right, because regardless of all that had been said, they'd solved nothing. Not that he'd expected to, but he'd had hope. He was as confused as he had been before. Only now, he'd wasted thirty minutes of precious time.

There was nothing left for him to do but resume the trip to Mena and try once more to change the mind of a certain crooked lawyer with a drinking problem.

The stars were bright that night—as bright, Lindsey imagined, as they had been on the first Christmas. The inky sky resembled diamonds on black velvet, sparkling and twinkling with such beauty, she wanted to stand forever here in the cold, hands in her coat, head tilted back to take in the wonder of God's creation.

"The sky does look pretty, doesn't it?" From behind her, Jesse's boots thudded softly against the hard ground.

It was closing time. He had turned off the music for the night and all but the security lights were now dark. Quiet lay over the land like a reverent prayer.

Turning, she smiled up at him. Her pulse bounded, reacting as it always did now that she knew she loved him. Having him here and near was enough, she'd told herself. Loving him was enough.

Jesse hadn't said a word about her admission that she cared for him. And she was grateful. Unless he could return her feelings, anything he might say would only embarrass them both.

At church, she'd prayed especially hard to understand the Lord's leading. Maybe Jesse and Jade had been sent for her to help them find the healing they needed. Maybe she'd been meant to love them back to health and then to let them go. She didn't know.

Pastor Cliff had preached on the scripture, "Trust in the Lord with all your heart and lean not unto your own understanding," and the message had seemed ready-made for her. But following through with the advice wasn't easy.

"I like to think about the days when God created the world. What an awesome thing to know He made all this beauty just for us to enjoy. He must love us so much more than we can ever understand."

"Pretty amazing, all right." Jesse stared into the

distance, the line of his face pensive. "I'm going out to feed the horse. Want to come with me?"

Though they'd already taken Puddin' and his wagon to the barn, a belated customer had interrupted them. The horse hadn't been properly groomed or fed.

She shook her head, though the temptation to spend every minute in his company was great. "Jade's finishing up your Christmas present. I told her I'd help her wrap it before you left tonight. She wants it under her tree at home."

She waited for his eyes to frost over and his face to close up the way it always did when Christmas gifts were mentioned. But this time proved different. Though he looked serious, he nodded. "She's getting pretty fired-up about Christmas."

"Have you bought her a present yet?" She knew Jesse had ignored Christmas last year. And Jade remembered all too well.

"No." He jammed his hands into his pockets.

"I could go shopping for you if you'd like."

"I'll do it."

Happiness bubbled up inside her. "You will?"

He shrugged and a grudging grin tugged at his mouth.

Before she could think better of the action, Lindsey threw her arms round his waist and laughed. When she started to pull away, Jesse held on a moment longer before letting her go.

"I'll be back in a few minutes." He started off across the semi-darkened field toward the barn.

"Don't hurry. Jade and I need time to wrap a certain present."

His chuckle echoed back to her on the chilly night breeze.

Suddenly lighthearted, Lindsey rushed inside the Snack Shack. The warm scent of sugar cookies made her stomach growl. She snitched a broken one and took a bite.

"Where's Daddy?" Jade was at the table laboring over the specially designed and decorated candies Lindsey had helped her make. From the looks of them, the finishing touches were almost in place.

"Gone to feed Puddin'."

The child looked up, affronted. "He said I could help him."

"I'm sorry, sweetie. I guess he forgot." Lindsey took some wrapping paper from beneath the counter and laid the roll on the table.

"I can catch up." Jade rushed to the door and shouted into the darkness. "Daddy, wait! I'm coming."

"What about wrapping your daddy's present?"

"You do it. Please, Lindsey. I saved something 'specially for Puddin'." She struggled into her coat, small fingers fumbling with the zipper until Lindsey reached down to help.

Lindsey followed her to the door and watched as she ran across the grass in pursuit of Jesse, pleased that Jade had a treat for the horse she'd once considered too big and scary.

The barn was less than a hundred yards away and Lindsey spotted Jesse's shadowy form beneath the diffused security lights. Satisfied that Jade would overtake her daddy, she turned back inside.

With a heart filled with gladness, she set to work wrapping Jesse's gift. Using candy molds, Lindsey had helped Jade create hearts and angels and various other chocolate delights for her daddy. Tonight Jade had added sprinkles and nuts.

After wrapping each piece in plastic wrap, Lindsey placed the treats into a pretty decorated tin she'd saved from last year. She wrapped the present and placed a big red bow on top, then set about cleaning up the Snack Shack for the night.

She was washing the coffeepot when the door opened and Jesse stepped inside. A small draught of cold air snaked in with him.

Smiling, she opened her mouth to speak, but the words died in her throat.

He was alone.

"Where's Jade?"

He looked around the room as if he expected the child to jump from beneath the table or from behind a chair. "Isn't she here?"

Slowly, Lindsey replaced the glass carafe and shook her head. "No. She wanted to go with you. I watched her until she was almost caught up. Didn't you see her?"

"Yes, but she came back here. She gave me a piece of apple for the horse. Then she said she was coming back to help you."

Lindsey pressed a hand to her mouth and fought down fear. "Where is she?"

"I don't know," Jesse answered grimly. "But I aim to find out."

He yanked the door open with such force the Shack rattled.

Going into the yard, he cupped his hands around his mouth and bellowed. "Jade!"

Trembling, Lindsey threw on her coat and followed. "I'll check the house."

"I'll head back to the barn."

They took off in a dead run, both returning in minutes without Jade. Lindsey had taken the time to grab her rifle and a pocketful of ammunition. If they had to go into the woods, they'd need it. Jesse eyed the weapon but didn't comment.

Together they searched the other out-buildings and the tree lot, calling Jade's name over and over, but there was no sign of the little girl.

Lindsey had thought she was panic-proof, but anxiety knotted her stomach and the nerves in her neck.

"She's terrified of the dark. Where could she be?"

"We know she was between here and the barn, so let's walk a circle around that area. If we don't find her, we'll widen the circle until we do. She's out here somewhere."

And likely crying her eyes out. The night was cold and dark, except for the stars. And there were wild animals in the woods and mountains behind Lindsey's farm.

Taking flashlights from the Snack Shack, they searched the grounds and then the area around the barn until finally reaching the wooded treeline that led up into the mountain.

"Surely, she wouldn't have gone into the woods alone," Lindsey said.

"Unless she got confused or something scared her and she ran without thinking." Suddenly, he stopped and shone his flashlight all around Lindsey. "Where is Sushi?"

"I don't know. She was outside earlier. I assumed she'd followed you to the barn." As soon as the words were out, she knew what Jesse was thinking. "Sushi wouldn't do anything to scare Jade. She knew Jade was easily frightened."

His jaw clenched, unconvinced. "Then where is she?"

"Maybe she went along with Jade, to protect her."

"Or maybe she chased her into the woods. Maybe she's the reason Jade ran away in the darkness."

"I don't believe that."

"Can you think of any other reason Jade would take off this way?"

She couldn't, but she also wouldn't believe the protective, loving German shepherd was responsible for Jade's disappearance. If anything, Sushi had followed Jade because she loved her and was worried about her. Convincing Jesse of that, however, was another matter.

"We'll find her, Jesse."

His jaw clenched and unclenched in barely controlled anger. "If that dog has hurt her, I'll kill it with my bare hands."

His assumption of the worst angered her. "You'd

better be more concerned about the real dangers out there."

"The real danger is the one I know about."

"Sushi is not a danger. She wouldn't harm anyone unless they threatened me. Jade was even beginning to accept her company."

"And maybe that wasn't a good thing. If you hadn't forced the situation, Jade wouldn't have felt she had to accept the dog to please you."

Hurt pierced her like a sharp nail. "That's not true. Jade knew I was trying to help her."

"Yeah? Well, look where that got us." He jerked around and stalked off into the darkness, calling back over his shoulders. "I mean it, Lindsey. That dog is dead if she's harmed my daughter."

Lindsey felt as if he'd slapped her. Did he really believe she'd force Jade to do something that would ultimately harm her? Did he really believe she'd bring an animal into Jade's life that would turn on her?

She trembled, not from cold, but from the harshness of Jesse's accusations. Tears burned inside her throat. Stiffening her spine, she swallowed and shook them off. Her own heartache had to take a back seat to the current crisis. She would cry later. Right now, a scared little girl waited.

Take care of her, Lord. And help us find her safe and sound.

She hoisted the rifle onto her shoulder, aimed the flashlight into the cold night...

And started walking.

Chapter 13

Sometime after midnight the wind died, and the temperature hovered in the upper thirties. Above the shadowy forest, the Milky Way smeared the indigo sky and stars danced and twinkled.

So beautiful…and so scary for a little girl alone.

Cold and more worried than he had ever been in his life, Jesse huddled deeper into his fleece jacket and thought about going back to the house to call the police. But Winding Stair was a small town manned by one police officer per shift. By the time the officer rounded up a search party, morning would be here. Surely, he'd find Jade before then.

Stomping on through the woods, twigs and branches snapping beneath his feet, he thought of how terrified Jade must be. Every sound magnified in the silence. For a child who feared the dark and suffered nightmares, the dark woods held unfathomable terrors.

He envisioned her as she'd been in the barn. Though warmly dressed in her coat and heavy jeans, her hood had been down. Would she think to put it up?

Was she cold? Was she crying? Was she hurt?

The torments of not knowing ate at him like hungry wolves.

For the first two hours he'd run on adrenaline. Now he was running on sheer determination.

From in front of him came a scratching, rustling noise.

A dark form loomed, and, with a swift surge of hope, he rushed forward. His boots snagged on twisted, twining tree roots growing above ground. He stumbled but managed to catch himself on the rough bark of an ancient blackjack, jarring his wrists in the process.

A startled possum drew back to hiss a warning, beady red eyes aglow in the flashlight beam. Jesse sagged in disappointment and hoped Jade didn't encounter any nocturnal animals.

He hoped she didn't encounter Sushi either.

Trudging onward, deeper into the thickening woods, he called her name over and over.

"Jade!"

The call was swallowed up in the dense trees. He paused to listen, longing for the answering call. Only the awful silence of a dark winter's night replied.

He had to find her. Soon. He was a grown man and

the cold and fatigue was wearing on him. How could a child hold out for long?

Fear and dread pulled at him, much stronger than the weariness.

If anything had happened to his baby, he couldn't go on. He would have no reason.

Another hour passed with no sign of the dark-haired angel. He found himself murmuring half-formed prayers.

"Please help me find her. Please protect her."

The weight on his chest grew until he thought he'd smother. Finally, when he could bear the stress no longer, he cried out, half in anger, half in hope-filled despair. "God, are You listening? Do You care?"

An owl hooted in the distance and, had the situation not been so serious, Jesse would have laughed. Leave it to Jesse Slater to pray to God and be answered by an owl.

But he didn't know what else to do. Lindsey believed in prayer. Clarence said God always answered, one way or the other. The way he figured it, no one was out here to hear him anyway or to know that Jesse had lost his reason along with his daughter. Praying would keep his mind from considering all the terrifying possibilities. And it sure couldn't hurt anything.

His prayers began in desperation.

"Lord, I know You're up there watching. I've always believed You were real, but I don't know You very well. Not like Lindsey and Clarence do. I have no right to ask favors, but maybe You'll do this one thing for Jade. Help me find her, Lord. Show me where she is."

A tree branch sliced across his face. He jerked back, fingered the skin and dismissed the scratch as inconsequential.

"Take care of her, God. Don't let her be scared. I know she is. I promised Erin I'd take care of our baby. Now look what I've done. I've lost her." A cry of grief pushed at his windpipe. "Don't let anything happen to her. I beg You not to take her, too."

The words of his prayer became jumbled, tumbling out from a heart filled with fear and seasoned with suffering.

"Was it me, Lord? Have I done something so bad that everyone I love gets taken away? Mama and Erin are gone. Don't take Jade. I'll do anything. Anything."

Somewhere—far too close for comfort—coyotes yipped and howled, raising the hair on Jesse's neck.

Pausing next to an outcropping of boulders, he shouted, "Jade! Jade!", until his voice broke.

As he collapsed exhausted onto the rocks, tears gathered behind his eyelids. He hadn't let himself cry when Erin died, fearing his grief would be too terrible for Jade to witness. Truth be told, he hadn't cried in a long time.

"Oh, God, I don't know what to do. She's out there and she's scared." He buried his cold, damp face in gloved hands. "Please help me."

Clarence claimed God was a friend who cared, who longed for friendship in return. Could that be true? All these years, he'd assumed he was last on God's Christmas list. Could he have been wrong all this time?

He began to pray in earnest then, pouring out the sorrow and agony of his past as if God didn't already know his life story. And yet the telling cleansed him, released him from the torment and anger he'd harbored so long, as though God Himself took on the load and carried his sorrows away.

He didn't know how long he sat there talking, but when he raised his face to the star-sprinkled heavens he was a new man—still terribly afraid for his child, but renewed in a way he couldn't begin to explain or understand.

All these years he'd thought God had abandoned him. But now he saw as clearly as he saw the Milky Way above—he'd been the one to pull away and forget the Lord. Now he understood what Lindsey had meant when she'd said that God would never leave or forsake us. God didn't. But man did.

At the reminder of Lindsey, regret pushed into his consciousness. Every time his own guilt started to eat at him, he lashed out at her, and he'd done it again tonight over the dog.

Maybe Jade had become frightened and run away from Sushi, but he couldn't blame Lindsey for that. She only meant good for Jade. She loved her.

And she loved him.

"Lord, I'm so unworthy. Of her. Of You. I hope she can forgive me." He raised his head and stared into the heavens. "I hope You will too."

A gentle warmth, startling in the cold, suffused him as if someone had draped an electric blanket over his shoulders.

With restored courage and a Friend to guide him, he pushed off the boulder and set out to find his daughter.

At the first gray promise of morning, Jesse turned back and headed out of the woods. All through the long night, he'd walked and searched and prayed. Twice he and Lindsey had crossed paths and then parted again to cover more ground. The wooded area expanded to the north and eventually became a state park. There were miles and miles to cover if Jade had gone in that direction. Now, he had little choice but to call in a search team.

Eyes scratchy and dry from cold and sleeplessness, he continued to strain at every shadow, hoping, praying. He was peering beneath a low-hanging cedar when a terrifying sound raised the hair on his neck.

Growling, snarling animal sounds—whether of dog or coyote or wolf, he couldn't tell—came from somewhere to his left. Breaking into a dead run, he headed toward the sound.

A gunshot ripped the morning quiet. Birds flapped up from the trees, filling the air with rushing wings and frightened calls.

Jesse's heart jump-started. Though beyond weary, the rush of adrenaline propelled him faster.

Barking and snarling became louder, and he recognized the sound—a dog. Sushi.

Fear mixed with anger whipped through him.

Breaking through the dense growth of trees, he glimpsed a purple coat. A small form, black hair spilled out all around, lay curled on the ground. Sushi, hair raised and teeth bared, stood over her.

Heart in his throat, Jesse cried out. "Jade!"

The dog spun toward the voice just as Lindsey arrived from the opposite direction.

"Daddy, Daddy!" Jade sat up, gripping Sushi's neck as though the dog was a lifeline.

Everything was happening too fast. Jesse couldn't comprehend anything except the sight of his little girl on the ground and the dog standing over her. Rushing forward, he fell to the earth and yanked Jade into his arms, away from the animal.

"Are you all right? Did the dog bite you? Did she hurt you?" Pushing her a little away, he frantically checked her for injuries. Her cheeks were red and her face dirty, but otherwise she appeared all right.

Lindsey's smoky voice, strained with exhaustion came toward them. She still carried the flashlight and her gun. "Sushi didn't hurt her, Jesse. She protected her."

Pressing his child close to him for warmth and safety, he looked up into Lindsey's red-rimmed eyes.

"What do you mean? She was standing over Jade's helpless body, ready to attack."

"No, Daddy, no." Jade pulled his face around to gain his full attention. "Sushi tried to fight the bad dogs that came."

Jesse blinked in bewilderment. "Bad dogs?"

He looked at the German shepherd sitting a few feet away, and then toward the woods from whence Lindsey had come.

His mind began to clear and reason returned. Lindsey had fired the shots and followed something into those woods. "Coyotes?"

Carefully placing her rifle on the ground, Lindsey knelt in front of him. With a soft smile, she stroked Jade's tangled hair. "Coyotes don't usually approach humans, but she was small and still and probably looked vulnerable. I heard Sushi's warning growl and arrived in time to chase them off. Thank God."

A shiver ripped through Jesse. He squeezed his eyes closed against the unthinkable image of Jade and a pack of coyotes. "Yes. Thank God."

Lindsey noticed the words of praise. Her eyes questioned him, but she made no comment. As naturally as if he'd done it forever, he pulled Lindsey against his other side and held her there. His girls, one on each side, where he wanted them.

"And Sushi, too, Daddy," Jade insisted. "She stayed the night with me. She snuggled me up and made me be warm. I cried, but she licked my face."

Jesse's heart ached at the image of his daughter alone and afraid and crying. But he was happy too, and relieved beyond words.

"Where were you, sweetheart? How did you get lost?"

Jade pointed at the sky. Her knit gloves were dirty and loaded with bits of grass and twigs.

"I wanted the star."

Lindsey appeared as puzzled as he. "What star, Jade?"

"The falling star. For Daddy." She cupped a hand over her mouth and leaned toward Lindsey. In a conspiratorial whisper, she said, "For a present. So he would like Christmas again."

A lump filled Jesse's throat. Jade had ventured into the dark and frightening night alone to capture a shooting star for him. To make him happy.

He pressed his face into her hair, chest aching enough to burst. "Oh, baby. Daddy's so sorry."

She patted his ears. "It's okay, Daddy. I didn't find the star, and I got lost. But my guarding angel was with me, just like Lindsey said. Sushi and me went to sleep, and I wasn't scared anymore."

The German shepherd sat on her haunches, tail sweeping the brown earth, eyes shining as if she knew she'd done a good thing. With a final hug, Jade pushed up from Jesse's lap and went to embrace the big furry dog.

"Sushi is my friend."

Who would think a guardian angel had a fur coat and four legs?

His gaze locked with Lindsey's.

Or had another kind of angel protected his daughter?

"I owe you an apology, and this dog a T-bone steak," he told Lindsey.

She shook her head, tangled, windblown hair swinging around her tired face. He thought she looked beautiful. "No apologies or steaks are needed. We can thank God He used Sushi to protect Jade when we couldn't."

"I was wrong about the dog." Now was his chance to tell her the rest. "I've been wrong about a lot of things. But last night, when I was scared out of my mind, God and I had a long talk."

Hope sprang into her expression. "You did?"

They were cold and tired and needed to get back to the house, but some things couldn't wait to be told.

"You were right. God was here all the time, waiting for me to make the first move. I'm only sorry I waited so long."

"Oh, Jesse." Lindsey threw her arms around his neck and kissed his rough, unshaven cheek. Then, as if she regretted the spontaneous act, she drew back, blushing.

Her golden eyes were inches away and the look of love was there for any fool to see. Suddenly all his reservations faded away as easily as the daybreak had chased away the night.

He loved Lindsey Mitchell. He wondered why he'd fought it so long. She was everything good and beautiful he wanted in his life.

He waited, expecting to be engulfed with guilt because of Erin. This time the feeling never came. Loving Lindsey in no way negated the love he'd had for his wife, but Erin was gone, and she would have handed him his head for not letting her go sooner. She would have expected him to take care of their daughter and to get on with living.

And that's exactly what he intended to do.

"Come back here, woman." Elbow locked around her neck, he drew Lindsey close again. He hardly noticed the cold ground seeping through his clothes. "A kiss on the cheek won't cut it."

Her eyes widened, but she didn't pull away.

With a silent prayer of thanks, Jesse bent his head and kissed Lindsey's sweet mouth.

"What was that?" she asked when they parted, her voice even huskier after a night in the cold.

"Something amazing has happened. Something I thought was impossible. I have a lot of things to tell you later, when we're rested and warm, but there's one thing that can't wait." He cupped her cheek, unable to take his eyes off her, now that he recognized the truth. "I love you, Lindsey."

A multitude of emotions played over her face.

"Oh, Jesse, I'm going to cry."

He winced in mock horror. "Don't even think about it. At least, not until you say you love me too."

Eyes glistening with unshed tears, she stroked a hand over his jaw. "I do. With everything in me."

Jesse's heart filled to the bursting point. This woman had done so much for him. She'd made him a better man than he'd ever dreamed of being. She'd loved him in a way that healed the gaping wound he'd carried around inside for so long. And most of all, she'd led him back to the Lord.

The morning sun broke over the eastern horizon, orange as a pumpkin, and as bright as the new light shining in Jesse's soul.

The increasing temperature was welcome, but the morning air was still cold enough to be uncomfortable.

"Time to get you and the butterbean back to the house."

"Time to go to work," she argued, but didn't move from her place in his arms. "Customers won't wait, no matter how tired we are."

Customers. All night, he'd been so preoccupied with finding his daughter that he hadn't thought of the long day ahead.

"I'll take care of the farm today." He kissed her on the nose and then set her on her feet. "You and Jade will have a good breakfast and plenty of sleep."

"I'll argue with you later," she said. "Right now that breakfast sounds too tempting to pass up."

Jesse chuckled, shaking his head at this special woman. He'd have to lock her in the house to keep her away from the tree patch, no matter how much sleep she did or didn't get. As for himself, he felt as invigorated as if he'd slept for days.

Holding hands, they started toward Jade. The little lost angel jogged around in circles with Sushi, appearing unfazed by her eventful night.

"From the looks of her, Jade had a lot more sleep than either of us."

"Thanks to Sushi," Jesse admitted.

A soft smile curved Lindsey's mouth. The light in her eyes spoke volumes. "And her guardian angel."

The situation with the farm and his rightful ownership tried to press in, but Jesse shoved the thoughts away. Right now, he wanted to bask in all the good things that had come from this strange night. Today he was happy to love and be loved. He'd worry about his dilemma some other time.

Chapter 14

"Hey, woman, get a move on." Eyes twinkling and step jaunty, Jesse burst through the front door of the farmhouse bringing the chill with him. "All work and no play—"

He stopped in his tracks when he spotted her.

"Whoa." A slow smile eased the perpetual sadness from his eyes. "If I'd known you'd look like that, I would have offered to take you Christmas shopping a long time ago."

Lindsey blushed, pleased but discomfited by the unaccustomed praise. "Slacks and a sweater aren't that impressive, Jesse."

He pumped his eyebrows. "Says who?"

Lindsey laughed, unable to resist this teasing, happy version of the man she loved. Since that anxiety-filled night of searching for the lost Jade, he'd been full of good humor and unbounded joy.

"I suppose after seeing me in pine-covered jeans and boots every day, anything is an improvement."

"What about me, Daddy? Am I pretty too?" Jade preened, showing off the red bow holding back her black satin hair.

"You are stunning." He swooped the child into his arms and blew onto her neck. Her giggle filled the room and brought Sushi in to investigate the commotion.

Jesse eased Jade to the floor and scratched the dog's ears. "Tom and his boy are all set to handle everything while we're gone. Any last-minute instructions you want to give them?"

Tom's teenage son had worked part-time for Lindsey last year and knew how the tree farm operated. She had no qualms about leaving the pair from her church in charge while she, Jesse and Jade spent a few hours in Mena. She looked forward to an afternoon of shopping, having dinner, and spending quality time with this pair that had won her heart.

"Tom and Jeff can handle it." She reached for his rough hand and squeezed, grateful and so full of love she could hardly see straight. "Thanks for thinking of this. I know how you feel about crowds and shopping."

He shrugged off the idea that he'd done anything special. "Everyone needs time off, even the invincible pioneer woman on Winding Stair Mountain."

She laughed. "I don't feel too invincible sometimes." Most of the time, to tell the truth.

She'd never admitted until now that she had insulated herself here on the mountain. Pastor Cliff had tried to talk to her once, and his gentle assessment had been correct. She'd used the tree farm as an excuse to distance herself from everyone but her church family, afraid of being hurt, afraid to trust.

Two nights ago, during their search for Jade, when Jesse had declared his love, her own fears had evaporated like morning mist. She'd seen Jesse's hard work around the farm, experienced his constant efforts to improve the place and to lighten her tasks. And she knew he was totally dedicated to his child. But there was something to the adage that adversity bonds.

Her gaze strayed to him, busily getting Jade into her coat and gloves. Jesse Slater's love had changed her. Something she'd never thought possible had happened. She trusted this good man with her life.

Most important of all, she trusted him with her heart.

A short time later in Mena, Jesse remained mildly surprised that he'd not only agreed to this trip, he'd suggested it. But Lindsey had that effect on him. He'd do anything in his power to see her smile. So here he was, in a crowded store where cashiers wore red Santa hats, Bing Crosby crooned "White Christmas" over the intercom, and he was almost enjoying himself.

Almost.

He would rather be on the farm or at a quiet little restaurant somewhere, but observing Lindsey's pleasure in such a simple outing made up for the discomfort on his part.

He let his gaze roam over the stacks of cologne sets, gloves, wallets, candy and back massagers. From floor to ceiling the place reeked of Christmas.

With a wry shake of his head, he realized how far he'd come—from a Scrooge who hated Christmas to a man in love who wanted to please his woman. And he couldn't think of anything in the world good enough to give her.

"What do you think, Jesse?" Lindsey held some kind of computer software box in one hand. "Would a boy like this?"

From the looks of her basket, Lindsey was buying for every kid in her church. "Depends on the boy. I always wanted sports stuff."

He'd gotten that kind of thing too before his mother had become ill. Those last two years before she died, he'd received nothing. Les Finch wasn't much of a shopper. Reason enough for him to do better.

A disembodied voice interrupted the music to remind kids that Santa was available in the toy department for picture-taking.

Jade, who'd been examining every baby doll on the shelf, tugged at his hand and requested for the fourth time, "Let's go see Santa."

Jesse was about to refuse when Lindsey caught his eye. "That might be a good idea, Dad," she said. "You two go back there while I do a little bit of *special* shopping."

She put enough emphasis on the word special that Jesse got the idea. She wanted to shop for Jade.

A frisson of energy passed between them. Maybe she wanted to shop for him too. His stomach lifted at the notion.

On the other hand, maybe the sensation was hunger pains. Dinner was beginning to sound good.

"Will you be ready to have dinner by then?"

Fingers curled around the handle of the shopping cart, she questioned pointedly, "Don't you have some shopping of your own to do?"

Jesse suppressed a shudder. Walking around in a huge department store, he could handle. But the pleasure in hassling through the jammed check-outs evaded him. He'd planned to buy Jade's gifts in Winding Stair. Run in the store, grab the doll, pay for it and run out. His way seemed much less trying.

"I don't suppose I could convince you to pick up a couple of things for me," he said hopefully.

Her cart was already littered with items. What would a few more matter? She knew what he wanted to buy Jade because they'd discussed it this morning over the phone.

A knowing twinkle lit her eyes. "Have we pushed you beyond the limits any male can endure?"

With a tilt of his head, he grinned. "Getting close."

Pushing up the sleeve of her blue sweater, Lindsey looked at her watch. "Okay. Tell you what. I'll gather up those last things and meet you back at the truck in thirty minutes. I'm starting to get antsy about leaving the farm for so long anyway."

He frowned. "Tom and Jeff will do fine."

"I know, but I don't want to impose on their kindness forever." She took a box of candy canes from the shelf and placed them in the basket, never mentioning the fact that she was paying her friends good money to run the tree lot. "Besides, shopping does me in, too. I'm always anxious to get back home to my peaceful little farm."

He studied her face, noticing the softness that appeared whenever she talked of her home. Guilt tugged at him. He'd been doing a lot of thinking about his claim on that place.

Looking around to see if anyone was listening, he leaned toward her and whispered, "I love you."

With a parting wink at her blushing face, he and Jade jostled their way toward the back of the store.

He did love Lindsey. And she loved him. And he hoped the words just now hadn't been spoken out of guilt. The farm was an issue that could tear them apart and change her loving to loathing. He couldn't bear that, not now that he'd recaptured the joy sorely missing in his life for so long.

Over the last few days, he'd spent a lot of time praying for answers about the Christmas Tree Farm, but the continual nag of doubt and worry plagued him yet. He had a right to that farm. He must have said that to the Lord a hundred times. Then he'd remember what Clarence said about rights, and how sometimes there was a big difference between being right and doing right.

Hurting Lindsey was wrong, regardless of his true

claim to the land. She trusted him—a huge leap of faith on her part. She put a lot of stock in loyalty and truth. If she discovered his original motive had been to repossess her land, would she reject him? Would her heart be broken at his deceit?

A lady elf, garbed in form-fitting tights and a short skirt greeted him with an interested smile as he and Jade joined the line waiting for Santa. Jesse barely noticed her. There was only one woman for him. And she wore flannel and denim and smelled as fresh as the pine trees.

In that moment, he knew the answer he'd been seeking. Loving Lindsey, in the way God intended man to love woman, meant doing what was best for her. *As Christ loved the church, so man should love his wife.* Jesse wasn't sure why he remembered the verse, but he was sure it came from the Bible. To the best of his ability, he wanted always to love Lindsey that way.

The farm belonged to her. She was the heart and soul of that place. He'd wondered what to give her for Christmas and now he knew. Even though she would never be aware of the secret gift, relinquishing his quest for the farm was the best present he could give. From this moment forward, the farm was hers. And he would no longer seek revenge for the wrongs done to him.

As if the shutters were opened and sunlight flooded in, Jesse saw the truth clearly. Jade had not been his motive. His rightful claim had not been his motive. He had wanted someone to suffer as much as he had—and that was wrong.

He would never again harass the pathetic old lawyer, Stuart Hardwick, to confess. And most of all, he would never hurt Lindsey by telling her of his original reasons for coming to the farm. She didn't ever need to know that the Christmas Tree Farm legally belonged to him.

He would find another way to provide well for Jade—and for Lindsey, if she'd have him. He had skills. He could work for any electric outfit in the area.

The final weight of his past lifted off his shoulders. Lindsey was his heart. Doing right *did* feel much better than being right.

Lindsey was in the house, wrapping all the gifts she and Jesse had purchased the day before. In exchange for her gift-wrapping favors, Jesse had agreed to man the tree lot. With only two days left until Christmas, business at the farm had begun to slack off. Only a few procrastinators waited this late to purchase a tree.

The grind and whine of a pickup coming up the drive rose above the television where Jimmy Stewart serenaded Donna Reed in "It's a Wonderful Life."

"Must be another of those procrastinators," she said to Sushi. The dog perked one ear, then rose and trotted to the door, whining.

"Need out, girl?" Lindsey put aside the silvery roll of foil paper and followed the dog.

The sheriff's SUV was parked in her drive, and Sheriff Kemp came across the yard.

Lindsey opened the door as he stomped up onto

the porch. "Hi, Sheriff. Forget to buy your Christmas tree?"

Ben Kemp had been county sheriff for as long as Lindsey could remember, but he was still tall and strong and fit with barely a hint of paunch beneath his wide silver belt buckle. His trademark gray Stetson and cowboy boots made him even taller. In the pleasant December sunshine, he shifted from one boot to the next, looking decidedly uncomfortable.

Worrying a toothpick to one corner of his mouth, he said, "Wish that was the situation, Lindsey, but I'm afraid I have bad news."

Pulse leaping in sudden fear, Lindsey gripped the doorpost. "My folks? Kim? Has something happened?"

"No, no." He took off his cowboy hat and studied the inside. "Mind if I come in for a minute? Got something here I need to show you."

He pulled a file folder from inside his zip-up jacket.

"Of course not. Please." She stepped back to let him in, relieved that her family was all right but troubled about the purpose of his visit. Sheriff Kemp was too busy to make unnecessary calls.

While the lawman made himself at home on the edge of her couch, Lindsey turned down the TV.

"Would you like some coffee, Sheriff?"

"Nothing, thanks." He placed the Stetson on the couch beside him. "A real odd situation has arisen, Lindsey."

She tilted her head. "That concerns me?"

"In a way. It's about this farm."

Now she was really puzzled. A butterfly fluttered up into her chest. "My farm?"

"Well, you see now, there's the trouble." Opening the manila file folder, he removed a sheet of paper and handed it to her. "When your granddaddy bought this place—in good faith, I'm sure—something was sorely amiss."

Lindsey read the paper and then looked up. "This is the deed to my farm."

"Yep. Now take a look at that signature." He took another paper from the folder. "And then have a look at this one."

She did as he asked, but what she read made no sense. Another butterfly joined the first.

"I don't understand."

Sheriff Kemp rubbed at his forehead, clearly disturbed with the news his job forced him to share. "Here's the upshot, Lindsey. This eighty acres belonged to a woman name of Madelyn Finch. She inherited it from her grandparents. When she died, her husband, Les Finch, hired a lawyer name of Hardwick to help him gain ownership of the place. I remember Hardwick. He was dirty to the core but so smart he always got away with his shenanigans."

Lindsey's pulse accelerated. The butterflies were in full flight by now. "Are you telling me that Mr. Finch illegally sold this farm to my grandfather?"

"I'm afraid so. The woman's will was clear. The farm was to go to her son. Somehow Hardwick and Finch forged the boy's name on the sale papers."

Dropping into the nearest chair, Lindsey covered

her mouth with her hand to keep from crying out. A dozen questions crowded her mind. "They cheated a child out of his home?"

Suddenly the truth hit her. That child, whoever he was, owned the tree farm—her tree farm.

"The boy must be grown by now. Does he know about this? Is that why you're here? He's filed a claim to regain possession?"

"Yes, ma'am. He's the one stirred things up after all this time. Seems Stuart Hardwick got himself a conscience after Jesse went to visit him. Hardwick brought all this information to my office this morning. Now, I don't know all the ins and outs. I figure the courts will have to look this over and hear some testimony from Hardwick and Jesse, but the evidence looks pretty clear to me."

"Jesse?" Her hands began to tremble. What did Jesse have to do with this? "Why do you keep saying Jesse?"

Sheriff Kemp blew out a gusty sigh. "Your hired man should have told you this himself, Lindsey. He's Madelyn Finch's son, the rightful owner of this land."

Blood thundered in her temples. She, who'd never fainted in her life, thought she might keel over on the coffee table and scatter gift wrap and ribbon everywhere.

She remembered, then, the times he'd taken off work to attend to personal business and the times someone had told her they'd seen Jesse at the courthouse. He'd been searching for proof that he, not she, owned this place.

Her voice, when she managed to speak, sounded small and faraway. "So that's the real reason Jesse came here."

She ached with the realization that his profession of love had been a lie.

"'Fraid so. Not that you can blame a man for trying to reclaim what was stolen from him. Especially since he has a little girl to care for. But he should have told you."

"Yes. He should have told me."

Her face felt hot enough to combust. Her whole body shook. Jesse had lied to her. She'd trusted him. Loved him.

Jesse had even gone as far as pretending to love her. There was always the chance he wouldn't find proof, but by marrying her, he could still take over the farm. Jesse had romanced her in order to regain the land any way he could.

Her heart shattered like a fragile Christmas ornament. Once more she'd been fooled by a handsome face.

Jimmy Stewart flickered across the silent television screen. He was sitting at a bar, tears in his eyes as he prayed in desperation.

Understanding perfectly, she stared bleakly at the screen, lost and broken.

"Could I get you something, Lindsey?" Sheriff Kemp's kind voice broke into her tumultuous thoughts. His weathered face studied her with concern.

Pulling the reins on her emotions, she shook her

head. "I'll be okay, but I need to be alone right now, if you don't mind."

"Understandable. Do you want to tell Jesse about this, or should I?"

Her pulse stumbled.

Jesse, no doubt, would be ecstatic.

"He'll have to come by my office," the sheriff went on. "He'll need to sign papers and such to get the ball rolling."

Lindsey gripped the edge of her chair, trying not to break down in front of the sheriff. She licked her lips, her mouth gone suddenly dry. "You tell him, please. He's down in the lot."

She'd trusted him. Oh, dear Lord, why had she trusted him?

"Maybe you should call a lawyer. There might be some way to fight this thing."

"I'll do that." Suddenly, she needed him gone. She needed to pray. And most of all, she needed Jesse to stay away from her until she could get her emotions under control. "Please, go talk to Jesse before he comes to the house." She despised the quaver in her voice. "I don't want to see him right now."

The poor sheriff was worried about her losing her farm. He didn't understand that she was losing that and a great deal more.

Jesse was halfway to the house when the sheriff came out onto the porch. His curiosity had been piqued from the moment the SUV pulled into the yard. But after the sheriff had stayed inside the house so long,

Jesse got a bad feeling in the pit of his stomach. Something was up.

Jesse broke into a lope. If Lindsey needed him…

"What's up?" he asked as soon as he reached the policeman. His heart pounded oddly, not only from the jog, but from some inner voice of warning.

Expression serious, Sheriff Kemp handed him a file folder. "Stuart Hardwick came to see me this morning and confessed his part in swindling you out of your inheritance."

Jesse's head swung toward the house. "Lindsey."

"I told her."

"Oh, no." He had to get to her, make her understand. Spinning away, he started that direction. The sheriff's big hand stopped him.

"Leave her be, Jesse. She doesn't want to see you right now. Give her some time alone."

"But I have to explain."

"Explain what? That you came here under false pretenses, looking for information that would take this farm from her and return it to you? That you've been dishonest with her from the start?"

Jesse relented. Remorse pinned his boots to the ground. The sheriff was right. He hadn't lied to her directly, but his silence had been as dishonest as his reasons for taking this job. Lindsey had trusted him with everything, and all the while, he'd gone right on with his devious plans.

No wonder she didn't want to see him now—or possibly ever. How could he expect her to forgive him for worming his way into her heart under such deceitful circumstances? She had been hurt before, betrayed by a man she loved. And now he had hurt her again. He didn't deserve a woman like Lindsey Mitchell.

Sadness shuddered through him.

His arms fell limply to his sides. "I don't know what to do."

Misunderstanding, the sheriff took the file folder from him and said, "Come by the office later today or tomorrow, and we'll get the ball rolling with the legal system."

With an aura of resigned disapproval, the man departed, leaving Jesse standing in the yard of his rightful home. The afternoon air was cool, but sweat covered his body.

He stared around at the quiet little farm that he'd coveted since he was fourteen. All his adult life he'd longed for this moment.

And now, instead of the exultant victory he'd expected, Jesse suffered a heartbreak so profound he nearly went to his knees.

Lindsey was hurting. She needed comfort. But as much as he longed to go to her, he resisted. Lindsey didn't want him. She'd told the sheriff as much. Going to her now, after what he'd done, would only compound the hurt. Nothing he could say would change the truth. Regardless of his good intentions, of his decision not to pursue ownership, he had betrayed her trust.

After one long last look toward the house and the woman who held his heart, he headed for his truck and the trailer park. He didn't know where he would go, but he'd done all the damage any one man should do in this quiet, loving little town.

At last he knew what to give Lindsey for Christmas. This farm wasn't enough, though he'd certainly leave that behind. What she deserved was a return to her peaceful life without him to bring her any more pain or humiliation.

Packing wouldn't take long. The Slaters traveled light. He'd have the truck loaded in time to pick Jade up from school.

The thought of his little girl gave him pause. She'd changed so much here on Winding Stair Mountain. She was happier, healthier and free from many of her fears, thanks mostly to Lindsey's love and care.

His poor baby. She'd be as heartbroken as he was.

But he had no choice now. Better to get out of Lindsey's life and leave her alone.

With a deep sigh of sadness, Jesse drove through the picturesque old town. The cheerful decorations mocked him.

Once more Christmas had brought him heartbreak, but this time, the fault was his own.

Chapter 15

"You can fight this, Miss Mitchell."

Stan Wright, a forty-something lawyer with a soothing baritone voice and intelligent brown eyes, regarded her across his littered desk. Having called the offices of Wright and Banks as quickly as she'd regained her equilibrium, Lindsey was relieved when he'd offered to see her within the hour.

"I don't want to fight it, Mr. Wright." She drew in a deep, steadying breath, determined to do the hardest thing she'd ever had to do. "The farm belongs to Jesse Slater and his daughter. They were cheated out of it through no fault of their own."

She didn't admit that the decision wasn't her original choice. Her first instinct had been anger and hurt and bitter resentment. She'd wanted to rail at Jesse and send him away. She'd wanted to keep the land to pay him back for lying to her, for making her believe he loved her when, all the while, he was plotting to evict her.

But as soon as the first rush of emotion passed, she'd prayed. And as hard as the decision was, she'd seen that Jesse was as much a victim as she. The land was rightfully his, and she wouldn't rest until he'd legally regained ownership.

"I understand the circumstances. But you've lived there in good faith and made the land productive. Even if the courts decide in his favor, he could be forced to pay you for all the improvements you've made, for the tree stock, etc."

She held out a hand to stop him. "No, sir. I want you to do whatever paperwork is required for me to sign away any claim to the entire eighty acres. I want Jesse Slater to take possession."

Shaking his head, Mr. Wright leaned back in his executive chair and rubbed a hand across his chin. Brown eyes studied her thoughtfully. "I wish you would take more time to think about this."

"I've had all the time I needed." Standing, she shook his hand, and if hers trembled the slightest bit, the attorney didn't comment. "Call me as soon as you have the papers drawn up."

With a final word of thanks, she left his office and went to her truck. She had a great deal to do between now and the first of the year. A job. A place to live. Maybe she'd go to Colorado and stay with her sister, Kim, for a while.

But for all her bravado, the ache in her chest grew to the exploding point. The Christmas Tree Farm was not only her home, it was her dream. Leaving would tear her in two. But more terrible than losing the farm, was the loss of Jesse and Jade and the sweet plans they'd begun to weave together.

"Why, Jesse?" she whispered to the windshield. But she knew why. He'd done what he'd had to do in order to retake the farm. And pretending to love her had been part of the plan.

Heading the Dakota through town, she let the tears come. As hard as talking to him would be, Jesse needed to know her decision. Harboring unforgiveness would destroy her relationship with Jesus. So she'd take the first, painful step and tell Jesse the farm was his—and that she bore him no ill.

And that was the truth. She wasn't angry. But oh, the hurt was far worse than anything she'd suffered before.

The palms of her hands were moist with sweat by the time her Dakota crunched over the narrow gravel lane leading into the mobile-home park. All the trailers looked sad and a little run-down, but strings of lights and green wreaths spread the joy of Christmas here as everywhere.

Lindsey wasn't feeling much joy at the moment. Swiping at her soggy face, she blew her nose and composed herself. The next few minutes would be hard, but she'd get through them.

As she neared his trailer, she spotted Jesse outside,

and her pulse leaped. Foolish heart, she loved him even though he'd betrayed her so terribly.

Jean jacket unbuttoned in the cold air, he was loading boxes into the back of his Silverado. Her stomach twisted at the implication. Was he planning to push her out of the house today?

As she pulled in to his parking area and killed the motor, Jesse looked up. Expression serious, his silver eyes bored into her like laser beams.

Stilling the awful trembling in her knees, Lindsey breathed a prayer for help and climbed out of the cab.

She stood on one side of the pickup bed. Jesse waited on the other.

"Lindsey." A muscle worked in his cheek. She recognized the movement as stress and longed to smooth her fingers over the spot and reassure him. No doubt he thought she hated him. But she couldn't.

From what she understood of the situation, Jesse was the victim of two unscrupulous men who'd stolen his birthright and left him to fend for himself. Thinking of a teenage Jesse scared and alone filled her with sadness.

Resisting the need to touch him, to feel his arms around her once more, she said what she'd come to say.

She hitched her chin up, struggling for control. "I would never keep something that isn't rightfully mine, Jesse. You didn't have to pretend to love me in order to get the farm back."

Her voice cracked the slightest bit on the last words. She bit her lip to keep from breaking down again.

Deep furrows appeared in Jesse's forehead. "What

are you talking about? I never pretended—" He stopped, his expression incredulous. "You thought—?" He stopped again, dropped the box he carried into the bed of the truck and started around to her side.

He strode toward her with the strangest look on his face. Lindsey wasn't sure whether to run or stand her ground. Her heart clattered against her rib cage.

Never a coward, she stood her ground.

Lindsey's words lit a spark of hope inside Jesse. The crazy woman thought he didn't love her?

Stalking around the truck, he jabbed a finger at the air. "Let's get one thing straight, Miss Mitchell. I didn't *pretend* to love you. I do love you. I didn't want to, never intended to, but you were too amazing to resist. When Erin died, I thought my capacity to love died with her, but you, with your sweet, caring, decent ways proved me wrong."

A curtain in the next trailer twitched, letting Jesse know his voice had carried and he'd attracted an audience. Across the road, in the other row of trailers, a woman came out on her porch and pretended to adjust the wreath on her front door. All the while, she cast surreptitious peeks toward Jesse and Lindsey. He heard the squeak and swish of windows being raised.

Jesse didn't care if the whole world listened in. All that mattered was the mystified, suffering expression in Lindsey's red-rimmed eyes. She'd been crying— because of him.

He reached for her hand, aching to touch her, but afraid at the same time. When she didn't yank away, he celebrated a small victory. At least, they could part on speaking terms.

"The one constant in all this mess is right here." He placed her hand over his heart. "My love for you is real and true. It has nothing to do with the farm."

She blinked, shaking her head in denial. Her tawny mane tossed around her shoulders and Jesse itched to smooth it, to comfort her somehow.

"I don't understand. I thought you purposely moved here to reclaim the land."

"I did."

She shrank away, forcing him to release her. How he longed to change the past, to take back his devious intentions. But it was too late for that. He'd hurt her too much to expect forgiveness.

Arms falling helplessly to his sides, Jesse knew defeat. He stared up into the tree growing behind the trailer. His insides felt as bare and empty as the naked, reaching limbs of the sycamore.

"Someday, sweet Lindsey, I hope you will try to forgive me." His gaze found her beloved face and soaked in every feature, storing the memory. "But whether you do or not, I will always be grateful for our time together. I'll leave Winding Stair a better man for having known you."

Tears gathered in her eyes, and Jesse despised himself for causing them. "The farm is yours, Jesse. I'm the one who will be leaving. I only ask that you wait until after the holidays so I'll have time to make some arrangements."

The idea of Lindsey moving away from the home

she loved cut through him like a chain saw. He stepped toward her again, desperately wanting to hold her, but the distrust in her expression stopped him. He shoved his hands in his jacket pockets instead.

"You're not going anywhere. I'm packed and ready. I'll inform the sheriff of my decision to renounce any claim to your land. As soon as I go by the school and get Jade, we'll be on our way."

Lindsey stared at him in disbelief. "After everything that's happened, you're leaving? You're giving up a home that's rightfully yours?"

"The place means nothing to me without you there."

Tears shoved at the back of his eyelids. If he didn't escape soon, he'd shame himself more than he already had. Spinning on his boot heel, he grabbed for the truck door and bounded inside. He cranked the engine, slammed the gear shift into Reverse and started to back out. One last glance at Lindsey's face stopped him.

Without understanding his new propensity for rejection, he rolled down the window and said, "Remember this much. I loved you. I still do."

Her sorrow turned to bewilderment. After a pregnant pause while time seemed to stand still and the nosy neighbors appeared to hold their collective breath, a trembling smile broke through her tears. In her flannel and denim, she looked radiant.

"Jesse," she said. "Oh, Jesse."

In the next minute, Lindsey yanked open the passenger door and bounded into the seat next to him.

He watched her, hoping, praying and utterly terrified to believe. "What are you doing?"

"I'm going with you," she said, alternately laughing and wiping tears. "To get Jade."

"You are?" Please say yes. Please say yes.

"And then we are all three going home, to *our* farm, where we belong." She gave him another of those tremulous smiles. "We have Christmas presents to wrap."

Understanding, pure and lovely, dawned. Jesse slammed the truck out of gear and did what he'd been yearning to do since her arrival. He pulled her into his arms. This time, she came willingly.

"I'm sorry, sweetheart. So sorry." Showering her face with kisses, he muttered apologies and professions of love. "I should have told you from the beginning, but I didn't know you. I didn't know I'd love you so much. I was wrong, so wrong."

"I'm sorry, too." She took his face between her palms, her golden eyes boring into him with a love so strong he felt humbled. "For all that happened to you as a boy. For my unwitting part in forcing you to take such drastic measures."

With a laugh of joy, Jesse hugged her to his happy heart. God had forgiven him and now Lindsey had too.

After years of searching, he had completely and finally come home. To his faith, to his farm, and to the woman who healed him in a thousand ways.

He was the luckiest man alive.

Epilogue

Lindsey was sure she would never be happier than she was this Christmas morning. She sat on the edge of an ottoman next to the Christmas tree, surveying her world like a queen.

The farmhouse smelled toasty warm with pumpkin bread and spiced cider and the promise of baked ham for dinner. Presents littered the living-room floor, some already unwrapped and exclaimed over while others still waited for their treasures to be discovered. And though these pleased her, the real joy came from the two people beneath her Christmas tree—Jesse and Jade—the loves of her life.

They'd arrived early, almost as soon as Lindsey was dressed in her Christmas best—an outfit she'd purchased especially for today—a silky emerald blouse, long black skirt, and matching dress boots. From Jesse's expression and brow-pumping compliments, she concluded she'd chosen well. She even felt pretty this morning.

"You open one now, Lindsey." Jade pushed a package at her.

Lindsey shook her head. She needed no other presents than the ones she'd already received. After considerable discussion during which each had tried to give the other everything, she and Jesse had agreed to share ownership of the farm. More importantly, she could spend this special Christmas Day with the man and child she'd come to love so deeply.

The Virginia pine in the living room had long since given up its stately status. Laden with ornaments and tinsel, popcorn strings and lights, homemade angels and clay-dough cookies, Lindsey's Christmas tree was loaded to the breaking point—thanks to Jade's daily additions. She thought it was the gaudiest, most beautiful tree ever.

"I want to see you open all of yours first." She lifted the camera from her lap and aimed.

Dressed in dark red velvet, her black hair pulled away from her face with a matching bow, the little girl was exquisite. With typical six-year-old exuberance, she hugged a stuffed dog to her white lace collar.

"This is my Sushi. I love her."

The real Sushi, watching from her spot next to the furnace, lifted her head and woofed once.

"She loves you too," Jesse said, his beloved mouth kicking up at the corners.

Snapping the ribbons from a box with one quick jerk, he opened a gift from Lindsey.

She held her breath as he lifted the sweater from the tissue.

"Wow." He held the rich blue garment beneath his chin. "Now I'll look decent enough to accompany you beautiful ladies to church this morning."

Lindsey snapped a picture, happiness bubbling inside her. Jesse was as eager as she to spend this holy day together in God's house.

"Do you like it?" She thought the blue looked stunning with his mysterious silver eyes.

"Love it." He leaned across the pile of discarded wrapping paper and grabbed her hand, charming her with a wink. "But I love you more."

Heart somersaulting in delight, she tapped him lightly on the head. "You'd better."

With a gentle tug, he pulled her off the ottoman onto her knees in front of him. "No problem there. But I do have another problem."

The sea-breeze scent of his cologne was almost as heady as the teasing, tender glint in his eyes. "What is it?"

"Some stubborn woman I know won't open her presents."

She'd been too busy relishing Jade's reaction to everything. "Christmas isn't about presents to me, Jesse. It's about loving and giving, the way God gave us Jesus."

"I couldn't agree more. And that's what I'm trying to do here."

Jade lay aside the gift she'd been about to unwrap and scooted toward the two adults. "Now, Daddy? Now?"

Her jittery behavior and dancing eyes told Lindsey something was up.

"Now, Jade. I don't think I can stand the suspense."

"Me either, me either, me either." Jade bounced like a rubber ball.

Lindsey laughed. "What are the two of you up to?"

Jesse left her long enough to go to his jacket and return with a small, gold-wrapped box. "This."

Her heart stuttered, stopped and then went crazy inside her chest. Mouth dry as August sand, she took the gift.

"Go on. Open it. It won't bite." Jesse tried to joke, but his eyes were serious and the muscle below those eyes quivered. Jade appeared excited enough to explode.

With trembling fingers, Lindsey removed the wrapping to find, as she'd suspected, a black velvet ring box.

"Oh, Jesse." Such a silly thing to say, but her mind was frozen.

Gently, he took the box from her fingers and flipped it open.

"Come on, Jade," he said. "Let's do this right."

He went down on one knee in front of her, and to Lindsey's great delight, Jade did the same. The sweetness of the picture overwhelmed her.

Jesse cleared his throat. "We've rehearsed this, so bear with us."

When he took her hand in his, she felt him tremble, and loved him all the more. "Lindsey Mitchell, I love you."

"I love you, Lindsey," Jade echoed.

The lump in Lindsey's throat thickened.

"I love you too," she whispered.

"We don't have much, but we can give you the most important things we own."

Jade touched her own chest. "Our hearts."

Tears welled in Lindsey's eyes. "You have mine too."

"Then, will you make our family complete and marry us? Will you be my wife?" Jesse slid the dainty solitaire onto her finger.

"And will you be my other mommy?"

"Yes. Oh yes." Lindsey could contain her joy no longer. She tumbled forward, grabbing both her loves into a giant hug.

First, she kissed Jade's cheek. "I promise to be the best mom I can."

And then while Jade giggled, Jesse took his turn, sealing the proposal with a kiss that promised a lifetime of love and honesty.

When at last they parted and sat smiling into one another's eyes, Jesse said, "Glad that's over. I didn't sleep a wink last night."

"Did you actually think I'd refuse?"

"I was afraid if I went to sleep, I'd wake up and discover you were a dream." His words melted her. "You are a dream. And I want to get married as soon as possible. Like tomorrow."

"Tomorrow?" Lindsey burst out in surprised laughter. In truth, she wanted the same thing. "Sorry, Mister Slater, but I've always dreamed of a Christmas wedding, and since it's too late for that this year, we'll have to wait until next Christmas."

"No way," Jesse howled.

"No way," Jade echoed, carefully sorting gifts into neat little piles.

Jesse thrust out a palm. "Hold it. I feel an idea coming on." An ornery twinkle lit the silvery eyes that had once been so wary and sad. "Not every place in the world celebrates Christmas on December twenty-fifth. Right?"

"Right." Lindsey agreed, unsure where he was heading. Not that she cared. She'd follow Jesse anywhere.

Suddenly, he clapped his hands together in victory. "Problem solved. According to a very famous song, there are really twelve days of Christmas. So there you have it. Christmas begins today and won't end until we're married twelve days from now." He squinted hopefully. "Okay?"

Happiness danced through Lindsey's veins. She'd only been teasing about waiting until next Christmas. She wanted to be Jesse's wife now.

"We'll talk to Pastor Cliff today and if he agrees, we'll be married among the trees on the twelfth day of Christmas. Just don't bring me any partridges or maids a-milking."

With a whoop of joy, Jesse grabbed her and twirled

her around in a circle. "This is the best Christmas of my life."

"Mine too."

He stilled and grew serious. "No kidding?"

"All my adult life, I've wanted my home filled with love and laughter. With a husband and children. This year, God has granted me those gifts."

"Do you think the people at church will be surprised? About our engagement, I mean."

"I don't know," she admitted. "But I'm eager to find out. Let's go early and tell everyone as they come in."

Jesse surveyed the disarrayed living room. "What about this mess and the unwrapped gifts?"

She slipped into the long wool coat she'd laid out earlier along with her purse and Bible. "They'll wait."

Jesse disappeared and came back wearing his new sweater. He was so handsome, he took her breath away. With a wide grin, he shrugged into his jacket and then helped Jade into hers.

Watching her two loves, Lindsey rejoiced. God was good. And on this glorious Christmas morning, He had blessed her exceedingly abundantly above all she could ever have thought or asked.

Jesse had come to Winding Stair with wrongful intent, but God had turned the bad to good. Only the Lord could have foreseen that the two of them, both with claims to the Christmas Tree Farm, needed each other to make their life circles complete. Only God could have made everything turn out so beautifully.

"Thank You, Jesus," she said, her cup overflowing.

"Amen to that." Jesse held out a hand and she took it. Jade clasped the other.

Then, together as a family, the trio headed out into the bright sunny morning, eager to celebrate the birth of their Savior and to announce their best Christmas present ever.

* * * * *

We hope you enjoyed reading

THE BRIDE

by *New York Times* bestselling author

MAYA BANKS and

IN THE RICH MAN'S WORLD

by reader-favorite author

Carol Marinelli

For more glamorous, passionate romances look for
the Harlequin Presents series!

Experience glamorous settings, powerful men and
passionate romances with Harlequin Presents®!

*Look for eight new romances every month from
Harlequin Presents!*

Available wherever books are sold.

Find us at

www.Harlequin.com

SPECIAL EXCERPT FROM

HARLEQUIN

Presents

Read on for an exclusive extract from
THE DIMITRAKOS PROPOSITION, the sensational
new story from Lynne Graham!

* * *

TABBY looked up at him and froze, literally not daring
to breathe. That close his eyes were no longer dark but
a downright amazing and glorious swirl of honey, gold
and caramel tones, enhanced by the spiky black lashes
she envied.

His fingers were feathering over hers with a gentleness she
had not expected from so big and powerful a man, and little
tremors of response were filtering through her, undermining
her self-control. She knew she wanted those expert hands on
her body, exploring much more secret places, and color rose
in her cheeks, because she also knew she was out of her depth
and drowning. In an abrupt movement, she wrenched her
hands free and turned away, momentarily shutting her eyes in
a gesture of angry self-loathing.

"Try on the rest of the clothes," Acheron instructed coolly,
not a flicker of lingering awareness in his dark deep voice.

Tension seethed through Acheron. What the hell was the
matter with him? He had been on the edge of crushing that
soft, luscious mouth beneath his, close to wrecking the non-
sexual relationship he envisaged between them. Impersonal
would work the best and it shouldn't be that difficult, he
reasoned impatiently, for they had nothing in common. She
cleaned up incredibly well, he acknowledged grudgingly

gritting his teeth together as his gaze instinctively dropped to the sweet pouting swell of her small breasts beneath the clingy top.

He had done what he had to do, he reminded himself grimly. She was perfect for his purposes, for she had as much riding on the success of their arrangement as he had. Thankfully nothing in his life was going to change in the slightest: he had found the perfect wife, a nonwife....

Two hours later, Acheron opened the safe in his bedroom wall to remove a ring case he hadn't touched in years. The fabled emerald, which had reputedly once adorned a maharajah's crown, had belonged to his late mother and would do duty as an engagement ring. The very thought of putting the priceless jewel on Tabby's finger chilled Acheron's anticommitment gene to the marrow, and he squared his broad shoulders, grateful that the engagement and the marriage that would follow would be 100 percent fake.

* * *

Will sharp-tongued, independent firestorm Tabby Glover accept Greek billionaire Acheron Dimitrakos's outrageous marriage proposal?

Find out in January 2014!

HPEXP1213-IR

HARLEQUIN
Presents

Save $1.00 on the purchase of

THE DIMITRAKOS PROPOSITION

by Lynne Graham

available December 17, 2013,
or on any other Harlequin® Presents® book.

Available wherever books are sold, including most bookstores, supermarkets, drugstores and discount stores.

- -

Save $1.00

on the purchase of
THE DIMITRAKOS PROPOSITION
by Lynne Graham
available December 17, 2013,
or on any other Harlequin® Presents® book.

Coupon valid until February 19, 2014. Redeemable at participating retail outlets in the U.S. and Canada only. Limit one coupon per customer.

52611201

Canadian Retailers: Harlequin Enterprises Limited will pay the face value of this coupon plus 10.25¢ if submitted by customer for this product only. Any other use constitutes fraud. Coupon is nonassignable. Void if taxed, prohibited or restricted by law. Consumer must pay any government taxes. Void if copied. Nielsen Clearing House ("NCH") customers submit coupons and proof of sales to Harlequin Enterprises Limited, P.O. Box 3000, Saint John, NB E2L 4L3, Canada. Non-NCH retailer—for reimbursement submit coupons and proof of sales directly to Harlequin Enterprises Limited, Retail Marketing Department, 225 Duncan Mill Rd., Don Mills, ON M3B 3K9, Canada.

U.S. Retailers: Harlequin Enterprises Limited will pay the face value of this coupon plus 8¢ if submitted by customer for this product only. Any other use constitutes fraud. Coupon is nonassignable. Void if taxed, prohibited or restricted by law. Consumer must pay any government taxes. Void if copied. For reimbursement submit coupons and proof of sales directly to Harlequin Enterprises Limited, P.O. Box 880478, El Paso, TX 88588-0478, U.S.A. Cash value 1/100 cents.

5 65373 00076 2 (8100)0 11890

® and TM are trademarks owned and used by the trademark owner and/or its licensee.
© 2013 Harlequin Enterprises Limited

REQUEST YOUR FREE BOOKS!

2 FREE NOVELS
FROM THE ROMANCE COLLECTION
PLUS 2 FREE GIFTS!

YES! Please send me 2 FREE novels from the Romance Collection and my 2 FREE gifts (gifts are worth about $10). After receiving them, if I don't wish to receive any more books, I can return the shipping statement marked "cancel." If I don't cancel, I will receive 4 brand-new novels every month and be billed just $6.24 per book in the U.S. or $6.74 per book in Canada. That's a savings of at least 22% off the cover price. It's quite a bargain! Shipping and handling is just 50¢ per book in the U.S. and 75¢ per book in Canada.* I understand that accepting the 2 free books and gifts places me under no obligation to buy anything. I can always return a shipment and cancel at any time. Even if I never buy another book, the two free books and gifts are mine to keep forever.

194/394 MDN F4XY

Name _____ (PLEASE PRINT) _____

Address _____ Apt. # _____

City _____ State/Prov. _____ Zip/Postal Code _____

Signature (if under 18, a parent or guardian must sign) _____

Mail to the Harlequin® Reader Service:
IN U.S.A.: P.O. Box 1867, Buffalo, NY 14240-1867
IN CANADA: P.O. Box 609, Fort Erie, Ontario L2A 5X3

**Want to try two free books from another line?
Call 1-800-873-8635 or visit www.ReaderService.com.**

* Terms and prices subject to change without notice. Prices do not include applicable taxes. Sales tax applicable in N.Y. Canadian residents will be charged applicable taxes. Offer not valid in Quebec. This offer is limited to one order per household. Not valid for current subscribers to the Romance Collection or the Romance/Suspense Collection. All orders subject to credit approval. Credit or debit balances in a customer's account(s) may be offset by any other outstanding balance owed by or to the customer. Please allow 4 to 6 weeks for delivery. Offer available while quantities last.

Your Privacy—The Harlequin® Reader Service is committed to protecting your privacy. Our Privacy Policy is available online at www.ReaderService.com or upon request from the Harlequin Reader Service.

We make a portion of our mailing list available to reputable third parties that offer products we believe may interest you. If you prefer that we not exchange your name with third parties, or if you wish to clarify or modify your communication preferences, please visit us at www.ReaderService.com/consumerchoice or write to us at Harlequin Reader Service Preference Service, P.O. Box 9062, Buffalo, NY 14269. Include your complete name and address.

ROM13R

HARLEQUIN® *Presents*®

Revenge and seduction intertwine…

**Miranda Lee brings you her stunning novel,
packed with power, temptation and excitement**

Don't miss

A MAN WITHOUT MERCY

January 2014

His out-of-hours invitation…

Dumped by her fiancé *via text,* Vivienne Swan
wants to nurse her shattered heart privately…until
an intriguing offer from Jack Stone tempts her from
her shell. But is Vivienne playing with fire? Jack's a
man used to taking what he wants, and now she's
at his mercy!

HP132

HARLEQUIN®

A *Romance* FOR EVERY MOOD™

Stay up-to-date on all your
romance-reading news with the
Harlequin Shopping Guide,
featuring bestselling authors, exciting new
miniseries, books to watch and more!

The newest issue will be delivered right to you
with our compliments! There are 4 each year.

Signing up is easy.

EMAIL

ShoppingGuide@Harlequin.ca

WRITE TO US

HARLEQUIN BOOKS
Attention: Customer Service Department
P.O. Box 9057, Buffalo, NY 14269-9057

OR PHONE

1-800-873-8635 in the United States
1-888-343-9777 in Canada

Please allow 4-6 weeks for delivery of the first issue by mail.

Love the Harlequin book you just read?

Your opinion matters.

Review this book on your favorite book site, review site, blog or your own social media properties and share your opinion with other readers!